ALINE
AND THE
BLUE BOTTLE

ALINE
AND THE
BLUE BOTTLE

CAROLINA UGAZ-MORÁN

For permissions contact:

admin@adventumbooks.com

First Edition: October 2019

Paperback: 978-1-7340728-0-8

Hardcover: 978-1-7340728-2-2

Printed in the United States of America

Visit: www.adventuresofaline.com

I dedicate this book to my husband and my wonderful two daughters, my first fans. To my husband, who patiently heard the story for fifteen years and saw it with me the moment I dreamt it. To my first fans, with every smile of excitement I knew I had created a world you would love.

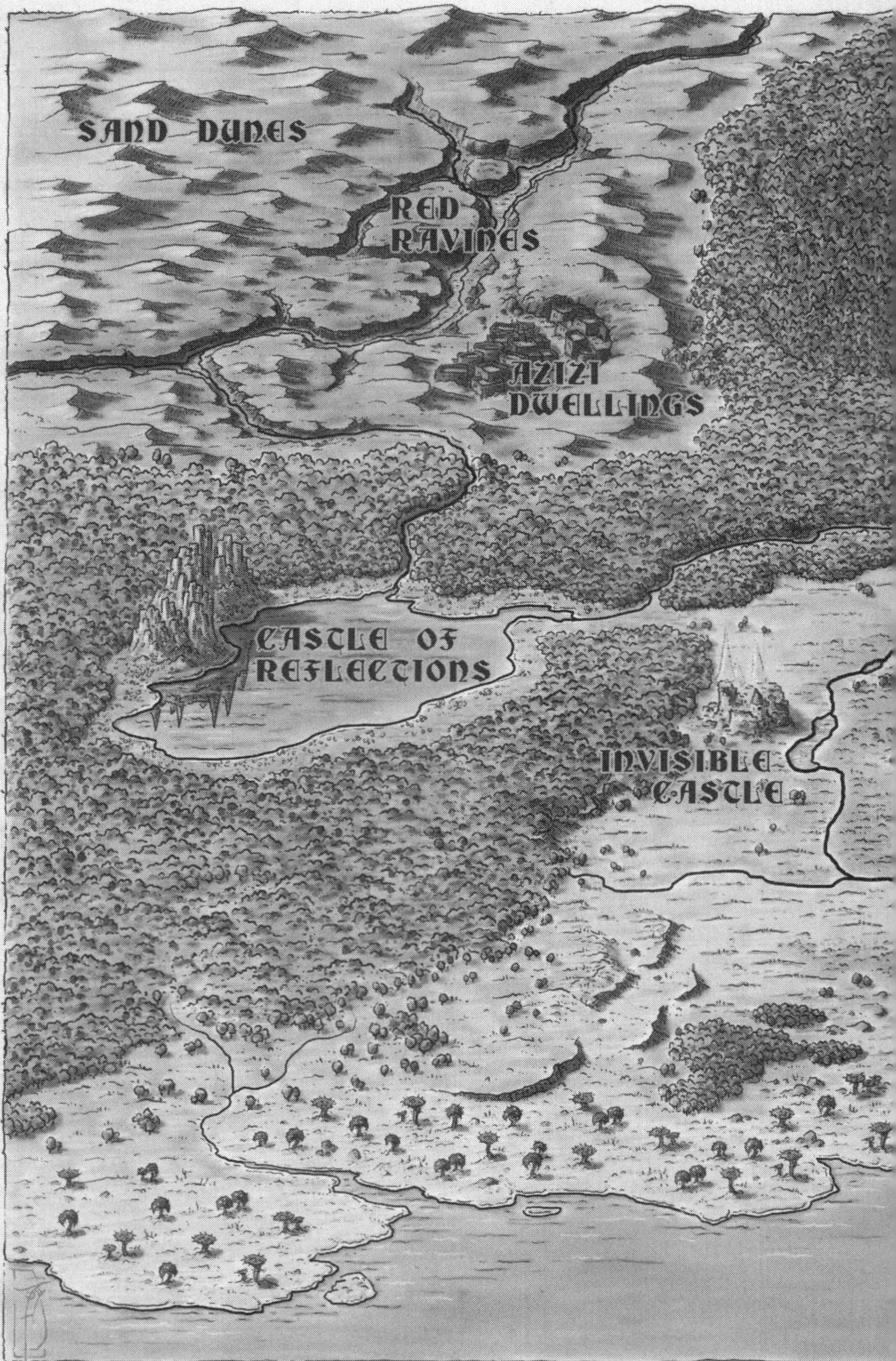
SAND DUNES
RED RAVINES
AZIZI DWELLINGS
CASTLE OF REFLECTIONS
INVISIBLE CASTLE

WIZARD'S
SUSPENDED CASTLE

PALACE

NORTHERN

MOUNTAINS

ATER

WINDING

FOREST

BLEAK

DISAPPEARING
WATERFALLS

FOREST

CAVE

SOUTHERN

SHORES

1

THE HOUSE OF HAUNTED GARGOYLES

Secrets

Most families have secrets. Locked deep within their family tree, these secrets are hidden from the rest of the world. Sometimes the secrets these families work hard to tuck away are indeed so wonderful you wish you could hear them. Then, there are families who lightly cover their secrets because they believe they are great; however, no one ever wants to know anything about them.

The truth is, the majority of family secrets are just plain ordinary secrets. Stories or even events that once they escape the circle of secrets, they either do not surprise you at all or maybe for a small amount of time. In the end, their impact is minor. These secrets feel more like gossip than uncovering a truly fascinating story. They reveal a common family fact to be forgotten by the next generation.

Now, it was said *most* families, because there is one family with one extraordinary secret. A secret so wonderful and terrific that its impact changed many lives forever. For millennia, it has been passed down from generation to generation. They understood the glorious and dangerous consequences that would arise if this secret was revealed.

You may just simply not believe that much power can exist within a single secret. That at the same time it saves and endangers lives. That it creates and destroys worlds. In the end, you will be the judge of this and you will choose how you would allow this secret to impact you.

Soon I will reveal this wonderful secret to you. And I will challenge you to see if you can find the other secrets around and within it. If by chance you are able to learn about the past. Pay great attention. For it will reveal to you more than just its history, more than the stories that took place eons of years ago. If indeed you get a hold of these stories, you have the choice whether to read them, to decode its many secrets, or to do nothing at all.

In the end, the choice is always yours!

Now that you know you have many choices, let me tell you the story about the family with a special secret.

Hallowing Wars

It was almost dusk, in a cold October, three days before Halloween. The chilly wind softly swept away the autumn leaves on Portico Street. The remaining sun rays faded away softly kissing the roof's tiles, giving them a scaly appearance of orange snakes or green lizards.

Portico was a dead-end street, with approximately fifteen houses on each side. It was a long strip of old stone and wood houses, with roomy porches, big trees, and large yards; some of the houses were over two hundred years old. A few of the trees were much older than the houses, with branches as thick as the trunks of a regular tree. There were cedars, redwoods, very curly junipers, aspens, and sugar maples. Just about all the trees on the street had changed colors— a funhouse of leaves, with the colors of pumpkin pie, caramel apple, lemon tart, carrot cake, and strawberries.

The houses were all dressed up for Halloween. Some had fake spider webs on the front porch and smiling skeletons on their doors, and some had cardboard tombstones on the front lawn. Little pumpkin lights and lighted bats adorned the porch steps. Others had little scarecrows made out of hay and many pumpkins carved into the shape of a ghost or a witch. Just like any neighborhood, there were houses that seemed to be in a never-ending decorating war. On Portico Street, there were two of those, kitty-corner to each other.

On the southeast corner of Portico & Cumbric Street—the side with even numbers—there was one house that looked like grey cotton candy. They had filled the entire house with fake spider webs. Webs were hanging from the windows on the second floor, from the door knobs, from the roof, on all of the bushes, and even on the fence. On the front lawn, carved pumpkins lit with candles lined each side of the path that led up to the porch steps. The pumpkin path continued up the seven steps towards the front door—each carving more elaborate with each step. They had put the pumpkins out so soon that a few were already saggy and looked as if they were just about to rot. The candles tickled the insides of the loopy pumpkins, and the air smelled like a pumpkin pie about to burn. The owner, Mr. O'Moghrain, had bought eight more pumpkins to create a pumpkin snake. Whistling in a low pitch, he sat on the back porch and made more intricate carvings to the largest pumpkin —the head of the snake.

They had five little scarecrows on each side of their front lawn, three witches, two mummies, and fifteen life-size rubber bats hanging on the lower branches of the only tree—the tallest redwood on the block. Seven human size glow-in-the-dark skeletons were hugging its massive trunk. Glow-in-the-dark rubber spiders, bats, snakes, and black cats swirled around the trunk starting at the tip of the skeleton's head, to as far up as Mr. O'Moghrain could climb. In addition to the bats, thirteen black and white plastic bags with smiling ghostly faces hung from the lowest branches, which were very high.

Fifty years ago, Mr. O'Moghrain's parents decided to cut down all the trees in their property. A five-year-old Mr. O'Moghrain cried while hugging the biggest tree begging his parents not to cut it down. It survived! From that moment, Mr. O'Moghrain would use any holiday as an excuse to decorate every inch of the tree. This Halloween he felt particularly inspired.

Leaning on the tree stumps of the front and back lawns, were so many gray styrofoam tombstones that their dog could only use one thin trail to and from the house to his little red doghouse. On the doghouse, there was a black sign with dripping orange writing that said, 'Sparky lies here'. The tombstones were all connected with fake spider web and if that was not enough, they had filled the webs with sufficient tiny rubber bats, spiders, scorpions, snakes, bugs, and ghosts to decorate the whole neighborhood.

At the northwest corner, on the side of the street with odd numbers, the Grant family had not used a single fake spider web. They had focused on Halloween lights. There were little shinning carrot-colored witches, bats, ghosts, pumpkins, spiders, vampires, Frankensteins, mummies, and waning crescent moons. It looked like one giant dirty orange light bulb. They had taped black and orange ribbons on all the white columns, window frames, doors, and along the white wooden fence.

This was the second house on the block with the most trees; and seen that as an advantage, they heavily decorated each one of them. They hung so many witches on their trees it looked like a witch gathering. Some were flying on broomsticks, some smiling immovable from a branch, others appearing to cook something in a big black smoky cauldron. Even more were merrily flying in front of a full moon with a black cat on their shoulder and big green hairy warts on their chin. For other witches, you could only see their legs sticking out in the air covered with white, green, and black striped tights, and black boots whose tips curled endlessly. One witch stood with a funny look on her face holding a broken broom and a crumbled hat onto her head. She had obviously smashed against a tree. More were standing on the ground and others missed the trees and crashed onto the grass.

Trying to keep up with the O'Moghrains, they had also carved multiple pumpkins. However, the Grants were horrible pumpkin carvers for the roof and the yard were full of unshaped orange swiss-cheeses. It seemed like zillions of mad termites decided to devour these orange leathery bowls, creating random holes of different shapes and sizes. At least, they were not rotten. Their back yard, besides the witches and pumpkins, was filled with plastic mummies, coffins, skeletons, hands, and feet which moved left, right, up, or down.

Almost the entire neighborhood was proud and tried to keep up with the decorations. Each year they came up with something new, scary, funny, and unique. Many visitors drove by just to see the Halloween decorations. They would drive slowly south down the street and spend time at each house, pointing at the new items or the ones they liked best. The O'Moghrain's carved pumpkins and the Grant's witch jamboree always seemed to be the decorations that pleased the crowd the most.

That is, until they reached the end of the street.

The House

UNLIKE MOST NEIGHBORHOODS, there was one house on Portico Street that required no decoration. This house howled when the wind touched it. The spider webs on the front porch were real, as were the bats hanging from nearby trees. The trees behind its iron fence looked uninviting. A strange forest it seemed, where the holes on tree trunks hid more than just squirrels. Overgrown roots grew in the front garden and cold winds whispered "get out." Strange sounds always emerged from the house, and those were accompanied by unusual stories. Some claimed that the house was haunted. Others blamed the house for any bizarre event that happened in the neighborhood, or in the house's many acres. The truth is that no one knew how much land belonged to the house and no one was willing to find out.

A tall, four-story ash colored house made of stone, it was the last house on the street. The one that marked the far edge of town. Its roof was surrounded by guarding gargoyles. They had shiny black or red jewels for eyes and wide-open mouths that hurled murky rain water creating dark waterfalls. On either side of it in front stood two imposing round towers topped with dark sharp cones. Four majestic stone columns, two on each side of the front door, protected the main entrance. The door was a large arched reddish-brown mahogany with black iron bolts and a little black iron door high in its center.

The balcony on the second floor, above the entryway, connected the two towers. A long and wide balcony, decorated with eight pairs of stain glass windows. Each pair had a predominant color with metallic undertones: golden, blue, purple, red, orange, green, black, or silver. When the windows were left opened, shiny white silk curtains flapped out of the house and onto the street. As if eight souls screamed for help with quivering white tongues. This was the only house with no Halloween lights.

Families would pass by the front of the house in slow motion at first, staring with open mouths in absolute silence. Once their brains processed what they were seeing, parents' fingers would seek their kids' hands and they would quickly scurry away without taking their eyes off the house. It was the only house were kids never stopped to ask for trick-or-treats, afraid they would get what they asked for. Tricks!

No one knew much about the house much less when it was really built. But there were rumors about this house. Stories heard by grandparents when they were children. Tales that the trees were alive, haunted by witches and monsters, and anyone who dared go near them would never come back.

At least that is what some said had happened to many of the O'Moghrains and the Grants over fifty years ago.

Most were certain the house was haunted—even cursed. They were certain the screams at night came from the ghosts trapped inside. A few claimed they had ventured into its forest and gotten lost in the forest. They had heard a cry coming from the trees and followed it, thinking someone was lost or hurt. Then once they got close to a tree, it tried to grab them and pull them into its branches. Several neighbors told how their great-grand-parents were invited in and never returned, and the few who did become mad or ill shortly after. This house was also blamed for the numbers of parentless children left in the neighborhood years ago.

There were also many opinions about the black dogs that lived in the house. Some said they were fed more than dog food. Others said they were the evil guardians of the iron black gates. But what most absolutely agreed on, was that the gargoyles in the house were there to make sure nothing or no one got out once they came in.

This house was known as the house of haunted gargoyles.

2

ALINE

Arrival

Most of the children had gone home to dinner. The fading sun and awakening lights on Portico Street revealed a shadow walking towards the house of haunted gargoyles. Fallen leaves swirled away from their resting place, as the cold wind arranged a bare path to the house of haunted gargoyles. A whistle echoed down the street, triggering a chain reaction of barks and howls from the neighborhood dogs. The rhythmic sound of shoes tapping on the pavement accompanied the whistle, and cats peeped out of alleys to see who it was. This arrival was announced by the cries from the crows as they flew onto the roof of the house of haunted gargoyles. The black gate moaned when it was pushed open. Hounds inside the house yowled and whined as the sound of footsteps and tinkling keys approached the front steps.

"Ugh," a faint voice complained. "So heavy!" The door creaked open and then slammed shut.

"Aline, is that you?" came a sweet, worried voice from deep inside the house. "Where have you been?"

"I was at the park, Mom."

"No! You didn't say anything to me about going to the park young lady!"

"Oh, no!" Aline whispered to herself. "Did I forget to write the note again? I thought for sure…huh…I wish I had written that note!"

"I was so worried," continued Aline's mother, "I looked for you all over the place. Called all your friends…"

"What friends? I don't have any friends remember." Aline replied sadly as she fixed the left strap of her backpack.

"Oh, Aline!" Her mother walked towards her with arms stretched wide to give her a hug. "Don't worry, you *will* have a lot of friends. I promise. You are a sweet, smart, and funny girl with the most beautiful heart I have ever seen."

With a warm smile, she looked at Aline, softly brushed her brown-copper hair away from her face, and tucked some wisps behind her ear. Aline smiled.

"You promise?" She tilted her head and her gray-green eyes glowed. Her smile got even bigger.

"Yes, I promise."

As she said this, they heard a loud bang. The dogs had managed to open the back door and were galloping towards them, their nails clicking and sliding on the wooden floor. Aline and her mom were soon surrounded by four big dogs that licked their hands and wagged their tails so hard that their butts wagged back and forth too.

"Calm down! Calm down!" Aline laughed. They immediately sat on the floor still wagging their tails and their butts.

"How did you four get in?" Aline's mom asked sternly as she walked towards the kitchen. "It doesn't matter how I close the door, they always manage to open it, especially if they hear you come in."

Aline giggled, and winked at the dogs.

"Go wash up Aline, dinner will be ready in a few minutes."

"Sure, Mom." She headed up the stairs smiling, all four dogs right behind her.

"Aline," her mom called her as she took the wine glasses out of the oak cabinets.

"Yes, mom?" Aline replied as she reached the top of the stairs.

"This is the last time you go to the park without telling me."

Aline knew what was coming. "Please don't ground me," she muttered. "How did I forget to write that note?" Frustrated, she pictured the note she thought she had written.

"Since your birthday is coming up," continued her mother as she went to the fridge to get some milk.

"I could have just clipped it on the purple clip," Aline sighed. In her mind, she could see her handwriting in blue ink on yellow paper. It looked so *real*. Her cheeks tingled, goosebumps appeared on her forearms, and she felt static on the tip of her fingers. "The purple clip...just...clipped it...on the..."

"I am not going to ground you, but don't do it again or..."

Her voice suddenly stopped and then Aline heard her gasp. She was looking at a note on the fridge. Stuck to the left-hand door above the water and ice dispenser with a magnetic purple clip. *Going to the park. Will be home before dark.* "Oh!" she said.

"Fridge..." Aline finished. Then, puzzled, she called out: "What, Mom?"

"I was certain...hmmmm, I supposed...er... well, I must have missed it," her mom whispered to herself. Then, out loud: "Sorry honey. The note's here after all. I guess I just didn't see..." She didn't finish her sentence. She read the note a third time to be sure she had read it right.

"Huh...I mean," Aline replied and then quickly shook her head as she headed to her room, dogs following close behind. The strap of her backpack slid off her left shoulder once more. "That's okay Mom," she said as she fixed the strap.

Once she was in her room with the door closed, she breathed a sigh of relief. "Phew! I really thought I forgot to write that note this morning," she said. "But I guess I wrote it after all."

Sitting on the bed lost in thought, she looked at her dogs. They all started to lick her hands, pushing each other away and tried to put their heads underneath her hands so she would pet them.

The Hounds

"Hey guys, I missed you." The dogs smiled, wagging their tails furiously. Licking her hands now became a competition.

"Hi Sky, Kay, Mach, and Ash."

As she said their names, she patted each one of their heads. Sky was a big black lab with long floppy ears—the oldest and shyest of the four. At fourteen, she was older than Aline. She was also the slowest, but this did not mean she was slow compared to other dogs. She was fast. They were all really fast.

Ash was the youngest, a puppy still, and the fastest. He definitely wanted all the attention. Part wolf and part Weimaraner, he had a shiny black and dark gray coat and blue eyes. He would chew anything in his way, especially Aline's shoes. She had to put her mom's heavy dark cedar and red velvet vanity chair in front of her closet so he would not open it and eat her shoes. One time she forgot to wipe the chair clean when she placed it back in her mom's room. Her mom was running late for work and sat on it to put on her makeup. When she got up, her back was covered in Ash's hair and drool. She screamed his name and he whined, hiding underneath Aline's bed, knowing he was in trouble.

Mach was definitely the most hyperactive of the four. Even more hyper than Ash. The two of them together were just pure trouble, but he knew better than to chew on shoes—or anything else for that matter. An old black Great Dane/Rhodesian ridgeback mix just a few months younger than Sky. He was a big softy when it came to Aline.

Kay, on the other hand, was calm and the most protective of Aline and her family. She was a black Rottweiler with brown eyes that liked to talk a lot. Kay would howl at Aline every time the girl asked something, as if she knew the answer. Maybe she did.

Grandmother

DID YOU MISS ME?" Aline asked.

"Auuuhhrrrr, auuuhhrrr, auu, au," Kay answered.

"Yes Kay, I know you did." All four wagged their tails and smiled.

"Did you guys have fun today?"

"Auuuhhrrrr, auuuhhrrr, auu, au." As Kay howled, Ash barked, and Sky licked Mach.

"It sounds like Ash had fun, huh?" Aline stroked Ash's head.

"Auuuhhrrrr, auuuhhrrr, auu, au." Kay looked at Mach as she answered Aline.

"Of course. I am sure Mach had a good day too," smiled Aline. Mach put his head underneath her hand and smiled innocently.

"Oh Mach, you always have fun." Aline was a bit sad when she finished her sentence. Sky licked her hands, Kay whined, Mach twisted his head to the side, and Ash nibbled her shoelaces.

"My day was not good. The girls in school are still mean to me. They say I look like a boy," she sighed, "and the boys make fun of me. They call me gigantor or tower girl. They point at me and laugh just because I am taller than everyone else. I am even taller than Mr. Strawser, but then again, he's as short as most of the kids in class."

Aline became quiet and then said, "why do I have to be so different?" A tear slid down her cheek and fell on Ash's head. He stopped chewing on her shoelaces and looked up at the ceiling to see where it had come from. Then he looked at her when he heard Kay whine.

"Oh my dear, don't worry." Aline looked up to see her grandmother standing tall and beautiful in her doorway. Her long white wavy hair illuminated her face and fell softly down to her waist. It almost had a shimmer to it that accentuated her eyes, which were of different colors. The left eye was violet with a blue undertone and the right eye was violet with a green undertone. Her smile was soothing, softening her strong jawline, and her skin, almost wrinkleless, was so beautiful it was tempting to touch it. She wore a silver silk blouse, a long black skirt, and black flats.

"You are very unique and beautiful. Your heart is pure, and it gives off love and happiness. This is a rare combination, and the kids from school simply don't know how to interact with someone like you. Being unique is a very good thing. You will soon learn to understand this. But I also know that because of the way humans are, being unique is a lot of work, of hard work. It is not easy when individuals do not understand what they see in front of them. Or when folks are nothing but blind to the beauty within someone who is only different. They plainly cannot see what I see," she walked towards Aline, cupped her face in her hands and wiped her tears, "an extraordinary young lady." She smiled at Aline, "you merely have to find a way for them to see this," and gently kissed her forehead.

"I don't understand why they judge me without knowing me. Without even speaking one word." She paused. "I think...I think I can be fun," she said and looked at her grandmother.

"I know you are fun." Her grandmother winked at her. "Do you trust me, Aline?"

"Auuuhhrrrr, auuuhhrrr, auu, au," Kay answered and they both laughed.

"Oh! I was not talking to you Kay, but thank you for saying that," she said, stroking Kay's head. Then she looked closely at Aline. "Well? Do you?"

"Yes, I do," Aline reassured her.

"Then believe me when I tell you that things will get better. You need to be patient and give it time…well, a little more time. Things will change. You will see this when the moment is right."

The wind entered through the open window, blowing softly on their faces. And just like that Aline was not sad anymore. Her eyes sparkled and she smiled at her grandmother. She felt good and warm all over. Like putting on clothes that had just come out of the drier on a very cold day. She hugged her grandmother.

"Oh, Abi!" Aline said with a bright smile. She always had called her grandmother by her first name. "What would I do without you and Mom?!" The four dogs, who had calmed down and lain on the floor, got up and started to shake their butts again, and Kay barked. "And the four of you, of course!" They all laughed.

"Now, let us go downstairs and join your mother. Dinner is probably ready. Plus we need to talk about…." she paused and had a mischievous look on her face, "…about Halloween, of course!"

"Yeah, right!" Aline knew what her grandmother had been about to say but she decided to follow along. Her birthday was coming up. She was turning twelve in three days.

Dinner

THEY WALKED down the stairs to the great entrance hall and then to the right, towards the family room where the smell of burning wood in the fireplace made them both briefly close their eyes and smile. Home felt great.

The large family room was separated from the dining room by big beautiful arched stained-glass doors, which reached all the way up to cathedral ceilings. They walked through the glass doors and into a five-corner dining room, with the fifth corner resting on the right side of the house. All the floors in the house were made out of fine oak wood. Like thin vines, the wood spread up each of the five corners, reaching and framing the ceiling. It was meticulously carved with ivy markings and stopped once it reached the light-gray Gothic ceiling molding which caved in twice like tiny inverted stairs leading you to its white center. Candelabras on the five white walls lightly lit the room, but it was the big chandelier in the center that brought the room to life. A big octagonal mahogany table surrounded by eight majestic reddish-brown chairs stood underneath the chandelier. Resting on the table was a white crochet tablecloth and on its center was a round blue glass vase. Set on the table were three china plates designed with little tiny gold and blue flowers and three wine glasses—two filled with red wine and one filled with milk. Close to the plates were two steaming large silver bowls.

"I made you your favorite, Aline." Aline's mom said as she placed a third steaming silver platter on the table. Aline lifted her head ever so slightly, as she inhaled her mom's cooking.

"Smells so good!" Her eyes got wide and her stomach rumbled. She suddenly realized that she was starving. Her gray eyes glowed green as her mother poured a yellow stew onto one of the plates. After adding rice and vegetables, she passed the plate to Aline, who was watching her every move. Aline placed the plate down and impatiently waited for her mother and grandmother to serve themselves. The smells of the food filled the room and the dogs whined a little. Their tongues were hanging out and drooling onto the floor. The wait felt almost eternal. Aline's feet eagerly tapped the floor while she looked at her golden food.

"We need to give thanks for this food. Abi would you please?" A half smile crept up on her mother's light pink lips, while her hazel eyes seemed to reminisce.

"Of course, Kani," said Aline's grandmother. "Please, hold hands."

The four dogs took a few steps closer to Aline and then stood motionless as they looked at Abi. The golden scent rose slowly from the stew and the air became thick. Abi's pale skin glimmered, her violet eyes looked upwards and her voice became soft and soothing. Aline concentrated on her breathing as her grandmother proceeded with what Aline felt was the longest prayer of her life. She looked up as her grandmother switch to silent prayer, and was not sure what to do. Her hand softened their hold on her mother's hand to grab the fork but this was quickly stopped by one hard squeeze. As soon as her grandmother finished, in a fraction of a second Aline was devouring her dinner.

"Aline, slow down" Kani cautioned.

"Sorry. I am just super hungry!" Aline did not miss one beat from one bite to the next, and her eyes were glowing.

Abi smiled at Kani and quickly changed the subject. "What do you both think our costumes should be this year? We have only three days until Halloween and I can only sew so fast!"

"You know, the other day someone mentioned a funny and simple idea and I thought we could try it," Kani said excitedly.

"It would be to dress up as tables! Aline can be a modern table, I can be a table from the '70s and you, Abi, can be an antique!" She felt more than saw Abi's expression.

"Hmm," She coughed a bit. "Tables."

Aline's spoon hung idle in midair as she looked at Abi and then at Kani.

"A possibility," Abi smiled. Then she brought up other ideas. "How about comets or asteroids? You know there are several very famous ones, and I still have shimmery organza, liquid lamè, and sequinned fabric from when we were fairies a few years ago."

"Oh, yes! And we can add flowing shiny veils too, for more effect," added Kani.

"Oh, no!" Aline's face showed her horror. "No, no, no! I am too old to be walking around in flowing shiny sequinned veils. Just no! Abi! The kids in school will tease me forever. Might as well dress me up like a gargoyle. At least they're afraid of the gargoyles on this house!"

"Ooh! Well, that's a great idea. A bit challenging, but I can make some wonderful wings and even get the dogs involved to create a full clan!" Abi was excited at the thought, and Aline was just stumped. Her objection had totally backfired.

"I can make horns out of paper maché. Yes! This will be great! Strong woman gargoyles protecting the humans. That's what they do, you know! A lot of people think they are evil but that's not correct." By now Abi had it all figured out in her head and Aline knew her expression all too well.

"Gargoyles, Abi? Could we be more normal, more standard? Like the three musketeers or superheroines like Wonder Woman, Supergirl, Batgirl, or...hmmmm, Catwoman! You know?" Aline pressed her advantage. She remembered when she was eight and Abi had created the most realistic amazon warrior princesses costumes. They had mohawks and amazing amounts of grass, branches, and feathers weaved into their outfits, even in their hair. *"The Amazon warriors blended in with their environment. They would completely disappear. Invisible. Until puff! You are getting attacked!"* Abi had said to them as she fixed their hair.

"Maybe in the jungle this was true, but not in the suburbs," Aline thought to herself. They had stood out like sore thumbs and some of the kids still teased her about that Halloween costume. Saying she was a tree with branches growing out of her hair.

"Hmmm! I can make little wings and dragon-like tails for each dog." Abi looked at Aline with a smile. Aline knew there was no coming back from this one. Plus, it would be the first time the dogs went trick or treating with them and they would look awesome in those costumes. With the dogs next to her, some of the kids might not get close and with luck may not even recognize her. Maybe this was not such a bad idea after all.

"This will be the grandest of any Halloweens we've ever had. Next year you'll be a teenager. This could be the last time all of us dress up. So let's be grand and get a bit crazy and creative! And most important of all let's have fun," Abi continued. Her eyes were a deep purple and as always, she exuded serenity, calm, peace, and pure joy. She looked just beautiful. With a simple and powerful smile she looked at Aline and without even thinking about it, Aline smiled back.

"Then, it is settled. Gargoyles it is!" Both Kani and Abi got up to take the dishes to the kitchen and Aline followed.

3

HALLOWEEN

Organza, Sequences, & Unfortunate Events

Both Abi and Kani were busy for the next two days. Abi was focusing on creating the costumes for all the family members, including the dogs. The house decorations were occupying Kani. Not that the house really needed any additional help—it looked perfect just the way it was. She would always fuss around and about, but every year the house looked the same. It looked scary! Not one person—child or adult—would dare to knock on their door, much less threaten them with tricks if treats were not provided.

In one day, Abi completed the dog's outfits and they were magnificent. They had beautiful bat-like wings made out of dark gray organza that shimmered the way a rock does at night in silvery moonlight. Their tails were very dragon-like and they had papier machè horns along their spines. The challenge was to keep the costumes on them. All four would walk backward in a circle trying to remove the wings. Ash would step on the tail and try to bite his costume. However, Abi immediately stopped what she was doing and gave him *the look*. The rest of the dogs immediately knew not to mess with their costumes. Only once, when Abi was not looking, did he try again to bite his tail. But as soon as he opened his mouth, Abi said his name in a low commanding voice and that was the end of that.

"They look great!" Aline exclaimed when she saw them all dressed up on the morning of the thirtieth. She was starting to like the idea more and more.

"Now it's time to focus on the humans," Abi laughed "Tomorrow is Halloween and I need to hurry."

"Do you need to measure me Abi?" Aline asked as she grabbed the measuring tape.

"No need."

"But how would you know if it fits?"

"You always ask me this question and what do I reply?" She said while she continued cutting a length of sequinned fabric.

"That you know me more than I realize. But how do you do this? You are going to have to teach this to me one day."

"One day I will teach you many things, but for now, please pass me the dark gray spindle on your left and go get ready for school."

"Yes, Abi. Have you seen Mom?" She asked as she passed her grandmother the spindle.

Abi paused for a second to think. "I believe she is outside working on the house." She looked at Aline, smiled, and then returned to her sewing.

"Thanks! I will see if I can find her."

"Is there anything I can help you with, dear? You know how she gets during this time."

"Yes, I know. I just wanted to give her a kiss goodbye."

"Well, give me one instead and go get ready because you are going to miss the bus," she said this as she pointed to the grandfather clock.

"Oh my goodness, I thought I had twenty more minutes. I have to go Abi." She kissed her grandmother on the cheek and started to run off.

"You have time for one quick hug, no?" Abi smiled at Aline as she was about to rush out of the room.

"Absolutely!" Aline quickly turned back and gave her grandmother a big hug. She felt her warmth and the smell of flowers. Abi always smelled of flowers and wood.

"Have a good day Aline."

"Bye, Abi!"

Aline rushed out of the sewing room full of joy and energy. As she got ready, she felt as if this was going to be a great day, a great Halloween, and maybe the best birthday ever. She hooked her backpack onto a shoulder and rushed out the door, all four dogs following her every move.

"You need to go back, guys. As much as I want you guys to come with me, dogs are not permitted in school." The four dogs sat down and looked at her while Kay whined in protest.

She speed-walked to the bus stop which was at the other end of Portico Street.

"I gotta hurry. I can make it if I cross Cumbric Street before I see the bus turn the corner," She said to herself. She looked to the right while crossing Cumbric Street. There she noticed that her mother was talking with the Mr. O'Moghrain behind the lonely grand tree on his property.

"Huh?" Surprised, Aline was just about to stop when she saw the bus out of the corner of her eye.

"Oh no!" She ran, barely making it onto the bus.

"That was weird!" she thought as she slid into her seat. *"Why is mom talking to Mr. O'Moghrain?"* The bus ride was long. She could see the light at the top of the bus illuminating the houses and their decorations. She was no longer on Portico Street.

As soon as she got off the bus, there, by the front door of the school, were Amanda and her followers. At least that is what Aline called them. Amanda's perfect mom had just dropped her off in their luxurious SUV. These girls were not nice in general, and they were flat out mean to Aline, especially Amanda. She had known Amanda since preschool. They had been friends then, but something had changed because once they got to elementary, Amanda stopped talking to her. In second grade she completely ignored her and by the time they reached middle school, she was downright mean to her.

"There she is," snarled one of Amanda's followers.

"Oh, the birthday girl. Do you girls know who has her birthday on Halloween?"

"Whooo?" asked the girls mockingly.

"Well, you know...evil giants." They all laughed in unison. Aline looked down at the ground and tried to pass them quickly far to their left, but one of them pushed her towards them and another tripped her. This time they all let out a belly laugh as poor Aline fell to the ground.

"Tomorrow I will have the best birthday surprise for you, Aline!" Amanda said with a crooked smile. Aline got up quickly and hurried away, hearing the followers still talking about her and her fall as she left them behind.

She spent the whole school day trying to avoid Amanda and her follow-ers. Went as far as eating lunch outside the school grounds, in what the kids called "The Forbidden Forest." Not one of the followers would dare to get their expensive shoes dirty, so she felt at peace there. She managed the second half of the day with no more encounters and made it safely to the bus, avoiding them one last time.

As she walked back to her house, she hoped that maybe, just maybe Amanda would be nice to her on her birthday. Trying to figure out what she could possibly have done to Amanda for her to treat her this way. As she crossed Cumbric Street she saw her mother speaking with Mr. Grant. The Grants were the decorating archenemies of the O'Moghrains, and the only reason Aline could come up with for these conversations was to obtain decorating tips.

"This is weird!" She forgot about the girls from school for a moment. "I need to ask Mom during dinner. I wonder what they could be talking about and why are they hiding behind the trees. Just like with Mr. O'Moghrain."

Before she knew it, she was opening her front door and the dogs once again got out to greet her. Aline walked up the stairs towards her room. They must have known something was wrong because Ash was not chewing on her shoelaces and they were all moving their butts like crazy pushing each other out of the way trying to reach Aline. Kay got to her first.

"Auuuhhrrrr auh auuu auhr." She looked at Aline as she gently nudged her hand with her nose. The other dogs sat, still moving their butts, and tilted their heads as they looked attentively at Aline. They felt her sadness. Both Mach and Sky licked her hand and Ash whined as he lay down.

"You know, there are good and bad days. Today was not a good day." A silent tear coursed down her cheek.

"Well, maybe this will change your day!" Abi said as she entered Aline's room. "I finished yours first. Take a look and tell me what you think." Abi shook out a beautiful gown. It looked like the dresses on Greek statues. Rock that had been chipped away creating folds, drapes, and fabric forever frozen in motion. That was her dress! Made out of different tones of gray organza over shimmering sequins. It was beautiful!

"That is not all!" Abi was feeding off Aline's smile. "Here is the cape!" This beautiful leathery cape draped down to the floor like dark gray water.

"A cape?" Aline tilted her head as the dogs had just a minute ago. The dogs were wagging their tails looking back and forth between Abi and Aline.

"Or is it!" Abi unhooked the clasps, that looked like long black claws, and two bat-like wings sprung open. All of the dogs started to bark.

"All of you, calm down this instant!" The dogs were quiet and Ash whined as he lay down again.

"Oh yes! Yes, yes, yes, yes! This is awesome!!!" Aline clapped her hands and jumped up and down at the sight of the wings. The tails on the dogs were moving and Ash was back up trying to find something to chew.

"Try it on!" Abi handed the dress and wings to her. Aline went behind the shōji room divider to change. She had no trouble at all putting this costume on. It was light and warm, delicate and strong.

"How were you able to do this? I just can't believe it…it is…it is just beautiful! Thank you, thank you very much Abi. This is your best costume by far." Aline smiled and try to give Abi a big hug, but on her way to Abi, she bumped both Mach and Ash on the head with her wings.

Abi and Aline laughed at the same time. You could say that the dogs joined them for they were all energetically jiggling their butts and turning in circles.

"You look mesmerizing Aline," Abi said with glistening eyes. "And wait until you see how I will paint your face, hands, and feet. They will look smooth like a stone with faint cracks."

"Will we go barefoot?" Aline asked.

"No," laughed Abi. "We will be wearing sandals. I was thinking about using the Amazon warrior sandals. They just need slight modifications so they fit you, and just a bit of gray paint." Aline nodded in enthusiastic agreement.

"Now, let's get you out of this costume so we can go and have supper."

"Yes, I am starving," said Aline, her stomach growling.

They sat down to dinner and had a salad with beautiful edible yellow flowers and ratatouille.

"This is delicious, Mom," Aline said, eating a flower followed by a big mouthful of ratatouille. Her eyes were glowing as she thought about the cool gargoyle costumes that Abi had made for them.

"Oh, Mom. By the way. I saw you talking to both Mr. O'Moghrain and

Mr. Grant today. I didn't know you knew them! What did you talk about? Did they want something?" Kani blinked as she looked at Aline.

"Well yes, I do know them, dear. They are our neighbors after all."

"But you never mentioned them before. Ever."

"There was nothing to talk about, Aline. It's not like we're friends. We're just...neighbors."

"Okay, so what neighborly thing did you talk about then?"

"They really wanted to ask me about the trees," Abi interjected. "You know how our trees are strong and beautiful. Well, they wanted to talk to me but since I was busy making the costumes, Kani went in my stead. Speaking of the costumes, what don't you tell your mom about the costume, Aline?"

Aline's expression changed from confused to excited.

"You will love them, Mom. They are just beautiful. And the wings. Oh! The wings are just so cool. They can be used as a cape you know."

"Oh Abi, you have outdone yourself. This is wonderful," Kani said. "And how are you going to do the faces, hands, and feet?"

"Aline?" Abi looked at Aline encouragingly.

"She is going to paint our faces, hands, and feet to look like stones with thin cracks. Oh, and she will modify the sandals we wore from when we were Amazon warriors. Mine are probably too small now, so I am not sure how you will fix them."

"Leave that to me, Aline. By tomorrow, they will fit like a glove."

"But you will have to work on them all night. How can I help?"

"No sweetie, this will be the easiest and fastest item for these costumes. Don't worry, I will finish them quick. Thank you for offering your help, Aline." Abi smiled. "Now, when you are done eating please help your mother and do the dishes my darling."

"Absolutely!" Aline thought this was the least she could do.

That night, Aline was awakened by the sound of rustling coming from the golden curtains in her room. She rubbed her eyes and realized that people were talking downstairs. With caution she put on her slippers, so not to disturb the dogs, who were sleeping on the floor all around her bed. Gently, she walked to the door and opened it, careful not to make a sound. She reached the top of the stairs where she could partially see her mom, Abi, and Mr. Grant. She could hear that more people were behind them.

"Tomorrow you say?" asked a low voice deep within the family room.

"Yes," replied Abi and Mr. Grant in unison.

"And no one else knows about this?" asked an airy female voice coming from further back in the family room. Aline could smell the firewood burning.

"No, and no one must know. At least not at this time," Abi responded.

"She does not know anything about this," said Kani.

"You mean the girl?" asked a man whose face Aline could not see.

"Yes, Aline," confirmed Mr. Grant.

Aline's eyes got really big. The sleepiness had completely left her and she was now listening very carefully. She heard a squeaking sound behind her and her whole body froze in waves preceded by goosebumps. She managed to gather her strength and turn her head to see who or what was behind her. The old house had betrayed her, the floor had squeaked as Kay approached her.

"Phew, it is you, Kay," she whispered.

"What was that?" Mr. Grant asked.

"Oh no, they heard Kay," Aline thought. She tiptoed back to her room as fast as she could, careful not to make any more noise, went in, closed the door, and got in the bed.

"Why are these people in my house? And what could they be talking about?" Aline asked in a whisper. "Could it be my birthday? Nah!"

She tried to stay awake to see if she could go back out to the stairs and listen some more, but she fell asleep. She dreamt that the curtains were flopping out of the second-floor windows creating a giant rainbow-colored worm that was chasing her in a hallway full of doors. As soon as she tried to touch these doors, they would evaporate leaving shiny fumes. She would then find herself again by the windows being chased by the worm and again she would run towards the hallway with many doors, which was now foggy. She repeated this until there was only one door left at the end. Running through the fog she reached the door handle and pulled the door open.

"Aliiiiiiiiiiiiiiiiiiine!!!!!!" a man's voice screamed her name.

In a jerking motion, she opened her eyes and sat up. She was breathing hard. Cold sweat ran down her back giving her the chills. Her alarm had gone off and with a heavy hand she turned it off. Parts of the horrible dream crawled through her mind and she rubbed her eyes. Suddenly it hit her.

It was Halloween. It was her birthday. She was finally twelve years old.

All Hallows Eve

ALINE PUT on black jeans and her favorite white shirt with blue and yellow flowers embroidered on the neck and on the end of its long sleeves. Abi had made that shirt for her. She thought it was elegant and beautiful. She put on her soft blue flats and ran towards the stairs. She got goosebumps again remembering what she had heard the night before. Without even thinking about it she walked into the family room.

"Oh my goodness!" Aline could not believe her eyes. The room was filled with white and pink flowers. The fragrance of the jasmines, lilies, and gardenias filled the room and her heart with joy. Above the room, there were tons of balloons that looked like floating crystal balls and in the middle of the coffee table was an octagonal white cake with three tiny fondant flowers. One was pink, one was yellow, and one was gray.

"Kani's is pink, Abi's is gray, and the dogs and mine are yellow," she smiled deeply. Next to the cake, there was a note that read

Go to the dining room. Love, Mom and Abi.

Aline ran to the dining room, which was decorated with purple azaleas, orchids, and more jasmine. Her costume was hanging on the fifth wall behind the dining room table, and on the table was a white box that whined.

"What?" She touched the box and it moved. Aline retracted her hand and tucked her hair behind her ear. She saw a note on the top of the box that read

Open with care for I love you and you can call me Alastair, Alis for short!

She opened it carefully. Inside was a beautiful dark puppy dressed up like a gargoyle. She licked Aline's hand and wagged her tail.

"Oh Alastair, I love you too!" Picking Alastair up out of the box she hugged her and petted her long black hair. She had that sweet puppy smell.

"She is an Australian shepherd mixed with giant Schnauzer..." Aline hugged Kani before she finished.

"She is just beautiful. Thank you, Mom."

"Look carefully at her fur, it has hints of purple when the light shines on her," explained Kani. "Abi and I worked last night with some of our neighbors. Mr. O'Moghrain helped us hide her for us and Mr. Grant invited his sister who owns a flower shop to decorate the room."

"Everything looks wonderful. You and Abi did not have to do any of this," Aline said as she pointed at both rooms. She could smell the gardenias all the way from the family room.

"Where is Abi? I want to thank her."

"In her room resting. She is not as young as she once was. Let her rest. You can thank her when you come home from school. Now, I made you several of your favorites. Pancakes, crepes with cream, strawberries and yellow syrup, and french toast."

"Yes!" Aline walked into the kitchen still holding Alastair. She heard the other dogs whining from outside.

"I had to take them out. These decorations with Alastair in the middle would not have lasted long." They both smiled.

Aline had an extra skip in her step that morning as she walked towards her bus.

"Happy birthday, Aline!" Mr. O'Moghrain said.

"Happy birthday, Aline!" Echoed Mr. Grant.

"Thanks Mr. O'Moghrain and Mr. Grant! And thank you for helping my mom and Abi set up the surprise."

They both waved and smiled. The bus was reaching the corner and Aline was at her stop.

The smell of the jasmine was still on her hair when she reached the school. Smiling, she walked towards the entrance. The school was full of Halloween decorations and most of the kids were dressed up. Aline wanted to save her costume for later. The rest of the day seemed to go fast and smooth. *"This is going to be an awesome day!"* She thought as she heard the school bell ring. It was time to go home. She went to her locker, put her books inside, closed the door, and turned to go to the bus. She caught a whiff of the gardenias when her hair moved as she pivoted. She smiled.

"Now!" Amanda ordered. The followers and Amanda threw rotten eggs at Aline. They hurt and they smelled.

"Stop" Aline pleaded.

"Happy witch day to you. Happy witch day to you. Happy witch day rotten egg. Happy witch day to you!" they sang as Aline covered her face with her arms.

"Happy birthday you little witch," Amanda said as she smashed the last egg on Aline's head. They all laughed as they walked away humming, and Amanda was still singing the cruel birthday song. The kids in the school bus sat far away from Aline; the smell of rotten eggs was really strong. The bus driver took pity on her, ordered all the children to put the windows down, and asked Aline to sit on the back seat on top of a plastic tarp.

Aline cried as she walked home from the bus. She felt ashamed that her mom and Abi were going to see her like this. She was embarrassed to have to see the kids from school again during trick or treating. All she wanted to do was to lock herself in her room and never come out.

The gate sighed as she pushed it opened and the dogs ran out to greet her. They wanted to lick her, even Alastair.

"Wow! You still want to be next to me even though I stink. But do not lick me. I do not think this will be good for you." They listened to her and licked Alastair instead. A tiny smile appeared in one corner of her mouth.

"Aline, is that you? For heaven's sake what is that smell?!" Abi asked as Aline walked up to the front door.

"Oh my goodness," she covered her mouth with both hands, partially covering her nose.

"The birthday present from the girls at school was not as nice as yours and moms."

"In the name of... what is that smell? Did one of the dogs vomit?" Kani asked. Abi and Aline looked at each other as Kani walked into the entrance hall covering her nose. Her whole face was pinched off. They both laughed.

"Don't worry Kani, I got this. I know just what to do."

"I don't think this smell will come out even if I take a thousand showers," Aline exclaimed.

"No showers. Just one bath. I'll use my magical bath salts."

"The ones that smell like roses? But you only use them on special occasions."

"I think this classifies as a special occasion. Now, up you go. Please try not to touch anything."

"I'll bring up a plastic bag for her to put her clothes in and her shoes." Kani turned quickly toward the kitchen still holding her nose.

"Good idea," said Abi as she walked up the stairs.

Abi prepared the bath in Aline's bathroom. Aline was in her room, carefully putting all of her clothes in a black trash bag. She could hear Abi pouring the pink crystals into the water. Normally she could smell them, but the smell of rotten eggs made it impossible. She looked at her favorite white shirt and let it go inside the bag. Aline could hear murmurs from the bathroom. She grabbed her towel, another item that would go in the trash, and quietly walked towards the bathroom.

"She must be preparing a strong concoction with her best salts to get this smell off my body," she thought. Then she noticed a piece of egg still stuck to her hair. *"...and my hair."* From the bathroom door, she saw Abi pour transparent blue crystals into the pink warm bath water. Then she waved her hand on top of the water and whispered a few words. The crystals dissolved quickly, changing the thickness of the water, and its color to light lavender.

"Uh!" she whispered.

"Aline?" Aline jumped, feeling she was caught watching something she shouldn't have seen. "Are you ready my darling?" Abi asked in a gentle tone with a warm smile. "Just go in and relax. Let the salts take away this bad experience..." she smelled the dirty towel, carefully grabbed it from Aline, and proceeded to take it to the wash.

"...and the smell?" Aline whispered. "Do I wash my hair?"

"Just float and relax. Forget about what happened and think about what you will make with the rest of the day. I will put the gargoyle costume on your bed and I will be back later to paint your face, hands, and feet." Aline looked at her grandmother in disbelief. Abi came back in and drew closer to Aline.

"Just float," she said, standing next to the tub while removing pieces of egg from Aline's hair. Then she turned and went back towards her room. "Don't worry about your white shirt. I will make it look brand new," she said, putting the towel in the trash bag and walking out of the room with stained clothes, pieces of rotten eggs, and some of Aline's sadness.

Aline sank gratefully into the rose water. A shy smile slipped from her lips while her thoughts of what happened floated away. She began to let go. The warmth of the water comforted her and the floral smell took away any traces of rotten egg. She felt good, calmed. Her mind wondered freely. First, to her gargoyle costume. Now, she found herself truly smiling. It was, without any doubt, the coolest costume she had ever seen. She pictured herself wearing it and how the kids from school would react. This thought stayed with her, as she relaxed more deeply. Lulled by the water, with the floral salts enclosing like a blanket, exhaustion overtook her and she fell asleep, floating.

Amanda's followers were praising the way Aline looked in her costume and Amanda wanted to go trick-or-treating together. She looked cool. She felt cool, strong, and fierce. The grandfather clock stroked, announcing it was eleven forty-five. Putting her candy bag down, she opened her cape and released her magnificent wings. All of the kids were in awe. She turned around and noticed that there were scales on her wings and she was able to control them. With open mouths, the kids surrounding her stared at Aline in amazement. She could move her wings and the power within them was invigorating.

Stretching the wings to their full span, she created a quick gust that blew the hats, wigs, and masks off the kids near her. Some of the kids now had looks of concern; others uttered sounds of fear. As she spun around to apologize, the scales on her wings scratched some of the kids. Their screams sent her into a panic. She opened her wings behind her and just as fast she closed the wings in front of her. Lifting herself off the ground, strongly pulsing her wings. The powerful gusts of wind from her wings pushed everyone around her to the ground, where they lay still looking up at her, watching her with horrified faces.

"Ah!" Aline screamed, sitting up and sending a wave of rose-scented water towards her feet. The bathroom was quiet except for the shushing water in the bathtub.

"It was a dream!" Aline noticed that the water had now a deep lilac color. Her skin felt soft and her fingers were pruney.

"What time is it? How long did I sleep? I need to get ready." She drained the water out of the tub and got her towel. The smell was gone from her skin and her hair. It was not in the water either. These salts had worked miracles against Amanda's rotten eggs. Aline was not just relieved, she felt strong.

Quickly she went into her room. All five dogs raised their heads and wagged their tails. Alastair was the first to get up. She licked the water droplets from her feet.

"That tickles!" Aline said. Alastair smiled and flipped her ears back but didn't stop.

"All right now," Aline said. Kay nudged Alastair away. Then she began to lick Aline's wet toes.

"Oh, I don't think so Kay." Aline moved her feet away from Kay.

"Auhhrrrr auh auhr," Kay apologized.

"It's okay. I need to get ready." She looked at the clock on her wall and realized that she had been in the tub for almost two hours.

"Oh my goodness. I am really late." Aline quickly towel-dried her hair. It was incredibly soft and had no knots. This was very unusual particularly after such a speedy towel-dry. That should have turned it into a bird's nest.

"I need to ask Abi to let me use more of those salts, they are incredible," she said out loud. She put on her Greek gown and then her gray Amazon warrior sandals. Her fingers touched the enormous wings. She was surprised again to feel how light they were. Shaking her dream off, she put them on. When she hooked the claws by her neck they resembled a cape from medieval times. There was no way around the electric feeling she got when she put them on. They were just awesome!

"Abi?" She called her grandmother as she left her room. "Abi," she sang her grandmother's name as she headed towards the stairs.

"Oh, Aline you look beautiful!" Kani responded as she came up the stairs already dressed up, with makeup on.

"Wow, mom! You look amazing!" Kani's cape flowed behind her on the stairs as she approached Aline.

"Abi is doing her own makeup. I will braid your hair and get you ready. She taught me what to do." They went back into Aline's room together, and Kani brushed her daughter's long brown-copper hair. While she was dividing Aline's hair into different strands, she looked up and saw Aline smiling back at her.

"Facing the wrong side of the mirror," Kani mumbled.

"Oh, would you like me to move, Mom?"

"No, it's okay, Aline. Something that Abi would have done first. Do not worry sweetie, this may just take longer than I thought," Kani said as she created an intricate braid crown around Aline's hairline, followed by multiple braids one on top of the other and finishing with a fishtail braid.

"Phew! All done," she said. "Turn around and tell me what you think" She grabbed the hand mirror and showed Aline the back of her hair.

"Wow!" Aline looked at her braids and gently traced them with her fingertips. "My hair looks amazing. I had no idea you could do these types of braids. Could you teach me, Mom?"

"Absolutely!"

Aline got up and gave her mother a big hug. They both heard the grand-father clock downstairs. It was seven o'clock and they were going to be late.

"Should I go get Abi?" Aline asked. "She may need some help."

"You're right, Aline. Wait here. I'll get her." Kani walked out of her room and down the stairs. Aline looked again at her braids, then her whole outfit, and finally she unhooked her wings. She looked like a powerful Greek goddess with her wings extended. She felt great! She was ready to face Amanda and the followers. She was ready to face any kid in school.

The grandfather clock struck again. It was seven-thirty and Aline found herself a bit jumpy. She looked out of the window. She could see the forest dark and deep in front of her and to the right, a multitude of kids and parents trick or treating up on Portico Street.

"Aline!"

"Oh, Abi you look fantastic! I understand now why you disappeared on us for such a long time," Aline said as she approached her grandmother. The makeup was everywhere except for her braided silky white hair. It was untouched by the gray paint, adding an additional layer to Abi's costume.

"Sorry, Aline. It took me longer than expected. Now have a seat," Abi said as she turned the chair so Aline would face her and not the vanity mirror. "Hurry up, sit, and close your eyes." Abi grabbed a powder box with what looked like gray dust and a makeup brush. Kani laid out the makeup on Aline's vanity table and grabbed another brush to help Abi. Aline closed her eyes and felt brushes alternating from her face, hands, and feet. After just a few minutes everything stopped.

"You are done! Open your eyes"

"So quick?" Aline asked Abi.

"Yes, I had two times to practice. I got it down to a science. Now, turn around and look."

Aline could not believe her eyes. She looked like a statue, but somehow dainty, with thin crack lines that softly highlighted age and time. It appeared she had tiny dust specks and slight discoloration from the long exposure to the sun; but she was beautiful, soft, and majestic. Aline was speechless.

"Here is your bag." A full smile was on Kani's face as she handed Aline a simple and delightful gray cloth bag with long, thick silver threads that looped around to keep it closed.

"Let's go," Kani whispered in Aline's ear. She was still admiring the full costume in the mirror. The grandfather clock struck again. It was a quarter till eight.

"Hook your wings, Aline, let's hunt for some of the good chocolate," Abi said. Her wings wrapped around her like a cape accentuating the brightness of her hair.

The three gargoyles surrounded by the four dogs (Alastair was too little to go) got several double takes from the trick-or-treaters. People opened a space for them to walk by, and Aline felt empowered.

Aline saw Amanda and the followers who had decided to dress up like superheroines not too far from them. Amanda was dressed up as Supergirl, with long golden curls falling on her red and blue costume. Her red cape paled in comparison to Aline's lustrous cape. Her jaw dropped when she realized that the girl she was admiring—in what Amanda could only describe as the best costume she had ever seen—was Aline. The followers were quiet for once.

Abi had managed to make some space around them, and winked at Aline who was between her mother and grandmother. She knew exactly what to do. In unison, the three of them unhooked their wings. The crowd moved backward in awe and in silence. Aline walked towards Amanda.

"Happy birthday to me!" She smiled, pivoted, and turned to the closest house to request candy.

The followers took several steps in Aline's direction and stopped, confused, when they saw Amanda was still looking at Aline without knowing what to say or do.

"Aline, enjoy your walk and your sweet price. Once you have acquired all the candy you want, you need to turn back and be Aline once again." Abi's soft eyes spoke to her more than her words. She knew what she had to do, and as hard as it was, she knew that Abi was right. She went trick-or-treating with only the dogs, who followed her every move. Ash almost attempted to eat some of her chocolate.

"No, Ash, you know chocolate is not good for dogs." All four whined in parallel.

Time flew. It was only measured as her bag got fuller, when each piece of the good chocolate hit the gray sack. Once she noticed it was half full, she turned around, hooked her wings, and walked towards Amanda with the dogs around her wagging their tails and shaking their fake wings.

"Do you want to go trick-or-treating with me?" She asked. Amanda's eyes showed the many conflicting thoughts going through her mind. Some of the followers looked at her in suspense, waiting for her response, and others spoke quietly into each other's ears. Stoic, Aline watched Amanda's face beginning to relax. She was filled with the happy memories of Amanda when they were kids. She remembered how closed they were—inseparable. Amanda had been Aline's best friend—almost family. Aline's whole body tingled and she brushed off the goosebumps on her forearm with her hand. It had been a long time, since pre-school really, since Aline had seen her best friend look back at her.

"Sure!" Amanda's lips curled into a small but solid smile. "Happy birthday, Aline. Great costume by the way." Just like that, almost magical, all of the tension was gone and they both felt the joy and happiness they had shared when they were in pre-school. The followers were right behind the dogs, who stayed close to Aline.

"Hey, Aline, do they bite?" One of the followers asked nervously.

"Not if you are nice to me. They are very protective." The followers looked concerned.

"Auhhrrrr auh auu auauuuhhrrr." Kay finished in a low growl.

"Ah!" All of the followers said at the same time while Kay licked Amanda's hands. "She is so cute," Amanda said.

"That is Kay and that was a warning," Aline laughed a bit. "She sure likes to talk a lot." Both Ash and Mach were shaking their butts so fast testing the dragon tails that Abi had created. Amanda and the followers could not resist petting Ash and Mach, who licked them in return. Sky was the only who did not lick them and remained close to Aline next to Kay.

"She is a bit shy," said Aline. Together, with the dogs, the gang continued forward to the next house.

For well over an hour and a half, all of them had a great time forging a new friendship. Their bags were almost full with their Halloween loot, when a woman dressed up in what appeared to be a very expensive Queen Elizabeth costume walked over to Amanda.

"What are you doing?" she demanded looking at Aline with disgust. "It is time for you to come home." Amanda's mom grabbed her by the arm and took her away from them, from Aline, as all four dogs growled. The followers were already dispersing, gossiping in each other's ears. Aline felt sad, more for Amanda than anyone else. She thought about how Abi and Kani would never treat her this way.

Watching Amanda follow her mother up Portico Street, Aline realized that if it weren't for the dogs, she would be totally alone. A few stragglers remained trying to get any candy from the last houses whose lights were still on. She looked around to see if Kani or Abi were anywhere near.

"This is weird," she said to the dogs. "Let's go home, guys."

"Auhhrrrr auh auu" replied Kay

"...and girls" added Aline after hearing Kay. With an extra skip in her step, she turned down Portico Street towards her house. She heard arguing in one of the houses nearby and realized that it came from Amanda's house. Without thinking, she stopped when she saw Amanda and her mom arguing by their living room window. Amanda's mother was really doing the arguing while Amanda looked at her mom with tears sliding down her cheeks. It all came back to Aline. She remembered seeing Amanda's mother being horrible to her right before Elementary school, and Amanda's face when she saw Aline feeling sad for her. It was right after this that Amanda stopped speaking with Aline. Amanda knew that Aline knew what her mom was really like.

"This is why Amanda was mean to me. All this time I have known the truth about what goes on in her house. All this time Amanda has been afraid that I would tell on her." Aline finally understood and felt nothing but sadness for Amanda. They could have been friends all of this time.

"Aline!" Startled by the unexpected voice, she turned around to see her grandmother. "You need to come with me, we need to go and meet with Kani."

"Abi, what's wrong?" Aline asked, hearing the concern in her grand-mother's voice. The dogs' ears pricked forward and their tails lowered.

"No time to explain. Come with me, Aline. Don't be scared." Abi took Aline's hand and looked at the dogs while she speed-walked, turning Aline's long steps into a sprint.

"You know what to do."

Immediately all four dogs ran towards Mr. O'Moghrain's only tree. But they didn't stop when they reached it. Instead, they completely disappeared!

"What!" Aline stopped running.

"Don't stop, we need to hurry!" Abi pressed.

Aline tried to focus on the tree but it was pitch dark. All of the houses had turned off their lights and she could not see the tree clearly. In the distance, she thought she heard her grandfather clock strike. It was quarter to ten. Aline felt cold sweat form on her forehead and some slid down her back.

To her disbelief, she saw Kay appear out of the tree and bark in what Aline thought was a whisper bark.

"It's clear, let's go. Kani is waiting for us. There is no time." Abi faced Aline and looked deep into her eyes. "You are in danger, child. It is no longer safe for you here."

She grabbed Aline's arm and nimbly walked Aline through the only tree in Mr. O'Moghrain's front yard.

4

A NEW WORLD

The Whole Truth

B linking. It feels like you are blinking with your whole body when you go through a portal, an entryway to another world. It was daylight and the greens in this world were radiant and vivid. Aline found herself in the outskirts of a forest. Behind her was the heart of a forest composed mostly of pine trees resembling the ones near her house…well, at least the saplings. The adult trees were at minimum ten times the pines within the iron gates of the house of haunted gargoyles. What was different was their shape, a lopsided "u." The trunk curved to one side then their only lower branch curved the opposite way forming a "u." The lower branch looked like another smaller pine tree growing out of the larger tree.

This magical world was in a perpetual cycle between spring and autumn. A banner of red, orange, and yellow leaves on the trees bordering the enormous "u" pine trees announced that it was now Fall. Beyond a few trees Aline could make out a valley, and in its center, there was a large rocky crater.

"There! You see the castle, Aline?" Abi's right soft hand touched Aline's shoulder, bringing her back to where she was standing. She noticed that on the ground there were now pebbles with scattered clusters of grass. Lifting her eyes, she followed Abi's left hand and had to blink a few times to see the castle. It was suspended in the air and anyone could miss it if they did not look twice, for it camouflaged itself as part of the crater. Like a boulder's reflection on a lake, it was not part of the crater but behind it. This made the crater seem bigger than it really was. Behind the castle were large mountains with white snowy peaks.

"The wizards live there," Abi said.

"Wizards?" Aline was confused and was about to ask more questions when she saw Kani running towards them.

"Kani, it is good to see you, my daughter," Abi said hugging her. "Does he know?"

"Yes, he will meet you in the white courtyard when you are ready. No need to hurry, mother. He understands you both have a lot to talk about," Kani said.

Then she held Aline's face gently in her two hands.

"I know this is confusing, Aline," she said. "But all will be answered shortly. The only thing I will ask is that you are patient for a bit longer. Abi will prepare you. You will soon meet someone very knowledgeable, really important, who will help us. But first I need to go back to the house of haunted gargoyles and speak with Mr. O'Moghrain and Mr. Grant before Akiya hides the entryway again." She paused and looked straight into Aline's eyes. "Abi will tell you everything. The truth about you, and us. The one truth I want you to remember is that I always have and will forever love you." The tone in her voice was strong and solid. Aline felt her words. "Goodbye, Aline," Kani said and softly kissed her forehead. Then she turned and ran off in the direction they had just come from.

"Come, child." Abi put her arm around Aline's shoulder and gave it a squeeze.

She led her granddaughter along a stone path around the crater, where some of the larger rocks had been chiseled to formed benches facing the enormous depression. Abi stopped at one of them.

"Aline," Abi gestured to Aline to sit down. Aline sank onto the bench and looked at the massive hole in front of her. It seemed to sparkle, and she realized there were two suns right above them. It dawned on her then just how beautiful and pure this world seemed, and just how far away she was from home.

"I am glad to finally be able to tell you the truth," exhaled Abi, exuding tranquility. Aline straightened her shoulders and fixed her eyes on Abi.

"Long ago there was only One World. In this world lived three kinds of creatures. Creatures with white magic, creatures with black magic, and creatures with no magic of any kind. This world was beautiful and rich with power. Magical power." Abi's purple eyes glistened as she spoke. Her voice and body were an ocean without waves, soft and calm and with a lot of life and secrets beneath the surface. "An evil warlock named Dashiok wanted to take all of the One World's magic. He thirsted for power and looked forward to reigning with darkness. It took a magical war to stop him and, in this war, we lost many, including the One World. A power blow created by the clashing of one white magical loving spell and one black ancient curse broke the One World into eight different worlds. We just came from what is known as the only world without magic, the human world.

"The war of magic took my mother. I was very young but I still feel, more than remember, as it was yesterday. My mother, Mawk'a, was one of the twelve Guardians selected to protect the One World. She was a dryad, and so am I." Abi gazed into Aline's eyes. Abi's words felt heavy and thick to Aline. She was having a hard time understanding anything that was said or that had happened in the last few minutes. Something felt heavy in her hand and realized that she was still holding her Halloween gray silk bag. It felt ages ago that she was trick-or-treating with Amanda and the followers.

"Let me show you," Abi said. She knew that words do not teach and would not be heard, nor could they explain what she was trying to say. A light glowed from within her purple eyes and her soft skin transformed into smooth gray wood; her gargoyle costume slid to the ground. White flowers grew out of her hair, connected by what seemed to be silk threads. Small branches draped downward along her body, forming a warm flowing gown. The smell of wood and flowers surrounded Aline, which took her home to the house of haunted gargoyles. However, Aline was no longer home, and she was no longer on Earth. She was sitting on the stone bench in front of a huge crater, talking with a magnificent and beautiful being the likes of which she had never imagined. Her heart beat faster with excitement as she tried to comprehend what she had just seen.

"I do not understand. Wh-what *are* you?" Aline stood up abruptly, dropping the gray silk bag. *"Was Abi not my grandmother?"* sounded over and over in her mind. She felt suddenly lost.

"I am a dryad. I possess magic, different from the magical creatures who live within the seven worlds. One of our powers is that we work in the world of whispers. We can receive and send messages through these whispers and know things that no one really does.

"Whispers? Other magical creatures?" Aline asked.

"Sylphs, wizards, witches, elves, many live here and more in other worlds," Abi explained. "For us, these whispers are alive and part of our spirits. They are a way in which we, the dryads, stay connected. A strong connection that links us with those who are no longer here in this physical world."

Aline extended her finger and gently touched Abi's hand. It was cold and smooth like bark that had been sanded down. She looked up at Abi, interested, and a bit worried. Until she saw her eyes. The left eye was violet with a blue undertone and her right eye was violet with a green undertone. Aline exhaled in relief.

"It *is* you!" she exclaimed.

"Yes, it is me. The same one that has cared for you from the first moment I saw you and the same one that still loves you."

Aline immediately felt such a strong sense of love and joy. A single tear fell from her eye.

"Is Mom also a... so, does this mean that I am also a..."

"Dryad," Abi finished her sentence. "Kani is indeed my daughter and thus a dryad. You, on the other hand, are far more special. This is why Kani, the dogs, and I were sent to be with you."

"The dogs???" She looked around for her dogs, realizing they were not by her side.

"You will see them shortly. Do not worry, they are fine," Abi assured her.

A warm feeling tingled first in her cheeks and then descended from the top of her head and down the back of her neck towards her back. Goosebumps appeared on her forearms, hidden by the wings still hooked together at her neck and draping around her like a cape. *"Special,"* she thought, as she replayed what Abi had just said to her.

"Wait, you were sent?"

"Mm-hmm," Abi affirmed. "Let me continue so you can understand this better. When the One World was destroyed, all of the creatures were dispersed to the new worlds. Everyone was accounted for except for Dashiok, the warlock who spoke the ancient black curse. Many thought he had perished. For several millennia we lived our lives filled with peace, joy, and happiness. The old stories stopped mentioning the dark warlock or the War of Magic. While time passed, history became stories, and stories turned into songs. These songs changed the original story, changed the truth, deleting the history of the war, forgetting the names of its warriors, erasing what happened. Life was quiet. Most of the white magical folks became naïve once more as they focused on their day-to-day living.

"Unnoticed in these quiet times, Dashiok's soul lingered within the emptiness that was left where the One World once stood. He had plenty of uninterrupted time to think, learn, and search. First, he found a way to regain a little strength from tiny specs of magic left from the destruction of the One World, which, after thousands of years, circled their way back to him. Enough power to allow him to connect inconspicuously through his magical binding contracts to a few old dark creatures. This then expanded to the creatures that his servants in turn encountered. Second, and most importantly, he found a loophole. A powerful wizard who craved power as much as he did. He tricked this wizard blinding him first by corrupting his heart.

"Using the last of his powers, Dashiok brought the wizard to where he was and inserted himself inside the wizard. Under this disguise, he took over the wizard and resurfaced once more, though in a weaker state than originally. Absorbing the energy of those under a magical binding contract, he soon became stronger. He did this right under the noses of the white wizards, the powerful wizards, learning exactly what he needed to do to gain more power. It was not long before he found out about the entryway.

"You see, Aline, power does not disappear. It is never really consumed, it is simply transferred from one state to the other, from one place to another. When the One World was destroyed, its power was transferred to what we now call the Entryway to All Worlds. It is a place that contains powerful energy ponds that lead to all of the worlds, including the human one."

She saw Aline's face wrinkle, and continue to clarify. "Think of it as a grand hallway with eight doors. Doors made of magic, containing nothing *but* magic, and consistently generating *more* magic. They resemble crystalline pools of water. Ponds of different colors, into which you can step, and travel to a new world in the blink of an eye. Imagine the energy the entryway holds."

Aline exhaled, realizing she had momentarily held her breath.

"Powerful," Abi continued. "And this is all Dashiok needed to know. It was now his new target. The high king wizard wanted to find the entryway and Dashiok managed to trick and convince him that he was the only wizard who could successfully lead such a quest, who could find the magical doors...and he did. Upon finding the entryway, he revealed who he was, and this led to the Battle of Wizards. Dashiok fought the high king wizard, and he would have won if it was not for Akiya."

"Akiya," Aline whispered, the name Kani had mentioned.

"A very powerful sylph who, like my mother, was one of the One World's Guardians and now guards the entryway. She defeated and wounded Dashiok, but he managed to escape with two of the ponds. To protect the entryway and all who could potentially be tempted by its enormous amount of power, she took two precautions. One, she casted a memory spell so the entryway was forgotten. Dashiok would not be able to use anyone to try to find its location or any information. Two, she ingeniously hid the entryway. She casted a separate spell that is constantly looking out for unknown, unwanted, or unusual places. It is never in one spot for too long. Quite brilliant, I think. No one will look for something that they do not know it exists. And it is very hard to find something that is always moving and hiding. For now, she is the only one who can find the entryway and possess the power to anchor the ponds to a particular object. We just came through one, but to protect it, Akiya will remove it soon."

"What happened to Dashiok?" Aline was curious.

"Vermin is indeed hard to vanquish. He not only survived but he grew in strength as the number of followers increased. See, the two doors he took led to where most of the dark creatures were transferred after the One World was destroyed. Where most of his army lay hidden.

"Believe it or not, evil is patient. He understood how much the white creatures had grown in power and in numbers. Clearly, he needed a powerful being to help him retrieve the entryway. If he could not find such an individual, then to create such a living soul was his only option. A new focus was born and with this, a new task. While he accomplished this new task, he also wanted to take vengeance on as many enemies as he could. Dashiok's strength is to identify other creature's need for power as well as find their weaknesses. First, he learned from the sylphs."

"Sylphs?" Aline asked.

"Fairies, dear. It was clear to him that purity within kin led to missed opportunities for power growth. He realized that where there was diversity, when the powers of different kinds of sylphs were mixed, the chimera twins were born. The twins were indeed a new development, and his biggest challenge during the War of Magic. Now, he observed how the sylphs had learned to expand the boundaries of their powers by straying away from the old purist culture. It was simple: when you mixed magical beings, you increased the power of their offspring, of their children.

"With this new found knowledge, he became interested in three different creatures whose paths were unlikely to cross without his intervention. Paying close attention, he found within these three creatures an unexpected and delightful surprise. He would become the father of brand new dark creatures.

Convincing the loner of the trio was no easy task. It took Dashiok decades to figure out what this solitary vampire—whose name was Yakar—desired the most. And it took even longer to decipher how he could speak with Yakar without triggering the vampire's instinct to feed.

"Vampires! At this point nothing surprises me!" Aline interjected. She found herself curiously unafraid at the mention of a vampire.

"Hmmm!" Abi looked deep into Aline's eyes, which at the moment were more blue than green. "It is good not to be surprised in any of the eight worlds. It may just save your life." She paused. Aline's eyes widened. "However, keeping your guard up is a must in magical worlds. The line that differentiates between dark and white magical creatures is no longer clear."

Aline nodded and Abi continued.

"There were two reasons why Dashiok picked Yakar to be part of the three creatures. One, he was almost defeated by Yakar before the War of Magic and he had sworn that he would get Yakar back. Two, Yakar possessed untouched magic that was just what Dashiok needed for his plan. Being the first creature ever created and the only one of his kind made him not just the oldest but also the loneliest. Yakar had never passed his magic down to any child or any family member. His magic was not diluted in any way. And it all resided within the lone vampire."

"How sad," Aline whispered.

A faint smile formed on Abi's face. "Only those pure of heart would feel what you just felt." She caressed Aline's cheek. "In his twisted mind, Dashiok felt opposite to the way you just did. He was filled with satisfaction instead of sadness. Knowing Yakar's weakness, his loneliness, is what gave Dashiok the upper hand. Conjuring powerful magic, Dashiok was able to put forward a proposal to Yakar that he could not refuse. A way for him to create a vampire coven made of humans."

"What?" asked Aline, surprised.

"Yes," Abi replied serenely. "Because there is no magic in the human world, Yakar could not absorb any magic from them. What he could feed on was the closest substance tied to the human heart. Their blood. Indeed a different power, which Yakar absolutely appreciated and dominated. Humans stood no chance against him. His fluorescent turquoise eyes shone bright as he fed. In the end, what bound Yakar to Dashiok was not access to this new power from the humans. No! Dashiok showed Yakar what else he could achieve when surrounded by inferior earthlings. When Yakar allowed humans to drink his blood, which contained specks of the One World's magic, a transmutation occurred that created new beings who resembled Yakar. Not quite children, but rather imitations he could control. Night beings that thirsted for blood, not power, and from whom all mortal emotions had been sucked dry. They had lost their humanity and had gained immortality, or at least very long lives.

"Through dreams, Dashiok showed Yakar what he could do and how he could create the closest thing to a family. In return, Dashiok requested Yakar's services. You see, Dashiok had the ability to move Yakar in and out of the human world. Using the magic of the two doors he had stolen, he was able to create just a few openings into the world with no magic. He controlled these gaps, opening and closing them as easily as he inhaled and exhaled. Yakar despised him for this and felt he had no choice but to agree with Dashiok's demands. Yakar's need not to be alone was so strong that there was no need for Dashiok to create a magical bind with Yakar.

"After he had Yakar, Dashiok then turned his focus on the two remaining creatures. This required combining two powerful beings of different kin. Magical creatures who love and marry another but were not within their own kind. You see, Dashiok had figured out that the same magical powers were passed from generation to generation of creatures who married within their kin. However, if a creature from one kin had an offspring with a creature from another kin, then these offspring were more powerful than both of their parents combined.

"You, Aline, were created out of a powerful love merged from two completely different creatures. Dragons and Krons."

"Dragons! Dragons! They exist?" Her pitch went from high to low as she was processing what Abi just told her. "I am part dragon? And part...?" she looked back at Abi.

"Kron." Abi picked Aline's gray silk bag, waved her hand, whispered a few words, and handed the bag to Aline. "Eat something dear," she suggested. "This is a perfectly good moment to have some chocolate. It is good for the soul, and yours at this very moment is troubled." Aline robotically took the bag from Abi, but in reality, she was in need of more answers.

"What are Krons? I do not understand. I am human, see?!" She extended her arm and pinched her skin.

"Eat your chocolate," Abi demanded, one eyebrow raised. Aline knew all too well that look, and it clearly came across even as a dryad. She grabbed one of the good chocolates and proceeded to eat it.

"Mmm!" Aline's eyes widen as the Halloween chocolate melted in her mouth. It was divine, calming, and warmed her from within. The chocolate tasted way better in this world. "You have to try this," she mumbled with her mouth full, licking her lips. "It is *so* good."

"Aline, do not speak with your mouth full." Abi corrected her with a smile. "Nonetheless, I will take you up on your offer. I added a bit of floral magic to them and they are truly delicious if I may say so myself." Aline watched as Abi's wooden fingers unwrapped the chocolate, broke a piece, and took it to her straw-like mouth.

"Do not worry Aline, by the time I am done I will have answered most of your questions. Where was I? Ah! Yes, an unexpected union," she said. "Pairing an unlikely pair required no effort from Dashiok's side and it partially fulfilled his desire for revenge.

Sañi, Zarkon's great-great-granddaughter, daughter of Gargon the new golden Kron clan leader, fell in love with Makaurrok, grandson of Rrok, son of Kaurrok the head of the dragon Superior Clan leader." Abi paused and looked at Aline, whose eyes were swallowing every word she had spoken. "Sañi and Makaurrok had a pure love. As simple and as logical as a smile. Regrettably, their love was absolutely prohibited by both clans. They did a tremendous job hiding their love and it was impressive that they lasted so many years. Years that were filled with happiness, unaware that another was watching.

"Unfortunately, some things can not be hidden forever, particularly for female Krons. A Kron expecting mother had a fantastic change that announced to all a new life was growing inside of her. Their golden shimmer changed to an enchanting silver glow. Sañi was no exception. Her beautiful skin had the silver glow of a pregnant Kron, as she was expecting Makaurrok's three offspring. Two males and one female were what Sañi could sense when she communicated with the eggs in the heart of her belly. Just like all dragons, Makaurrok's chest filled with pride and fire when he found out he was going to become a father. This pride was soon infected with worry once he started to figure out what this could mean to either clan. He now feared for the safety of his new family.

"When Gargon found out that Sañi was expecting Makaurrok's offspring, his eyes turned red and he cried out for the second time the battle call of the Krons. A deep and loud growl which echoed and vibrated with the aid of his wings. The first cry was produced by Zarkon— another Guardian of the One World—during the War of Magic.

"Gargon was now hunting for Makaurrok. Once he reached the top of a bare and rocky mountain, the domain of the dragon's Superior Clan, instead of finding Makaurrok, he encountered his brother, Moikaurrok who tried to defend his brother's honor. However, Gargon was too enraged and made his first mistake. He began to fight with Moikaurrok. Alerted by the call, many Krons and dragons flew towards them and joined the fight, including Gargon's twenty-seven sons. Fueled by uncharacteristic anger, the clans went from trying to stop the fight, to blaming each other. It is sad that love created new beautiful creatures, and in mere months, fear and hate for these new creatures turned into a battle that destroyed equally beautiful creatures. It was the clash that ended the dragons. Gargon, older, stronger, and enraged made his second mistake. He killed Moikaurrok."

"Oh no!" Aline exclaimed, feeling Abi's sadness.

"Large shifts in emotion and power impacted Sañi, who was hiding in a cave not too far from the battle. Every pore in her body sensed Makaurrok's pain when he felt his brother's death and the fall of his fellow dragons. She also sensed the rage of her family and the vast loss within her clan. It was at that moment when the turbulence and the sorrow were at their highest that she felt the first jerk deep within her belly. Makaurrok put his pain aside and rushed to help Sañi. He knew this would now move very fast and he could lose the four of them.

"Normally other Kron females are present to provide not just support, but magic to the little ones and the mother. Sañi had propped herself against the rocky walls of the cave for support and looked into Makaurrok's eyes. Not able to speak, she created an energy sphere which surrounded her and her eggs and focused only on having her babies safely. He felt helpless and as a non-magical creature, the only thing he could do was to send his life energy towards her. Sañi was filling her eggs with her magic, his life energy, and their love when a strong feeling of weakness paralyzed every massive muscle in Makaurrok's body.

"Dashiok was making his presence known. His new servant, Yakar, was absorbing the energy from Makaurrok while Sañi could only watch with glossy eyes as her beloved turned gray and fell on the ground. Dashiok then moved forward with his plan. The only thing Sañi could do was to transform her love into energy and focus this towards her eggs. At once, Dashiok sent his dark magic towards Sañi, forcing her to give birth to the three eggs: two blue eggs and one golden egg. Her energy could still be seen swiveling around all three eggs like golden silk lace around a gift. It then moved up and inside the eggs, creating golden veins. Sañi smiled and turned to face Dashiok, ready to fight. Using black oozing spindly long arms, Dashiok attacked Sañi. She used her wings to cut off his dark energy and growled back at him.

"She fought with all of her energy. He projected black oozing balls towards her. She immediately jumped to the ceiling and sprang to Dashiok twisting her body and wiping him with her tail, landing in front of the eggs. Her wings covering her new born, leaving her body exposed. He touched the blood on his forehead, and looked back at Sañi. She was exhausted and weak and he noticed. Sending multiple rays of black magic, he tired her until he was able to wrap her with his dark energy and forcibly transfer all of her energy to the three eggs.

"This killed Sañi instantly.

"Finally, Dashiok used a dark and powerful spell to cut out energy and blood from Yakar, without his permission and incorporated all of it first into the golden egg. This drained Dashiok.

"It was at this moment that the wizard Benowit entered the cave with a blast of white magic, pushing both dark creatures away from the eggs. While Dashiok fought against Benowit, Yakar managed to take the two blue eggs out of the cave. Dashiok, weakened by the ritual, barely managed to escape the white wizard.

"Benowit saw his two dear friends lying on the floor and wept while carefully picking up the remaining golden egg. It had fine florescent turquoise veins where Dashiok had inserted Yakar's energy.

"The dragons were lost and only four Krons remained, all with broken wings. In the midst of battle, the dragons had burned the yellow flowers that powered the Krons. Even if the few remaining Krons survived their injuries, they would have nothing to eat."

Abi glanced over at Aline and saw the sad expression on her face. "I think we need to take a pause," she said. "This may be too much to explain in one sitting."

"No!" Aline screamed. "I mean, please continue Abi. I need to know what happened."

"All right." Abi exhaled and continued. "These were very dark times. The rumors whispered to us that Dashiok had completed the ritual on the two eggs he stole. Two blue creatures hatched from these eggs, significantly smaller than a Kron. Now he was coming back for the golden egg. He had spies everywhere learning of its whereabouts and was getting closer and closer. Benowit hid the egg for many years in this world. Passed to different white magical creatures where the wizards, elf, and sylphs tried to provide pure white energy to the egg; however, no change could be seen or felt.

"When Dashiok was getting too close, about 2000 years ago, Benowit sent the egg to a powerful magical clan who hid in the east within the human world. He wanted to see if they could reverse any magic that Dashiok had infused into it. This clan was on the move to an island in the North Atlantic inhabited by the Celts. Three things happened in this transition.

"One, when the egg reached the human world, it shrank in size. Two, Dashiok knew about the move and sent his dark creatures—the hobgoblins —to the human world for the first time, to get the egg. They were nasty monsters who entered the human world painfully and attacked a human village. You see, Dashiok had used some of the power from the stolen energy ponds. Remember, these magical ponds led to different worlds. He used strong black magic to control which world to enter. However, since he only took a small piece from the ponds, even with his dark magic, he could not create a regular door to another world. Instead, he created weak windows. Because these openings were weak, they cause pain to the crea-tures as they passed through them. Akiya has been working ever since to remove the windows that Dashiok created in the human world.

"Three, the hobgoblins attacked the magical clan then hiding in a small village. Even though their magic was not as strong in the human world, the magical clan fought them back and escaped with the egg. They rid the human world of the hobgoblins and saved most of the villagers.

"This attack and the ensuing victory inspired the ancient Celtic festival, which is the reason you are now holding a gray bag full of chocolates. At least something good came out of this small battle. Even though the people of that time may not have agreed, for they were terrified and many died.

"The golden egg stayed with the magical clan for almost two thousand years. Besides the magical clan creating a fantastic bond with the egg, nothing else really happened or changed in the egg. It was 50 years ago when Benowit and the High Magical Council decided that it was time to move the egg again. They thought that the dryads may not only be able to protect the egg better, but could potentially hear whispers from within the egg. They were right. This time the magical clan was living in the house of haunted gargoyles, and the entryway was in the majestic redwood tree on the property of the O'Moghrains.

"Dashiok once more knew about the exchange. His dark creatures suffered when passing through the window to enter the human world one last time. At least, the last time that we are aware of. Dashiok placed his windows in the trees around the properties of the O'Moghrains and the Grant's, deceiving everyone. The humans helped us fight the dark creatures. Many children lost their parents that day, but a strong bond was formed with the O'Moghrains and the Grants that witchy night. Akiya finally destroyed the last of Dashiok's windows, but not before some of his creatures escaped back to this world. That night, Kani and I stayed."

Aline looked intensely at Abi and was about to speak when Abi continued. "Our magic is not as strong in the human world, so it took us many decades of listening. But finally, during the night where the veil between the human world and the magical world is at thinnest, you answered."

Small tears were spilling from Aline's eyes. "I always told you that you were special!" Abi's smooth finger wiped away her tears. You, Aline, were created out of pure love, and your life was fought for against all odds. I guess there is magic after all in the human world, because it changed you, for once the egg broke open, instead of a dragon or a Kron, there was a beautiful, perfect pink human-looking baby. Not even Dashiok could have predicted this; and because of it, we were able to hide you for so long. And could probably have hidden you for longer.

"One of your brothers has grown impressively strong and he is now helping Dashiok create an army. Yesterday the rumors told us that this army is now stronger than we thought and he could have the power to find you, Aline. You see, now Dashiok hungers for revenge and is looking for you once again. He believes that with you he can finally obtain all of the doors from the entryway."

Abi shifted her weight slightly. "Did you hear or feel something different today?" she asked. Aline tried to think but she was dizzy with all of the new information she had just heard. The gray bag of trick-or-treats felt heavy in her hand once again, and Amanda's face popped into her mind. Aline got goosebumps.

"Amanda!" Aline whispered and unsuccessfully tried to brush them away with the palm of her hand. Abi looked at her intently, head tilted.

"When I spoke with Amanda, my body tingled," said Aline, showing Abi her goosebumps.

"Hmmm!"

Aline could not get this chilly sensation to go away, and she remembered the voice on the morning of her birthday. It was a man, and he had screamed her name.

"Interesting...possible!" Abi paused and thought for a few seconds. "Kani and I always wondered if a specific age would trigger a connection. I think it did; 12 years ago today you appeared to us as a tiny human baby. Whatever it was, it created ripples through different worlds and Dashiok felt you for the first time. This alerted Dashiok, because he knew where you were and is one of the reasons why Kani stayed—to protect you."

Aline suddenly missed her mother desperately and she felt a tear grow in one of her eyes.

"We had no choice, Aline, but to get you here where we are stronger to protect you...where you can find your own powers, and learn how to defend yourself."

"I have powers?" It was more of a statement than a question. Aline was not aware she was carefully looking at her hands. *He is looking for me,* she thought as the voice screaming her name echoed in her mind.

"Yes, Aline, you are stronger than you—or anyone, in any of the eight worlds—could ever imagine. We do not know what type of powers you have, but we know one way to turn all of them on."

Aline looked up at Abi.

"How?"

"There is a ceremony that it is done every year for all of the younglings in this world to obtain their powers. We call it the Endowing Ceremony. It is a magical meteor shower. Each meteor is filled with different types of magic. Many think these were created when the One World was destroyed and orbited around all of the magical worlds reaching the next generations of magic folk. It was the One World's last attempt to control the magic, so it was never all in one place for one person to take, but rather equally spread among all creatures."

"How can a world think or try to do something?"

"Oh, dear, the One World was very much alive. I think the One World still *is* alive, somewhere. Now, I know that you have many questions. I will answer many more before we meet the high king wizard. For now, it is time to change out of your Halloween clothes and rest for a bit." Abi touched the wings on Aline's costume. Aline had forgotten she was still wearing it.

"Will I ever return to the human world?" she asked.

"Interesting. That is really a question for you to answer," Abi replied.

Aline's face wrinkled again.

"When the time is right, the decision will be yours. As far as we sense, you are more human than Kron or dragon, but things may change in this world. Now, follow me."

Abi took her to what seemed never-ending gardens connected by either labyrinths, ponds, or flower beds. At the far right side, there was a palace made of smooth rock with beautiful gothic carvings.

"Wow!" That is all Aline could manage to say. The palace was small compared to the wizard's suspended castle, but Aline could have easily called this a castle.

"Let us go inside and freshen up." Abi showed Aline the way towards the palace.

Aline walked into a floor bathed by multiple colors. A partnership between the sun rays from both suns and the few selected stained glass windows scattered throughout the palace. As the day progressed, the sun rays became stencils painting on canvas made out of the floors and walls of the palace. Most windows were shaped as inverted water drops.

Her steps echoed across the open space surrounding the large front doors. Aline followed Abi through wide twisted stairs that separated and led towards the east and west wings of the palace. They walked into a room that was as big as the entire house of haunted gargoyles. It was dome shaped with a large bed in the middle. Vines descended from the ceiling, draping the walls, mimicking the upside-down water drop windows in the main entrance of the palace. Aline could not tell if there were windows on the roof or not, for the vines seemed to move. Sun rays entered from the openings through the top of the rounded ceiling and shone on the wall, right on the spaces between the vines that looked like panels. Seven archways went past the bed, leading to a large balcony facing the gardens with the crater as a backdrop. To the left of the bed was another circular room with what seemed like a small pool in its center.

"For now, this will be your room."

"This is my room? All of this? Really?" Abi could not help but release a small laugh.

"Yes, Aline."

"And you? Will you be here with me as well? There is enough room for both of us. There is even a pool, I think."

"That is not a pool. That is your bath." Warmly Abi grabbed her hand. Aline could feel the cold bark and the heat of her magic. "I will be near you. Let me show you." Gently Abi led her towards the wall to the right of the bed. Aline realized that Abi did not make any noise when she walked. Her steps did not echo like her own footsteps did. Ever so slightly, one sun ray was a tiny bit smaller than the others and it was not straight, as if the air had broken and shifted its direction so it did not fall in the center of the panel surrounded by the vines.

"This will also happen with the rays from our two moons, so you will always see it," assured Abi while she softly touched this long panel and it opened. It was a hidden door.

"Ha!" Exclaimed Aline.

"My room is a mirror image of yours. You can come in whenever you want, and besides..." Abi paused and right on cue, Sky, Kay, Mach, Ash, and Alastair ran in the room, "you will not be alone."

"Oh, how I missed you guys." This is exactly what Aline needed and for a brief moment, it felt like she was home.

"They are weredogs. Shapeshifters. Originally, they were spies working for the magical clan that hid you in the human world. They have been in the human world for so long as dogs that they prefer to be in this shape. When they are dogs, they are not able to speak but they can communicate in other ways. Try it?"

Aline stood still, not really knowing what to do. All five dogs looked intently at her. Her eyes then narrowed filled with curiosity.

"I do not hear anything."

"Yes, but what do you feel, child?"

"Feel?" Aline knelt down and Kay came closer to her, looked at her for a few seconds, then licked her cheek.

"They also feel like home when they are with me." She opened her eyes wide. She *could* feel their thoughts! "Oh my goodness, I can feel what they think!" The butts on all of the dogs were wiggling hard trying to keep up with their tails. Mach, Ash, and Alastair could not help it and started to jump. Her room did not seem so big anymore.

"If you want anything, anything at all, just ask. This is a magical palace, after all."

"Anything?"

"Yes, anything. Clothes, food, books, toothbrush, anything. The palace will provide you with whatever you need. Now, relax. I recommend that you take a bath in the pool and ask for jasmine water. It is most refreshing and will calm the many more questions that I am sure you still have so you can sleep for a bit. I will wake you up so we can eat on the balcony. Eventually I will take you to meet the high king wizard. But for right now you just settle in."

Aline felt excited, tired, hungry, overwhelmed, confused, and still very human. Snippets of what Abi had just revealed to her took turns weighing on her mind. There was so much to understand. She had powers. This excited her. Abi and Kani were not her grandmother or mother, They were magical trees. She was not sure how to feel about this. Her real mother was a Kron and her father was a dragon. They were both dead. She felt sad. She had two brothers and one was helping a dark warlock named Dashiok. This scared her. He was after her and now she was in a magical world, in a magical palace. A palace that can give her anything she asked. She was thirsty.

"Palace, may I please have a cookies and cream shake and a glass of water? Oh, and pirate booty? Please?" A table appeared in front of her and on it was exactly a glass of water, a shake, and a large bowl of pirate booty.

"Yes!" She fist pumped. "Oh, Abi would not approve of this at all." As she got close to the table, a chair popped out of nowhere. "Ha! I did not even ask for a chair. Thanks, palace!" She was about to sit down when Ash whined and a bowl with shredded chicken and bacon appeared on the table. Kay looked at Ash and barked. Four more bowls emerged from nowhere. Aline then proceeded to gobble down her snacks.

"Now, let's try the pool. Taking a bath in a pool, who comes up with this stuff?" She walked towards the pool and only Kay, Sky and Alastair followed her. "Uh! Now I get why only you gals followed me to the bathroom. Okay, what did Abi say I should ask for? Oh yes, Jasmine water." In that very moment, it rained on top of the pool. A powerful rain that quickly filled the pool without getting any other part of the enormous bathroom wet. The air was thick with mist and the scent of jasmine. Aline took her costume off and the vines took the gargoyle outfit from her and hid it in one of the panels on the wall. "I guess they all open," she concluded. The feeling she got from touching the water was something she had never felt before. Not even when Abi used her salt waters, which now she realized were indeed magical.

This was a cozy and calming sensation that also filled her with energy and allowed her mind to wander and focus at the same time. Floating on this wonderful pool of jasmine goodness, Aline's mind drifted. No longer thinking about what Abi had revealed in pieces; but rather, she replayed every word again exactly how it was told. By doing this she answered more questions and felt slightly more at peace. In a soothing manner, she repeated this again and again until there were no more questions left. Now what floated away were Abi's words telling the truth about who she was and where she came from.

On the surface of the pool, she found herself enjoying her blank mind and the silence the water provided. Dimly, a blue light began to appear in the corner of her mind. It grew until she could tell there was a small yet powerful object in front of her. Blinded by the blue shimmer, she could not make out what it was.

"Aline," a whisper startled her out of her slumber. This seemed familiar to her. The jasmine water helped her focus and she remembered. On the morning of her birthday, she had heard this voice screaming for her. She stood up. *"Could it be Dashiok?"* she thought, distracted by the vines, which moved quickly. First, they dried her using a long, fuzzy towel. Later, they provided her with extremely comfortable pajamas.

"Oh my! I do not think I would ever get out of these," she told Kay, Sky, and Alastair. They all smiled. "I am really tired. It seems that I have been awake forever." Dragging more than walking, she made it to the bed and fell asleep right on top of the covers. The vines gently lifted her and tucked her in.

Unexpected Friends

"Aline, my darling, it is time to wake up."

"Is it time to go to school? Did I miss the bus again?" She sat up and everything came back to her all at once. She was no longer home; she was no longer on Earth. There would be no need to get up early to take the bus again. For a long, long time. The last part made her smile.

"Are you hungry?" Abi asked, handing her clean clothes.

"I am starving!" She looked up and saw her favorite white blouse. "You fixed it?" Plunging her nose into the blouse, she inhaled hard. She could only smell wildflowers.

"Did you ever have a doubt?"

"Never. Not once!" It all became clear. Through magic, Abi was able to make impossible things happen and at a speed not doable for humans.

"Let's go to the balcony. Your favorite yellow stew is ready. This will help wash down the not so healthy snack you had."

"You know about that?"

"Dear, the whispers tell the dryads just about everything."

"Dryads, that's what it was," she looked towards Abi apologetically.

"That is all right Aline. I understand. Everything is new and it will take a while to remember it all."

The palace had set a beautiful table with flowers, cold nectar water, yellow stew, and wonderful sweet treats that resembled cookies. Aline slept right through breakfast, so she had thirds of everything. Quenching a thirst she was not aware of, the nectar water was one of the most refreshing things that she had ever drunk. For the five dogs, the palace had prepared what looked like scrambled eggs with bacon and toast—their second break-fast. All five joined Abi and Aline at the table.

Both suns shone high above the crater. Soaking in their rays, Aline sensed the energy flowing with each breath, in each bite of food, on every-thing she heard or touched in this world. She felt stronger. Like she could run forever and never get tire nor feel any pain.

Abi turned towards Aline and took a deep breath. A cool breeze gently blew Aline's hair and she felt connected. Everything around Aline spoke to her and filled her in a way that made sense. She had experienced similar sensations back in the human world, but they were not clear, they were jumbled up like white noise. Music that was muffled. You could hear there was music, but could not tell the melody apart from the lyrics.

"Do you feel something, Aline?" Abi asked while she exhaled.

"Yes." She barely managed to speak she was so busy pushing another spoon full of stew into her mouth. Abi looked at her with one raised eyebrow. Aline swallowed hard and immediately slowed down.

"I can't explain it, but I feel strong. Not like I can pick up heavy things with my hands that I couldn't before, but more like I can feel things that I could not before. Does this make sense?" Abi nodded and Aline continued. "This world lets me hear things that I could almost hear back home. That I ignored because they never made any sense. I am not sure what it is saying to me now, but I am closer and could possibly figure it out."

"Yes, it speaks. I like to think that the whispers are part of it. We will rest here for a while and maybe you can try to connect with this new world," Abi suggested.

After their meal, Abi showed Aline around the palace and gardens, and answered as many questions as Aline could throw at her. Kani would always come up first, and the answer was always the same...*she had to stay on earth to protect you.* Aline missed her terribly.

During their stay, Abi would walk Aline through the gardens, and around the crater. She really enjoyed these walks. She particularly enjoyed walking underneath the suspended castle. As Aline looked up, she could see the forceful waterfall falling right above their heads, but it never touched the ground, as if it hit an invisible wall. It was magic. The waterfall roared, as enormous amounts of water would disappear and a cool mist was the only thing that reached Aline, lightly touching her face and hands.

"It is grand, isn't it?" Abi mused. Aline just nodded, raising her hands, tilting her face back, and laughing out loud. Abi enjoyed Aline's reaction. "Only a small portion of the majestic waters are turned into mist," she explained. "It is this magical mist that waters all of the gardens in the castle grounds, including the gardens around the palace. Well, a bit of the mist is also used to make the nectar water that you love so much." Abi moved her head slightly to point south. Aline noticed the mist was floating down towards the palace and on its way, it would gently kiss all the leaves and flowers. She felt their joy. "The whispers always tell me how happy the gardens are here," said Abi. Now Abi was the one to tilt her head back. Aline could see the mist touch her smooth gray wooden skin, creating water droplets that moved around and then look as if they pushed their way into her skin. Aline realized that Abi was drinking the mist.

"The wizards cast a wonder spell," she said, and Aline noticed that some of the white flowers that created her hair began to bloom, and moss grew on the small branches that draped downward, turning her flowing gown to a mossy green. Abi's purple eyes glistened as she continued, "for the rest of the waters are gathered and magically transported to the rivers flowing south from the Northern Mountains. These then support all life as they make their way down to Southern Shores." She pointed at the grand Northern mountains behind and to the right of the wizard's suspended castle and traced her wooden finger south. Aline was filled with joy. Even with all of the questions in her head, she felt at ease. The cooling mist had broadened her connection to the One World. This was one of Aline's favorite walks with Abi.

When Abi was not around, Aline would ask the palace for crazy food and share it with the weredogs. She always asked for the nectar water as this was a treat for her in more ways than just quenching a thirst.

For the next few months, Aline learned more and more about this new magical world and the many creatures that roamed it. She finally relaxed and let the world speak to her. She still had questions, but believed that the ones that mattered now had been answered. More questions would be answered in their own good time. She was content. A tiny smile peaked through her lips. For the first time, a small part of her felt she was home.

In one of their many walks Abi decided to tell Aline how the children of this world learn what they needed to in order to become good, strong, magical young adults.

"In our world, education for our younglings is very strong and robust;

however, we do not have schools. The world itself, our forests, mountains, deserts, and oceans are the institutions where our youngling truly learn everything there is to know to become better than the generation before," she explained. "Nature, life experiences, and the elders are the best teachers. Nature teaches us magic, science, and math. The elders teach us about the past, our history. They teach us how all creatures applied magic, science, and math. Finally, our life experiences teach us what magical powers we have, when to use magic, and how to grow this magic. Our life experiences help us refine what Nature and the elders have taught us. In the end, words do not teach, only life experience does."

Aline was surprised that there were worlds out there where children did not go to school but rather a backyard, a park, or a forest was the school.

"This is awesome! I love this world even more now," Aline responded excitedly.

"It is much harder than you think. It requires more discipline, better listening skills, and more understanding of the individual self and how you fit as a whole in the world we live in. By far this is better than any earthly educational institution could ever capture in their programs, much less teach or guide another to do. It works because children—all children including human children—are natural learners.

"Nature is an innate teacher and takes many forms. Learning that is bound by four walls is slow, limited, and conditioned by the four walls and one individual, the teacher. Not to blame the human teachers, for I know they do a wonderful job without any magic. And they are absolutely under-estimated and underappreciated sometimes for the wonders they achieve without a single drop of magic. Relying on passion and love—if applied correctly, these feelings can be stronger than magic. They do the best they can. But in the end, they are only one, where Nature is composed of thousands upon thousands of teachers.

"Now, it is the time for you to listen and understand before you make any decisions or changes. Lesson number one Aline. For everyone—and there are no exceptions—the path to learning is different. On your path, you will need to learn fast and maybe even teach others sooner that you or anyone could have anticipated.

"Lesson number two. Everyone's choices are endless, and so is what they are capable of creating. All we need to do is feel, really feel deep in our hearts what we truly want, what genuinely makes us happy. It is the feeling, not at all what we see or have in front of us, that creates things in our life."

Abi turned to look at Aline. "For you, my dear, I believe this could not be more true. Regardless of what anyone says, thinks, has done or tries to do to you Aline, ultimately, you decide who you are, what magical powers you have, and what you will do with those powers as you develop them." Abi gently moved her hair behind her ear and smiled at her.

One late afternoon, when the two suns were high and the air was fresh and light, Aline was enjoying lunch with the weredogs and Abi. She was admiring the reflection of the sun rays on the castle's gardens as well as on the crater. The crater looked like a large bowl that was filling up with sunlight.

"Aline, after we are done eating, we'll go to the white courtyard and meet with the high wizard king. He has only seen the golden egg. So this will be the first time he will see you, my beautiful Aline."

She gently brushed Aline's hair. Aline smiled back at Abi while picking up her first cookie. The vines of the palace moved quickly to pick up the dirty dishes and give the dogs biscuits and fruits. With their tongues sticking out, all five wagged their tails. This made Aline smile wider. Abi continued, ignoring the dogs. "He has been around for a long time, Aline, and he knows more than you could ever imagine. However, one of the few things he does not know is you and your capabilities. You, Aline, represent something new that touches all eight worlds. He knew that coming here would trigger some of your powers, and we all hope that the meteor shower would wake up the rest. Ultimately, it is up to the type of meteors that choose you, and it is up to you, Aline, to discover yourself and your powers."

"A meteor shower where meteors choose...er...hit me?"

"Choose not hit. They are quite gentle, and yes, indeed they knowingly choose. There are many kinds and sizes of meteors. These meteors are attracted to and select only the children they know the powers they bring will flourish with. As I mentioned, everyone's path is different. This has been the way every year, for years. It is how I enhanced my powers and how Kani obtained hers. We believe that the right meteors will be attracted to you and choose you and that this event will wake something deep inside you."

"Do you really believe this will work? I mean, that my powers will wake up?"

"We believe so, but it will take patience," she paused, "...and time. I am afraid that Dashiok may not need as much time as we do." Aline continued eating her cookie while looking at the crater. She was thinking about Dashiok and the calls she had heard in her dreams.

"I do not think we have much time," she thought.

"Ready?" Abi asked once Aline had finished her third cookie.

"I am," she said, standing tall in blue jeans and her favorite white shirt, feeling a bit better. The cookies were delicious.

They walked through a small labyrinth made of waist-high bushes that led them to the stone path they were on when she first arrived in this magical world. Slowly, Aline's eyes followed the crater far to the right, where once again she had to blink twice to see the wizard's suspended castle.

Once they reached the right side of the crater, there was a semicircle of stepping stones facing the crater. Its edges hugged the mouth of the crater. It was a stage or amphitheater of some kind with several tiers of seats made out of slate behind it, echoing the semicircle. Beautiful long silk blue-green grass grew between each slab. Tall thin pine trees created archways separating the amphitheater from the rest of the gardens.

As they continued on the main path of the front gardens, on each side there were sections containing different flowers, fountains, arches, aqueducts, benches, or gazebos. If you did not look up to see the castle, the gardens seemed endless.

"We need to go there," Abi pointed at tall white aqueducts that boxed in a garden. To Aline, they appeared to be giant spiderwebs. White arches surrounding two narrow, drawn out pools with white lily pads scattered throughout. There were benches on both sides following each pool and in between the pools, there was a beautiful white stone gazebo. On its columns, there were alternating blossoming flowers that reminded Aline of the fragrance in her family room on the morning of her birthday. Looking down at the light gray stone on the ground, she found herself missing the house of haunted gargoyles, missing Kani. She still thought of her as her mother.

Lifting her head, she noticed that in the gazebo, there was a tall, bald man admiring the lily pads on one of the pools.

"Benowit," Abi called softly. Aline's eyes widened when she realized that

Benowit and the high wizard king were one and the same. "I would like to introduce you to Aline."

The first thing Aline noticed was his long silky beard, which ended in a perfect cloud of curls. Then, she noticed his gentle brown eyes surrounded by thousands of fine wrinkles. These lines became deeper on his hands for it seemed that the history of the universe was written on his light-brown skin. What really surprised Aline was his voice. It was soft and powerful, young and wise.

"Hello, Aline." His smile was warm and inviting. "Mmm! You remind me of Sañi, your mother," he continued without changing the expression on his eyes though his voice was now a bit sad. "She would have been so happy to see you. I knew your mother and your father well, Aline, and you were deeply loved by both."

Aline was not expecting to feel the way she did about the two beings whose names she had just learned, and was surprised to experience a strong surge of happiness.

"Now, I know that all of this is new and that at such young age it is a lot to understand," Benowit continued kindly. "You must have many questions. Is there anything you would like me to tell you?"

"Could you please tell me more about my mom and dad?" Aline was stunned at her own question, but deep inside, she was desperate to learn more.

"Ah, yes! We should arrange more time for this, for there are many tales I can tell about both from the time they were younglings. Maybe we can ask the palace to prepare tea and sweets and I can tell you in more detail about them." Aline's heart sank, realizing she would have to wait to hear more about her real parents. But as Benowit talked, she felt better.

"I knew them since they were mere hatchlings. Oh boy, I have many stories to tell you," Benowit laughed out loud. He had a heavy laugh and she found herself smiling, knowing that even though she might have to wait, she would hear about her parents beginning with when they were young.

"This will take many cookies and will require that I spread our reunions out a bit. But there is something I can tell you now about both your mother and your father." Aline's eyes widened, and he continued, "Sañi was incredibly smart, very astute. Always a few steps ahead, figuring out what most of us would say or do before it was said or done. This is how she was able to save you. In those last minutes, she knew what Dashiok was about to do and she used the love between her and your father to protect you." Aline was absorbing everything Benowit was telling her almost without blinking.

"Now, what I can tell you about your father, Makaurrok, is that he was never afraid to move forward, even when he was really afraid." Aline's brows knit as she tried to figure out the puzzle that had just been laid in front of her. The high wizard king smiled slightly and he continued.

"Child, there is not one being in any world who is never truly not afraid. In reality, what they are is courageous. Even though they are afraid or unsure, they do not shy away. They face whatever it is that they need to face. I see all of this and more in you: your mother's intelligence, your father's courage, and their loving energy."

"You can see energy in me?" Aline asked.

"I can see enormous amounts of energy in you, stirring inside, with no flow or sense of direction. This is why going to tonight's Endowing Ceremony is important. You see Aline, we attract what we need, what we ask for. We sometimes do not even know we are asking for something we want. To be more specific, we attract what we wish. When it comes to magic, most younglings wish for certain types of powers. This is not just merely asking for what they want. They desire this with their whole body. Picturing themselves with these powers and feeling in their bones the happiness that these powers will bring them and others. It is not all about them.

"When they do this, the right meteors sense those pure wishes filled with good intent and they choose. It has been so for many generations. We—the representatives of each magical creature—have agreed that it would be best for you to participate in the Endowing Ceremony." Looking straight into Aline's eyes, he continued, "Now, it is my turn, Aline, to ask you questions. First, tell me, child, do you truly know what your heart wishes for?"

Aline sat down, looking at Benowit. Understanding the perturbed expression on her face, the wise king offered her some guidance.

"Take a deep breath, close your eyes, and when you exhale listen, Aline. Inside of you, there is an answer."

So she did. Aline looked into the pool of water in front of her, inhaled, and closed her eyes. Because it felt good and it just made sense, she held her breath for a few seconds. Her body felt heavy against the bench and her mind felt it was floating in a lightless opening. Soon, little stars appeared and her hair moved as if she were under water. Feeling a strong light above, she opened her eyes and could see the surface not far above her head. Exhaling, she swam up as fast as she could, breaking the surface, taking another breath. However, her body did not stay in the water. She floated up to what seemed to be the middle of space.

The stars were now bright, bigger, all different colors, and moving towards her fast. Her first instinct was to run away. Desperately she made running motions, but in truth she was barely moving. Then she remembered Benowit's words about her father. Even though she was afraid, she decided to turn and face the moving stars. As they got closer, she realized they were not stars at all, but large rocks surrounded by glowing fumes. Dozens of glowing rocks started to pass right by her. Without knowing why, she wanted to stop one but had no idea how to do it, or even how to move.

"My mother would have known what to do!" she thought. Not too far away she saw an immense orange rock with a purple and blue tail moving towards her. She wanted this rock and noticed that it would miss her, moving right above her heard. She felt desperate. Waving her arms and legs, she began to spin in place.

"What do I want?" she screamed. "Magical powers, I need a magical power. What powers do I want? What do I..." At that moment, she saw a tall golden being in the shape of a human. Surprisingly, she was not scared, but rather calm and at peace.

"Aline, Aline, Aline..." many whispers echoed her name. "Aline," this time a female voice stood out from the echoes. "My beautiful child." Warm air wrapped itself around Aline. It felt like a hug. "I have waited for a long time, and here you are, full of love and kindness." The golden shape was fuzzy so Aline could not make out who it was.

"Who are you?" she asked.

"Tell me, what does your heart tell you?"

She knew it all along, it was her mother, the golden Kron.

"Mother!" The words caressed Aline's lips, leaving a smile as they escaped and tears in her eyes. "How is this possible?"

"Only the most powerful magic has allowed me to do this, Aline. You, my child, are my last message. In the end, Aline, magic, which is what most seek, does not really matter. There is only one power that is victorious over all others. You, my child, have this power. You need nothing else. Use it well."

Aline's tense muscles relaxed and she was about to speak when the rock hit her dead center.

"Aline" the male voice from her dreams screamed and she opened her eyes. Catching herself on the bench, she noticed Abi and Benowit looking at her.

"Are you all right Aline?" Abi asked, a bit concerned.

"I am fine." She looked at Benowit and said, "I do not know what powers I want, but I do know which meteor I shall choose."

"Interesting! Tell me more."

"It is orange with a purple and blue tail and very large."

"This just became really exciting," Benowit exclaimed. The smile of a young child was painted on his face between the fine wrinkles. "Originally there were all larger meteors like the one you just described. With time they had clashed one against another, forming more smaller meteors with just one color. The smaller ones are what most of the younglings have received for the last millennia. Everyone waits to see who will receive the remaining five original meteors."

"It is impressive Aline, that you got all of this from one small breath," Abi added. Aline saw the puzzled look on Abi's face and realized that what had just happened to her took but a few seconds. Then she remembered the warm air hugging her. She had just seen her mother.

"Did you see anything else?" Benowit asked upon seeing her smile.

"No...eh...it was all weird and really fast." Aline decided to keep the encounter with her mother to herself. After all, it was a very private moment, special, and it was all hers.

"I do have a second question for you Aline," he continued, now a bit more serious. "Is there anything else you wish to tell me?"

Aline hesitated. She was not sure what to do. Should she tell them about her dreams? What could she really tell them? That she dreamt about a blurry blue light? There really was not much to tell them at this point. If she dreamed of something more clear, she would let them know. But for now it was just a dream.

"No, not really," she said. Once she knew more, and if it was important, she would tell them. At least, this is what she told herself to feel a bit better.

"If you do see, hear, or feel anything different, out of the ordinary, you can come to me and tell me. I may be able to help you, Aline." Benowit's gentle voice was followed by a soft pat on the hand and a kind smile. She did not feel bad for keeping to herself that she had seen her mother; however, she felt a little bad not telling them about the blue light and the voice.

"The voice," she thought, *"who could it be?"* Now she had heard it a third time, and was no longer sure it was Dashiok. She imagined that her mother would not allow Dashiok, not even his voice, to get close to them. *"No, it had to be someone else,"* she argued, *"or maybe it is just a dream. Oh, boy I am not sure."* She brushed off her thoughts of dreams and came back to the conversation that Benowit and Abi were having.

"Yes, you are right Abi," Benowit concluded. "It is agreed then, we will ask the members of the High Magical Council to witness the event and stand guard in case Dashiok decides to show up." Aline was at a loss.

"What! Dashiok will be here?" A shot of panic gripped her.

"It is not likely, but we can not let our guard down," Benowit reassured her. "If anything, he is counting on tonight to be a success. Do not worry child, he has no idea that you look human, nor the strength of your humanity. Indeed you are blessed, for you carry the best of all of us."

"Now, come Aline, we need to get you ready for tonight's ceremony." Abi bowed her head to Benowit and guided Aline out with one hand on her shoulder.

All five dogs were waiting for them at the palace. Aline had fun again asking the palace for snacks. This time she was more creative and requested french fries, tiny meatballs, caramel popcorn, and blueberry pancakes with a glass of warm milk. The five dogs mimicked her but with a doggie twist. They selected peanut butter pancakes, tiny bacon balls, sweet potatoes, and chicken strips. Abi was not really happy with any of the snacks they selected and Aline compromised by having more vegetables and fruits during dinner.

Apparently, the Endowing Ceremony was a bigger deal than Aline thought. All of the magic recipients dressed up in fancy clothes. This was another area where Aline had tons of fun. She asked the palace for different clothes, for the dogs. She dressed Mach and Ash with bowties and matching vests. They did not like this at all, but all of the girls enjoyed it very much. Particularly Alastair, who wagged her tail so much she fell on her butt and rolled backward. What made everyone laugh even more was when she got up quickly, not knowing what had just happened.

Then several funny dresses appeared on Aline's bed. There was a clown dress, a monkey dress, and an ostrich dress. Aline could sense the dog's voices laughing just as much as she could hear their barks and whines. The ostrich one came from Alastair.

"Alastair, an ostrich dress, really?" she laughed. Alastair got really quiet and very close to her.

"What is it, Alastair?" Aline got two distinct messages. One was to call her Alis; her name was given by a Scottish little boy thinking she was a boy puppy and it had just stuck. Two, a picture came through of little Alis standing on the amphitheater stepping stones.

"Alastair, I mean Alis, you got your powers last year?" When Alis raised her little paw, Aline saw a purple meteor moving towards her, adding the hint of purple on her black fur.

"Thank you for sharing Alis. This gives me hope!" Aline said. This sent all five dogs into a butt-shaking outburst. Once they calmed down, they all selected simple outfits for the ceremony.

In the end, Aline decided on a white silk dress, with elbow length draped and split sleeves, delicate jewels creating an empire waistline, and layers below it imitating white rose petals. No shoes, as it was a tradition. It was thought that feeling the grass between their feet grounded them when receiving their powers. Excitement began to fill Aline when all five dogs and Abi exhaled as soon as they saw her. Aline asked the palace to choose whatever it like for her hair. It was the first time that someone asked the palace to choose for itself. Its vines carefully brushed her copper brown hair leaving most of it loose with the exception of a few little braids held in place by tiny white flowers.

Before they reached the semicircle, Aline could hear that it was bursting with different creatures. For the first time, she saw elves, sylphs flying around, other dryads, small little square creatures she later learned they were called Apotequils, witches, and wizards. Tons of children of all ages were standing on the stepping stones of the semicircle. All the other magical creatures were either sitting down on the stone slabs or chatting around the amphitheater. Many of the creatures looked at her and then whispered to each other, which made her feel uncomfortable. The two suns had just touched the crater and Aline choose to stand at the right end of the semicircle.

"Hi. I am Cristina," a decisive voice spoke up. Aline turned around to see a sylph addressing her. She looked about one year younger than Aline with long wavy brown hair, hazel eyes, and one dimple that could only be seen when she curled her right cheek.

"My name is Sofia..." the sylph right next to Cristina smiled. A nine-year-old looking girl with long brown hair and very long eyelashes. Her big brown almond-shaped eyes looked at Aline, hinting it was her turn to speak.

"My name is Aline!"

"It is really nice to meet you, Aline," Sofia replied.

"It is nice to meet yo...," Aline began, but Sofia continued talking.

"I love your dress, it is really beautiful," she started to pick up the petal-like layers and began to smell them.

"Stop Sofia, it is not made from real flowers," Cristina said crossly.

"I know Cristina, but it does smell like roses!" She winked at Aline, and continued sticking her nose deep into a petal. "And stop telling me what to do!"

"Really, it smells like roses? Let me see." Next thing Aline knew she was being hugged and smelled by two sylphs, and it tickled.

"Ha, ha, ha. Oh no! Ha, ha, ha, ha. Please stop it tickles, stop," Aline managed to say before breaking into uncontrollable laughter.

"My goodness, you are extremely ticklish," observed Cristina. Sofia was still sniffing the petal on her dress, looking at Aline with a playful smile.

"I am sorry, but I did tell you that I loved your dress," Sofia said.

"It is all right...er...I guess," Aline responded, not knowing what else to say and still wiping tears of laughter off her face. "So you two are fairies?"

"We prefer to be called sylphs," Cristina corrected her.

"I am a sense sylph. I can make you feel things. Want me to show you?" Sofia asked.

"Sure," Aline said, curious. Instantly she wanted desperately to eat oranges. Lots of oranges and only oranges.

"Hungry for oranges?" Sofia asked proudly.

"That is all she can do now," Cristina explained proudly, for Sofia was her sister. "But soon will be able to control other feelings, like happy, sad, confused, and more. Mom and Dad say that she may possibly control some-one's power if their powers are linked to their feelings. Which it is true for most magical creatures. I am a nature sylph. Let me show you."

She did not even ask or wait for a response. Aline felt a tug on her shoulder and when she turned around she saw a long vine that twisted and turned into the shape of a smiley face.

"Wow, that is amazing!" she exclaimed. "Both of your powers are incredible."

"What are your powers?" Sofia asked.

"I am not sure," Aline replied. "It is one of the reasons why I am here tonight."

"That is okay, I just recently got mine and I am still figuring them out," Sofia said matter-of-factly.

"You got yours three years earlier than me," Cristina said, "which is pretty amazing considering I waited forever to get my wings and to increase my powers." As she spoke, her crystal-like wings opened and closed softly. Aline noticed they had a soft hint of green and blue.

"The meteors help grow the powers for those who already have powers," said Cristina, "I wonder what I will be able to do after the meteor chooses me!"

"Oooh! Maybe you will get one of the five," Sofia said.

"That would be awesome," Cristina said. "It has been forever since someone got an original meteor. You know, there are only two marbled ones left."

"How exciting. Even before I got my wings I have been wishing really hard for us to be the only sisters to get similar meteors, to get the marbled ones," Sofia said, flickering her wings, which had a yellow and pink shimmer. "They are called, *The Twins*. Is there one meteor that you are wishing for?"

"Sofia! You know we only talk about our wishes after the Endowing Ceremony." Cristina quickly corrected Sofia.

"I know, I was just curious. You do not have to answer me."

"It's okay," Aline grinned. "I think I wish for the orange one with a purple and blue tail."

"Uh-huh! That's a big one all right! Stick with us Aline, maybe when the three of us wish together for original meteors, they will have no choice but to be attracted to us and move in our direction."

"Yes, worst case, maybe just one of us will get lucky. I like how you think Sofia." Cristina looked at her sister and then at Aline. "...I am in!"

"Me two," Sofia cheered.

"I am in as well," Aline beamed.

"You are supposed to say 'me three'," Sofia corrected her.

"Oops, me three," Aline giggled, and the sisters joined her.

Meteor Shower

BOTH SUNS WERE NOW SLIDING behind the crater, triggering the light sylphs and the Yachaq (or white elves) to send flickering flames around the semicircle. The magical creatures were all seated now on the tiers of the amphitheater. Several creatures were humming spells and creating a translucent dome to cover the amphitheater.

"It is time," Cristina said.

"That is new," Sofia added, pointing at the transparent energy atop the roofless theater. Aline knew that it was there to protect them from Dashiok in case he decided to show up, and the ones humming must be the members of the High Magical Council.

Benowit stood in the middle of the semicircle facing the younglings, with his back towards the crater. The Northern Mountains stood silently to his left. Only their white peaks were visible under the night sky.

"Our young magical children. Many of you have been waiting for this since you were little saplings. You are now ready. This is one of the most important magical moments of your lives. What you desire tonight will define the type of magic you shall receive and/or grow, and how you will choose to use it throughout your life. Remember to fill your hearts with strong wishes and good intent. Choose well."

He stepped to the side. The light that the sylphs and the Yachaq had created, descended downward until it went out, leaving the night sky pitch dark.

In a distance, Aline noticed tiny dots of different colors. She knew exactly what these were and that initial fear she got when she was in the gazebo came back, flooding her senses. Sofia grabbed her hand.

"If it helps, I can make you really hungry for chocolate. It is very hard to get some here." This distracted Aline, and she turned again to face the dots, which were now big fuming rocks moving in their direction. Loud roars emanated from the meteors, followed by strong gusts of wind. Cristina grabbed Aline's hand.

"There!" She and Sofia pointed at the same time. Aline saw large marbled green, pink, blue, golden, purple, white, and black meteors barreling towards them. And right between them was the giant orange rock with a purple and blue tail. The closer they got, the more she would see their beaming magical fumes. Squinting, she noticed that the front was not orange at all, but yellow, white, and red that looked orange from afar.

"Do you see that? It is not orange!" Aline said.

"It isn't?" both asked, tilting their heads and squinting up.

"You do not see it?"

"No," they said in unison.

This made Aline want the meteor even more. Turning to ask Cristina a question, she noticed her eyes were closed and that she was muttering the word "wish" over and over. Sofia was doing exactly the same thing as her big sister. Aline took a deep breath and looked at the meteor. A warm air swirled around her and she remembered what her mother had told her:

There is only one power that is victorious over all others. You, my child, have this power. You need nothing else. Use it well.

"I already possess this power," she murmured. "I already possess a power. My mother gave me her power. Her power is the only thing I need. So I don't really need the meteor."

All tension left her body. What she now wished for was to see her mother one more time. She wished Dashiok would stop looking for her. She wished for her brothers to be good so they could be together as a family. Feeling both Sofia's and Cristina's hands, she wished for them to get the marbled meteors. She glanced up once more to focus on the meteors and realized that the orange meteor was about to hit her.

Bathed with an enormous amount of energy, Aline felt a rush of happiness that she had never felt before. She felt the warm air that was her mother hugging her once again. The meteor had not hit her. Nor had it gone through her. It was inside her, igniting her eyes to an incandescent green.

Aline had awoken her powers.

5

BLUE DREAMS

Training

"Aline, darling, there are a few people here to see you." Abi's smooth fingers caressed her face. Aline brushed the sleep out of her eyes, trying to remember how she got back. Opening her eyes wide, she remembered it all at once. It felt like a movie winding backward. She went from the palace back to the amphitheater. Benowit had given a congratulatory speech, then all of the creatures were clapping. Cristina, Sofia, and Aline were jumping up and down, hugging each other. Finally, she saw the marbled meteor floating before the sisters, and the giant one standing still in front of Aline. The glimmering fumes turned into tentacles that cradled Aline. Its massive body began to dissolve and its dust-like particles entered her body.

"Dear, you need to get up. Sofia and Cristina are downstairs waiting for you," Abi pressed.

"Cristina and Sofia are here?" Aline leapt out of bed, which made Ash and Alastair hop up and down like crazy sheep.

"Indeed, they are. I need to take care of a few things, Aline. I will be gone for some time." She saw Aline's curious look and continued. "Dryad stuff. You seem to know your way around and it may be good for you to try things without me for a bit. Plus, you will have the dogs with you."

"It's alright, I guess," Aline nodded back and then turned her attention to the very energetic dogs. Abi kissed Aline's head and Aline gave her a big hug.

"You will be just fine. Plus, it will be a lot of fun to train with Cristina and Sofia and for all of you to discover your powers," Abi said, stroking her hair. Abi smiled at Aline and then walked out of the room.

All of the dogs lifted their noses and Aline got the message they could smell Sofia and Cristina below.

"You guys like them, right?" she asked, pausing briefly to pick up their answer. It took less time for Aline to feel what the dogs were thinking now. They sent her the image of her hugging Cristina and Sofia at the Endowing Ceremony and she felt happy.

"Hey, I am getting better at feeling your thoughts. Wait, I do not remember seeing you there last night. Where did you guys go?" Kay barked, and Aline quickly got the message that they went to the Endowing Ceremony shaped like humans.

"Uh! How come you shifted?"

"Auuuhhrrrr, auuuhhrrr, auu, au." This time Sky answered and Kay barked.

"Ha! She beat you fair and square Kay." The urgent need to speak with Benowit crawled into Aline's mind and she then saw all five weredogs in human shape doing just that. All five dogs began to whine, sending Aline scrambled thoughts and pictures.

"Kani asked us to go back to the human world, Aline, to search for any remaining creatures serving the dark warlock." Mach's voice was as clear to her as Abi's had been just a few minutes ago.

"But we want to stay with you Aline," Kay said.

"Yes! So after the Endowing Ceremony, we met with Benowit and explained to him that we will be of better use here, next to you, protecting you," added Sky.

"We love you, Aline. We have since the moment you hatched," Ash continued.

"Since the moment we first saw you," Alis said.

"For weredogs, a pack is a family, and you are part of our pack," Kay concluded.

Happy tears began to form in Aline's eyes.

"I feel the same way," she gushed, kneeling down and hugging them all and receiving multiple licks on the face in return. "But Kani needs you too." She missed her mother terribly and was now worried about her. "Maybe you should go with her. What are you going to do? Will you stay?" She asked timidly, for she was not sure if she was ready to hear a "no;" but all concerns left when she received a robust "Yes!" along with whines, barks, and more tail wagging.

"Yes, this is awesome!" Aline said, breaking into a dance. She could hear the dogs reassuring her that Kani was going to be fine and was on her way to find reinforcements. As they felt her excitement grow they all started to join Aline in a dance...well it was more like butts and tails swaying around.

"Aha, I like the way you wake up," Cristina sang. Sofia just shimmied her way towards the group and started to dance with Aline and the dogs. It did not take long for Cristina to join them as well.

"Join us palace?" Aline asked. Music started to play in her room.

"Look up," Kay suggested. The vines in Aline's room were swaying and bobbing. The palace was dancing with them too!

"Well we certainly got the 'warm-up' part of the training completed," Cristina laughed.

Sofia nodded in agreement. "Yes, it is fun training with you, Aline. Do you have anything to eat in here? I am hungry."

"You are always hungry Sofia. Maybe some water?" Cristina said.

"Let me show you." Aline wanted to ask them about the training, but it seemed more important to first show them what the palace could do.

"Palace what delicious surprise would you like to prepare for us for breakfast today?"

A table and eight chairs appeared in the middle of the balcony. On it, there was a spread of waffles, french toast, and pancakes, all topped with cream and colorful sprinkles. Next, were scrambled, fried, and boiled eggs, followed by fruits, donuts, nectar water, orange juice, and of course, hot chocolate.

"Oh, my..." Sofia did not finish, she just ran towards the balcony and sat down. "Come on guys let's eat!" she said as she stuffed food into her mouth. They all laughed, followed her to the balcony, and had a magnificent breakfast together. Finally, when they all felt that they could not eat one more bite, Aline asked them about the training.

"Well, our aunt is part of the High Magical Council, and she told us that after the Endowing Ceremony they met to talk about us," Cristina began.

"Did you hear the gasps when the original meteors choose us? It was epic!" Sofia remarked, drinking her hot cocoa. She had a chocolate mustache that Alastair wiped clean with one lick.

"How dare you?" Sofia gasped.

"Hey! You are not supposed to eat chocolate, it is not good for you," Aline added sternly.

"This would be true if we were regular dogs. Since we are weredogs, we can eat just about anything," Ash explained, still nibbling the waffles.

"Anyway," Cristina continued, "it has been over a thousand years since any of the original meteors has chosen a child. And last night all three of us were chosen!"

"I know! We got the marbled meteors, Sis! Still get goosebumps!" Sofia said. Her words were followed by a yawn. She was excited but had eaten too much and was now hugging her belly. Cristina carried on with a smile.

"They thought it would be better if we all stuck together as we learned more about our powers," she continued. "Our aunt said that the meteors enhanced the sylph's existing powers, and suggested that we help you, Aline, discover your powers as we are learning to control ours. To train you, in a way. So here we are."

"Where should we train?" Aline asked. "This room is big enough we can try it here if you like."

"I am a nature sylph. It is easier for me if we go outside," Cristina responded.

"Okay, let's go," Aline said. She was ready to start.

"We may need to wait a bit," Kay said, pointing at Sofia with her nose, "I think this youngling has eaten herself to sleep." Sofia snored a bit and they all laughed.

"Fair enough. I will go change and then we can wake up Sofia," Aline suggested. The palace picked up all of the dishes, including Sofia, lightly carrying her to Aline's bed.

They decided to go to the open fields behind the castle to train. The three girls and the five dogs walked below the wizard's suspended castle looking up at the disappearing roaring waterfalls.

"Wow!" They all said at once.

"Let's do that again!" Sofia said, and they all ran beneath the castle one more time. The cooling mist had further reenergized them. They all felt ready to train.

"Okay, Aline!" Cristina faced Aline and proceeded, "How my aunt explained it to us is that there is something inside of you that you can actually...touch. Like a thread that you can tug on. The first thing you need to do is find the thread. The best way to do that is to relax. Focus on it, but do not think about it."

"How do I do that?"

"You know when you are daydreaming? You are really looking out somewhere, but you are not really looking at anything. It's something like that," Sofia explained. "For me, if I wanted to make you feel something, I would start by facing you. Not really looking at you, but looking at you. You know what I mean?"

Aline nodded.

"Then I would connect with my thread. It takes me a few minutes." Sofia closed her eyes. When she was ready, she continued. "Once I have my thread I will tug on the part that touches you. Then I will begin to think about...let's see... a fruit. I let the thought of this fruit go and just focus on its smell. Maybe the way it tastes. How to pronounce its name. How you would pronounce its name. Your nose picking up its scent and that you want to hold this fruit and take a bite. Finally, how you feel when you taste it."

"Now I am craving strawberries. At least Abi will be happy it is a fruit," Aline said.

"I love strawberries, they are my favorite," said Sofia licking her lips. "I am hungry." Both Aline and Cristina looked at her in disbelief.

"Me too," added Ash. The girls looked at Ash, smiled, and then proceeded with their training. Sofia winked at him and took out buttery buns from one pocket and chocolate muffins from the other. Ash pointed at the buttery buns with his nose and Sofia tossed it to him; then, she began to eat the muffins.

"Easier said than done. It took me nine months just to find the thread. Now, it is easy peasy lemon squeezy. I can do this in under a minute," Cristina said, looking at Ash and Sofia eating.

"Nine months!"

"For me, it was almost a year. But do not worry, you have the meteor and we did not," added Sofia, chewing on her second chocolate muffin.

"Yes, the meteor," exhaled Aline. "Okay, I think I understand what I need to do. Let me try."

"Remember, do not think about the thread, just find it," said Cristina, who was now blossoming flowers around her.

"Okay! Find the thread but do not think about the thread. Find it. Do not think about it." This was harder than it seemed. The more Aline said the word "thread," the more she thought about a thread. Its color, shape, its length...it was very hard for her not to picture a thread.

"Argh. This is really difficult. How can you even say the word thread and not think about a thread? It is impossible!" She was frustrated.

"Let me help you," Mach thought to her. "It is really hard for a were-animal to shift through free will. For most, something in nature needs to ignite the change. Like a full moon for werewolves. If it is through free will, there has to be a strong feeling or desire to make such a powerful shift. That is why we were able to change last night. We had a strong feeling that needed to be expressed. Find that strong feeling and let it grow. See where it takes you."

Aline spent the rest of the afternoon either letting the strong desire of finding her powers grow or trying to find a thread by not thinking about a thread and failing for she only saw a thread. The heat of the two suns started to diminish. Weird butterfly-like bugs began to fly into Aline's face while she was trying to concentrate or to let go.

"It is useless, and I am hungry," she said, exhaling. "I wonder if the palace magic reaches the castle gardens."

"You are thinking too hard, Aline," thought Alis. "You just need to stop going around in circles and just do it. Like this." She stood behind a bush and was able to change from dog to human several times. In her human form, she looked like a teenager, with dark purple eyes and black hair. Feeling slightly irritated and a bit mortified, Mach tried to shift but he had eaten so much he could not focus on any strong desire besides sleeping.

Ash made fun of Mach, and Mach immediately challenged Ash to change back and forth three times. Ash cockily agreed. First, he concentrated quietly, then huffed and puffed to no avail. He tried again before Mach could say anything. This time, he used all of his strength, and without meaning to, he let out a loud bursting noise through his butt. This ceased all activity at once. Cristina, Sofia, Aline, and the four dogs laughed so hard that there was no sound coming out from their mouths. For some, their knees gave and just laughed on the ground. They started to calm down, but as soon as one lost it, they all lost all composure again, even Ash. It took them several minutes to gather themselves, and stop laughing. By then, they were all really hungry. They discovered that the magic of the palace indeed reached the castle gardens and asked the palace to make them a wonderful and rich dinner.

For several months after that, Aline met with the sisters and the dogs to train. It was similar to that first day. Large breakfast, walking twice underneath the wizard's suspended castle, training with the same results, Ash or Mach doing something funny, followed by a large dinner. They always ate so much for breakfast that they were never hungry during lunch, and training always started late since Sofia and Ash had to take a nap after they ate. This pattern was about to repeat itself on the day Abi finally returned from her dryad errands.

But instead Abi woke Aline up really early. "Good morning Aline. Time to train."

"Is it you, Abi?" Aline asked half asleep. She could see the two moons shining above the castle gardens.

"Yes, dear and you need to get up," Abi said firmly.

"It is still night!" She pulled the silk green and white covers over her head and rolled over.

"Go on now, your bath is ready. You need to be fresh and ready for the sun's first rays."

"What about breakfast?"

"Not until after we have our morning practice," Abi said. "Now go, Aline, and hurry up. The sisters will be there waiting for us."

"She has come back very serious," Aline thought.

Dragging herself out of bed, she walked to the bathing pool to find it filled with ginger, as well as mint and peppermint leaves. The bath refreshed her completely and woke her body up. On the white chiffon fainting sofa, she saw the clothes that Abi had left for her.

"I guess I will not be wearing my jeans today," Aline said to herself as she put on dark leathery pants that were made out of what appeared to be vines, with a white silk blouse, and a black plush silk cape. Surprisingly, the clothes were very comfortable.

When they reached the open fields blanketed by the light of dawn, she could see that Cristina and Sofia were waiting for her next to an older fairy. She was slender and fair with long white hair, crystalline wings, and icy blue eyes.

"Hi Akiya, it is good to see you again. Thank you for coming. I think these youngsters can benefit from your wisdom."

"Akiya!" Aline blurted. "I, er, mean, it is nice to meet you. I have heard many things about you."

"So have I about you, Aline." Her voice sounded like humming crystals set off by water droplets. "My great-nieces tell me that you are having a hard time finding your thread."

"Akiya is your great-aunt?" Aline looked at Cristina and Sofia in shock.

Sofia nodded. "We just call her aunt. It is easier"

"Akiya and I are here to help you with your training," Abi said. "She will come on and off and I will be here every day until the end. Now, Akiya, please start us off, the sun rays are about to reach us." The three girls turned around and saw flaming red tints in the sky where the two suns were about to show themselves. Sofia's stomach growls disrupted the silence, making Aline and Cristina smile.

"Sorry," Sofia apologized, holding her stomach. "I am really hungry."

"Well, then it is a good thing that I brought my cookies for after the training."

"Oh yes!" Cristina exclaimed. "They are the best cookies ever. The lemon cookie is awesome, but the chocolate is the best by far. Now I am hungry." She looked at her stomach.

"Nope! The best one is the peanut butter one *with* chocolate," Sofia said.

"All right. Then it is settled. First, we train, then we eat the cookies," Akiya said.

"Aw!" the sisters complained in unison.

"I need all of you to sit wherever you like, the only thing I ask is that you do not face the sun. Once you are comfortable, I need you to close your eyes. Cristina and Sofia, I need you to hum your wings." Akiya winked at the girls and they both gasped with excitement.

Aline's eyes widened. She had not seen the sisters fly and was thrilled as the girls began to gently move their wings. The hues of green, blue, yellow, and pink softly kissing their wings became more noticeable the faster their wings beat. They lifted from the ground ever so slightly while their wings beat even faster, creating the most beautiful humming sound Aline had ever heard. It was like singing crystals.

"Aline, you need to close your eyes," Akiya's gentle voice brought her back and she realized she did not remember sitting down. She was sitting down in the middle of the floating humming sisters.

"Now, I want you to let go of your thoughts and only let the humming sound in," Akiya instructed her. All three girls followed her guidance and lost themselves in the singing of the sylph's wings.

Aline felt the green around her from the open fields and noticed a fading blue light not too far from her. She let this go and focused on the humming. She was back on the grassy field alone. The humming grew, creating crystal notes that floated and clicked around her. When she touched one, it complained and quickly joined the others around it, giving her a dirty look even though it did not have any eyes.

"Now, you will feel a warmth on the back of your heads. The suns are rising. Let this energy bathe you and just focus on finding the thread but do not look for it," Akiya coached them.

The first thing that Aline felt was an intense warmth on her head, surprisingly starting on her forehead. It felt nice and intensified the smell of wet dirt and of dew on the grass. When Aline looked again at the crystal notes, they were all reflecting an inward light. They were forming a path, and she decided to follow the humming notes. She walked until she reached a labyrinth made with bushes which seemed to lead towards the castle gardens. As she went deeper inside the maze, the notes sped up. She began to run after them turning in and about the labyrinth. She stopped when the notes floated away and she was in front of two paths. The path to the left had a golden shimmer to it and the path on the right had a thin blue light.

"All right, I need to find the thread. I need to focus on the thread, but not look for it. That is so confusing. Okay, if I looked for the thread which path would I take? Hm! I guess the golden path. Then, the blue path it is," Aline spoke out loud to herself and turned to the right. The further she moved towards the blue side of the labyrinth, the more intense the light got, until she reached an opening in the shape of an octagon and right on the middle she saw a blue bottle. Her steps made scratching sounds against the gravel as she walked towards the glass bottle.

"This little thing is creating this strong light," she knelt down and looked more carefully at the bottle. Rather than a smooth cylinder, its body was shaped like a star. It looked like two long rectangles overlaid on top of each other. Where one rectangle was shifted ever so slightly that its corners stuck out the middle of the sides of the other rectangle. Markings adorned each of the eight sides.

"Uh! These look like some type of writing,"

Aline stretched her hand to touch the bottle but right before she reached it, she felt a tug on her blouse. Goosebumps dressed the skin on her neck and back. Just like if someone had blown warm air on the back of her neck during a cold, cold day. She paused and remained very sill, trying to hear for something or maybe trying not be heard nor seen. Once she relaxed the muscles on shoulders, it happened again. This time it was a strong tug, almost annoyed at her for not turning around. Benowit's words about her father's courage came to mind, so, she took a deep breath, stood up, and pivot to face whatever had tugged her white blouse. In front of her stood two liquid-like substances. One green and one blue-violet that twirled and twisted around each other. She instantly knew, or rather felt what it was.

"My thread!" A rush of happiness bathed her from the inside. She reached her hand and touched her thread. At first, it felt cool to Aline, but soon it became warm and comforting. It felt like home. Whispers were now all around Aline, as if thirty people were mumbling next to her and she could not make out what they were saying. The whispers started to go in circles around her making it difficult for her to hear, feeling like she was going to lose her footing and fall. Then, Aline tugged back at her thread, stabilizing her stance, making the whispers hum along with the sister's flickering wings.

"You can do this Aline, I believe in you." Akiya's voice was sweet among the whispers.

"It is not the right time to give her news about Dashiok. This will absolutely distract her, she just started and we need to give her more time," pleaded Abi; however, her voice was different compared to Akiya's. It was as if Abi was talking on the phone to someone else and Aline was listening in on the conversation.

"Focus. Let the thread guide you, Aline" Akiya's voice continued to peer through the whispers.

"Maybe we can take her to the seen witch. She could help us…she could help Aline," continued Abi.

"What do you see Aline? What do you feel?" asked Akiya.

"Alineee!" A scream dampened Akiya's words and silenced all other whispers. It was the same male voice she had heard before. Aline opened her eyes. It was spring.

The sisters were still floating like hummingbirds next to her, and far away, slightly to the right, Abi was quietly talking to Akiya, who was looking at Aline.

"Is everything all right Aline?" Akiya asked as the two of them approached her. She seemed very interested in her answer.

"I...I believe I found my thread. I have found my power!" Aline said excitedly.

"*One* of your powers," Akiya corrected her. "Tell me more, child." The sisters stopped their humming, not very gracefully. Both Cristina and Sofia fell hard on the ground and were rubbing their bums.

"You found your thread?" They both asked in unison, as Cristina continued to rub her rear end, and Sofia she stood up wincing a bit.

"Yes! I did," Aline grinned proudly. "I was able to hear what you were thinking," she pointed at Akiya, "and what you were saying Abi, but not with my ears...you were too far away." It hit Aline as soon as she said it. It was physically impossible for Aline to have heard either one of them talk.

"Ah! A telepath. A powerful one. Most telepaths can only hear thoughts. Only a few can hear another speak when they are far, cities, or even another world away." Akiya could tell that Aline and both sisters were very interested. "Almost always, what you say and what you think does not happen at the exact time, or with the same frequency. Most humans would argue this, but we sylphs know better."

"Frequency?" Sofia asked.

"Yes! All living and non-living things are energy. Not magical power, just energy. Energy is always vibrating and these vibrations create waves. How many waves can travel in a period of time is known as frequency. Speed, sound, colors, light, cells, molecules...everything and anything has a frequency. Think of it this way, when your wings go fast enough they vibrate moving the air around, creating sound waves. These waves then move or vibrate the little hairs in your ears which help your brain translate this energy into sound. Energy leads to vibrations, which leads to waves, which leads to frequency."

"Ah!" Exclaimed the girls at the same time. Aline and Cristina nodded while Sofia looked at them, following their lead.

"Now, most telepaths can only connect with one speed, one-time frequency. The lower frequency or slower speed. That is, they are capable of hearing somebody else's first layer of thoughts. Known as still thoughts. Thoughts that happen when someone is not doing much. No action nor motion. This is where most of the telepath's abilities can be found.

"The faster frequency, or faster speed, is connecting with someone's mind as it thinks and acts *at the same time*. For example, sensing the words that are about to be said before they are said. This means thinking or rather feeling significantly faster than the speed of sound or light. You, Aline, can tap into both speeds."

Silence. The girls were digesting what she had just said in disbelief.

"You can think or hear, not sure which one, does not matter, you can do this faster than the speed of sound or light...that is just cool!!!" Cristina said, and Sofia smiled and nodded.

"Our training will now focus on finding out how far you can stretch your telepathic hearing and how deeply you can listen to thoughts" Akiya continued, "and then...let us push those boundaries."

"Wow!" Sofia said.

Aline swallowed hard.

"Question, Aline," Akiya asked. "Before you were able to hear my thoughts, was there silence or were there other voices?"

"Whispers! I heard a lot of whispers. At first, the whispers made it very hard to understand anything. Once I tugged on my thread, then I was able to hear both you and Abi." Aline was becoming more and more intrigued.

"Interesting! Most telepaths can only hear the first layer of thoughts. For them, it is almost like walking into an empty room and hearing or for some even reading a ribbon of letters that tell them a person's first thoughts. They are not able to dig deeper than what they just heard. That on its own is impressive. However, you Aline, can hear the ripples that one thought can make." The faces on all three girls were pinched off.

"I will try to explain this; however, it is not easy to understand," added Akiya with a focused look. "A mere thought has more power than most can fathom. Not from the spoken words, but from the sensations it can create. It can impact someone else's feelings and thoughts. Are you with me so far?" The girls nodded.

"This is how a powerful sense sylph can introduce fear or happiness into another being. The difference is that most telepaths do not insert a feeling or a thought onto others. Yet, when you can hear all of the ripples created from a first layer thought, you may be able to connect them."

Aline looked like she was about to figure it out and Cristina and Sofia were right behind her.

"You may be able to connect a thought from one creature to another or maybe between several creatures. The whispers represent the root of a thought. This is when it gets messy, so pay attention."

All of them nodded, including Abi.

"Most of the time, the first layer of thoughts are quick, impulsive, and easier to hear. However, deep-rooted thoughts are more complicated. These are thoughts that have been brewing for a long time and with time, maybe through intense life experiences, they have changed, shifted, and evolved. So, an original root thought could be very different than its first layer thought. Like a planet. The top layer is very different from the inner layer. The question is, Aline, can you peel these layers to see what is at the bottom? Let me make this even more interesting. Could you connect thoughts?"

Sofia began to smack Cristina on the shoulder and said, "How cool is that? How cool is that!"

"It is cool, Sofia, but stop smacking me," said Cristina and brushed her sister's hand away.

"I am curious to see if you can peel off the layers of deep-rooted thoughts and sense their humble beginnings," Akiya said. "Regardless, it is *all* very impressive. If both are true—if you can sense deep-rooted thoughts and you are able to connect thoughts among different creatures—then you will be pushing the boundaries of telepathy. I do not know of anyone who can connect thoughts. I only know of one other who can peel off the layers of deep-rooted thoughts."

"Who?" They all asked at the same time.

"Me!" she said.

"You are a telepath?" Aline gasped.

"Sense sylphs by nature are powerful empaths. Almost all can know if you have good or bad intentions right away. A handful are telepaths and can hear the first layer thought from others regardless of the distance." She paused, shifted her tone and continued. "And I am the only one who can sense deep rooted thoughts."

"Wow," Cristina and Sofia said, exhaling. Then they both shouted "Jinx!"

but Cristina went further. "Double jinx!" she screeched, laughing victoriously.

"Ohhh," Sofia groaned.

"Now, now girls. I trust that you both are getting better at finding your threads?" Akiya asked, bringing them back the subject at hand.

"Yes," responded both at the same time. Sofia was about to say "jinx" once more time but then she saw Akiya's raised eyebrow.

"Let us start the training then," Abi said proudly.

"There is something else," Aline interjected.

"There is more?" Cristina asked eagerly as Sofia drew near to her.

"Before I found my thread—or rather my thread found me—I saw a blue light. I decided to follow the path towards the blue light and it led me to an opening. On the floor, there was something weird."

"What was it? What did you see? Tell us. The suspense is killing me!" Sofia interrupted; she was thrilled and her voice was filled with enthusiasm.

"Go on, go on. Tell us what you found" pleaded Cristina, leaning even closer to Aline.

"Well, on the floor was a crystal blue bottle. I think it was a bottle...I... have never seen a bottle like this before. It had some sort of...symbols...or maybe...writing on it."

"Tell me, Aline," Abi chimed in. "Was this bottle shaped like a star?"

"Shaped like a star? Now, this is getting really interesting," Cristina said.

"Agreed, I have only seen round bottles," added Sofia.

"You mean cylindrical," suggested Cristina.

"Yes, that is what I meant," mumbled Sofia.

"How did you know?" Aline asked Abi.

"Many, many years ago the whispers shared with the dryads the existence of an enchanted bottle. A blue bottle. Not created by any magical creature, white or black, but it rather just existed once the One World broke. Maybe it was part of the One World. This bottle can create enormous magical rooms where anything can be placed inside regardless of its size, magical powers, or desires. It is not bound by the laws of magic, space, nor physics stated in any of the eight worlds. Many have tried to find the blue bottle to no avail. As part of the One World, it calls upon nature to protect it, to hide it. So, it is only found by those whom the blue bottle allows or wants." Turning to Akiya regally, with a troubled look, she continued. "Imagine what this power could do for whomever possessed the blue bottle."

"Did it tell you or show you where it is?" Akiya asked Aline.

"Did it tell me…? No, my thread tugged me before I was able to touch it."

"This is good," Akiya responded. "I will help you connect back with the blue bottle, but we will need the power of both moons…we may just get by with the second moon. It is our largest moon, and we need it to be full. In forty-five days we shall find out if the blue bottle wants to tell you its location."

A soft breeze blew around them and Abi became really quiet.

"This could be a big opportunity," Abi was now talking directly to Akiya, with an urgency in her voice. "The whispers just told me that if the blue bottle already let Aline see it, then it is a wise assumption that it will let her find it. I will go and meet with the other dryads and then go to Benowit to prepare him. We need to be ready for what could happen afterward."

"Agreed," Akiya said. Abi turned and strode purposefully towards the castle without another word.

"All right," Akiya said, turning back to the girls. "Let's train then!"

"Wait," said Sofia without hesitation. "I thought we were going to have cookies." Her stomach grumbled so loudly they all heard it. Aline realized that she was hungry as well.

"And breakfast! I am starving!" Cristina added emphatically. "Good call, Sofia!" And with that she high-fived her sister.

"Yes, I almost forgot. There you go."

All three girls turned around to face the risen suns. In front of them, the palace had prepared a feast. There were waffles & crepes topped with hazelnut butter, strawberries, and bananas. Scrambled eggs, nuts, fresh orange juice, nectar water, and Akiya's famous cookies completed the sumptuous repast, all placed on a round table. The three girls first tried the cookies and Aline felt that she had never had a cookie before. Not if you compared them to Akiya's cookies. They were magnificent! Anything else was not a cookie; it was just a lie. The five weredogs joined them for breakfast and the girls shared with them the experience they had at dawn. They all found out just how fantastically refreshing the nectar water was after the training.

After a robust breakfast and filled by the rays from the two suns, the girls felt strong and energetic. Aline felt more at home with her furry friends near her.

"Cristina, I need you to work with Kay and Sky. Use nature to move them away," Akiya said. Then to the weredogs she said, "Kay and Sky, do not get caught. Cristina, you will get cookies if you catch them, and you two if you evade Cristina's traps."

"Yes! It is on!" thought Kay.

"Sofia, you will work with Mach and Ash. I need you to provide strong emotions or feelings that will send them running away. Mach and Ash, you need to sit still and fight these new emotions or feelings."

"Why do we have to sit down? I am faster than Sky and Kay combined," whined Ash, and Mach nodded.

"Oh hush! Staying still and fighting magical powers are both of your weaknesses. This training is for you as well," Akiya said with a stern look. Both dogs did not complain for the rest of the training sessions.

"Ha!" Kay barked. "Faster than us? That is nonsense!"

"For you Aline, the first half of the day, I need you to hear what Alis says when she is far and running further away from you. Alis, you need to trick her. What you say has to be different or opposite to what you are going to do. Aline, hearing words in motion is much harder. If you can master this, you can master any motionless word said. Alis, first I need you to change to human form. Then, do not think about Aline or try to connect with her when you are speaking. If you both get this right, then both of you get a cookie."

"Yes!" Alis thought, and Aline smiled at her.

"After lunch, I need you to find root thoughts. Alis, you will think of something and gradually morph it into something completely different. When you are ready, let Aline see if she can find the first layer. Then, Aline, you need to peel this thought away to get to or as close to the original thought, to the deep rooted thought. Finally, this is the last challenge. You, Aline, get to choose any of those thoughts and try to connect them to anyone here except for Alis."

Both Alis and Aline were both completely confused by these instructions.

"This can be confusing, so I shall give you an example, but you cannot use any of it. Say that you, Alis, think about how eating an apple as a weredog tastes like eating chocolate as a human. Then this thought shifts to working with the Apotequils and organizing a group whose sole purpose is to create magical chocolate bars, which in turn makes you think about their magical lances. And finally, that evolves to you trying to find a magical weapon of your own. In this case, your first layer thought is a magical weapon. Now Aline, once you hear the thought about magical weapons, then you can dig deep to get all the way back to the deep rooted thought: *for weredogs, apples taste like chocolates do for humans.* With me so far?"

Akiya paused for a moment and looked at each of them. They looked at each other and then nodded. Then she said "Good. And finally, Aline, you will choose someone, let us say Ash, and connect his thoughts to Apotequils. If he expresses that he is thinking about the Apotequils, you have succeeded. Make sense?"

Aline and Alis nodded again, hesitantly.

"Wow! That is hard," Sofia said. "I am glad I do not have to do that."

"All right, what are you waiting for? Get started! Alis, here are some clothes."

Aline was impressed to see that even though Alis looked like a teenage human girl, in many ways she still behaved like a dog. Sometimes showing her teeth and growling. Alis was very short with long black hair. Wearing the red and black clothes that Akiya handed to her, and with her purple eyes, she looked like a samurai warrior.

All of them had a miserable time and none of the girls ate additional cookies by the time lunch arrived. They were exhausted, frustrated, and were not looking forward to the second half of the day. Even after drinking what appeared to be several gallons of nectar water, both Sky and Kay were still panting from all that running. Their tongues were hanging out and their mouths were too dry for cookies.

Aline had only managed to get letters from Alis, no words, not even a partial word. Not able to focus, she let the whispers overpower any one word that might have reached her. She was absolutely dreading the training for the second part of the day, it seemed so much harder.

They all dragged themselves back to work, except for Mach and Ash who had a pep in their step and were licking the remaining cookie crumbles on their fur as they trotted out to their positions.

The second part of the day was a disaster. By the time it ended they all felt defeated and tired. Even Mach and Ash's spirits were down.

"Girls, and boys," Akiya said. "This is what real training is like. Not the playing around you were doing while Abi was gone. Real training is a big challenge. You cannot expect to be perfect the first day. Having been chosen by magical meteors does not mean that you are immediately powerful, or that you can use all of your powers at once. *Having* powers and *mastering* your powers are two very different things. One is given, the other must be earned. The only way to earn anything in any life, in any world, is by doing two things: working hard and wanting it even harder. For this you must have determination, you absolutely need to believe it, and it is essential to have trust in yourselves. Easy to remember. Focus, faith, and trust. This is all you need…and of course, a lot of patience," she smiled at this last bit of advice. Akiya knew it was far easier said than done. "Go home. Eat, rest, for we need to train again tomorrow before first light."

All shoulders dropped at once as tired long faces stared back at Akiya.

"First have a few cookies and nectar water." She moved her lips and whispered a few words. A green silk bag appeared in midair.

"These may lift your spirits a bit."

The bag opened and cookies floated their way to each one of them. With zero resistance they took a bite and felt much better. By the time they finished their first cookie and had a few gulps of nectar water, their muscles felt stronger and their hearts had lifted. Another cookie was soon on its way to them, followed by more gulps of nectar water.

"When you wake up tomorrow for your training, think about the three words that can help you master your powers," Akiya said. "Do you remember what they are?"

"Focus, faith, and trust," responded the eight of them at the same time.

"Good," said Akiya and they all walked back in silence.

Grey Feather

THEY TRAINED for weeks with very little improvement. Well, they would have argued that the only things that improved were the aches in their muscles, the increased hunger, and how tired they felt right after dinner.

The training sessions were all similar, with minor tweaks here and there. Aline was able to find her thread but never saw the blue bottle.

"Remember, you must have focus, faith, trust…and patience. Let's try it again tomorrow," Akiya would encourage them at the end of each day. The lack of progress only fed their feeling of discouragement.

On one particular training, the day just felt longer than normal. Akiya magically handed them the green bag of cookies which they had all waited for anxiously. Sometimes, those cookies and the nectar water were the only reason they made it to the end of the day. Before the group ate and walked home in silence, Akiya turned to Aline.

"Aline, I will find you after dinner," she said. "I suggest that you eat well and then take a relaxing bath, because tonight we are going to find where the blue bottle is hiding."

Aline and the five weredogs dragged their feet home. The palace had set the table for them. After eating several bowls of the yellow stew, Aline asked the palace for a relaxing bath. The palace made it rain. This always surprised her. Big gentle warm droplets rained from the middle of nowhere. They filled the bathroom pool with a lavender scent, while chamomile flowers started to bubble up from below Aline and then float around her. Her muscles began to loosen and her thoughts about the training started to drift away. It was the longest bath Aline had taken in her life.

"You look relaxed," Kay thought to Aline.

"I agree," Sky added.

"If you ask me, you look too relaxed," Ash interjected. "If you want to find the bottle, just go out and start running. It is the best way to find things, I say."

"So you say!" Alis scoffed.

"Yes, even better at night," Mach agreed. "The moons are bright and it is not too hot."

"Boys!" Alastair snorted.

Walking towards the balcony, Aline thanked the palace once more for helping her with her bath. She heard a wind chime go off right after she spoke, and felt the palace had smiled back at her.

As she stood on the balcony watching both suns set behind the crater, Aline wondered how Akiya would help her connect again with the blue bottle. Her gaze followed the crater toward the castle gardens, where her thoughts were now focused on the strange insects flying about and around. The last rays disappeared and she could not see the bugs. Night had reached the palace, and Aline's eyes felt heavy. She felt like going to sleep, when a hue of silver gently gave light to the view. Aline looked back to see where this light was coming from and saw the two moons were peaking up from behind the palace. One moon was full and the smallest was a waning gibbous.

She looked back down and noticed a small but strong light that zig-zagged through the gardens. She marveled at its sharp movements and remembered the summer fireflies in the back yard of the house of haunted gargoyles. She missed her mother. It had only been a few months, but her mother Kani, the house of haunted gargoyles, Amanda, the followers, and her life on the human world seemed like an eternity ago. These thoughts were quickly erased by the fact that the little light was becoming much, much bigger than a firefly and it was moving fast towards her. Now, she could make out the silhouette of a human with piercing eyes. Ash, protec-tively, lifted his head from a chewed up shoe the palace had provided. He squinted his eyes and his ears perked up like two antennae.

"We are good," he reassured Aline and when he saw her face, he contin-ued, "I know who it is. Want me to tell you?"

"What?" Aline looked at Ash and when she returned to look back out the balcony she was startled to find someone floating right in front of her.

"Hi Aline, may I come in?" Akiya asked gently. Her long white hair was emitting most of the light that Aline had seen earlier, and her glass-like wings were not making a sound. They did not hum like the sister's wings did on the open fields behind the castle.

"Yes," answered Aline marveling Akiya's stealth, strength, and beauty. "Of course, come in." She caught herself staring. "Would you...er...like something to drink?"

"Thank you. Yes, hot water," replied Akiya. "I have brought special herbs that will help you relax even more than the lavender-chamomile bath you took."

"How did you...sure," Aline leaned in to take the cloth with herb. As she did so, she caught the scent of Akiya's. It also smelled of lavender and chamomile.

"Palace, could you please provide us with hot water and two cups?" Aline asked.

"It is nice to hear you asking rather than ordering the palace. Many find it easier to just order magic and forget that magic is indeed alive and it does have feelings," Akiya said while handing Aline a cup of tea.

It took Aline several sips to get used to the strange, strong taste of the herbs. She thought maybe Akiya had brought the wrong herbs, because nothing tasting this strong could help any creature to relax. Akiya, however, remained unaware of Aline's troubles and watched her until she finished every drop in her cup.

"The air is still nice and warm. We can do this out here," Akiya thought out loud. "Palace, could you please bring a phuru feather for Aline. A blue-gray one, please. They are not only the biggest but the softest of all the phurus. Interesting creatures, they are. Big, but not really too smart," she explained. At that moment a feather as big as Aline's bed appeared in front of them. Akiya whispered a few words and the feather stayed put in mid-air. "Climb up Aline. You will find it quite sturdy and soft."

Aline touched one of the fluffy grayish blue plummets that came out from the central shaft of the large feather. It was incredibly soft, almost like air. She grabbed the feather with both hands and gently pushed on it to test how strong it was. It did not budge.

"Mmm!" she breathed.

"Go on now, child. You need to climb up before the effect of the herbs begins to set in," said Akiya.

This time, Aline grabbed the feather firmly and pushed herself up. Carefully, she crawled forward, turned, and lay down. The shaft of the feather ran along Aline's back, while its veins curled around her. It felt like being wrapped in a cocoon, or lying in a hammock when the top comes around like a clam about to close.

Maybe it was Akiya's herbs, but Aline thought this could be the closest she could ever come to sleeping on a cloud. At this point, her head felt heavy. One of the veins lifted ever so slightly, imitating a pillow, releasing any strain on her neck. Aline could not resist the temptation to sleep. Closing her eyes, she let herself float away like the chamomile flowers in the bathing pool. She desperately wanted to sleep, but found herself awake in a perpetual slumber, half asleep and half awake.

Through the open space on top, between the veins of the phuru feather, the moonlight from the second moon illuminated Aline's face and body. In this weird sleepy state, Aline found herself walking in the castle's gardens.

"Aline, find your way back to the path with the blue light. Once you are there, follow it like you did the first time. You will get distracted by other thoughts. Just ignore them and follow the path," suggested Akiya.

Upon hearing Akiya, Aline found herself in the labyrinth at the place where the two paths began. This time she felt even more curious about the path with the golden shimmer. Shaking that off, she shifted towards the right and followed the path with the blue light until she arrived at the opening space shaped like an octagon. The blue bottle was not there.

"It is not here!" she exclaimed out loud.

"Good!"

"Good? How can this be good?" Aline thought. "No! I mean, the bottle is *not here*," she repeated, this time slowly, in case there was a misunderstanding. After all, who knows how she sounded under the special herbs.

"I was not expecting it to be," Akiya said. "What do you hear, or smell, or sense?"

"I do not sense anything. Zero points for my telepathy."

"Do not get distracted. Relax and breathe in the silence. You will find there is no silence."

"There is no silence! What? Why are things so contradictory in this world?" Aline said. "Can't things just be a bit more clear and simple?" The blue tinge within the open space began to fade. "Oh, no! I am getting distracted. Okay, listen and breathe." She took a deep breath and focused a bit more. "I have done this before, so I should be able to do this once more." She took another deep breath. "I was trying not to find my thread and I decided to follow the blue light. Which was the opposite to looking for my thread." Another breath. "I reached the two paths, maybe I can go to the golden path."

Aline began to run back but rather than finding the golden path, she was now exiting a forest. First walking on moss and then walking on grass, passing fewer trees with each step. She could hear ocean waves not too far away and could smell the salty breeze blowing on her face. The grass blades turned purple and became thicker, like succulents. Sand was now on the ground instead of dirt.

"I am walking towards a beach," Aline reported.

Patches of purple grass began to scatter throughout the beach until the sand sloped down towards the shore. Aline could see the two suns rising from the ocean and a few small mounds of sand on the flat portion of the beach. To her right, between two trees, the sand descended like a path and curved into a cave.

"I see a cave nearby. I will try and get a bit closer," she said.

She had a strong urge to go inside the cave, and began to move past the trees. The blue hue of the blue bottle could be seen from where she was standing, and the sand felt hard under her feet. Once she reached the front of the cave, a loud, clear growl stopped her right on her tracks. It was a warning. This was very clear to Aline.

"There is something inside the cave. It is attracted to the power of the bottle and it is not letting me inside," she told Akiya.

"Can you see the bottle?"

"I see its light, but not the bottle."

"You must *see* the bottle, Aline," Akiya insisted.

"Are you sure?" Aline asked. "Whatever is inside does not want me to enter, and it sounds big."

"Nothing will happen Aline. I am here with you," Akiya reassured her.

"I am not too sure about this," Aline thought to herself. Once she took a few steps closer, another growl came from the cave, clearly louder than the last. "I do not think it is a good idea to go in," she told Akiya.

"It is safe. I promise. Go on now. Go inside the cave," said Akiya encouraging Aline to move forward. "Do not try to defend yourself, Aline. No weapons of any kind. Walk in as you are."

"Okay," Aline responded anxiously. Taking more steps right up to the cave's mouth, Aline heard the powerful growl echo against the cave's walls and the sound of claws hitting its rocky ground.

"I can do this," Aline comforted herself nervously. "I know I can do this." She took a cautious step into the cave. Then she went deeper in, moving softly and quietly. The blue bottle was inside, and it provided the cave's only light. Aline walked towards it, as well as towards the growls and the hisses. She felt that she was going to be attacked any minute. An eternity seemed to pass. To Aline it felt like the end was never going to arrive. And she was certain she'd soon find a beast who wanted more than ever to devour her for entering the cave after so many warnings.

"Aline!" An airy voice called to her. Not a scary voice, but rather light and breezy.

"Aline, come to me!" It called once more between the beastly growls.

Aline was now curious. *"What fragile creature could be near such an awful beast?"* she wondered, pressing forward. Finally, she could see a gap filled with blue light. As she reached the opening, the growls grew deeper and louder and she was positive there would be an attack. Out of instinct, Aline knelt down and grabbed a rock to defend herself.

"Aline," the airy voice called. "Just you."

Hesitantly, she put the rock down and pushed herself to move forward. Closing her eyes, she walked through the clearing expecting a ravenous beast to pounce on her.

Silence.

Cool air softly brushed her hair back and Aline opened her eyes. The blue light shimmered, and Aline realized she could hear the ocean.

There was no beast, just the bottle in the middle of an opening once more shaped like an octagon. She walked towards the blue bottle and sat down right next to it. In this little clearing of the cave, so close to the ocean and filled with blue light, Aline felt like she was underwater.

"Aline, you finally heard me," the airy voice now filled the entire clearing. "It is your time. I have let you find me because you need my help, Aline."

Looking down, Aline gently touched the blue bottle with her left hand. She felt a cold electric current touching it in response. Even though it did not hurt her, she pulled her hand back fast. Then, with her finger, she traced the palm of her left hand and examined where she had felt the cold current. Besides feeling cool to the touch, it was fine.

"It is okay, I will not hurt you," she heard. "You may pick me up."

The blue bottle was speaking to Aline. She picked up the bottle and observed its unique shape and markings. It was indeed beautiful.

"Thank you!" The bottle said.

"But I didn't say anything!" Aline exclaimed.

"You did not have to, I am now connected with you and know what you think. You thought I was beautiful, and I wanted to thank you," the blue bottle explained.

"This is amazing," Aline looked up. She wanted to share this with the sylph sisters and her furry friends, but she realized that she was in the cave alone. She suddenly felt cold.

"We do not have much time. You need to hurry and find me, Aline. You are not the only one looking for me. I do not want him to find me, but he is very powerful."

"Okay, so what do I do? I am not sure where to go."

"Describe to Akiya all that you have seen. She will know where to go. Once you find your surroundings, you will realize where to look and how to find me. Now hurry!"

Aline found herself resting on the feather, holding her hands out. They felt empty without the blue bottle. Akiya was looking at the hand she had used to touch the bottle and then she looked deeply into Aline's eyes.

"We need to hurry!" Aline told Akiya everything she had seen right down to the most minor detail.

"The Southern Shores," concluded Akiya and Sky barked in agreement. "We need to see Benowit," she added. "Ash," immediately he sat up and looked attentively at Akiya, "go ask Abi to gather the High Magical Council. Let her know that we will be in the castle tomorrow at first light. Then, tell Cristina and Sofia to meet us in the castle. Ash, tonight, I need your speed."

Proudly, Ash bowed his head and sped out of Aline's room.

"Now rest, Aline."

Facing the remaining four dogs she said, "Please, tomorrow escort Aline to the castle's great hall."

Akiya looked at Aline one last time. "You should be proud. Very few could have done so quickly what you did today. I am impressed, Aline."

She straightened her crystal clear wings, and finally said, "I shall see you tomorrow. Good night, Aline."

Her wings pulsed and she flew out of the balcony.

"Good night, Akiya," Aline responded, but she was gone.

Summit

FEELING that something was looking at her, Aline opened her eyes. Alis was on the bed hovering over her. She smiled and then licked Aline on the cheek. Aline had slept deeply. She could see on her bed that she had barely moved. And it had been a dreamless night. *"It must have been the herbs Akiya gave me,"* she thought.

"Good morning! Time to get up," Alis added and then jumped off the bed. "Mach is working with the palace to get breakfast and Kay and Sky are getting your bath ready. It seems like lemon, ginger, and passion fruit are the choices for your bath. Bright and fresh!" Her teeth were displaying what Aline would call a sarcastic smile. "That's what they said, not me," Alis clarified in case there was any confusion.

The bath did indeed wake her up and breakfast was just what she needed as the vines of the palace worked on her hair.

"It's okay palace, I can do my hair," she said once she had finished her strawberry and banana porridge.

"Ready?" Kay asked when Aline had finished brushing her teeth.

"Yes," said Aline. "Do you know what will happen?" Aline had no expectations of what was going to happen next. She was still wrapping her head around being in a magical world and having powers.

Once they reached the main entrance gate of the castle, Aline got a shot of excitement. This was the first time she was going inside the wizard's suspended castle. If it was anything like the palace, she was bound to be impressed.

"Morning Aline!" Cristina called out to her. Sofia was walking right next to her big sister and Ash next to Sofia.

"Hi, Cristina, Sofia, and Ash! It is good to see you."

"It seems like you had a good session with our aunt!" Sofia said. "I just love going inside the castle. Any excuse will do, and this one is a big one."

"I know," Cristina said. "The great room, we are going to the great room. Let me tell you, IT is GREAT!"

Both sisters looked at each other, grabbed hands, and instead of jumping up and down, they fluttered their wings and bounced in the air. Aline was impressed. She would have called it a day at that point, but just then the castle gates rumbled open.

As soon as they took the first few steps, the girls looked left and right towards the magnificent waterfalls they had seen when they walked below the castle on their way to train. This time they felt their power. The cool breeze the waterfalls created gently moved their hair back and forth. Aline was in awe. The suns were finally high enough that their rays were touching the waterfalls giving them different tones of gold, blue, purple, red, orange, black, green and silver.

"I bet you I can see more rainbows this time," Cristina said in a competitive tone.

"You know I can sense them right before they appear. You can only hear them after they appear, right?" Sofia replied with a wink and a smile, "but I am in!"

"Alright!" Cristina said with a smile.

"Yup, see there is one right...there," Sofia pointed. Both Aline and Cristina turned to look. "There. Ah! There is another, and another. That is three so far."

"There is one! And there is number two!" Cristina said excitedly.

Aline blinked her eyes and then saw that in the layer of mist created by the waterfalls there were thousands of rainbows swimming around like fish in a pond. She realized that the sisters were not pointing at the rainbows that were already there but the ones that were just about to be created as the sun rays shifted when they took another step.

The girls walked up to what felt like thousands of floating stairs that arched up towards the giant castle doors. The doors opened as soon as they got close enough. The wizard's suspended castle was immense. Aline thought that its ceilings were so high you could measure it in buildings or miles rather than stories or floors. There were many windows and arches letting in tons of light from every direction.

From the main entrance, they walked up the stairs that curved to the right, down a long hallway, and finally made it to the great hall. Cristina was not kidding. It was great.

It was in the shape of a long rectangle. Rows of arches held by majestic columns that rose up on the long sides of the room marked the space as the great hall. On top of each arch, there were smaller arches. These smaller arches hugged windows made of scales which let rays of light in that crossed right in the middle of the hall. Within this tunnel of light rays sat a long table with many grand chairs.

On one end, two huge arches separated the hall from the southern courtyard where the same arches of the great hall continued on each side. Long pools of water were below the grand arches that faced the crater nestled to the west. The pools had stairs that allowed you to watch the water cascading down to the ground from a bit closer. Even though the water would cascade down at high velocities, the pools in the courtyard remained magically serene and calm.

The roaring of the cascades was echoed by those falling from the courtyard in the northern wing of the castle. Aline could feel their breezes. The morning suns' rays were kissing the grand arches facing west—facing the cascades and the crater—turning them into golden crowns on the waterfalls.

In the center of the courtyard were several stone benches forming a circle where Akiya, Abi, Benowit, among other fantastic creatures, were sitting and having an animated discussion.

"Aline, it is good to see you my darling," Abi welcomed Aline with a big hug. "Come," she gestured, "all of you." All eight of them walked towards the High Magical Council. There were creatures there that Aline had never seen, exuding a sense of respect, of power.

"Aline," Benowit spoke and all were now quiet, "these are the members of the High Magical Council. Kunaq and Atik are representing the Yachaq, or white elves." Both bowed their heads to Aline.

"Unan and Kawayu represent the pegacorns." Two beautiful unicorns with thick scars across their midsections bowed their heads to Aline.

"Khallma and Uskhay represent the Apotequils, our lightening warriors." Two short, square, fierce-looking fighters bowed their heads.

"Saywa and Urpi represent the witches. You already know Akiya, who represents the sylphs, Abi, who represents the dryads, and me, the wizards."

Aline was in awe. These powerful beings had all just bowed to her. She looked at Abi for comfort, who was seating directly to her right, and then to Akiya, who was in front of her.

"The High Magical Council is very interested in learning more about what the blue bottle showed you," Benowit said.

"We are all particularly curious about what the creature protecting the cave sounded like," added Khallma.

"Could you please start from the first time you think you heard or saw the blue bottle?" Saywa asked.

"Well, ahem," Aline was a bit nervous speaking up. She composed herself and continued. "the first time I heard and saw the blue bottle's light was when I first arrived at the palace and was taking a bath. It called my name... I think. The second time was during the training. I saw the light and was about to touch the bottle but then I found my thread." She said this last bit proudly, but the only reaction came from Abi who smiled at her. "Then, the last time was in the palace with Akiya's help. This time I saw the light and I was able to talk to the blue bottle."

Mumbles from the High Magical Council interrupted her story.

"You are the first creature who has ever spoken to the blue bottle. Until today, we did not know such a thing was possible." Aline heard in her mind a deep voice. It was the pegacorn Unan.

"Spoke with the blue bottle," Kunaq repeated gently. "What did it say?"

"Well. It took me to a beach, and showed me a cave where I could hear something big growling. Protecting the bottle," Aline explained. She looked at Abi who still smiled at her. Then she continued. "I walked into the cave and found myself in the same place I was when I first saw it. This time…this time, I was able to touch it."

Aline opened the palm of her left hand and the High Magical Council leaned towards her to get a better look. They began to whisper as they looked at something, but Aline was not sure what it was.

"Continue, child," said Saywa.

"Okay," Aline responded. "The bottle told me to hurry up and find it because there was another looking for it and 'he' was powerful. Then it told me to tell Akiya everything. That she would know where it is and once I am there that I will know where to look and how to find her."

"This alone is a sign of your potential powers," the witch Urpi said. "How do you know the bottle is a 'her'?"

"I…I just do," responded Aline.

"The bottle has given Aline a warning. We know who that powerful creature looking for her is. Dashiok. The bottle is right, we need to hurry up!" Benowit exclaimed.

"Aline! It is Aline who has to hurry and find the blue bottle," Akiya corrected him.

"But she is only a child," said the pegacorn Kawayu, "who is still finding her powers."

"Her powers will develop. We all agree on this. She has just started to show us the beginning of courage and her eagerness to learn. We need to give her the opportunities to push and explore her powers. Better to be on our turf than on his," the Apotequil Khallma argued.

"It is too dangerous," said both Benowit and Saywa.

"It is more dangerous if she stays and does nothing," stressed Uskhay, Khallma's older sister.

"Nothing, no! She will be training and should be training with all of us!" Atik said.

"*His* turf? *He* is powerful, the bottle said. Who is, *He?*" Aline asked out loud. All turned to look at her. She had a feeling that they were referring to someone else besides Dashiok.

"It is our time to give you information," Akiya responded.

"Akiya, maybe we should not," Abi cautioned.

"We vowed after the War of Magic to include all equally. Plus, she must know in order to be prepared. The best way to stay true to our vow and to help her is to be transparent," Akiya said.

With hesitation, Abi nodded her head. She looked at Aline and said, "The whispers recently told us that your brother has spotters in this world. He sent them to search for something. We first thought these spotters were trying to find you, and still many of us think this to be so. Now, with the message from the blue bottle we believe that your brother's spotters are looking for both, you and the blue bottle," Aline's eyes widened and Abi softly squeezed her hand.

"Hmm! There are many things Dashiok and your bother could do with this power," explained Akiya. "One possibility could be to create a loophole among worlds."

"The whispers heard one spotter moving towards the Winding Forest near the Northern Mountains. This is on the opposite end of the forest where you first arrived to this world," said Abi. The picture of the 'u' trees came into Aline's mind. "They are getting too close," continued Abi. "Another spotter was heard on the southeast edge of the Bleak Forest. The Bleak Forest reaches both, the Winding Forest and the Southern Shores. What this means, Aline, is that they have picked up your trail and possibly the location of the blue bottle."

"Oh!" Aline's mind became overfilled with whispers. She felt both Cristina's and Sofia's arms on her shoulders. She had forgotten they were right behind her.

"We can go with her and help," Cristina suggested shyly.

"Yes, and we will go with them as well," Sky thought to the group.

"She must not go, under any circumstances. None of them should go. They are just children." thought Benowit.

Aline looked at him. He was sitting quietly looking at Saywa who was arguing why Aline should stay and the sylph sisters should absolutely not participate at all. She was asking why they were even in this council.

"There is no other choice, she must go. The real question is if we can trust her with all this power. After all, she has been dwelling with the humans. Being human is all she knows," he looked at Akiya, "another lesson from the Wars of Magic is not to trust humans," thought Unan.

Quickly, Atik began to argue why she should go and continue her training on the journey.

"What if she fails, then we will all die. Should we trust a child with our lives? I do not think so," Kawayu thought quietly, while Khallma was suggesting that he and others should go with Aline to help her with her training.

"Oh my child, how can I best protect you if you go. Whatever happens, whatever you decide, I will be there," thought Abi as she looked up quietly towards Aline. She could see the concern on Abi's wooden face.

She was having a hard time following the heated conversation while hearing their thoughts at the same time. The whispers were getting louder and louder, making her almost dizzy. The sister's hands on her shoulders were helping her anchor herself down and keeping her steady.

Suddenly a voice became very clear to Aline. She saw more than heard a thought, and then another and another. Pearls of thoughts, one linked to the other exploring paths, leading to different possibilities, reading different endings.

The first thought was of Aline making it to the Southern Shores with Cristina, Sofia, the weredogs, and members from the council of magic. She finds the bottle and is able to come back.

The second thought was for Aline to go with Cristina, Sofia, and the weredogs, but they never make it to the shores. Her brother captures her and takes them to Dashiok, who uses her to find the bottle. They all perish.

The next thought was for Aline to go with members of the council. They make it to the shores, but are all captured in battle by her brother's army who take her to Dashiok. He uses her to find the bottle and they all perish.

Then this led to the next thought which was for Aline to stay in the palace and members of the council to go find the bottle. While Aline is training, the bottle does not allow them to find it. They perish fighting her brother's army. Dashiok goes himself and retrieves the bottle. Without key member of the council, he attacks, captures Aline, and they all perish.

The last thought she heard was, "We must protect Aline at all cost. If she survives, then they all live."

These multiple scenarios kept on playing back and forth. Changing here and there trying to seek for the best outcome. The only outcome that worked was the one where Aline went with her friends and some members of the council. If the council did not push their emotions aside and search for the correct path—the logical as well as the hardest and most dangerous path—then Dashiok had already won.

Aline just heard Akiya's first layer of thought. And then she peeled it all the way back to her deep rooted thought.

Benowit spoke up over all members. He was opposed to Aline's and the sister's participation, for this could be far too dangerous for her, for them, and for everyone. He insisted that this is exactly what Dashiok wanted and that they were all falling in his trap.

Aline focused on his thoughts. She felt as well his fear of losing her and loosing everyone. The thought of failing her father and mother was more than he could bear. How he could not allow himself to be tricked by Dashiok a second time. This all led to his deep rooted thought: he had failed the One World. It was his fault that it had shattered into eight pieces. The different spells he could have used to save the One World circled around and around in his mind. Never achieving the possibility for all creatures to live together, safe, and happy.

Aline had Akiya's thoughts on her right and Benowit's thoughts on her left. She was able to move these thoughts forwards and backward like toy trains. Each wagon was one thought and just like that she was able to draw an energy line from Akiya's first thought to Benowit's first thought. She then watched him as he looked at Akiya and then at Aline.

He knew. Akiya was right. Aline had to go and the sylphs, the weredogs, and members of the council must accompany her. He realized he had underestimated her just like he had with Ihxu and Akiya thousands of years ago. He would never do this again.

Taking a deep breath, the great wizard king closed his eyes and said, "Aline needs to go and so do the sylph sisters, and the weredogs. Some of us will need to accompany them."

The council was quiet. The strongest voice and power opposing Aline to go had just changed sides.

"Why?" Saywa asked.

He answered simply. "Because it is the only logical path where we may have a chance to succeed and to survive."

It did not take long for the council to conclude. They decided that in addition to Cristina, Sofia, and the weredogs, Kunaq, Khallma, Uskhay, Urpi, and Kawayu would also accompany Aline and help them the girls with their training.

Aline was to leave in one week and that would be all the time she had to train with Abi and Akiya before going on her quest to find the blue bottle. Abi was devastated she could not go with her, and Akiya spoke with her, barely calming her down.

"You continue to impress me, Aline," said Akiya as they were walking back inside the great hall. "Not only did you find my original thought, but you connected it to Benowit."

"You knew?" Aline asked, surprised.

"Mmhmm! I am a sense fairy, remember? What is interesting is that he does not know and believes he came up with all of the scenarios on his own." Akiya winked at Aline, who was in awe, and then walked a bit faster to catch up with Abi.

Aline was now next to Sofia, Cristina, and the five weredogs.

"Well played Aline!" said Sofia.

"What do you mean?" Cristina asked.

"Ha! Do not worry, it is a sense thing. I do have one question to ask. We are all embarking on this quest and we know the dangers that we may face." Both Aline and Cristina were intrigued. "I have been playing this in my mind and I am a bit worried. It sounded like we need to journey through the Winding Forest and then the Bleak Forest, until we make it to the Southern Shores. Not one council member mentioned meeting up with anyone or going to any house."

"Yes," responded both Cristina and Aline trying to figure out her concern. Did the council miss something major? Are there creatures they did not account for?

"Well, then...er...where are we going to go when we need to...you know...go?" Sofia asked.

"Go where?" Aline asked, confused.

"To the bathroom," Sofia whispered.

"What?" Cristina barked.

"The same as we do it. Just dig a whole and kick some dirt on top when you are done," Ash explained.

"Ew!" All three girls cringed.

"Boys!" scoffed Alis.

6

THE QUEST

Forest Monsters

The week breezed by as Aline, Cristina, Sofia, and the weredogs spent every day training. With new-found motivation everyone was able to get more cookies during the training.

Aline was able to hear more of what Alis said when she was far away. Even peeled some of her thoughts, including some Alis did not mean to reveal. Something Alis was not really too happy about.

Cristina caught Kay and Sky three times, even though both Kay and Sky were getting faster. The first time, she used a slab of grass to block their way. Then, she went from using grass to vines to sending dirt balls and wind gusts their way. At least with the wind gusts, she was able to blow away some of the dirt on their fur. The palace smelled like flowers from the many baths it prepared that week.

Sofia had been able to make both Mach and Ash feel like their fur was full of tree sap, which caused uncontrollable licking. She also made them feel that they had a persistent fly flying around their noses. This was most annoying for them since they could never get rid of the tiny bug. A third time Sofia made them feel like they had hiccups and the girls thought it was hilarious. Quickly, both Ash and Mach calmed their emotions and became really happy, which got rid of the hiccups. Really, they were laughing uncontrollably and this overpowered the impulse to hiccup. No one was really sure if the laughter was just another sense sent by Sofia. And she was not telling.

Finally, the day came. It was time to leave. Aline was feeling nervous as she waited in the amphitheater where six months ago she had received her powers from the orange meteor. Now that she could hear more often what others thought, she was not sure she liked her power. In general, folks put on a brave face, but they were really scared—particularly those who were leaders. They were just better at not only hiding their true feelings but also emanating a sense of security.

The palace had put together a small backpack for Aline that was connected with one of the many secret compartments in her room. Once, when she opened it, she even saw her gargoyle costume. She really was set for this trip.

"Aline, my beautiful darling. You may not be my granddaughter, but you are *my granddaughter*. Understand?" Abi's eyes were filled with love and concern.

"I know," Aline answered.

"Please be careful. Use your powers, as they will protect you. Telepathy is just one of them. The other powers will come when you need them the most," Abi advised.

"I will. I promise," Aline said solemnly.

Cristina and Sofia were next to her, hugging and saying their goodbyes to their parents, who were as worried as Abi. All three adults held back tears to look strong for the girls.

Aline could not help herself as she stared at their mother Azel. She stared for two reasons. She missed Kani terribly; and she was mesmerized to think that Azel, Cristina's and Sofia's mother, was really the daughter of Ihxu and not Akiya. The similarities between her and Akiya were striking. The only differences were that Azel had golden eyes with green specs, was younger, and had a more peaceful look. Akiya's look was intense, as if she were piercing into your soul. Aline guessed that this was part of the hardship she had endured. The sisters told her that Ihxu, her parents, her brother-in-law, and her only love had died in the War of Magic, leaving her to care for her niece Azel.

Akiya approached the sisters and spoke softly to them. By accident,

Aline heard their thoughts and realized that Akiya was not full of sadness, but rather full of love for Azel, Cristina, and Sofia.

"Aline," called Akiya as she waved her hand for her to come closer. "I want to continue your training."

"Absolutely. As soon as I am back we can start again," Aline responded.

"There are many things you still need to learn, child. I mean, we should continue your training while you are on your quest."

"With the other quest carriers?" Aline was certain she had asked the wrong question.

"With me!"

"I thought…are you coming with us?"

"No," answered Akiya very matter of fact. She seemed to be enjoying this interaction with Aline.

"I do not follow. Oh! You want me to see if I can hear you speaking to me telepathically during the quest," she paused. "Right?" She was certain she got it correct.

"So close. Try again."

"Hmm!" Aline thought really hard and then she realized all she had to do was to dig deep within Akiya's thoughts. She tried to search within the sylph's mind but hit a brick wall.

"Nice try." Akiya said. "Let me help you. What do you think we can do on your way to the Southern Shores?"

"For me to hear your thoughts?" Aline answered. And then she thought: *There has to be more.*

"Of course there is more Aline," Akiya said. Aline looked at Akiya and realized that she had not moved her mouth. From the beginning, the whole conversation had been done telepathically.

"That is awesome!" Aline said out loud.

"Let's continue this conversation later," added Akiya. "In the meantime, be alert. There are eyes and ears everywhere. Using your powers may come in handy, more than you could know." She hugged Aline and whispered in her ear, "Trust only your friends."

"Come close, quest carriers," requested Benowit. All thirteen walked up to him. "It is in my power to send you with one protection spell," his voice echoed across the amphitheater. He spoke over the group in another language. Aline saw the energy surrounding the theater rise, combine, and then cover each of the thirteen quest carriers.

"May the One World protect us,' said Benowit.

"May the One World protect us," Aline watched as everyone responded in unison.

All thirteen began to walk southwest towards the Winding Forest, not too far from where Aline had arrived in this new magical world. Now she was leaving Abi, Akiya, Benowit, and the palace. She felt that she was leaving her home all over again.

It did not take them long to arrive at the entrance of the forest. She took one step onto its mossy floor, and just like that Aline's quest to find the blue bottle began.

They walked southeast in silence for several hours. Every so often Kunaq—the Yachaq or white elf—would run ahead to check their path. The three girls looked at the 'u' trees and resisted the urged to climb them. Aline looked at the endless rows of 'u' trees and decided that when they returned from their journey she was going to spend more time in the Winding Forest. After one of those scouting expeditions, Kunaq came back and explained their options to the quest carriers.

"We have two choices," said the Yachaq. "We can continue heading southeast. It will be a two-week journey. The advantage is that it will take us four days to cross the Bleak forest. The Yachaq region is right before the frontier between forests. We could rest there and resupply. Then it will take us three more days on the Southern Shores to make it to the shorter point on the coast where we believe the blue bottle is.

"The disadvantage is that if we continue walking in this direction we may risk being seen by the inhabitants of the southeastern portion of the Winding Forest. They are so close to the Bleak Forest that it is hard to tell who spies for Dashiok and who is an ally. Another disadvantage is that the portion of the Bleak Forest we will need to cross is the most dangerous one."

Aline noticed the other council members and the weredogs shuffle their bodies uncomfortably.

"The other option is to go from here directly south. This means that we will reach the Bleak forest in three days. There is a small group of Yachaq who patrol this border. We can meet with them and hear their guidance for the best path through the Bleak Forest. I believe I know which one it is, and it may take us about eight days. If we all make it out of the Bleak Forest we will arrive at the most southern point and we will cut our journey by almost half the time."

His purple eyes gazed at each member while he spoke and once he finished they rested on Aline. The feeling that he was trying to connect with her became apparent. She remembered Akiya's brick wall so she built one in her mind. Kunaq tilted his head ever so slightly and Aline knew she had succeeded.

"Since all Yachaq are connected, can you ask the Yachaq near the southern border for guidance now?" Kawayu asked.

"No," Kunaq answered dryly. "They are so close to the Bleak Forest they have blocked themselves to prevent spies from acquiring any information. The only way to obtain it is to go there."

"It is obvious, we must take the safest route!" exclaimed Urpi the witch. Her long black wavy hair bounced when she looked at Aline and the sisters. It was the first time that Aline saw deep black eyes that sparkled.

"Both paths are dangerous, so there is no safe path." Kawayu said. "We are also time bound. Risking time would be risking Dashiok's spies finding the location of the blue bottle before we do. The question is what are we willing to risk?"

"That is the correct question," agreed Urpi. "Thus my answer remains the same. We must take the path that exposes Aline, Cristina, and Sofia to the least amount of danger. We should not risk them."

"Both Uskhay and I have traveled the Bleak Forest and know of its perils," added Khallma.

Aline was mesmerized by his square gem-like eyes and stocky presence. Even though their head and torso were very square, she noticed she could see every bone on their hands and feet. Skin that was like a thin layer of leather that half hid the mechanical motion made by each bone when their fingers moved.

"We are powerful, even though we are not many. Minimizing our stay in the Bleak Forest may appear to be the best route, but do not underestimate that forest. The short path that Kunaq mentioned is indeed the most savage and treacherous one. Keeping Urpi's words in mind, it may be best to take the southern path," Khallma added. Both Kawayu and Urpi nodded in agreement.

"We weredogs also believe that the southern path is the best path to take," Kay said. "The five of us will walk surrounding the three girls. We can allow Kunaq to connect with us while he treks ahead. If he finds danger, we will be the first to know and can guard the girls."

"I can stay behind guarding our rear," Kawayu offered.

"Both Khallma and I can cover the left and right flanks on higher grounds," suggested Uskhay as she pointed to the 'u' trees.

"I will share the front with Kunaq. When he is trekking, I can cast spells protecting the group," Urpi said.

"Then it is settled," Kawayu said.

"Wait! Don't we get a say in this?" Sofia asked with a smile. Not waiting for a response, she continued, "I agree. We should take the shortest path because of the warning that the blue bottle gave to Aline. The bottle was clear. It said to hurry."

All of the council members smiled. "What is so funny?" asked Sofia, confused. She was serious.

"I am with you Sofia," Cristina said. "For me, the correct question is which path will allow us to be both safer *and* fast. Risking our lives is out of the question, and so is time. Speed is a huge risk that I do not believe the quest carriers should take. If Dashiok has the blue bottle and we fail, it is the same as risking our lives. So I wholeheartedly agree with Sofia. What do you think Aline?"

Aline admired both Sofia and Cristina. Sofia for speaking up and ensuring that all voices were heard and Cristina for defending her sister and providing a great point that was missed by the adults.

"I will stand by what both Cristina and Sofia pointed out. We must travel south." Aline felt proud of her friends and found that their bravery empowered her.

Kunaq bowed his head and guided the quest carriers south. They stayed on this course for the rest of the journey towards the Southern Shores.

In just two jumps Khallma and Uskhay climbed to the top branches of the 'u' trees. Both moved swiftly from tree to tree so quietly that Aline sometimes forgot they were up there guarding them. They only came down when they stopped to eat and rest. It was here that Aline enjoyed seeing the dynamic between brother and sister. Uskhay was spunky and liked to compete with her brother a lot. Whether it was the faster eater, climber, or the one who jumped the highest, it did not matter, she was ready to compete. He always took her up on these challenges and it was impressive seeing them go at it. They were fast and powerful. The things they were capable of doing were unimaginable, even more so for someone their size and with square bodies.

They walked for the rest of the day and Sofia and Cristina told Aline about the adventure of how they got their wings. Aline was surprised to know that sylphs are not born with wings but have to earn them, and that the quest they were on now was the sisters' second one. Both Cristina and Sofia were very excited to tell Aline about their adventures last year where they had to fight a terrible sorceress, and saved two witches and two sylph brothers.

"Wow! This is incredible. Both of you had such an amazing adventure." Aline realized that she was the only one who had no experience in quests or adventures. "I think I am the only one here who has not had any experience with quests. Come to think about it, I am the only one who does not really know how to use her powers. I feel like the underdog."

"Hey, what is wrong with been a dog?" Ash asked, a bit insulted.

"It is just an expression. All I meant is that I am maybe holding the quest carriers back," Aline explained.

"Don't listen to him. He knows what underdog means. He just never liked that expression since the moment he heard it in the human world. First in Britain and then in the United States of America," said Sky, giving Ash a dirty look. "And by the way. YOU are most likely the most powerful creature among the quest carriers."

"That is what folks keep telling me. I am not sure if it is the case," Aline confessed. "I mean, what if all this mixing of creatures and their powers canceled each other's magic out?"

"Well, we know that is not true Aline, for you have telepathy," Kay asserted. "Besides, you are in the midst of your adventure. Enjoy it! The good and the bad, as you learn on the go."

Aline smiled. Kay was right. She *was* in the midst of her own adventure. And right now, they were walking a lot. Sofia continued by telling Aline their adventure story and Aline listened carefully. Maybe there is something she could learn and apply it to hers.

That night, Aline telepathically communicated to Akiya the route the team had decided to take. To her relief, Akiya was pleased with their decision to go south.

The next day was pretty much a repeat of the first day. What started to change was that the 'u' trees were now closer together and not in neat rows as they had been a day ago. Cristina and Sofia continued telling Aline their story while Kunaq's treks proceeded to show them the safe path forward. When they rested to eat, the Apotequils would swiftly climb down and chat with the group. The girls very much enjoyed speaking with them. They would talk about the One World, about how each Guardian found their powers. About the War of Magic and the creation of the eight worlds. Aline took mental notes of everything. For her, these were all lessons, part of her training. During these talks, she began to telepathically communicate with Akiya, who would fill in the gaps for her.

By late afternoon on the third day, they reached the white elves patrolling the border. During dinner, they spoke to the group about the Bleak Forest.

"There is one path and only one path you can take that will possibly guarantee your safe passage," said the Yachaq with long brown hair and gray eyes.

"Possibly?!" asked Cristina, surprised.

"Yes, child." He looked at her intensely and gave her a dry smile. "You must stay together as a group. Numbers matter in this forest and you are barely enough."

"The path is marked by 'u' trees on either side; a smooth river rock is next to each tree. The forest will deceive you, so look for both—'u' trees next to a river rock. Before the Bleak Forest was created, there used to be a river leading all the way to the Southern Shores. Some of the Laqha and warlocks transformed the forests and its inhabitants into what you see today," added the second white elf.

Aline could see his pointy ears sticking out of his long blond hair. She did not like his black eyes—they did not shimmer like Urpi's.

"Laqha? Black elves are here?" Sofia asked, concerned. Both white elves nodded.

"You should be more concerned about the colossals who were not able to escape the transformation. They changed. They went dark. Devoted to the Laqha and the warlocks now, they will try anything to trap you and take you to them," warned the elf with brown hair.

"The only advantage that this path provides is that the 'u' trees create a small opening." the second Yachaq continued talking as if no one had said a word after he spoke the first time. "A tiny one really," he looked down a bit sad, remembering something. "Barely visible by most, but it allows just enough light into the forest to repel most of the dark colossals away."

He continued in a solemn tone. "There are three rules you must abide in order to survive." His dimmed black eyes looked up at the group. "Only travel under full daylight, not even during dusk or dawn. You are lucky to have the Yachaq with you. He will be the only one who can truly tell when there is full daylight. Do not climb any trees, this includes the 'u' trees. Even if you think you can see a light between its branches. Stay on the ground."

When he said this, both Khallma and Uskhay bowed their heads and murmured a small conversation to each other in a different language. Then Uskhay softly elbowed Khallma and he elbowed her back.

"Lastly," the elf continued, ignoring the Apotequils, "without exception, you must stay together. You will be tricked and tested many times. By all means, do not, I repeat, *do not* separate." His instruction struck a chord, for the group remained silent.

"Has anyone ever made it through this path?" Aline asked, breaking the stillness.

"A few," answered the gray-eyed Yachaq.

"*Very* few," confirmed the blond-haired Yachaq. "We have done this the most times. More times trying to rescue as many as we could, but this has come at a price."

"Now rest. You need to leave at first light," the first elf said.

It was hard for anyone there to have a peaceful sleep. Aline felt like she was partially awake, in a repeating dream, with no control and no say. Becoming aware of her surroundings every time she turned, and she turned a lot. She could feel the sisters moving as well as the weredogs softly whining, growling, and moving their paws.

Her dream that night was a little similar to the one she had on the night of her birthday. She was in the middle of a meadow filled with yellow flowers, looking out towards the mountains, when she saw different color rocks that would shake and then smashed against each other. Afraid they would break she tried to grab them but they were stronger and would slip from her fingers. She continues until they form a giant worm which begins to chase her. Running away, she saw several open doors back-to-back on the meadow. Behind the first door were Cristina and Sofia desperately calling her to get in, but when she was just about to reach the door it would close and disappear revealing the next door. She could see Kay and Sky, but again, this door would disappear too before she could get there. Her friends were behind each door and she could never reach them. When the last door disappeared she would find herself back again in the meadow staring at the mountains and finding the colored rocks. Even though she knew the rocks would turn into the giant worm, she still tried to grab them no matter how hard she told herself to leave. The more it repeated, the more she would warn herself, but nothing worked.

She was awoken by Mach licking her cheeks and she felt she had finally reached her friends without a door disappearing.

"Time to go, Aline," Mach's nose softly nudged her face and Aline could hear his breathing almost tickling her ear. "Stay close to me," he urged.

"I will, my gentle giant," promised Aline, holding his enormous head between her hands.

The only supplies the two Yachaq had given the quest carriers was wood for kindling.

"You have a witch with you that has enough magic to make each one count and last. This is more precious than any food we can supply you with," they explained "Use them well, and you may survive."

In the middle of dawn, they quietly gathered their belongings and followed the two Yachaq towards the path. Aline noticed the bark on the 'u' trees was getting darker and darker as they walked south. The air was thin and she felt she had to inhale a bit longer to fill her lungs. The leaves on top of the trees were getting bushier and tangled with each other forming a canopy. A green tent that blocked the first lights of dawn. The elves were right. It felt too real for Aline and she began to feel afraid. Then both Cristina and Sofia grabbed her hands. They were walking next to her and they also looked scared. They did not shy away; they moved on, and with a new-found strength so did Aline.

They entered a tunnel made of nature and watchful eyes. Aline noticed that as soon as they touched the dark grass on the path, their presence had rung a bell that many were ready and willing to answer. To her, it felt wrong, and every bone and muscle in her body screamed for her to run the other way.

The group trotted lightly, trying to make as little noise as possible. This path was narrower than the one they had traveled before, so they advanced in smaller groups, closer to each other. Kunaq, and Urpi were in the front, Mach and Kay were next, followed by the girls, then Sky, Ash, and Alis, and finally Khallma, Kawayu, and Uskhay. It was only when Kunaq announced that it was time for lunch, that everyone realized half the day had already passed.

It felt like an eternity to Aline. There were hardly any sounds and those she heard made her think that something beyond the trees was spying on them. For the girls, the little light battling through the green blanket held by the dark 'u' trees was fighting for dear life, and it did not look like it was going to win.

Whispers more than words were exchanged during lunch and Aline, Sofia, and Cristina felt like they were in their school library. They missed hearing Khallma's and Uskhay's stories. They walked the second half of the day dreading dusk. Kunaq began to slow his pace. He signaled to Aline, Sofia, Kawayu, and the weredogs first. They told the others that he had sensed something get closer to the path. This made the girls really anxious and Aline did not like that maybe Kunaq was aware of her fears. Mach, who the whole time was right in front of Aline, got closer to her, lifted both ears, and his nose. Nothing was getting close without him smelling or hearing it. Aline felt a bit better. The other weredogs followed his lead and Cristina and Sofia felt better as well.

Rustle. This time all of them heard a clear movement coming from not too far behind the 'u' trees. Then it was on the move again. They all stopped breathing for a few seconds, trying to figure out where it went.

"Kawayu." The pegacorn stopped, for he had heard Uni's calling as clear as if he were standing next to him. "Why are you walking with a human? Look at you. Aren't your scars evidence enough that they cannot be trusted? You are betraying our kind. Leave this instant."

The pegacorn was troubled and had to find, buried within, the strength to move forward with the group. Khallma and Uskhay warned the others that something had affected Kawayu, but they did not know who or what, as neither had heard or seen anything.

The team gathered in front of the pegacorn and he told them that whatever was out there had magic and explained to them what happened. Kunaq suggested that they needed to camp once they reached a spot where the path widened just enough. Based on what he had learned from the two elves, it was not too far.

As they continued on, the quest carriers walked closer together and as fast as they could. It was no longer a concern to be quiet, but rather to get where they needed to and quick. When they got to the open spot, Khallma took some wood out and with Uspi's white magic they created a strong fire that lasted all night. This did not mean that any of them got any sleep. That night, it was eerie quiet.

The next day at dawn, Kunaq let everyone know it was time to get ready. Breakfast had a bitter aftertaste. They had seven more days to go and whatever was out there had just started to play with them. With a heavy feeling, the quest carriers headed out.

It was not long before all of the weredogs stopped mid-track and faced out in five different directions. With all of their might, they fought the urge to run out towards the smell and noise that was making them itch to hunt. It was so powerful that the team had to stop, and only the combination of both Urpi's and Kawayu's magic was able to snap the five weredogs out of this dark enchanted. It was their loyalty to their pack and to the quest carriers that enabled them to resist. What brought a smile to Cristina and Sofia in this tense moment was to learn that they were considered part of the pack.

The rest of the day, any little noise they heard made them jump. There were many little noises throughout the day and more during the night. It was the second night the quest carriers had little to no sleep. Rotating watch was pointless for they were all awake, their thoughts were not as clear, and they started to lose their focus.

Breakfast on the third day was tasteless. They knew they were not going to last long if they did not eat, so they forced themselves to finish. It was a dense and quiet day. They knew something was going to happen, but they did not know when. The anxiety of not knowing made it worse. Two hours before dusk, Kunaq told them that soon they would reach a safe spot to camp for the night. The quest carriers relaxed just a nudge.

"Cristina!"

"Mom?"

"Cristina, your dad is hurt. We need you."

"What is wrong with Dad, Mom? Where are you? I am coming," she called out desperately. The team felt a blow on the heart—this time one of the girls was being tricked.

"No!" Urpi yelled. "Hold her!" she instructed Kunaq and Uskhay. "That is enough!" With a commanding voice, she sent a strong pulse of light out from within her towards the trees. A magical ring striking whatever had played with Cristina. Whatever was there had left for now, but the team was concerned. The attack on Cristina hurt them more emotionally than anything else.

Every day Aline had reached out to Akiya letting her know what they had experienced, their plans for the next day, and her concerns. Aline was not sure how much this forest was affecting the team, and always felt better after speaking with Akiya. A little relief to bounce their ideas and plans off someone outside of the Bleak Forest. Akiya was the balance she needed. Not only did she quietly train and learn from her, but the sylph always gave her the right guidance when she needed it. Tonight, in particular, her wise words motivated Aline.

"We knew this was going to happen before we came in," Aline broke the silence during dinner. "This is what the two Yachaq told us. *'You should be more concerned about the colossals that were not able to escape the transformation...they will try anything to trap you and take you to them'*, remember? Why are we acting surprised that whatever is out there decided to attack Cristina? Did you really believe that Cristina, Sofia, and I were not going to be bothered at all?" She had a strength in her voice that made Kawayu see her for what she really was, and it was not just her humanity. "If we let them break us apart like this, then they've already won. I know Cristina and Sofia. They are the bravest girls I have ever met. It is because of them that I am here. I will not give up. Will you?"

"No," Cristina said, strong and clear. "I will never give up."

Sofia was proud of her sister. "I am with you, Sis!"

The rest of the quest carriers smiled. They were all in.

That night the council members and the weredogs took turns keeping watch. The others resting had the best sleep yet since entering the Bleak Forest.

On the morning of the fourth day, breakfast did not taste good but they were hungry. With risen spirits, they began their journey. The first half of the day passed a bit faster and they even though they heard some birds. During lunch, Khallma and Uskhay irritated each other a bit and all three girls smiled. They ventured towards the second half of the day a little lighter.

It was not long before the quest carriers realized that Khallma had paused to look at one of the 'u' trees. When they got close to him, Uskhay did the same in the opposite direction.

"No Uskhay, stop," pleaded Sofia.

"You can't climb, remember!" urged Cristina.

Kunaq did not wait for a response, he knew their strength and their weakness. They were having an internal struggle and if they lost, the carriers were not going to have a chance to stop them. Connecting with them, Kunaq used some of their power to reach both of them in record time. He went to Khallma as he was the first to be enchanted and sent him shocking energy similar to the power wielded by the Apotequils. This released him immediately. Then, he repeated this with Uskhay.

"Wow, that stings," said Uskhay.

"Thank you," added Khallma, and Uskhay nodded. Urpi was ready to send her light ring when Sofia stopped her.

"Wait!" An idea had dawned on Sofia. "With Urpi's and Kawayu's magic, Aline, Kunaq, and I could create a way for all of us to speak with one another without making a sound—no one could hear us but us. We could communicate telepathically. We could all be connected. We would all know if someone was getting attacked."

"Brilliant, Sis!" Exclaimed Cristina.

"It is worth a try," said Kunaq.

"A good idea indeed," agreed Kawayu.

"I knew I liked you," approved Uskhay.

With a new sense of hope, the quest carriers gave this experiment a try. They failed on their first attempt because the weredogs, the pegacorn, and Urpi were attacked with dark magic at the same time. Again it was the speed of the Khallma and Uskhay that save the quest carriers.

It all happened in a matter of seconds. They immediately sent their lances up, piercing the green canopy and letting in more light. Horrible screeches echoed from the creatures around them as the enchanted quest carriers were released. The leaves quickly closed the holes and extinguished the new light. The quest carriers were captured once more. But lightning rays pierced the bushes on their way down to Khallma and Uskhay letting more light enter the forest. It was accompanied by horrific screams. The creatures moved to the darkness trapping once more the same quest carriers. Brother and sister guided the rays in opposite directions, creating explosions of light that freed their companions. At the same time, with his left hand Kunaq had sent a ball of energy to protect the girls and with his right had entered the whirlpool of energy. There he was able to learn crucial information from their injured enemies.

"Their attack means they are desperate and afraid," Kunaq told the group. "We must try again, quickly!" He knew they had very little time before their enemy grew in numbers and took them. "Aline! Sofia! Grab my hands and hold on to each other," he said, reaching out for the girls. The girls also held each other's hands.

Urpi was mad. She immediately created a sphere of pure white energy, which swiveled around her. "Now Kawayu," she screamed and sent with one finger this energy towards his horn. Swiftly, glimmering pink, purple, and green rays shot out at once from his horn towards her energy, pushing it through Sofia, Aline, and Kunaq. They were ready. Opening their powers, they received these pulses of energy and changed them into colorful threads that touched the quest carriers on their foreheads.

The quest carriers were connected. Now they could speak to each other telepathically. Silence was all that anyone from the outside could observe around them. Inside the quest carrier's minds, their communication was vibrant and loud. They were all able to hear if an enemy was trying to attack any one of them without being affected by the enchantment.

Reaching a spot to camp, the quest carriers rested and had supper. They like speaking to one another in their minds while their ears only heard silence in the dark forest. The silence was a bit eerie, for they could feel eyes watching them.

"So...hm...I need to...er...go," thought Ash and they all stopped what they were doing and looked at him a bit confused. "...nature is calling," he said, clearing his throat.

"Do not go too far," Kunaq said, ignoring the looks on some of the quest carrier's faces.

"But make sure it is far enough," Uskhay said sarcastically. Ash just ignored her and walked a bit away from camp. The rest of the quest carriers began to clean up from supper and set up camp as they talked telepathically with one another.

"You know, the fact that we can all hear each other's thoughts is great and all...er...but I cannot concentrate," Ash thought. All of the quest carriers exploded in laughter, breaking up the eerie silence.

Their spirits were up; however, they knew that revenge was near. Taking turns to watch was easier to do telepathically. Sleeping was another issue. Their dreams or rather nightmares kept waking each other up. Kawayu had to use his powers once more to help the group rest peacefully. He connected them to one peaceful dream where the quest carriers walked in a beautiful meadow.

Before going to sleep, Aline met with Akiya again. She was happy. Now she understood why Akiya had pushed her so much when she was practicing making a wall the moment they walked out of the amphitheater towards the Winding Forest.

Unknown to the other quest carriers, she had been mentally attacked even before she had entered the Bleak Forest. The wall she had created when meeting the two elves had saved her. This is why the elves looked at her funny. They could not reach her at all. She had kept the wall up, with Akiya's help, all this time, even when the powerful magic that connected the quest carriers passed through her. To their surprise, Akiya could now hear the others too. In an indirect way, she was also connected with them. Now, all Aline had to do was step behind the wall to speak with Akiya and the others could not hear them.

"Aline, you have done well. This wall is strong," said Akiya.

"Thank you, but I have you. I was only able to do this because of you," responded Aline.

"No child. The help I provided was that of guidance, nothing more. I never sent any magic to you."

"No way. I felt you. You had to!" Aline did not believe her.

"I do not lie, child," Akiya reminded her. "It is the truth. My support has been as your mentor. You have only felt my magic used to guide you, that is all. The magic was yours."

Aline could not believe it. Even so, Akiya went on.

"It is time, child, that you expand your magic. If the quest carriers do not have your protection, they will perish. You must broaden the wall to cover all of the carriers."

"I cannot..." Aline's human nature was about to say she was not able to do something this big. Then she remembered, as a human, she would not have been able to create an enchanted protective wall in the first place. Nor communicate telepathically or be in a quest to find a magical bottle in a magical world. She took a deep breath and changed her statement into a question. "Do you believe I can do this?"

"During the time in the One World, I grew up with sylphs who limited their powers based on the belief of others." Akiya said. "Those others created rules to make themselves feel better. It was only when sylphs let go of these rules and beliefs that we began to scratch the surface of our powers. The truth is that each one of us possesses the only power to unleash our true potential. Trust me, every single being has some sort of power hidden deep within them. There are no exceptions. Their beliefs can either free and grow this power, or limit, even lock their powers away. We put too much emphasis on what others believe we can or cannot do. How many barriers do we need to overcome before we realize that we have added these obstacles ourselves? The only thing that matters is what we believe we can do or not. With this awareness, what do you believe, Aline?"

Aline was able to see Akiya's words as they illustrated the sylphs in the One World limiting their powers and then Cristina's and Sofia's powers surpassing the original sylphs. She was happy to have Akiya as a teacher. She felt empowered. That she could take anything on, like a magical superhero.

"Cristina and Sofia are super lucky to have an aunt like Akiya. Just her cookies alone would have done it for me. She is amazing, I am so glad that she is helping me out," Aline thought to herself, forgetting that Akiya was linked with her telepathically even in her hiding place. She blushed.

"Okay," she said. "What do I need to do?" She sensed Akiya's smile.

The fifth day had finally arrived and the quest carriers thought they had camouflaged some of the noise they made by speaking by using only their minds. The path no longer ran straight. It appeared to weave about in different directions. To ensure they were not tricked, they slowed their pace and checked for river rocks next to the 'u' trees.

This pace helped Aline practice expanding her wall. It was hard. For her, this was as crazy as trying to stretch a real brick wall. She thought that if she was sitting still by herself surrounded by silence, maybe, just maybe she could accomplish this. But extending a wall while hearing the thoughts of twelve other beings was nearly impossible.

Many thoughts crossed her mind while she practiced. By the end of the fifth day, the one thought Aline could not remove was that she was a fake. Akiya instructed her to try again, that she did not have the luxury to give up, since the life of the quest carriers depended on her. She explained to Aline that she was trying something that would be considered advanced for most adults. But in the end, when Aline saw the faces of her friends struggling in a quest that had only begun because she said they needed to hurry to get the blue bottle, she knew she had no other choice but to make it happen.

That night, Akiya thought Aline needed additional help. After a lengthy talk, they both agreed that they would tell the rest of the quest carriers in the morning. During breakfast, Aline faced her companions, but she was not alone.

"When Kunaq, Sofia, and I connected you telepathically, something happened that you were not aware of," she began.

"What? Are you okay Aline?" Kay asked, concerned.

"Yes, I am all right. It is nothing like that," she said. "It's just that... well...there is an additional member who is also connected with us."

"Who, child? There are dark forces in this forest," Kawayu said sternly.

"Do not be afraid, my friends. It is I, Akiya." Hearing this voice, the quest carriers were confused. They thought they had been tricked by their enemy.

"It is her," confessed Aline. "I have been speaking with Akiya telepathically since the day we left. It was a way to enhance my training." She looked apologetically at Cristina and Sofia, not for what she had done, but for not telling them.

"Sofia, I let her know about your plan to connect the group and she thought it was brilliant." She looked proudly at Sofia, who smiled back. Aline could sense she had already forgiven her. "But we realized that being linked may not be enough against the creatures in the Bleak Forest. So Akiya suggested that I help protect the group. Yesterday, I practiced all day, but I am not able to do this by myself. I need your help."

"That is why you were more quiet than usual," teased Uskhay.

"She is not quiet! You heard her, she has been practicing!" Cristina jumped to Aline's defense. Aline knew that she too had forgiven her.

"Well, that is not entirely true, Aline. In fact, it is quite the opposite. This is why I am here, to help them help you to protect them," added Akiya. All the weredogs tilted their heads.

"I do not understand," said Aline.

"It is rather simple," Akiya said. "They just need to be quiet. This would be easier if it were just as simple as closing their mouths. But you are linked with your minds. And quieting the mind, well, only a few originals have been able to master that."

They all faced Kunaq.

"I do not think that you could help my sister's mind. She has already lost it!" Khallma joked. They all laughed. An interesting sight to see if you were looking at them, with their mouths opened obviously laughing, but no sound coming out at all.

"We do not have much time," Akiya said. "I will send your way what I can only describe as a warm thought. I want you not to just *focus* on this thought, but to walk into it and stay there. It will put you in a sort of silence slumber or trance. I will release you once it is completed."

Then she said, "Aline, you know what to do."

Silence. This was what Aline had been wishing for yesterday, and finally here it was. It became an empty room where she could hear each step she took echo in the vast nothingness. She closed her eyes, sat down, and breathed. With each inhale, Aline pulled white energy from within the wall and gathered it around her. With each exhale, she doubled this energy in size. After a few seconds, Aline heard a noise from behind the 'u' trees and lost her focus. Like electric shots, the energy returned to her wall. She looked, but could not see anything but her friends sitting still with open eyes, not really looking at anything.

"Focus, Aline. Ignore what you hear, smell, or feel, just focus," Akiya reassured her. Once again, Aline closed her eyes and began to breathe. She had managed to take several breaths and the energy had quadrupled in size.

"I can do this. I can really do this!" Aline was feeling great. This was far beyond what she had been able to achieve all day yesterday. This time she felt something hit her and bounce on the ground. She opened her eyes, immediately dropping the energy disc that surrounded her.

It was a stick and her arm was red. At that moment, several sticks and rocks began to hit them. She saw Urpi fall, bleeding from her forehead. Next Mach, Alis, and Kawayu hit the ground.

"Oh no! You need to wake up. Akiya, they need to wake up, you need to release them!" Aline pleaded.

"No! You need to focus, otherwise, all of you will die." Akiya said sternly. "Now *focus!*"

Aline was desperate. All she wanted to do was to stop these rocks and sticks from hitting their friends.

"No, no, no, noooo. *You* need to stop! Akiya! *Stop!*" She screamed as she stood up and was hit even more. "Stop, *please* stop."

Tears began to well over. When she saw Cristina fall next, she stood in front of her to protect them. She felt a warm liquid sliding from the side of her face and a rock dropped hard on the ground with blood on it. Then, she saw Sofia and Kay drop to the ground.

This time she was mad. An intense heat rushed to her hands and she screamed "*Stop!*"

A blurry translucent ripple peeled off Aline and flew towards the objects that were heading to her and her friends. Every rock and stick that was on its way to them froze in mid-air and then shot forcefully right back to its source. Screeches, followed by rustling, faded away from the quest carriers. Aline did not know how or what had happened, but she was glad it did. Sitting down, she closed her eyes and focused once more. She knew she did not have much time until they returned.

Back in the empty room, she pulled the energy and breathed until the center of the room was filled with an electric white light.

"It is time Aline," said Akiya

With a swift hand movement, Aline pushed the energy towards the wall with such force that the wall began to slide backward enlarging the space around her. It continued to slide until Aline saw her frozen friends pass through the wall.

Once they were all in, Akiya stopped the warm thought. It was noisy again, and Aline welcomed the many thoughts on the other side of the wall. The quest carriers just realized that a pressure had been on them ever since they entered the Bleak Forest and now it was gone. They were safe from any magical hold these dark creatures would send their way.

"Kawayu, we need your healing powers," said Akiya. All of them focused now outside and realized what had happened.

"How...why did they stop?" Kunaq asked, looking at Aline.

"It seems that another of Aline's powers is beginning to show. I am not sure what it is yet, but it appeared when she needed it the most, like most good magical powers. Anything you can do to aid her as she develops this power will be very helpful for Aline. And for this quest," Akiya said.

The weredogs pricked their ears and wagged their tails. They would always help Aline.

"How cool," mused Cristina, Sofia, and Alis.

"Jinx," Alis added quickly, sticking her tongue out at Sofia. She was surprised Alis said it first and made a face like she had just missed out on something big.

Most of the wounds were small, so Kawayu was able to use his magic and heal everyone, including Aline. They packed their belongings and were ready to continue on their quest for the sixth day.

There was no way anyone could play any mind tricks with the quest carriers. In this matter, they were absolutely safe. What they were expecting was a physical attack much worse than yesterday, so they moved with caution. The weredog's ears were up. One was facing forward and the others moving in all directions. Urpi swiveled her magic back and forth between her fingers. The Apotequils gripped their lances tightly behind them with the tops resting on their shoulder blades. Kawayu's horn had a dim glow. Kunaq was focused but no one knew on what, since whatever he was doing was not in his thoughts.

"I think it is on," said Sofia to the other girls, referring to Kawayu's horn. The sisters' wings were out and Aline knew they were ready to use their powers against any enemy who dare to attack the quest carriers. Aline herself was prepared. She concentrated on hearing any of the enemy's thoughts behind the 'u' trees. "Finding their location would be a great advantage," she thought to the others, and they all nodded.

They walked like this until it was time for lunch. They decided to eat in turns. Aline wanted to eat last. The longer she could concentrate on hearing their enemy's thoughts, the safer her friends would be. Before sitting down with Kunaq, Khallma, and Ash, Aline circled their surroundings with her mind. Nothing, not even a bug. The woods seemed eerily quiet. When she finally ate, it was so fast that Ash told her to slow down.

"Wow, if you are telling me to slow down, then I must be going way too fast," she smiled back.

"Do not confuse this with me insinuating that you are faster than me. Not at all. I am merely suggesting for you to enjoy your lunch. That is all," Ash explained.

"Oh my goodness Ash. You are so competitive. I bet I was eating faster than you," Aline teased.

"No way. I can finish this meal in two gulps."

"I do not think so!"

"Are you challenging me? Is it a race I hear you asking for?" thought Ash.

"See! So competitive. I never asked..." She was not able to finish her sentence. Kunaq immediately got up from his seat and looked down towards the path and then looked west.

What happened next played out in slow motion. Running towards them were giant creatures, dark, and mad. She found out later they were centipedes, wolf spiders, bleached earless lizards, spadefoot toads, tarantula hawk wasps, and velvet ants. She felt the darkness that emanated from their eyes and heard their dark thoughts. These creatures meant to harm them and they were coming their way from two directions.

Uskhay sent her spear to the sky letting light in, which split the creatures coming from the west into two rows. Quickly she shot a ray their way, sending several creatures flying back. The weredogs took off running, teeth out, unleashing deep growls towards their enemy. There was no room in the narrow path for them to change.

Cristina created a jail with vines holding some of the creatures and the creatures that Sofia focused on took off running away. More infected creatures began to approach from the south and Urpi sent some away with her magic. The tarantula hawk wasps flew straight towards Aline with their powerful stingers out, but Kunaq swiftly moved in front of her and grew wasp wings on his back. Tapping into whirlpool of energy, he copied the powers of the wasp. Using these new powers, he mimicked their venom and sent it right back at the wasps melting its wings off. Kawayu was using his horn to send several creatures away whining, and Khallma was now shooting lighting rods, creating a powerful explosion of lights which repelled even more of these nasty creatures.

The more the quest carriers fought the more creatures appeared, and Aline thought they were not going to win. The quest carriers began moving in different directions. Urpi ordered them to stay together. When Aline realized they were not hearing Urpi, she screamed it mentally. This stopped them all for a moment. They touched their heads.

"No need to scream it, girl. We can hear you just fine," said Uskhay.

The quest carriers gathered together in a circle, fighting off the multiple creatures attacking them via air and land. Aline watched as Kawayu walked forward, showering the colored lights from his horn and pushing four of the creatures back.

"Stay in the circle," said Uskhay as she took out a wolf tarantula that had climbed on the pegacorn's back and was about to bite him with its giant jaws. In that moment a centipede pushed her forward, curled its body around her and began to take her away. Khallma ran towards her, but a giant spadefoot toad spat its tongue out, stuck it on him, and rolled him into his mouth. The toad also began to follow the centipede.

"No!" Screamed Sofia. who flew towards them, pointing her index finger at them. Immediately the disgusting creatures released their prey and took off running. Until a huge velvet ant jumped behind Sofia and grabbed her. Its stinger was out. The quest carrier's circle broke trying to save Sofia. All of them were pushed in different directions by the creatures, who began to overpower them.

"Aline," Akiya called, "these creature's minds are very simple. Just find the original thought that sent them there and change it. It is shared by all, one thought that they have in common. Change this thought with one of your own. You can send them all away at once."

"How?" Aline asked, as she desperately watched her friends fighting fiercely and being taken one by one.

"Close your eyes, Aline," instructed Akiya.

"What! Now?" Aline was not really comfortable closing her eyes in the midst of an attack.

"Yes, Aline. You need to trust more and ask fewer questions. Now, close your eyes."

Right before closing her eyes, Aline noticed that everything around her had slowed down to almost a halt.

"I have given us more time. This will only last a few seconds so you need to listen carefully." Akiya had sent a powerful spell and all Aline could do was nod and focus. "The whispers around you are many. Within these, you will find there is noise, almost a buzz. Go to it and pay attention to the rhythm of this buzz. It should come in and out in waves. It is the in wave that you must focus on, for this is a command. Take this with your own thought, but without altering the overall pace. I believe in you, Aline. Now go!"

Aline, was back again in the room where she had heard the whispers of the creatures for the first time. She quickly identified the buzz within the noise. However, it seemed to come from all directions at all times. It was like trying to find a rhythm in a maze.

"No! Cristina!" She heard Urpi's thoughts in slow motion.

"Oh no," Aline said. She knew that those creatures had taken Cristina and that Akiya's spell was weakening.

"Where are you, rhythm?" Aline looked at the gray, black, and white dots that made up the buzzing. It was all scattered. She thought her task was impossible. But then she noticed the buzzing had a center. In it, things seemed to move together. With a wave of her hands, she moved out the scattered noise and looked at its center. It was only gray. A dark gray with a bustling noise that came in and out. She could hear it, broken and fuzzy, like someone speaking behind an electric fan on high.

"Find them and bring them to me. Find them and bring them to me..." It kept repeating on and off.

"Got ya! A thought of my own. What is my thought?" She asked herself. A random memory popped in her mind; she remembered Amanda and the follower and how easily she had forgiven them that Halloween night on her birthday.

"I know!"

Timing the in pulses only, Aline grabbed it with one hand and quickly pushed her thought, a cloudy white fume, in its stead right before it went back out. Then, she opened her eyes.

All of the creatures dropped their friends and began to change. Their eyes were no longer black, but more alive. The colors in their skin, hair, and wings were more vibrant. They had transformed back to their original forms. Bowing their heads to Aline, they turned around and left.

"What happened?" Sky asked, amazed.

"Aline was able to change the command to trap you and take you with a thought of her own...what did you think of?"

"Well, I feel that all of you are my friends, my new family, and I am clear on how important you all are to me." Aline, paused, put her hair behind her ear and continued. "I am also aware of all of the changes that I have gone through since my birthday." She remembered Kani suddenly and missed her terribly. She swallowed hard, held her tears back and continued, "because of these thoughts, my own thoughts, I have created my own decisions since I arrived here...really, I have made my own decisions even before I left the human world. The first thought that came to me was one that had led to a decision that made me really happy. This is when I was back on earth, on Halloween, on my birthday, right before I came here." Amanda's face was in her mind and she remembered what happened as if it was yesterday.

"I chose to simple forgive someone who was horrible to me, and that gave me the opportunity to regain a friend," she continued. "A best friend that once I thought was family, just like you. If I am given a choice now to forgive and go back to my family, Kani, my mother, my father...I would take it in an instant. So I changed the original thought to attack and capture us with the thought that they had a choice and could be with their family and friends. To be with their family, with their loved ones, they only needed to make their minds, make a decision to use the same magic that transformed them, to leave whenever and however they wanted. It was their choice at the end, which was what was taken from them."

"Interesting," responded Akiya. "There is magic in freedom." It was more of an inward thought than a general summary.

Once again Kawayu healed those who were hurt. Then the quest carriers walked until dusk. They knew they were going to be okay on the last two days on the Bleak Forest. For Aline, the last day and a half were a blur. It all became clear when they saw a light at the end of the path. With renewed spirits, almost in a trot, the quest carriers ran out of the Bleak Forest and into the Southern Shores.

Sunlight bathed the forest trees that were on the Southern Shores. There was so much light that sun rays spilled between the tall trees on either side of them. The trees had dark brown trunks and the green foliage was either flat, like a table top with small red flowers, or were moon shaped filled with small white flowers.

The quest carriers continued walking fast, with open arms embracing the sun and the fresh air. They could hear the ocean waves nearby and Aline recognized the mounds on the ground. As they walked closer to shore, the moist earth began to change to sand and the trees were now far in between. Aline bent down and grabbed the sand, feeling its heat in her fingers. They had been exposed to dim light and dampness for so many days that she welcomed the dryness on her skin and the warmth in her heart.

Out of the corner of her eye, Aline saw two tabletop trees with a downward sandy ramp between them. She could see the ocean very close behind the two trees and smelled the salt on the air. She walked toward the trees. Swirling the grains of sand between her fingertips, she looked down and saw the cave.

"There! It is there!" she pointed towards the cave. "We need to hurry!" she called to the others. And began to run towards its mouth.

"Wait," yelled Kunaq.

A massive growl echoed through the walls of the cave and out its mouth. Creating gusts of wind which shook off the sand on Aline's hands. The loudest growl that Aline had ever heard in her life. She had forgotten, and it all came back to her really quick. The blue bottle calling her and a beast near it, guarding it, attracted by its power. The quest carriers now had to face a new monster.

Shore Monsters

QUIETLY, Aline stepped back. With the second wave of growls, Aline felt the warm air on her hair and face. Whatever was inside was big. She worked her way back past the tabletop trees, where her friends were waiting for her. They set camp not far from the two trees and planned the best way to enter the cave.

"Maybe I can reach out to this animal. I am a nature sylph after all," said Cristina, closing her eyes and focusing on the cave. "I can sense it is deep in the cave, and it is one of the colossals." The group looked intently at her. Maybe it would be this easy; maybe Cristina would talk to it, they could just walk inside the cave, take the blue bottle, and leave the beast be.

"Nope," Cristina said after a few minutes. "It is not letting me in. It is like something or someone is protecting it, blocking anything going its way. Why don't you try to read its thoughts, Aline? It is worth a shot." So Aline closed her eyes and focused on the cave. The quest carriers held their breath one more time, hoping to get good news.

"No, nothing! Just like you said Cristina, there is something protecting the beast. I got only silence in the cave," Aline said.

Each one of the quest carriers used their powers to see if they could possibly connect with the beast or better understand the layout of the cave, but to no avail. All of them had the same experience. There was something shielding both the beast and the cave and they all knew what it was—the blue bottle.

"But why is the beast there in the first place?" Ash asked.

"To protect them. It is an even exchanged, and the bottle is all about fairness," explained Kunaq. "The only way to get the bottle is for a few of us to go inside the cave. I believe it should be Aline, Cristina, and Sofia."

"Why?" Ash asked.

"I am not leaving them alone," Mach growled.

"Nor I," said Kay, Sky, and Alis at the same time.

"We need to remember, the bottle asked for Aline only," Kunaq explained. "Think about it. The beast and the cave were selected by the blue bottle for its protection. Aline was chosen by the blue bottle. This means that Aline must go. Cristina can connect with animals and Sofia's power may be used with the cave. Their powers can help Aline without threatening the blue bottle. It is either this, or she goes completely alone. Something I would not suggest.

"The rest of us need to be here to safeguard the entrance in case other transformed colossals are commanded to go to the shores," Kunaq continued. "The girls may choose to have one more join them, but I would counsel against this. Khallma and Uskhay cannot use their powers underground. Any of the weredog's senses will be tricked by the cave and I have been shut down by the bottle. My powers would be useless there and better used here. So this leaves Urpi and Kawayu. They are the only two that could accompany the girls if they so choose."

The girls looked at each other. Aline could see that concern on her friends' faces. She smiled at them and said "I should go by myself." With shaking fingers she pulled her backpack onto her shoulders. "Like you said Kunaq, the blue bottle selected me and I am the only one that has to go. So, I will go. By myself."

"That *sounds* really nice. Super brave and all," said Cristina, grabbing Sofia's hand, "but you know it is not happening, right?" The sisters smiled at Aline and then grabbed her hands.

"Ha! You thought you had a choice," laughed Sofia, and the quest carriers smiled with her.

"Can we all still communicate telepathically while the girls are in the cave?" Kawayu asked.

"Well, we can try, but I believe the blue bottle chose this cave for a reason, and stopping any communication with the outside world is one of them," Kunaq replied.

"Wait, so this means we will not be able to speak with them? I do not like this one bit," Kay growled.

"I agree," said Uskhay, and Khallma nodded.

"Then Urpi and I must accompany them," said Kawayu, and Urpi nodded.

Aline got closer to Kawayu, she touched his forehead and gently moved her hand all the way to the tip of this nose. It felt like velvet to her. She kissed it and said, "thank you." Then she looked at Urpi, "But you know you cannot come. Your powers are really strong, we are just learning ours. The bottle will feel you as a threat. We cannot miss this chance, it is the only one we'll get."

Urpi hesitantly lowered her head and Kawayu kneeled uncomfortably to the ground with his front left leg.

"Aline is right," said Akiya. "They must go alone. It is already enough of a risk for Cristina and Sofia to accompany her."

Even though the weredogs complained, it was settled. The three girls were going into the cave alone. They left almost everything in the camp, taking their training, their bravery, and their belief in their powers and in each other.

While the quest carriers watched behind the two trees, the girls moved forward. A small breeze blew as they walked down the sandy ramp towards the roaring cave. The beast must have smelled them because as soon as they set foot on the ramp, the growls began. They squeezed each other's hands.

"Are you ready?" asked Cristina, looking at Aline and her sister and gently moving her wings in and out.

"I am," said Sofia with a twinkle in her eye, shaking her wings.

"If she is, then I am too," said Aline looking at both girls on either side of her. The strap of her backpack slid off her shoulder and she slide it back in place.

"Focus, faith, and trust," said Cristina.

"Focus, faith, and trust," repeated Aline and Sofia.

They took one step closer. The roars were so strong they blew the girl's hair back. They paused for a second, took a deep breath, and took the second step. This step took the girls inside the cave and out of view of the rest of the quest carries.

Panic set in for the weredogs, who began to move closer to the trees.

"No," said Kunaq sternly. "They must do this alone. We may put their lives and everyone else's in danger if we go." The weredogs whined and sat behind the trees looking at the cave's mouth. The rest of the quest carriers stood by them, and they all whined in silence.

IT WAS DARK. Aline was expecting the blue bottle to shine their way as it had in her visions, but this was not the case.

"Do not worry, we come with light," said Cristina. She held her nose as if she were going to dive into a pool of water and the subtle lines within her wings lit up, releasing lovely lights. Like bioluminescent jellyfish swimming deep in the ocean, they glimmered back and forth between green and purple. Sofia smiled and repeated her sister's movements, illuminating the dark tunnel even more with shades of pink and yellow. The long cold stones called stalagmites and stalactites shimmered with the sylph's lights.

"Wow!" said all three girls when they looked into the cave. It was covered in crystals that reflected the lights from the sister's wings, illuminating the way in front of them.

"This is not that bad," said Sofia with a smile. A massive roar echoed deep within the gut of the cave, blowing their hair again. "Never mind," she added.

Aline tried to connect telepathically with the quest carriers or with Akiya, but as Kunaq had guessed it was not possible. After taking a few steps, they found themselves in front of many possible paths and were now at a standstill.

"What do we do?" Sofia wondered.

"Do you remember where to go, Aline?" Cristina asked.

"No! This looks very different. There was only one path and a blue light showing me the way to the bottle," Aline replied. The growls were getting stronger.

"Sofia, could you sense the right path?" Cristina asked.

"That is brilliant. Let's try!" Aline agreed.

Holding tight to her sister and Aline, Sofia closed her eyes. Finding her thread, in her mind she saw many lights that moved in several directions. Through her feet, she felt the energy of the cave and searched for the right path. Out of all of the light around them, Sofia found an ocean blue light that wound forward. This light called her to it.

"This must be it," she thought. "I know the direction we should go!" she said, and Cristina and Aline smiled at her.

"I knew you could do it!" Cristina said proudly.

"To be clear, it is the way that feels right to me, but may not tell us exactly where the bottle is," Sofia said.

"Close enough," Cristina said. "I am going to send my energy out to see if I can connect with the beast. You never know."

"Great idea! We need all the help we can get," Aline said. The wind from the roars was so powerful that the girls had to hold on to each other to stay their ground. Against all odds, they continued to walk forward deep within the cave. The roars and hisses increased to the point that they couldn't hear each's spoken words. They could still communicate telepathically. It became the only way the girls could speak with one another when the roars were too loud.

It was a quest of the will. Their muscles, wings, and feet wanted to run back to the entrance of the cave and out into safety. It was their will to save the magic worlds and not let Dashiok win that kept them going. This courage shifted every thought from the entrance towards the cave's guts. They tightened the grip on each other's' hands and continued moving forward. Cristina did not stop trying to communicate with the beast and Sofia guided them through the cave.

Everything looked so different. To Aline, the shimmering crystals and silver stones reflected a cave filled with long stone teeth growing from the ceiling and the ground. She needed to find an entrance to the opening and she thought she saw it on every other stalagmite. They walked for a few hours in silence. The path took a downward turn and Aline stopped.

"Something is off," she said.

"What?" Cristina asked. "Do you see something?

"No," she answered. "That is exactly it. I do not see or hear *anything*."

"You are right," said Sofia. "We are speaking out loud...the beast is not roaring anymore."

"We need to turn back," said Cristina.

"Yes," said Aline. "We need to look for a gap. An entrance that will lead us to the blue bottle. I have been trying to find the one on my vision, but it is hard with all these stones. I think I see one and when we get close I realize that my eyes were tricked."

"Well," said Cristina, "the beast roars when we get close to the bottle. Let's listen for the roars as we get back. They might guide us to where this entrance is."

"Excellent idea, Cristina!" Sofia said.

"I agree. That was pretty smart," said Aline. Cristina smiled.

The three girls turned back and the wings of the sylphs shone on the stone around them. The cave was impressively beautiful. The rows of stalagmites looked like miniature stone towers placed in perfect and exact locations. If you stood in front of one, you could not see the others behind until you moved slightly to either side.

Once again, they walked towards the beast's roars. At least this path was leading them towards the entrance of the cave. For the girls, this slight change gave them hope. They looked for a gap between the long stalagmites that resembled an opening to another room. With each step, they could hear the echoes made by their feet as smaller rocks scratched against the ground. The water drops, falling from the stalactites to the stalagmites, echoed. For a while, they thought they were walking in circles until the first roar blew their hair back. They were getting close.

MEANWHILE, at the trees outside the cave, the others were beginning to worry.

"They should have connected with us telepathically by now. How, do we know they are alright?" Kay asked.

"This means that the cave is enchanted. The blue bottle is not letting them connect with anyone and is probably blocking some of their magic," Urpi said.

"Blocking their magic?" Ash asked, surprised.

"Some, I said some of their magic. The same would happen to us if we were to go in," Urpi replied.

"Yes, and the blue bottle could consider us a threat. Remember, it asked for Aline," Kunaq said.

"So why do the sylphs get to go with her? I want to go as well. I have known Aline since she hatched!" Mach protested.

"They are still young," Khallma explained. "Children possess a power that adults do not. This is why most of the Apotequil's trials are done before adulthood. When the young still have pure hearts and possess more resilience. We believe that children better remember the connection to the lightning gods since they were recently with them. I think that the blue bottle's magic comes from something bigger than us and I know that the girl's hearts are still pure. They pose no threat to the blue bottle and are the only ones that can accompany Aline."

Mach sighed, laid down, and looked towards the cave's mouth.

"We need to stay focused. Because Aline and Sofia are in the cave, our telepathy is not as strong," Kunaq warned.

"I do not like waiting. I am going to look around the area," said Uskhay impatiently. "Anyone wants to join me?"

"I will accompany you," said Urpi. "We used most of the wooden sticks in the Bleak Forest. I will gather more in case we need to make a fire."

"I will go with you as well. Maybe I can sense where the girls are from above the cave," said Kunaq. The three walked around the table top trees until they were above the cave's mouth. From that point on, Kunaq walked with his palm facing the sand while Urpi gathered sticks and Uskhay observed the lay of the land. They continued walking until they disappeared from sight behind the sand mounds.

Ash and Alis walked around the camp sniffing the ground and the air every so often until they were satisfied that nothing had recently passed by or was on its way towards the campsite. Kawayu closed his eyes and faced the shore. He was trying to pick up any vibrations through his horn. Not just the girls but anything else that may come from behind the sand mounds. Khallma knelt down staring at the cave. Kay and Sky looked in the direction they had come from, towards the Bleak Forest, and Mach stared at the cave. He would sniff it once in a while and whine a bit.

"They should have come back already," said Mach after a few hours.

"The girls or Uskhay, Kunaq, and Urpi?" Kay asked.

"Both," answered Ash, and Mach nodded.

"Kunaq was right, our telepathy is not as strong while Aline is in the cave. I can hear you guys fine, but not Uskhay, Kunaq, and Urpi," said Kay and they all nodded in agreement.

"I will prepare lunch. It will be more like an early dinner at this point," said Ash.

"Lunch sounds good," said Alis.

"I am not really hungry," added Sky.

"Count me in," said Kawayu, without changing position. His eyes were still closed.

"I will help you, Ash," said Khallma.

"You just do not want me to use my muzzle to prepare your food, right?" Ash teased.

"Well, I cannot lie. I am very thankful; however, I prefer my food without slobber," Khallma confessed.

"Now you say something? In this group, there are almost more muzzles than hands you know," laughed Ash.

"It is a hard choice since the weredogs cooking is better than my sisters, Urpi's, or Kunaq's." Khallma paused. His gem like eyes opened even wider "But please, do not tell them I said this!"

"We will not. Right, Ash?" Kay said.

"You know, I am confused. I was just insulted and praised at the same time. Not sure what to do next," said Ash. "I guess I accept your help." He asked more than said it, then he turned his head towards Sky and Alis and raised his shoulder. He was unsure of what was an acceptable response for the Apotequils. They both got busy preparing lunch for the quest carriers.

"Hush!" Kawayu hissed. Khallma noticed that Ash, Mach, and Kawayu had turned their heads towards the sandy mounds while Kay, Sky, and Alis faced the Bleak forest. All five weredogs discharged a faint growl.

"WE MUST BE near and I do not like it one bit," said Sofia, holding her sister's hand tighter.

"This thing has to be huge," thought Cristina. The nature sylph side of her was very interested in this animal. In understanding what it wanted, why, and what made it happy.

"Not the best thing to say right when you are walking towards the 'huge thing,' you know," Sofia said.

"My bad," said Cristina shrugging apologetically. "It's the nature sylph in me. I just can't help but wonder why he is here and how can I help him."

"How do you know it is a he?" Aline asked.

"I have not connected with him like I wanted to, but I have...hmm, how can I put it...heard him, I guess," Christina said. "His voice is male and one that demands respect. When we are there, we need to show respect. And we can not show any fear at all. That is all I have been able to feel."

"No fear!" Sofia sputtered. "How can we show no fear in front of something humungous that probably wants to eat us?"

"We do not know that he wants to eat us. All we know is that the blue bottle chose him to protect it," Cristina replied.

"Well, I do not want to hang out and ask him if he is hungry," Sofia muttered. A roar stopped the conversation, making Sofia jump and tighten her grip on both Aline and her sister's hands.

"No fear," whispered Cristina to Sofia.

"No fear," Sofia repeated in a mocking voice.

Their hair was blown back again and again. The roars and hisses were getting louder and more frequent muting their words again and forcing the girls to communicate telepathically. They were getting closer and all three of them looked more carefully around to find an entrance. Finding an opening within the many gaps between the stalagmites seemed like an impossible task and the girls were losing hope.

A massive roar hit them again, blowing their hair in front of their faces. They stopped. Not just to push their hair back in order to see, but because they knew the beast was once again behind them. This meant that the entrance was also behind them. Turning around with excitement and nervousness, they looked for the gap. The beast did not stop roaring and they knew that it was right there. The problem is that they could not find the opening. They moved back and forth getting their hair blown forward and backward, but with no luck.

"Do any of you see it?" asked Sofia.

"No," Cristina replied.

"It's like it is invisible," said Aline, frustrated.

"Wait! Aline, you are brilliant!" said Sofia.

"What do you mean?" Aline asked.

"Well, just like the beast, the cave is also protecting the bottle. Don't you see! The blue bottle connects with nature," beamed Sofia. "Cristina, you need to connect with the cave just like you did with the beast. Maybe it will tell you something."

"Yes, that is it! Remember what Abi told us about the blue bottle? It is part of the One World and uses nature to hide, only letting the ones it wants to find where it has hidden."

"Alright! I will give it a go," Cristina said. "Give me your hand Sofia. I may need your sense magic."

She grabbed her sister's hand, lifted her other to touch the stalagmite in front of her, and then closed her eyes. Her training had paid off, she immediately found her thread. She tugged on the part that linked with the cave and listened.

The damp smell within the cave surrounded Cristina. She felt the coolness of the water and the warmth of sun rays touching the cave's entrance. It was proud of its size, for it was almost endless. It was transferred to this magical planet when the One World broke off. Ever since, it had been busy creating its many paths, perfecting the small stone towers, creating new tricks. This cave was known for the complex maze within its bowels. No one dared to venture deep inside for fear of never finding their way back. However, this cave was lonely. It craved companionship and had been fond of housing the blue bottle and the beast all this time. Now, it was enjoying the girls' company and it was happy that they were trying to communicate with it.

The beast stopped roaring.

"It is alive," Cristina said. "It has been alone for so long. It does not want to be lonely anymore. It is afraid that if we find the blue bottle, everyone will leave and it will be all by itself once more."

"I felt it too," said Sofia wiping a tear from her eye. "It is so sad, you know. To be alone for so long."

Aline put her arm around Sofia. "What can we do to help?" she asked.

"We could come and visit," Sofia offered. The other girls shook their heads emphatically.

"There has to be a better way than to come to the Southern Shores!" Aline said. She felt sad, but she remembered how hard it had been crossing the Bleak Forest.

"We'll find a way to come and see you," Cristina promised. Both Cristina and Sofia looked at Aline. Aline felt in her heart that was the right thing to do and she smiled.

"Promise!" she said wholeheartedly.

A soft vibration began to gently shake the stone towers that were right in front of them. They moved to either side, creating a pathway towards a small opening in the cave's wall.

"Thank you!" Aline said.

The three girls stood at the edge of the opening. They remembered the beast and were nervous once again for it was all too quiet. Slowly walking through the gap, the girls reached a massive opening. A cave within the cave. Eight stalagmites & eight stalactites circled the cave, creating an optical illusion. They made the opening look like it had an octagonal shape. In its center was the blue bottle on top of a single broad and short stalagmite. In front was a feline-looking creature bigger than any elephant Aline had ever seen back on earth.

"Oh boy!" said Aline, and Sofia swallowed hard.

"No fear," reminded Cristina as she reached for Aline's and Sofia's trembling hands.

FOR SEVERAL HOURS Kunaq tried to trace the cave when walking on the sand with Uskhay and Urpi. There were just a few trees scattered between the sandy mounds. Urpi had sent out a string of magic that grabbed each stick she pointed at, magically gathering them above her head. Firmly, Uskhay held her lance while she touched the trees and certain stones on the ground.

"What is wrong?" Urspi asked.

"Not sure," responded Uskhay, "maybe…it is too empty. Both the trees and rocks are quiet."

"Yes," admitted Kunaq, "over four hundred years ago this was a place filled with life. After the transformation of the Bleak Forest, very few dwell on the Southern Shores. No one really knows if the shores were transformed too—magic sometimes comes with side effects."

Kunaq began to walk closer to the water. To their right were the table top and moon-shaped trees, and behind the trees, they could see the shadow from the Bleak Forest. It was indeed very quiet. Urpi realized that she could not even see small animals in the air or on the sand. The sound of the waves crashing on the shore was too loud to hear anything else. Uskhay got more uneasy.

"We should walk on the sandy mounds back to our camp," she suggested. She felt better where there were trees around her.

"Yes," nodded Kunaq. "I can tell there are tunnels underground leading towards the water, but I can not feel the girls. The blue bottle's protective magic is very powerful. If it does not want to be found, it will get lost. The cave itself is also blocking my powers."

"I agree, and there are no sticks closer to the shore," added Urpi.

The three of them walked inland for a few hours until Urpi saw a moon-shaped tree with sand sloping downward away from its trunk, with a lot of sticks for kindling lying around. The green foliage on the tree looked like a table cloth that had been pulled too far on one end. The branches and leaves on the side facing the Bleak Forest touched the ground creating a large green curtain. On the other side, the branches and leaves were higher, barely touching the top of Kunaq's head, the tallest of the three.

"After this we should have enough wood. Plus we have strayed far too long from the others. We should head back," said Urpi walking towards the tree trunk.

"Agreed," added Uskhay.

Kunaq cordially let the other two pass in front of him while he guarded the back. The branches swayed when the females passed below them entering the green canopy. Kunaq paused right before it was his turn to enter. There was no breeze.

"Wait." He managed to say right before a branch lowered, coiled around his neck, and pulled him up. Uskhay used the sharp end of her lance to cut off the branches but a heavy blanket of leaves and branches fell on her, pushing her face towards the sand. She used her elbows to keep her head up. The branches on the large moon-shaped tree began to move closer, like a closing curtain after a play, and the white flowers had turned around, spilling toxic nectar that dried and pulverized the kindling on the ground into sand.

With a quick spell, Urpi sharpened the wood above her and cut the branches that were pulling Kunaq up and pushing Uskhay down, freeing her friends. Kunaq took a deep breath and then used his magic to stop the tree, which was now sending long vines their way to get them inside before it closed. All three began to run away from the tree and towards the camp.

"Stop!" urged Uskhay. All three hovered close to a tabletop tree keeping their distance from the moon-shaped trees.

"What is it?" asked Urpi.

"Do you hear that?" Uskhay replied. "There is something in the Bleak Forest! We need to get to the others...run!"

KHALLMA KNEW what was coming their way. He could smell them.

"Prepare to fight," he said grasping his lance. "Do not let them get near you. Especially the ones with the red eyes."

Kawayu lit up his horn and all five dogs released their claws.

"They are coming from the north and the west," added Khallma.

"That's the direction Kunaq, Urpi, and Uskhay traveled," said Sky, worried.

"Aye," responded Khallma, "so focus more on the north. Uskhay will take care of the ones coming from the west."

A multitude of hobgoblins emerged from the Bleak Forest and fanned out once they reached the trees on the Southern Shores. They were massive gray creatures with deep scars on their bodies, exceptionally long and muscular arms that carried immense axes. Their white unruly hair was braided, revealing pointy ears and short horns on their foreheads. Angry faces with long sharp ashen teeth and noses that had rotted away revealing triangular holes. But it was their feral green, almost chalky eyes that really conveyed how much they despised white magical creatures. They ran growling, breathing hard, and spitting towards the quest carriers. But it was their stench that reached the group first.

"Wait..." said Khallma. "Wait for it..."

More of the beasts were arriving each second that passed. They heard lighting shots to their left and knew that Uskhay, Urpi, and Kunaq were fighting their enemy. Khallma tightened the grip on his lance and with his right foot he pulled a dark green bag he had carried throughout their journey closer to him.

"Wait..."

Using his toes, he opened the bag, revealing lances from the One World's Magical Forest. The tails on the weredogs were shaking more towards their left, their heart rate had increased and they were ready to attack.

"Nowww!!!" Screamed Khallma.

He shot his lance and ten more from the bag to the sky, sending multiple bolts of lightning towards the first hobgoblins that arrived. The lightning from the special lances were wider and more powerful.

With astounding synchronicity, Kawayu used his horns to push out the next fifteen hobgoblins to the left and the following twenty to the right. The few beasts that made it through were attacked by the weredogs. In the rush of battle, to everyone's surprise, the weredog's bodies had increase twice, if not thrice in size. Their jaws were now massive and their bulging muscles far more powerful.

Khallma stuck his hands out, whispered something in a different language, and all of his lances came back to him. He was ready to send more lightning shots towards the hobgoblins, who continue to spill out into the Southern Shores.

Kawayu had decided that they needed to go back to where they came from. Standing firmly on the ground, his horn produced multiple bubbles, which floated towards the revolting creatures. Once above the hobgoblins, these bubbles pushed down on them, capturing them inside. Like plucking out weeds. They repeated this bobbing until they were full of hobgoblins. Then the pegacorn flew them far, far back into the Bleak Forest.

"Send them into the ocean!" screamed Mach.

"These beasts can not swim!" yelled Sky as she dragged a huge one towards the shore with her huge jaws. She got close to the water, and with brutal strength, she launched the beast miles behind the foamy waves.

They began to move as many hobgoblins as they could towards the ocean. The quest carriers were powerful. Nonetheless, if they threw one away, three more would appear from the Bleak Forest. Like ants spilling out of their nest after it was poked.

"We need to organize ourselves," said Khallma telepathically to his friends. "I will use my rays to force them into a narrower entryway. Then you can cast them in the water."

"Sounds like a mighty plan," said Alis. "Start rounding them up!" She had grown larger than any of the weredogs and was excited to take on more hobgoblins.

Creating a nice rhythm, the quest carriers began to hurl hobgoblins far and deep into the ocean. It seemed that less were coming their way and, in their minds, they began to breathe a little easier. Even Alis shrank to the size of Mach, who was the second largest fighting weredog.

"Any more and we would have been in trouble," said Alis.

"You do not say things like that, Alis," said Ash. "Does she not know?" He looked at the other quest carriers. "You've gone and done it now. Get back to your bigger size."

"Oh, come on! You are so superstitious. We've won. I do not hear anything from the west which means the others are fine," snarled Alis.

"I am not superstitious," said Kawayu. "But I've learned my lesson not to think of victory until you are indeed victorious." His scars glittered under the two suns.

"It is not over," affirmed Khallma as he looked to the north. "More are coming. Get ready."

KUNAQ WAS the first to take off towards the other quest carriers. He knew he had to warn them. Glistening over the sand, barely disturbing the tiny rocks. Until he turned his head around to look at Urpi and Uskhay one last time. This is when he saw the yawares. Red-eyed bloodthirsty humans who were running almost as fast as he was from the west towards his two friends. Sliding with one hand on the sand he pivoted and took off once more, this time to the west, towards Urpi and Uskhay.

Uskhay saw Kunaq running their way and looked back. She knew exactly what these eager monsters were and sent her lance straight to the air. Jumping an incredible distance for her height, she twisted while sending a powerful lightning ray towards the yawares, throwing many backwards. Then she somersaulted on the sand, called her lance, grabbed it, and continued to run at an even faster pace.

In parallel, Urpi saw these long pale faces not too far behind. A massive stampede, moving towards the east, towards the cave. All of the shaking and vibrations woke up the moon-shaped trees, who began to close fast. She saw some of the yawares fighting with the moon-shaped trees as they were closing up.

"Well, I can work with that," she thought. While running, Urpi cast a spell that sent a huge sphere of magic. It pinned several yawares to the inside of the moon-shaped tree, which immediately sent vines and entangled these creatures. Then she sent one more spell smashing the sand creating a long ditch filled with quicksand, into which many of the red-eyed beasts fell and disappeared.

Urpi's magic and Uskhay's bolts gave them an advantage. They were about to reach Kunaq, who had stopped running. He looked to his right, towards the Bleak Forest.

"Urpi, do you allow me to link with your magic?" He asked telepathically never taking his eyes from the north.

"Yes! Link away," Urpi affirmed.

He lifted his arms and she slightly pulsated back, smiled, and then continued running towards Kunaq.

Whispering something, Kunaq waved his hands and created a shield around the three of them just in time. For a shower of arrows were casted their way breaking against the shield.

"Let's go! We need to get to the rest of the quest carriers," said Kunaq. Urpi and Uskhay looked to the enemies in the north and then to those in the west and took off right behind Kunaq, who was keeping pace with his companions in order to maintain the shield. They heard the screams before they saw the hobgoblins spill out from the north and the yawares not too far behind coming from the west. They could see the two tabletop trees next to the camp. They were still far away. The hobgoblins were attacking their friends. Uskhay shot and retrieved her lance ten times in a row at lightning speed, increasing once more the gap between them and the yawares behind them.

"Hold my hand," Kunaq shouted, extending his hands towards Uskhay and Urpi. The two females took his hand and felt his speed running through their bodies. He had shared his power with them. The shield was now down and the three took off running as fast as Kunaq. The camp was closer. They could see their friends sending these foul creatures deep into the ocean. For a split second, it seemed that most of them were drowning in the Southern Shores.

With his uncanny vision, Kunaq saw who was leading the hobgoblins and the bloodthirsty humans.

"We need to protect Aline," he whispered to himself.

Yakar the vampire was emerging from the Bleak Forest, striding in the direction of the cave with several of the strongest hobgoblins the quest carriers had ever encountered. He was the spotter working for Dashiok and Aline's brothers. Clouds moved onto the Southern Shores covering any rays coming from the two suns.

"We must hurry," urged Kunaq.

———

THE MUSCLES on this creature's body were lean and powerful. The head was lower than his shoulders in a hunter's pose and his wild yellow eyes were mad with adrenaline. He was crunched down with its claws fully extended and its ears back, ready to pounce. His long brown, black, and white fur remained still as he quietly inhaled, smelling the girls. He opened his mouth wide, crunching his nose, curling his tongue in a u-shape and hissed. It echoed so loud that the girls had to cover their ears.

They were petrified. Everything appeared quieter after the dreadful hiss. Cristina felt her thread tug her and she knew what she had to do.

"Focus, faith, and trust," she thought. She swallowed hard, took a deep breath, and spoke up.

"My name is Cristina." She broke the silence with a calm voice. Her hands shook against Aline's and her sister's. "This is my sister Sofia and my friend Aline."

She cordially bowed her head and told both Aline and Sofia to do the same and not to look directly into his eyes. His tail flicked a few times but he remained in the same position.

"Where do I look?" Sofia asked nervously. "I do not know where to look."

"Look at his nose," Aline replied.

"Yes, his nose. And be quiet. This is hard enough as it is," added Cristina. She took another deep breath and relaxed her shoulders, which had raised and tightened after the hiss. "We are here on a quest and ask your permission to pass," she said. "May we pass?"

The beast lifted his head.

"My name is Liyun," he replied in a deep raspy voice, bowing back to the girls. "What is your quest and why should I let you pass?"

Aline knew it was her turn to speak. Gathering all her strength, she took a step forward, still holding on to Cristina's and Sofia's hands.

"The blue bottle reached out to me," she started to explain, and then felt that she had to catch her breath. "She guided me here and showed me that you and the cave were here to protect her from those who are not supposed to find her. I believe I am supposed to find her to protect others. A bad warlock name Dashiok is also looking for the bottle and wants to use her to do bad things."

Aline took another step forward, and Cristina and Sofia followed her still holding her hand. "We do not want this to happen, but we need your help to stop it."

"Hmm!" Liyun purred. He raised his head, finally emerging from the crouched position. "This is an honorable reason."

With the utmost grace, he sat down and continued talking. "Most self-claimed warriors who have faced me have not been able to do what you have done just now. They could barely look at me, let alone speak to me. All they wanted to do was either to run or to fight me. Cowards!" He growled on the 'r'.

"You are indeed very courageous young ones, because I know that you are afraid," he licked his lips and continued, "yet you choose respect, trust, and faith. I will let you pass Aline. However, allowing you to take the bottle is not up to me."

Without making another sound, Liyun got up and moved to the side, granting the girls passage to the blue bottle.

"Thank you, Liyun," said Aline. All three girls had huge smiles on their faces. Hearing that they were brave from such an outstanding animal was humbling. Aline walked up to the stalagmite where the blue bottle rested. She began to hear whispers and looked around nervously. Her friends were giving her encouraging looks and Liyun looked like a regal statue. Reaching the stone, she marveled at the bottle and her unique shape and symbols. The whispers increased. Lifting her finger she was about to touch the bottle when the whispers got even louder. She hesitated. Then she placed the palm of her left hand on the blue bottle. Blue light illuminated the grand space where the bottle rested. Aline could see another gap on the other side of the room. She heard a soft airy voice at first speaking to her and then it became loud and clear.

"You have found me," she said. "I hear hesitation in your heart. Ask me, child?"

"Why me?" asked Aline

"What do you mean?" the blue bottle asked in return.

"I am just a child and there are so many powerful creatures in this world that can help you much better than I ever could. I do not understand."

"Power and age hold no value to me, child. In the end, they truly do not matter. It is what I see in you, Aline that is significant to me, But I can not tell you what that is, you will need to find it on your own."

Aline still did not understand why the blue bottle had chosen her, but at that moment, she appreciated knowing that she was chosen.

"Alright! What do you need me to do?" she asked, ready for her next task. At that moment, a loud bang coming from above was heard. Dust and water began to fall from the cave's ceiling.

"Take me, child, and hurry. Your friends are in danger. Ride with Liyun. He will help you."

Aline grabbed the bottle. She was incredibly light. She put the bottle in her backpack, and ran towards her friends. Liyun was hovering over them protecting them from any falling debris. Sofia and Cristina were pressing against his chest and secretly enjoying his fluffiness. He moved to the side and knelt down.

"Climb on, we need to leave."

The cave widened its gap and the path back to its entrance so all five could get out. "Hold on tight, I would not like to lose any of you."

The girls gripped his long fur and looked down the tunnel. Liyun was super fast so it was not too long before Aline and the sisters saw the light coming from the cave's mouth. Cristina tells the story differently. She believed that the cave shortened the path so they were able to reach its entrance faster. Nonetheless, Liyun leaped out of the cave landing next to the two trees, releasing a fantastic roar.

Surprises

IT TOOK a few seconds for the girls to adjust their eyes even though the suns were covered by a blanket of clouds. This was not the same for Liyun, even though he had been years inside the cave, for his eyes adapted to the light immediately. He jumped out swiping the remaining hobgoblins away with his tail and pawing others to create a large clearing.

When Aline was finally able to open both eyes and focus, she saw the quest carriers looking at the girls riding on Liyun in disbelief. Kunaq, Urpi, and Uskhay ran in from the west and Khallma, Kawayu, and the weredogs were joining them from the shore. Aline could not believe her eyes when she saw the weredogs. They were not as big as Liyun, but they were huge, especially Alis.

"You finally decided to join us, sister," said Khallma after calling his lances back.

"Yes, we got detained a little," Uskhay replied as she threw a lightning rod towards the few persisting hobgoblins moving towards them.

"I am happy to see that all of you are all right. Were you able to find what you were looking for Aline? Kunaq asked.

"Yes!" She said grasping a bit more the situation at hand. "What happened? Are you okay?" she asked, noticing that her friends had wounds.

"Just fine, Aline. Nothing to worry about," said Kay licking a small scratch on her paw.

"We have no time to explain. Yakar is here," Kunaq told her. "He is bringing more hobgoblins and an army of yawares."

He walked towards the camp, knelt by his sack, and pulled out a sheathed sword. "The Yachaq only used weapons as a last resort," he explained as he tightened the sword to his waist. He looked to the north and the west. The quest carriers had defeated the first wave of hobgoblins, but more were coming their way.

"Yawares? How is this possible? They are not supposed to be in this world," said Kawayu.

"It does not matter," said Urpi. "What matters is that we need to protect the girls."

"Agreed," answered Kawayu.

"I see you brought a cat to the fight," said Ash.

"You are just jealous because he is much bigger than you," said Alis.

"We mean no disrespect," said Khallma, giving Ash a stern look, "we are honored to fight by your side." Liyun bowed his head towards Khallma and then softly growled at Ash.

"Now you done it," said Mach mockingly, licking some of his wounds.

"His name is Liyun and he is our friend," said Sofia. Liyun smiled.

"We know that the hobgoblins cannot swim. We have been throwing them in the ocean and this has worked so far," Kawayu told the newcomers.

"What is coming our way is much stronger, bigger, and faster," Kunaq warned. "You weredogs will need to reach your full capacity if you are to fight them once more."

"Wait, you can get bigger?" asked Sofia.

"A bit more," Sky said, "and that is all we need to fling these foul vermin back in the water," Aline noticed that she had the fewest scratches on her.

"All right then," said Cristina, stunned these words were coming from the shiest weredog.

"Was that...really...you Sky?" Aline asked in pure amazement.

"She is one of, nope, she is *the* best fighter among *all* of the weredogs. When we are back I'll tell you the stories, for I reckon she won't," said Mach proudly. All the weredogs nodded and Sky bowed back to them.

"Then we can count on the five of you to send the hobgoblins to the ocean," Kunaq said. "While you fight off the hobgoblins, the rest of us will focus on the yawares. We will create a semicircle in front of the girls, where you," he pointed at the weredogs, "will create another to ensure that no one from Yakar's army reaches them. Liyun, you will be in the middle of this circle with the girls on your back. Anyone who makes it through our barrier will be all yours."

"It will be my pleasure," Liyun assured Kunaq.

Uskhay opened her bag, freeing many lances. "We are good to go my younger brother. May the best warrior win," she winked at him, "you know it is always me." Khallma smiled back at her.

"They are close. Get ready," Kunaq warned.

Yakar was walking behind several of his hobgoblins. Not a minute later, the yawares joined his right flank. They were all calmed. Not running towards the quest carriers. Some were even smiling, showing their ashen teeth or sharp canines.

Aline followed the rows of monsters with her eyes until she saw Yakar. He was looking intensely at her. Only her. She immediately looked away. He scared her. Tightening the grip on Liyun's fur, Aline searched for her thread.

Both Khallma and Uskhay sent lightning rays towards the yawares and the hobgoblins. Knocking a lot of them to the ground. Most got back up, growled, and began to run towards the quest carriers.

"It is time!" Ash roared.

It did not take long for the creatures to arrive. Cristina and Sofia found their threads quickly and were ready. They were the first to fight, surprising all of the quest carriers. Cristina moved the sand under several hobgoblins, sliding them towards the weredogs like groceries on a fast conveyor belt in a supermarket's checkout lane. Cristina also moved the table top and moon-shaped trees in front of their enemy, creating a forest barrier before they could reach the quest carriers. A brilliant and impressive tactic.

Sofia did things slightly differently and had a bit of fun with her strategies. The first one was when she pointed at several of the hobgoblins. Stopping straight in their tracks with contracted faces, they dropped their axes, held their butts, and ran back towards the Bleak Forest screaming.

"This is how I felt this whole quest," she whispered, and had her own internal laugh.

The next thing she did was make the hobgoblins afraid of whatever was attacking their toenails. They ran away looking down, jumping and screaming in a race they never won. Lastly, she gave them a sensation of thirst. Making them feel like their throats were filled with sand and only huge amounts of water from the ocean would remove the sand, moisten their throats, and quench their thirst. These fellows ran towards the ocean where the weredogs would throw them further in.

However, the yawares were too fast for the girls, and this is where Urpi, Kawayu, and Kunaq stepped in without breaking the front of the circle around Liyun and the girls.

Whispering a spell, Urpi moved her hands in sharp movements, then joined her hands, and made her fingers dance creating deep glowing lights that swerved and pulsed around her like a pumping heart. She sent the magical glowing veins towards the nearest yawar. They created a cocoon around the beast, a sac that shrunk as it absorbed the creature's powers. Once it opened, it dropped a motionless pruned-up monster whose eyes were now void of light. It was a drying spell. She sent many of these veins out towards the yawares like pulsing electric shocks.

Kawayu used his horn to alternate creating the bubbles and what Aline thought looked like magical plastic sheets. The bubbles would send the hobgoblins to the weredogs. The plastic sheets were a completely different magical power. They would shoot out like pellets, opening mid-drift, and slamming several of these creatures towards the trees. When he saw that the moon-shaped trees would close up and then open once again with mounds of sand by their trunks, he only shot them towards the moon-trees.

Kunaq moved fast towards the yawares. In seconds, he linked with each of them, absorbing their strength and combining it with his own. Both magical beings were very powerful. Using his speed, he swerved around any hands or fists thrusting his way. Keeping the momentum, he would pull on the flying arms and throw the yawares above the tabletop trees, which would fold in half spitting out sticky toxic nectar from their red flowers, trapping the creatures inside. The trees would then shake off, creating small mounds of sand on either side.

Very few creatures made it past the protective circle and Liyun quickly flung these creatures far away. He moved so elegantly and stealthily that the girls barely felt anything. Aline had finally grasped her thread and was trying to use her new power to help Liyun. However, the yawares were so fast that she would hit sand, flinging it everywhere.

As a unit, the quest carriers were working together and defeating the putrid creatures. Sofia smiled at her sister and Aline. She could feel that they were going to make it home. More comfortable, the quest carriers began to venture a bit farther from the circle to get to the creatures faster.

It was here that Aline saw Yakar raised his arm up and sharply bring it down. A swarm of giant tarantula hawk wasps flew in from the Bleak Forest. Since they were coming from pitch darkness, they curled their heads inwards to prevent themselves from being blinded by the light on the Southern Shores. Filled with dark magic, they could see through the eyes of hobgoblins and yawares and their hearing and sense of smell were enhanced. Picking up Aline's scent, they flew towards the circle, disrupting the unity within the quest carriers. The circle around the girls was broken.

Kunaq saw Yakar heading towards the girls. He unsheathed his sword and began to run towards him. A silver blade that sang as it cut the air and quieted down when it cut through the enemy. Desperately he swung his sword, making way against the massive wasps, the hobgoblins, and the yawares. He felt every blow. The Yachaq felt the energy within all living creature, so the white elf felt their light dim out as well, and this pained him. But there was no time for sorrow if he wanted to help his friends save all living creatures in all of the eight worlds.

The weredogs saw this as well and Ash was about to reach Yakar when a yawar tackled him to the ground, making him exhale a powerful yelp. Many more yawares joined in as he fought from the ground, growling and biting.

"Nooo!" Screamed Aline, seeing the yawares hurting her friend. Tears fell from her eyes while she watched. Without a thought, she jumped of Liyun and ran past the cave towards Ash. Feeling her thread tugging at her, she used her magical powers to release a translucent ripple that pushed the monsters off of him, sending them deep inside the cave. The cave shifted and moved. These monsters were lost and Aline knew the cave was going to enjoy toying with them. Then, something pushed her away hard, knocking the breath out of her. She turned around to see a hobgoblin lifting his ax. She thrust him away with her magical powers, and crawled back towards Ash. More of these creatures were coming their way. Too many for her. She leaned forward to protect him with her body.

The quest carriers were desperately trying to fight off the hobgoblins, the yawares, and the giant wasps to get to Aline. Even more enemies spilled from the north and the west and they were barely making a dent among the putrefied creatures. Without losing hope, they fought as hard as they could, trying to regroup and make it towards Aline. It was at that moment that a translucent pulse of light exploded out of the quest carriers, taking down several of their enemies. The force of it created a huge clearing, giving them just what they needed.

It was Benowit's spell. They all felt and saw what it did to their enemies.

It gave them the speck of hope they needed to fight back. Aline was thankful for Benowit's spell. She raised her head and looked down at Ash.

"Ash? Ash? Please answer me. Are you okay?" She kissed and caressed her furry friend, whose eyes were closed. "Please, please, please. Stay with me. I love you, please stay." Her tears slid furiously from her face onto this black and dark grey fur. She hugged and kissed him, but he did not move.

"No!" Suddenly she was angry. She shook him, shouting "You wake up! Wake up this instant! You hear me?"

"You know...that hurts," his bright blue eyes opened to look at her and he licked her face.

"Do not scare me like this ever again, you hear me?" her tears were pouring out of her eyes. She wiped her eyes and kissed her friend once more. "Now, you need to get up."

Aline was helping her friend up when a scream made her look up.

"Aline," Akiya screamed, "Always keep an eye on your enemy." They were coming back, tons of them and fast.

Lifting her gaze, she saw that Yakar was almost on top of her. The next thing she heard was Kunaq's sword singing above her and Yakar jumping back. Kunaq pushed Aline out of the way and ran towards Yakar. He fought Yakar, pushing him north, towards the Bleak Forest.

Yakar seemed to get pleasure from this fight. He avoided every blow from Kunaq who masterfully swung the sword towards him. It was a dance, and Yakar was leading. Kunaq focused his eyes on Yakar and thrust his body forward. Yakar shifted to the left and hit Kunaq square on the chest. Kunaq slid backwards forcefully. He stuck his sword on the ground to stop himself.

He focused once more on Yakar, and boosted himself towards the vampire. Getting very close, he stuck one hand out while the other moved the sword in a figure eight between him and Yakar. With his opened hand, he began to connect with the vampire's energy. He was now as fast as Yakar. Swinging his sword from left to right, he struck the surprised vampire, slashing his left arm. The dance stopped. Yakar looked at his arm, his wound had already healed.

"You know, I will enjoy fighting you," he snarled. "But not today." As he spoke, a tarantula hawk wasp soaring overhead swung down and grabbed Kunaq, flying him away from Yakar, from Aline, and from his friends.

Yakar was now walking towards Aline. She ran, but he was too fast. Once he was a few steps away he stopped. Ash leaped towards him but the vampire flung him far away as if he were a mere pup. His fluorescent turquoise eyes focused only on Aline. He got very close to her. Slightly raising his head he breathed in the air around the girl and smiled.

"You smell sweet," his voice was soft, inviting. Not what Aline expected. "Or rather, your powers do."

He began to walk around her. He was toying with her like a cat does with its prey.

"The moment your friends entered the Bleak Forest I knew. It alerted my spies. They could not sense you were there, but I was certain that you were with your friends. Maybe it is one of your powers Aline, to hide," he said.

She did not like at all how her name sounded under his cold and empty words. He was facing her once again. Taking one step forward, Aline felt the air thick. She took two steps back and began to search for her thread. She was ready to fight.

"Why even bother?" He mocked her. "You are outnumbered. Look at your friends."

Aline looked around and saw her friends desperately fighting against Yakar's army. While protecting Sofia and Cristina, Liyun was receiving massive blows to his paws and tail. The weredogs had several creatures swarming them. She could not find Kunaq. Kawayu was frantically kicking the creatures around him so he could send his magic out. Urpi was valiantly fighting three hobgoblins with magical whips, and the Apotequils were defensively sending lightning rays.

Sadness filled her; she did not want her friends to get hurt, but she could not give up. There was no way she was going to give him the blue bottle. She was not giving up, not today, not ever, or all of this was for nothing. He took another step forward and Aline used her new magical translucent ripples to expel him out and away from her. She began to run towards the two tabletop trees, towards the cave's mouth, but Yakar was already running after her. He was really angry.

In the blink of an eye, he grabbed Aline tight. She looked into his crazed eyes. Her arms hurt as he bent her back. She saw there was a golden ring in the middle of each of his eyes. He began to absorb her magic. His eyes shimmered. Magical echoes transferred from her body towards him. Aline felt she could not breathe even though she was taking deep breaths. She felt something dark deep within her and for the first time, she realized that this dark thing inside of her was connected with Dashiok. It came from Dashiok, and it was his. Part of her was Dashiok's.

Yakar stopped. Surprised, he softened his grip on Aline. The golden rings in his eyes were wider.

"No," he whispered.

He could feel his own energy in Aline and remembered. Dashiok had used his energy and blood without his permission and had given it to the golden egg. This had scarred his eyes with a golden ring as a painful reminder of that day. So many years he had felt forsaken by the One World, where he was the only creature of his kind. The one thing he had desired for so long was not to be alone. This need had allowed Dashiok to imprison him in order to create the yawares which were mere shells of Yakar.

Aline was more than a shell. He was about to kill the only real magical family he had. He gently stood her up as the golden rings in his eyes glistened.

"I am sorry," he said. "I am so sorry, Aline. You must go."

Hardly believing her ears, Aline looked at Yakar and began to back away.

"Wait," he said.

She stopped. He wanted to return back to her the power he had stolen. This was something he had never done before. He freed a magical echo from his body. Aline raised her hand and absorbed her magic, along with some of his. This was new. Something that Yakar, the oldest creature ever created had never once felt.

Kindness.

Aline turned around and ran back towards her friends. With her power and some of Yakar's, she sent a ripple that freed her friends, knocking down many of her enemies in a series of circles around the campsite.

"Aline, you need to get out. Use the backpack," advised Akiya.

She remembered. The palace had made it specially for her. She had felt her gargoyle costume, which was stored in one of the compartments in her room at the palace. Using her telepathic powers, she created a clear connection with all of the quest carriers, including Liyun.

"Come to me. Now!" she commanded.

Sky and Mach were helping Ash get to her. She could see them all getting there except for Kunaq.

"This is a magical backpack." She took it off and opened all of its hooks. Like a large tepee, the backpack created an entrance with two curtains for a door. It was so big that even Liyun could fit.

"Get in," instructed Aline. One by one, they got in as she asked. Aline saw Yakar enter the Bleak Forest and disappear. As her gaze lowered, she could see that some of the yawares were moving towards them.

"Hurry!" she demanded, looking desperately for Kunaq. Sofia and Cristina entered next. She saw her friends were proud of her just as she was of them. Kunaq was still nowhere to be seen and now the yawares were getting up after she had knocked them down hard with her power. Still no sight of Kunaq. Kay was the last to get in.

"You need to get in Aline," she urged.

"I can not see Kunaq," Aline answered hopelessly.

"Hurry, Aline," she said looking at the yawares who were stumbling towards them and the hobgoblins who were now moving on the ground.

"I will. I promise," she said.

Glancing left and right, Aline searched for Kunaq. She grabbed the strap of the backpack ready to go in and the tepee-backpack entrance became smaller. Right behind the tepee-backpack, there was a blur moving towards her. It was Kunaq running to Aline.

"Get in, get in," she screamed. He ran right in through the entrance and Aline followed him, pulling on the strap, reversing the backpack and taking it with her into the palace.

They all disappeared from the Southern Shores and were now safe in the palace, in Aline's room. Aline was holding the backpack. It was back to its normal size.

"The blue bottle," she whispered in a panic. When she opened the backpack, she was afraid she would see the beach, but she did not. It was empty.

"Oh no!" She exhaled and became pale. The blood had left her face and she felt like she was going to faint. A chair appeared right behind her and a vine very gently brought the blue bottle to her.

"Oh my goodness! Thank you, palace." As soon as she had placed the bottle in the backpack, the palace had taken it and kept it safe.

The vines in the palace went about healing everyone. They were all hurt. Akiya and Benowit arrived soon afterwards and began to heal them as well.

Aline was exhausted. Her back hurt, really, her whole body ached. She closed her eyes, still holding on to the blue bottle, and decided it was the perfect time to sleep. The vines gently carried her and the bottle to her bed. The quest was over.

7

DECISIONS

New World, New Family

Aline opened her eyes to find all of the weredogs back in their normal sizes and sleeping on the bed with her. She smiled. In her hand was the blue bottle. They did it! It was over. They had successfully completed their quest and made it out of there alive.

Then Aline remembered her encounter with Yakar. Putting her hand on her heart, she took a deep breath and felt the darkness within her. Dashiok had put more than Yakar's energy and blood into the golden egg. A piece of his dark magic was inside of her and she felt its darkness there. Ash licked her, bringing a smile back to her face. She swallowed hard and pushed her thoughts of Dashiok away.

"Are you okay?" She asked, petting his soft fur.

"Yes, Aline, thanks to you I am okay," he said to her. She scratched behind his ear.

"Sofia and Cristina! Are they okay?" She was concerned. "Is everyone all right?"

"The sisters are okay. Fine young warriors, I might add," said Mach.

"Agreed," said Alis.

"Everyone is fine, Aline. Nothing that Akiya, Benowit, or the palace could not heal," answered Kay.

She exhaled and began to relax. "Wow! I am hungry," she realized.

That is all Aline had to say for the palace to put together a table with a hearty breakfast for her.

"Do I smell bacon?" Sofia said as she walked into the room.

"Hmm! And hot chocolate. Yum!" Added Cristina.

Both sisters ran towards Aline and gave her a big hug. Abi was right behind them with Akiya. They had big smiles on their faces, which Aline returned.

"They have been waiting downstairs for you to wake up every day for the past four days," added Abi.

"Four days?" said Aline, surprised.

"Yup! I slept for two days, and Cristina slept for one," added Sofia.

"I am happy you finally decided to wake up," Christina said. "That was the longest nap I have ever seen anyone take," she added with a wink and a smile.

"I knew you would like the company." Abi gave Aline the biggest hug and the floral smell reminded her of home and her mother. "I am so glad you are okay. Akiya kept all of us informed, but I was so worried," she said, tucking Aline's hair behind her ear. "I am so proud of you." Then she looked up, and added "I am so proud of all of you."

"I will second that," said Akiya. "You have made all of us very proud. Very few adults can demonstrate the bravery that you have shown, and your powers are beginning to blossom in the most spectacular manner. You should be very proud of yourselves. That includes you as well," she motioned to the weredogs.

During breakfast, the girls recounted their quest step by step. Aline realized that their journey had been a powerful one and now that it was over, she appreciated it even more. However, every so often her thoughts would drift to Yakar and the darkness inside of her. She was not sure what to do about this, but it was too soon for her to talk about it with anyone.

"Did you hear, Aline?" Cristina asked excitedly.

"Hear what?" Aline asked.

"That means no," Sofia giggled. "There is going to be a ceremony in honor of the quest carriers..." she paused, grabbed Aline's hands, shrugged her shoulders and raised the pitch in her voice. "That is us! Can you believe it? A ceremony for us? This is unheard of!"

"Really? For us?" Aline was surprised. "When?"

"In one month," responded Cristina. "I am already thinking about what to wear."

Sofia turned to look at Akiya, and asked, "What do you wear to something like that?" She was a bit concerned.

"Do not worry, we will help you," Akiya said.

Aline handed the bottle to Akiya, "Here," she said, "You should take her."

"Well, I am not sure that is the case, nor that it is up to any of us, but if the bottle allows it, I will hold her for you until the ceremony." Akiya carefully extended her hand towards the bottle. Nothing happened, so she softly took the bottle from Aline. "The bottle chose you, Aline, to find her, and she may choose someone else to do whatever is needed next. Hopefully, she will tell us before the ceremony."

The rest of the month was very relaxed. Aline, Cristina, Sofia, and the weredogs met every day. They chatted about the quest, the ceremony, and food of course. Almost every night, they met with the rest of the quest carriers for dinner, including Liyun. He had become the fourteenth quest carrier. It was nice to see them all happy, relaxed, and clean. Indeed, Sofia whispered an observation to the two girls: "We all smell much better."

"You know, I was thinking," said Cristina to the girls and Liyun. "We made a promise to the cave that we would be back. I have been thinking about this and I do not know how we can keep it." Her eyes were filled with guilt.

"That is not a problem," responded Liyun. "She has created an entrance not too far from here, near the Winding Forest. Hidden.

"How do you know?" asked Cristina.

"I have picked up her scent. I can probably smell the entrance's location. We can go there any time you like."

"Really?" Cristina was elated and gave him a hug. Sofia did the same.

"Sorry, you are just so fluffy. I could not help myself," Sofia admitted.

"Not a problem at all. You are welcome to hug me any time you like, little one," he said politely in his deep raspy voice.

"Let's go tomorrow, after the ceremony! Then we can tell her all about it," suggested Cristina.

"Sounds like a plan," said Sofia, and Aline smiled in agreement.

Compared to the quest, the month passed by very slowly. To Aline, it felt like a year. The weight in her heart did not help her either. Ultimately, she was content with her new friends, her new powers, and her new home.

They filled her in a different way, lifting some of the heaviness away and bringing, without doubt, happiness. She always had a smile on her face when she was with them. When she was alone, things were very different.

Finally, the day of the ceremony arrived and the girls wanted to go together to the castle. Aline was wearing a dress that the palace had selected. It was soft pink silk on top with little white roses around the neckline that went all the way around to the back. The bottom was made up of many layers of lilac organza with a wide hem. On the front, the dress reached the ground and, on the back, there was a semi-long train. The train would behave like the wind was always softly blowing on it, so it never really touched the ground. More small white flowers were on the back, right where the silk met the organza. Her brownish-copper hair was mostly up with tiny white flowers placed here and there, and soft curls that fell down around her face. The dress and her hair smelled like lavender and wild lily.

Sofia had a chiffon white dress, and on one side the skirt opened up to reveal different shades of pink and yellow flowers matching her wings. Her shoes were made of flowers and she had decided to wear a pink hat. It smelled like roses and daffodils.

Cristina had decided to do something new. She had asked green and purple butterflies to pose as her dress and they politely agreed. So her dress was alive, and every time the butterflies closed their wings they would reveal bright green leaves below. The dress absolutely mirrored the color on her wings.

The weredogs decided not to wear anything. They felt more comfortable as they were with shiny and fluffy furs. However, removing the knots on Ash and Mach's fur was not a pleasant task for either Ash, Mach, or the palace.

It was a pleasant evening with a soft fall breeze. The ceremony was in the castle's great hall. Small enchanted spheres floated around the hall and courtyard generating light, and the waterfalls had bioluminescent magical fish swimming up and down. The girls could see these colors from the palace as they excitedly walked towards the castle gate that evening. On the way, Aline thought she saw someone looking at them when they were crossing the labyrinth but in a blink whatever it was, was gone.

They walked past the castle gates, through the main entrance, towards the stairs. On top of the stairs, they met with all of the quest carriers and together they walked to the great hall. Aline had forgotten how great it was. Maybe that is part of its magic. Every time you saw it you got the same or even a better feeling than when you laid eyes on it for the first time. It was magnificent.

For the ceremony, the long table in the middle was removed and replaced with an ice sculpture of dancing sylphs holding the blue bottle. Aline thought it was neat that the sylphs were really dancing and laughing and she wondered if they were real. Smaller tables were added in each of the four corners with food. Sofia and Ash walked towards the table far to the left next to the courtyard doors, which were closed for the ceremony.

Chattered filled the great hall, and many new magical creatures reached out to Aline and the quest carriers to congratulate them or hug them. After all, they had saved their lives.

Aline received a large number of hugs that night. However, the same could not be said of Liyun. Therefore, Sofia gave him extra hugs to make sure he was not left out. Sofia and Liyun seemed to have formed a special bond. Just like Cristina and the cave.

When the ceremony was about to start, all of the floating lights circled around gently and then faster. They pivoted and moved towards the center and up circling back to their original places. Benowit with the High Magical Council next to him stood at the far right, the opposite end of the courtyard.

"My fellow magical kin," he said in a clear voice. "We are gathered here this evening to honor the remarkable achievement of fourteen brave and courageous individuals. We, the High Magical Council, thank you for joining us for tonight's ceremony. Please may the quest carriers come up."

The fourteen quest carriers gathered in front of Benowit and the High Magical Council. Aline could feel the many eyes looking at them. Her hands became clammy, tiny droplets grew on her forehead, and her fingers were slightly shaky.

"Tonight, in front of all these magical and non-magical creatures, we want to honor your camaraderie, your grit, and your courage."

At that moment the members of the council, including Benowit, walked towards the quest carriers. In front of them were floating purple crystal-rocks. These were presented to each of the quest carriers. "May the One World's light forever shine."

"May the One World's light forever shine," the members in the great hall repeated and they all applauded. Each quest carrier extended their hand and the crystals floated next to them for the rest of the night.

"Now, let us enjoy the rest of the evening," said Benowit and the lights above exploded into many pieces, several times, finally regrouping back to where they were. Music began to play above from flying sylphs. A long table appeared next to the arches, filled with delicious food. The smiles on the girl's faces barely fit their heads. Sofia once again walked along the long table grabbing one of everything.

"You know, the castle is starting to compete with the palace," Sofia said.

"Do not let the palace hear you or you will not get more goodies," Aline warned her friend.

"You are right," said Sofia. "I take it back. I love your food palace."

When most of the magical creatures began to dance, Abi asked Aline, Cristina, and Sofia to follow her. She opened the door to the courtyard and then locked it again with magic, right after the girls passed through. It was empty, and Aline appreciated the moon rays illuminating the courtyard giving it an ethereal look. She walked down the stairs, into the pool of water on the third arch before the waterfalls. Abi touched the wall in a peculiar sequence and a door opened.

"Come in, quick," she instructed.

The three girls felt a spark of excitement as they walked down towards the pool. Critina's butterflies flew above her and followed her without getting wet. The water glowed and fizzed when the water touched their skin, bubbling their dresses up and the girls giggled as they walked back up through the secret door. The passage took them to the northern courtyard that was part of the second hall. This hall was a mirror image of the great hall, but the mountains behind the castle blocked the moonlight so it was not as bright. Close to the arch Benowit and Akiya waited for them in secrecy, concealed from the rest of the party attendees who were still celebrating and dancing in the great hall. Benowit whispered a spell and Abi and the girls were dry.

"I am glad you are here." He spoke calmly, but Aline could tell he was eager to speak with them. "There is something all of you need to decide," he said, "but before any decisions take place, we need to share with you, Aline, a piece of information from the past and one from the present. For you Cristina and Sofia what is next is part of your current main journey."

The girls were very curious and leaned in a bit closer. Aline looked at

Sofia and Cristina. She had not known the girls were already on another journey.

"Do you remember, Aline, when I told you that both Kani and I went to the human world to take care for you? To take care of the golden egg?" Abi asked. Aline nodded.

"It was about fifty years ago when Kani and I went to the human world," Abi continued. "The magical clan who was taking care of the golden egg before us was hiding there from Dashiok. When Kani and I travelled to earth, they travelled back to this world to hide. Before today's ceremony, the whispers told me that the magical clan had finally come out of hiding to find you, Aline." Abi looked carefully at her.

"Find me? Why?" asked Aline, confused.

"You were not the only egg they hid." Aline looked at Abi in disbelief. "After the clash that ended the dragons, the magical clan took care of the four remaining Krons. Unfortunately, they did not survive. But they did reveal to the clan where the mothers had taken the Kron eggs. During the clash, in order to protect the eggs, the mothers took them deep within the mountain caves. The Krons breathed on the eggs and turned them into smooth rocks, camouflaging them from the enemy.

"Using magic to sense life within the rocks, the clan found 257 eggs in the cave. With help from Benowit and Akiya, they hid in the human world in the far east and only moved when they feared danger was near. In all of these years, both in the human world and in this world, nothing had changed. The eggs remained stone and the magical clan could no longer sense life within them and thought that after so many years they were just that, stone. However, the magical clan leader remained hopeful.

"A few months ago, just a few days after you entered this world Aline, some of the eggs moved. Last night the pale gray stones changed into the eight different colors of the Kron clans. That is why the magical clan came out of hiding. That is the reason they are looking for you. They need to leave; however, the colored eggs are using magic and are not letting the magical clan move them. The eggs are alive, Aline."

Cristina and Sofia looked at Aline with bright glistening eyes.

"You are the closest living relative to these eggs Aline," added Akiya. "You may be the only key to waking them up."

Aline was in shock. Eggs. Krons.

"You are the daughter of Sañi," said Benowit, his voice filled with honor.

"Zarkon's great-great-granddaughter, daughter of Gargon the leader of the golden Kron clan. Just as much as you are the daughter of Makaurrok, grandson of Rrok, son of Kaurrok who was the head of the dragon Superior Clan leader. These eggs are your flesh and blood. They are your family, Aline, and you are theirs."

Aline felt the pride in Benowit's voice when he pronounced her parents' names. Family. She had a family that was alive in this world.

"There is more," added Benowit. "The whispers believe that Dashiok somehow has found out about the magical clan. We do not believe he knows about the eggs. However, the clan possesses knowledge on Krons and Dashiok wants this knowledge for himself. We believe that you have a new quest if you choose to take it. This quest will help to bring the magical clan and all of the eggs here, safely, to the castle."

"Before you tell us your decision, we need to provide Sofia and Cristina more information about their journey," said Akiya. Both sisters wanted to hear Aline's decision before moving forward, and Akiya had figured this out. "It is important that all three of you see this first."

The sisters nodded. Akiya used magic to draw a rectangle in the air, opening a window to a vault. When she twitched her index finger, the vault opened, revealing the blue bottle. She whispered something, put her hand through the window and picked up the bottle.

"That is a neat trick," exclaimed Cristina.

"No trick dear," asserted Akiya. "It is time to let the blue bottle decide what the next step is and who will be her carrier."

They all looked at the blue bottle. Each of the eight sides, created by the two long rectangles which overlaid on top of each other giving the bottle her star shape, were still adorned with strange markings. The bottle floated up from Akiya's hand, and as she did so, the rectangles shifted around, changing the symbols on her panels.

She was now above their heads. A blue dust dripped from the tip of the bottle right between their eyes. The blue bottle then showed all of them images of Cristina and Sofia receiving the entryway from Akiya, hiding the entryway in the blue bottle, and then hiding the blue bottle.

Aline looked at her hand. She could still feel the connecting energy of the blue bottle pulsating. "You have a different quest than I do," she said a bit sadly. "I need to help bring the Kron eggs here to the palace." Her eyebrows knit together as she spoke.

"We know," said Cristina. "To keep our wings, we need to complete our quest, which is to hide the entryway. It is the reason we went to the meteor shower. We needed to enhance our powers to do this."

"This is true," added Sofia wiping tears from her eyes. "This is true," she whispered and hugged Aline. Cristina grabbed the blue bottle and hugged Aline. She could not help it as tears slid down her cheeks as well.

"I do not like this," Sofia protested.

"Me neither," Cristina affirmed.

"Agreed," said Aline, wiping her eyes.

"So why do we need to do something we do not like?" asked Cristina a bit frustrated. "I mean, there is a reason why the three of us got the original meteors." An idea was forming in Cristina's mind and it started to feel good.

"No!" She said. They all looked at her surprised.

"What do you mean by no, Cristina?" Akiya asked gently.

"I mean, we are not going on separate journeys," said Cristina with a smile. Aline always admired the way the sisters spoke their minds. They were fearless.

"You are right, Cristina," added Sofia. "Aline, Our quests are connected. If we help you, then at the same time you help us. Dashiok is after you and he is also after the entryway. Anything he does is to get the entryway, and this includes getting the Kron eggs. He needs the eggs to get to Aline, and he needs Aline to get the entryway. So no! I agree with Cristina." Cristina smiled at her sister. It always made her happy when Sofia had her back.

"We will go with you, Aline, to bring the Kron eggs here..." said Sofia.

"And then," responded Aline with a smile, "I will help you hide the entryway. It is perfect!"

Benowit, Abi, and Akiya looked at each other and smiled. They had been hopeful the girls would make this decision.

"I shall guard this for you while you help Aline," Akiya opened the magical window and placed the blue bottle back in the vault.

"Okay, when are we leaving?" Aline asked.

"As soon as the whispers tell us where the magical clan is located," Benowit answered, "Knowing the magical clan leader, I believe this will be in about a month or so. The fact that they are out of hiding does not mean that they are easily found. In the meantime, we will talk to the quest carriers and the High Magical Council to see who can join you."

The girls were excited. A new quest together! A new adventure! And it was going to be great!

The rest of the evening the girls danced and Sofia ate even more. They enjoyed each other's company and burned off some of the adrenaline they got from the secret meeting with Benowit, Abi, and Akiya. Later in the evening, the girls hugged goodbye by the castle gates and Aline walked back to the palace. The weredogs wanted to come with her, but she convinced them to stay and enjoy the party. For the first time in this new magical world, she really needed to think and to walk alone.

The crisp air felt good to Aline and the two moons were high, illuminating the ponds in the labyrinths by the gardens. Her purple crystal still floated by her side and lit her path, giving everything a funny shade. She looked at it more carefully and noticed that the crystal was encrusted in a silver ring. Its light hid the ring.

"That is a neat trick," she thought, and smiled.

As she continued to walk, she could still smell the floral scent on her dress and she smiled. It was a great night. She had a family. Her thoughts bounced from the Kron eggs, to the magical clan, to helping the sisters, and back again.

Once more, out of the corner of her eye, Aline saw not too far away someone looking at her and then moving away.

"Who is there?" A rush of energy and goosebumps flooded her body and Aline started to look for her thread. The outline of a person began to walk towards her. It was Yakar. Aline froze.

"Please do not be afraid. I will not harm you," Yakar assured her. There was a hint of sadness in his voice. "I just wanted to make sure you are okay. May I walk you home?"

Aline looked to either side, unsure what to do. She remembered their encounter on the Southern Shores. Her hand immediately clutched her heart. Then she remembered what he had said and that he had let her go. Deep in her heart, she felt sad for him. To an extent, as a human, she understood how alone he felt, and through their magical connection, she felt his sadness.

"Okay," she said once she had found her thread. They walked in silence until they reached the palace doors. In those few minutes, while he walked by her side, she learned something that she did not expect. Even though walking next to Yakar was like walking next to a hungry lion, she felt safe.

Not because she had finally reached the palace, but because at the end of it all she knew deep in her heart that he indeed would never hurt her. He was as desperate to find his family as she was to find hers. The difference between them was that she was not alone.

"I'll be around," he said and, in a blink, he vanished.

She saw Yakar two more times. Once, when she visited the cave near the 'u' trees and another time when the girls were playing on the fields behind the castle. She knew that he would always be close. Even though he was not good, she was certain he was not bad either. Not anymore anyway. She felt that he was going to be good to her.

It had been about ten months since Aline had arrived in this magical world, but to Aline, it felt like several years. Some days she could feel darkness pressing against her heart. There was a part of her that was connected to Dashiok, to her brothers, and to Yakar. She knew this and it bothered her. So, she would push it down, deep, deep down, until she stopped thinking about it, at least for a while.

When she was with her friends this horrible feeling would float away. They were so magical and powerful that she felt magical. They were so humble and simple that they reminded her of a part within her that was human. They brought out the best in her and she loved them. This was her home now and these magical creatures were her family. Very soon she would embark on a new quest to bring the rest of her family home.

Three weeks after the ceremony, Abi reached out to Aline and the sylph sisters. The whispers had finally found the magical clan. They heard that the magical clan was in the northwest, in the Red Ravines. Benowit had confirmed who was joining Aline, Cristina, and Sofia in their new journey, their new adventure.

On the day they were heading out, they all waited for Aline by the amphitheater. Aline grabbed her backpack and walked with her friends towards the 'u' trees.

She had found her thread. She was ready.

ACKNOWLEDGMENTS

Most of the people who helped me know that the idea of Aline started about 15 years ago, and boy you stuck by me. It took a long time, as life provided wonderful interruptions, making this book more rewarding than I could have ever imagined.

None of this would have been possible without the support, love, and encouragement of my husband Ricardo—oh...did I mention patience? The same could be said about my two wonderful daughters Monica and Veronica—you know you are my inspiration!

To my mother Lili, what can I say? You read this book many, many times and were right there with me. You helped me get Aline out into the world—and let the secrets out!!!

My kid beta readers, Fabian, Alejandro, and Stella, it was so encouraging to hear your thoughts and excitement. You confirmed that I was going in the right direction!

To my adult beta readers, Deven Mehta, Dan Sorgen, and Todd Kyger, in your busy lives you found time to share your thoughts and recommendations. This meant a lot to me!

John Stevenson, my illustrator, boy you took on the crazy task of completing two maps and a character tree in impossible timelines. I take my hat off!

To my fellow author, Brad Haakenson (http://www.bradhaakenson.com)

—those long bus rides from work were golden to learn and obtain your very much needed guidance. May your books flourish!!!

Chansonette Buck, my dear editor, I am so thankful for all the guidance, humor, and dedication you provided. You made it fun—and your encouragement and confirmation were invaluable. I look forward to our upcoming adventures with Aline.

SPELLS

The Night Song (English version)
   The dark veil has fallen,
   the stars are bright.
   Together we are,
   not alone tonight.
   Our love is strong,
   and it sings this song.
   Family is magic,
   do not fright.
   For magic will bring the light tonight.

El Canto Nocturno (Spanish version)
   Cayó un oscuro velo,
   y estrellas brillantes reveló.
   Esta noche no estaremos solos, si no juntos, lo prometo.
   Poderoso es nuestro amor,
   y canta una canción.
   Magia vive en la familia, una revelación.
   No tengas miedo,
   tu sonrisa surgirá.
   Por que la magia, esta noche iluminará.

Tutapi Candana Taqui (Quechua version)
   Indi ñami pacajurca,
   lucerocuna inti shina ninanda punllayachin.
   Kunan tutapi mana ñucanchigllachu canchig.
   Ñucanchig cuyay sinchimari can,

shinami, cay sumag candotaca candajuni.
Ayllucuna magia shinami can.
Ama manchaychu,
cunan tutapi ninandami punllayachinga, michagu shina.

———

GLOSSARY: QUECHUA TO ENGLISH

- Achkyi: Light
- Akiya: Comes from the word Akilla, which means chosen one, chosen among many
- Apotequil: Comes from the word Apocatequils, which means Incan God of Lightning
- Atiq: Victor; the one who can achieve something
- Azel: Nobel*
- Illapa: Fire arm, lightning
- Ihxu: To be born a leader (astrological term)*
- Kachi: Taken from the word Kachichay, which means to crystallize, rennet and salt
- Kani: I am
- K'antu: Song or sacred Incan flower
- Khallma: Shuttle
- Kawayu: Horse
- Killa: Electricity
- Kunaq: The one who advises, counselor/advisor
- Kuti: Taken from the word Ch'ilikuti, which means small, minute
- Laqha: Darkness
- Liyun: Lion
- Mayu: River
- Mawk'a: Old, history of... (e.g. History of Greece, History of Egypt, etc.)
- Micha: Energy
- Muyu: Taken from Muyuriq pacha amachay, which means environmental protection
- Nina: Fire, light, candle, restless and vivacious like fire
- Ninan: Is nominative of Nina
- Paya: Grandmother, old woman, ancient

* Not originated or derived from the Quechua Language

- Phuru: Feather
- Phuyu: Fog, haze, cloud
- Pusaq: Guide, companion, leader, conductor, boss
- Q'axniy: Thunder, deafening sound v. Thunder, explode
- Qhispi: Taken from the words Qhispi Umiña, which mean diamond
- Qori: Golden, gold
- Qucha: Lake
- Ruku: Taken from the word Machuruku, which means ancient, old
- Sañi: Golden
- Saywa: Who indicates the way, points the way, frontier, border
- Surux: Taken from the word Suruxchi, which means to asphyxiate due to lack of air and due to fatigue
- Tiksi: Dirt or earth
- Thuru: Hard, stand strong
- Tuj: Taken from, Tujllaki, which means hunter
- Umi: Taken from the words Qhispi Umiña, which mean diamond
- Unan: Taken from Unanchay, which means to understand, consider, discern
- Urpi: Dove, bird, tortola
- Uqi: Ashen, lead, gray
- Urqu: Hill, mount, mountain
- Uskhay: Comes from Usqhay, which means hurriedly, quickly
- Uspha: Ash
- Ut'u: Taken from Ñut'u jallp'a which means dust
- Yachaq: Wise, wisdom
- Yaku: Water
- Yana: Black
- Yakar: Derived from Yawar, which means blood
- Wallqa: Hualca, from Hualca Hualca which is an extinct volcano in Arequipa Region in the Andes of Peru. Hualca Hualca forms a volcanic complex with the two southerly volcanoes Sabancaya and Ampato. It is older and more heavily eroded than these two volcanoes
- Wayra: Wind

ON LINE SOURCES:

- EN.WIKIPEDIA.ORG 2019. HTTPS://EN.WIKIPEDIA.ORGWIKI/HUALCA_HUALCA (21 SEP 2019)
- KATARI.COM 2019. HTTP://WWW.KATARI.ORG/DICCIONARIO/DICCIONARIO.PHP (21 SEP 2019)
- GLOSBE.COM N.D. HTTPS://ES.GLOSBE.COM/QU/ES (21 SEP 2019)

GLOSSARY: QUECHUA TO SPANISH

- Achkyi: Luz
- Akiya: Viene de la palabra Akilla, que quiere decir elegida, escogida entre todas
- Apotequil: Viene de la palabra Apocatequils, que es un Dios Inca del Rayo
- Atiq: Vencedor; el que puede lograr algo
- Azel: Noble*
- Illapa: Arma de fuego, rayo, relámpago
- Ihxu: Nacer como un líder (astrología)*
- Kachi: Viene de la palabra Kachichay, que quiere decir cristalizar, cuajarse la sal
- Kani: Soy, estoy
- K'antu: Canto or flor sagrada de los Incas
- Khallma: Lanzadera, cohete
- Kawayu: Caballo
- Killa: Electricidad
- Kunaq: El que aconseja, consejero
- Kuti: Viene de la palabra Ch'ilikuti, que quiere decir Pequeño, diminuto
- Laqha: Oscuridad
- Liyun: León
- Mayu: Rio
- Mawk'a: Antigua, historia de... (e.g. Historia de Grecia, Historia de Egipto, etc.)
- Micha: Energía
- Muyu: Viene de la palabras Muyuriq pacha amachay, que quiere decir protección medioambiental
- Nina: Fuego, candela, inquieto y vivaz como el fuego
- Ninan: Nominativo de Nina
- Paya: Abuela, anciana, vieja

* Palabra no originada o derivada del idioma Quechua

- Phuru: Pluma
- Phuyu: Neblina, nube
- Pusaq: Guía, acompañador, líder, conductor, jefe
- Q'axniy: Trueno, ruido ensordecedor. v. Tronar, estallar
- Qhispi: Viene de las palabras Qhispi Umiña, que quiere decir diamante
- Qori: Oro, dorado
- Qucha: Lago
- Ruku: Viene de la palabra Machuruku, que quiere decir viejo, anciano
- Sañi: Dorada
- Saywa: Quien indica el camino, señala el camino, frontera, borde
- Surux: Viene de las palabras Suruxchi, que quiere decir asfixia por la falta de aire y por la fatiga
- Tiksi: Tierra
- Thuru: Quiere decir duro, pararse fuerte
- Tuj: Viene de las palabra Tujllaki, que quiere decir cazador
- Umi: Viene de las palabras Qhispi Umiña, que quiere decir diamante
- Unan: Viene de la palabra Unanchay, que quiere decir enterder, considerar, discernir
- Urpi: Paloma, pájaro, tórtola
- Uqi: Ceniciento, plomo, gris
- Urqu: Quiere decir cerro, monte, montaña. adj. Macho de los animales
- Uskhay: Viene de la palabra Usqhay, que quiere decir apresuradamente, rapidamente
- Uspha: Ceniza
- Yachaq: Sabio, sabiduría
- Yaku: Agua
- Yana: Negro
- Yakar: Derivado de Yawar, que quiere decir sangre
- Wallqa: Hulca, vine de Hualca Hualca, es un volcán de tipo estratovolcán al sur del Perú. Está localizado en la Cordillera de los Andes a 6.025 msnm, en el departamento de Arequipa. Es el volcán más antiguo de un complejo volcánico que incluye otros dos volcanes: El Ampato y el Sabancaya

- Wayra: Viento

On line sources:

- EN.WIKIPEDIA.ORG 2019. HTTPS://EN.WIKIPEDIA.ORG/WIKI/HUALCA_HUALCA (21 SEP 2019)
- KATARI.COM 2019. HTTP://WWW.KATARI.ORG/DICCIONARIO/DICCIONARIO.PHP (21 SEP 2019)
- GLOSBE.COM N.D. HTTPS://ES.GLOSBE.COM/QU/ES (21 SEP 2019)

A LITTLE HELP

- Accentuated: to give more emphasis to; draw attention to
- Arduous: entailing great difficulty, exertion, or endurance; laborious
- Astute: keen in understanding and judgment; shrewd
- Bioluminescent: light given off naturally by certain kinds of insects, fish, or bacteria
- Camaraderie: friendship, good humor, and closeness among a group; comradeship
- Candelabras: a large decorative candle holder with branches for several candles
- Canopy: a covering made of cloth and hung over a bed or dining area
- Chimeras: animals or humans that contain the cells of two or more individuals. Their bodies contain two different sets of DNA
- Colossal: extremely large in size, magnitude, or effect; enormous; gigantic; huge
- Comprehend: to understand or grasp the meaning of
- Composure: calmness in thinking or acting; self control
- Condensation: the act or process of changing from a gas to a liquid
- Conflicting: to disagree strongly; to differ in opinion
- Contraptions: a mechanical device, sometimes of odd design or construction; gadget
- Conveyor: a mechanical device, such as a continuous chain or belt, used to convey materials from one place to another
- Crazed: having lost one's reason, or having or giving the appearance of being insane
- Cull: to select from a group; choose
- Deceive: to cause to believe something that is not true; trick or fool
- Differ: to be not the same as; be unlike
- Differentiate: to perceive differences or distinctions between

- Diluted: to make thinner or weaker by adding a liquid
- Dispersed: to drive away in all directions; scatter
- Dwindling: to become or cause to become gradually smaller or less until almost nothing remains; shrink
- Ecstatic: in a condition of extreme delight, overpowering emotion, or religious trance; enraptured
- Elongated: to make longer; lengthen
- Emanated: to come or send forth; issue or emit
- Emit: to send out or give off
- Endowing: to provide with some ability or quality
- Eons: a very long period of time
- Erudite: having or showing a high level of scholarly knowledge; learned
- Exuberance: the quality or condition of being exuberant
- Exuberant: vigorously enthusiastic or happy; high spirited
- Exude: to emit or give off from, or as if from, the pores of the skin
- Fathom: to get to the bottom of or understand completely
- Fellowship: the condition of being companions; company or friendship
- Hapless: not favored by chance; unlucky; unfortunate
- Humanoid: having humanlike qualities of structure and appearance
- Immobilize: to make incapable of motion or action
- Imperceptible: so gradual or subtle as to be unnoticed or unnoticeable
- Impose: to set as something that needs to be followed, done, or obeyed
- Incandescent: giving off light as a result of being heated
- Incessantly: never stopping; constant
- Incomprehensible: impossible to understand
- Inconspicuously: not likely to be seen or noticed
- Innate: belonging to or existing in someone or some organism from the time of birth; inborn
- Insinuating: suggest or hint (something bad or reprehensible) subtly and indirectly
- Intensified: to make stronger, more acute, or more intense
- Intermingled: to mix or mingle together

- Intuition: the power to know or understand something without thinking it through in a logical way
- Inverted: to reverse the order, position, or direction of
- Invigorating: giving or causing a feeling of being filled with energy or strength
- Lumbering: to move in a heavy, clumsy way
- Mahogany: an evergreen tree that grows in tropical North and South America. It has hard, reddish brown wood
- Mesmerized: to induce a hypnotic trance in; hypnotize
- Meticulously: very careful or precise
- Midsection: the middle part or section of something, esp. the human torso
- Millennia: one thousand years
- Multitude: a large number of people, animals, or things
- Octagonal: a flat closed figure with eight straight sides
- Pegacorn: a horned Pegasus or a winged unicorn
- Pint: a unit of measure equal to sixteen fluid ounces or one half quart (abbreviated: pt.)
- Plentiful: large in amount; more than enough
- Predominant: being the most common, frequent, or prominent; prevailing
- Potent: having strength, powerful
- Refine: to make pure or fine
- Reminisce: to recall past experiences, often with fondness or pleasure
- Repercussions: consequences; a result or effect of an action or event, often occurring indirectly or unexpectedly
- Resplendent: full of splendor; radiant; shining
- Singular: having to do with or designating the form of a word that indicates only one
- Stalactites: a rock formation that looks like an icicle and hangs from the roof of a cave. Stalactites are built up from minerals in dripping water
- Stalagmites: a rock formation that looks like a cone and is built upward from the floor of a cave. Stalagmites are built up from minerals in dripping water
- Stoic: not affected by or showing passion or feeling

- Surpass: to be greater or larger than; go beyond. To be better than in talent or accomplishment
- Taunted: to make fun of, tease, or challenge using mean language
- Tormented: to cause to feel great pain or distress. To annoy, tease, or cause to feel worry
- Transmute: to change into another form, substance, state, or the like; transform
- Transmutation: the act or process of transmuting or the state of being transmuted; transformation
- Vermin: an animal that causes harm or damage or is difficult to control; pest. Rats and cockroaches are thought of as vermin

On line sources:
Merriam-Webster.com. 2019. https://www.merriam-webster.com (21 Sep 2019)
Wordsmith.com 2019. https://kids.wordsmyth.net/we/?ent=Singular (21 Sep 2019)

BONUS MATERIAL

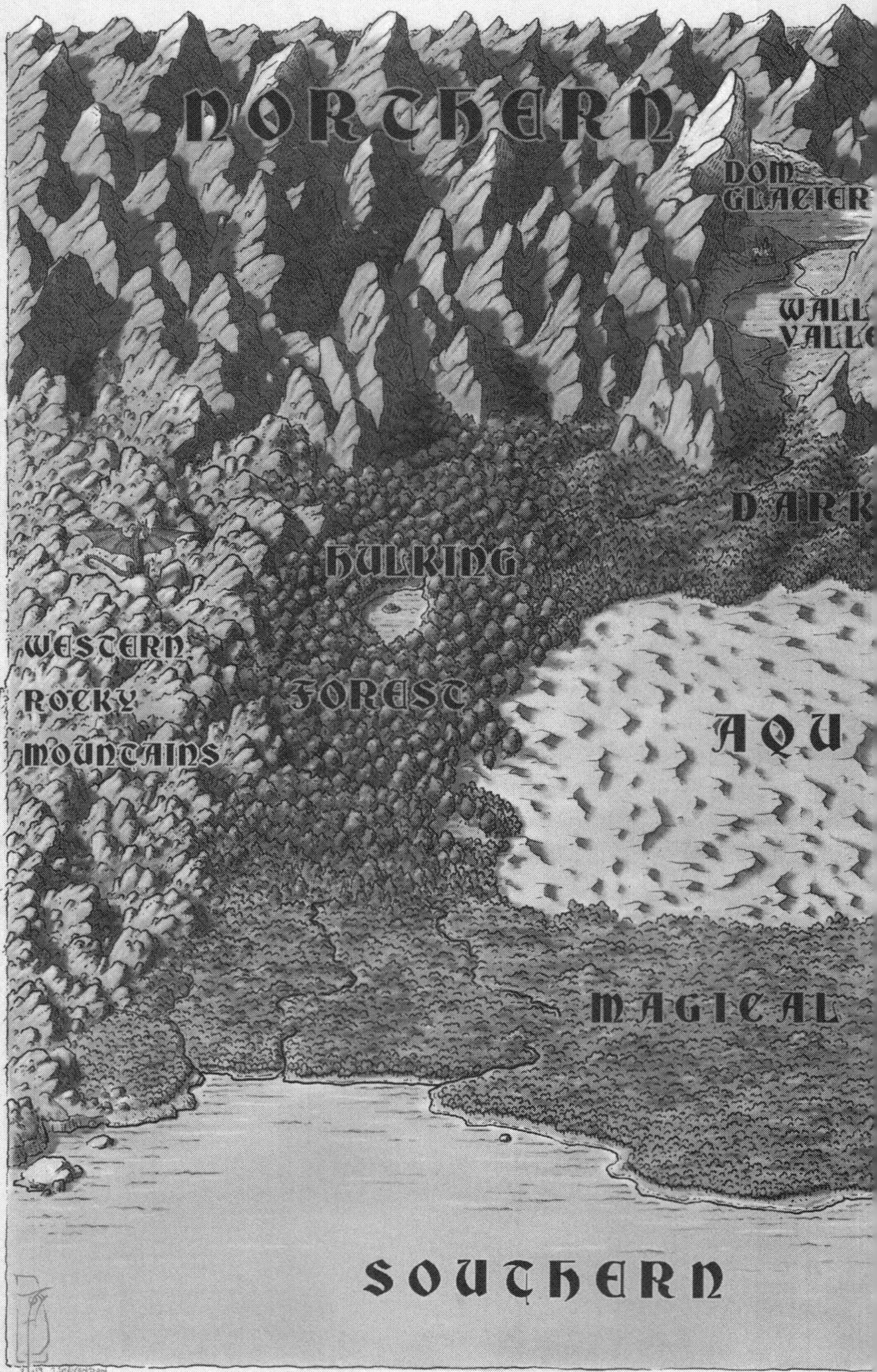
NORTHERN
DOM
GLACIER
WALL
VALLE
DARK
HULKING
WESTERN
ROCKY
MOUNTAINS
FOREST
AQU
MAGICAL
SOUTHERN

MOUNTAINS

FOREST

EASTERN
FLOATING
ROCKS

COURSE
SAND
DUNES

DESERT

FOREST

SEAS

THE BEGINNING

The One World

Eons ago, there was only One World. A vast world. Very different from any world we know today. Its soil was filled with magic. A single speck of its dust contained the most potent power ever known. This rich powder was everywhere. Deep beneath its entire surface. In its mountains all the way to the top. And even below its massive oceans and remarkable bodies of water. This magic fed all of nature on the One World. Including the first beings ever created.

These fascinating and extraordinary creatures cohabited and roamed this One World's colossal and resplendent landscape. Nevertheless, it was not the magical earth nor the creatures that made this world so different from ours. The One World was alive.

It was its own creature. The beings walking its land were there because it allowed their existence. Just as a shark allows the tiny remora fish to clean its body from parasites, and in return protects them and allows them to eat scraps of food that float away, knowing that at any moment it could just change its mind and have a little snack.

Do not let this scare you or confuse you. This world was a fair world who kept the balance between all creatures, for this One World was old and knowledgeable and very, very wise. Some say it was the source of all life. It understood and respected all forms of life in ways that have escaped the most erudite of creatures to ever live in any world created after it.

There is no true knowledge about the quantity or the types of creatures that lived on this world. The only thing that can be said for certain is that there were three kinds of creatures: creatures with white magic, creatures with dark magic, and creatures with no magic at all.

Stories do not always evolve or end as we expect them to. In fact, because life always finds a way to move on, all stories have no end. And now I will tell you a part of the great secret that has been kept for generations: one way or another, we can be traced back to one of the creatures wandering on this One World!

Only a selected few knew and maintained this secret. Measures were put in place so that we only remember what is necessary. And there was never any collective knowledge of this original world, at least not among the humans. But in the end, all of us have more in common and are more connected than we realize.

But for now, let's not get ahead of the story. More will be revealed at the right time. In the meantime, let me share a little about these creatures.

CREATURES

Creatures with White Magic

As I told you before, in this One World, there were creatures with white magic, creatures with dark magic, and creatures with no magic at all. Saying there were creatures with white magic escapes one's lips almost too easily, making it seem ordinary. This couldn't be further from the truth. Thriving in this One World was the rarest and purest form of good. It was a raw goodness. And it was young. This is where the Yachaq, Krons, sylphs, dryads, pegacorns, Apotequils, wizards, and witches wandered free and lived in enchanted forests, mountains, and oceans.

Although magic was everywhere, and all creatures were surrounded with it, the One World granted an extra tiny portion of its magical dust to the creatures with the purest hearts and intentions. These special creatures were the One World's keepers—its Guardians. Blessed by this dust, the Guardians swore with their souls to protect this fantastic world. Most of the other creatures did not even know there was magic in the soil. And those few trusted white magical beings that had an inkling it was there did not know how to harvest it or how to use it. For years the Guardians ensured that it stayed that way—a secret.

The Yachaq, also known as white elves, were pure and majestic creatures with unearthly beauty. A true splendor within the One World. The white elves were stealthy in their movements and deep in their emotions. They were creatures of few words, with sharp features. Their hair trailed down their long lean bodies, broken only by their pointy ears and framing their brilliant eyes. Their bodies were built for speed. Their eye color reflected the color of their source power. An internal essence that tapped into a whirlpool of collective energy, this source power provided them access to a central fountain of information, feelings, and new abilities. Both their spirit and their power were deeply rooted in this whirlpool of energy.

There was a natural fellowship among the white elves. It strengthened when pairs or groups gravitated towards each other because of the style and the stealth of their speed. You see, it wasn't just any speed the white elves loved. It was *silent* speed that thrilled them. A velocity so high it eliminated sound. This kind of speed forced them to pay immense attention to every movement they made. And they loved the challenge of it. They loved being aware of all their muscles in order to control the strength with which they hit the ground and then furiously pushed off again to build to even higher speed.

Kunaq and Atik were best friends. They loved running side by side, helping each other go faster and quieter. They shared every detail of their experiences with each other. How it felt. The feel of the earth, the scent that rose from the ground as they pushed against it. The coldness of the air as they sped through it. And what they learned each time they ran.

It was this camaraderie that led them to higher and higher speeds. Not only were they fast, but they were looking for new ways to be silent. They explored quiet movements. Not by focusing on their bodies, but rather by focusing on speed and letting go of the very concept of a body, of weight, so they could run faster without noise. This technique they were creating together was the exact opposite of the traditional way the Yachaq quieted their steps. The unspoken rule was to remain absolutely focused on every single muscle movement, from the smallest of movements to the most complex and powerful.

It was Kunaq who was the first to feel and connect with the whirlpool of energy. By pure accident really. One morning, as a soft breeze blew a leaf off a tree they were standing near, Atik challenged Kunaq to a race by just looking at him and then at the gliding leaf. Kunaq bowed his head slightly, in acceptance.

Waiting for the leaf to touch the ground, both Atik and Kunaq turned to face the same direction. Their goal was to cross the pond on the other side of the forest without disturbing the giant phurus. Whoever did that would win. As you will learn later in the story, phurus were large ancient birds that were very sensitive. And when they were disturbed they would thrust their sharp beaks out from their necks in all directions. Phurus would attack blindly first and check to see if they really needed to later. An elf could get pretty badly hurt scaring a phuru.

A pocket of silence surrounded them as the leaf gently made its way down. As it settled softly on the ground, it sent out sound waves, like the ripples created when we drop a pebble in the water. Both elves felt the waves, which triggered their liftoff. They moved fast, barely disrupting the dry leaves or dirt on the ground. Kunaq was winning. He was not aware of it, since white elves live in the now. They do not pay attention to the "what could be" but only to the "what is."

He stopped feeling his body, letting go of his weight, breath, limbs, and heart. He was only left with what he felt within him—magic. And suddenly, looking inward, he tapped into the endless swirling energy that allowed him to sense everything and everyone. By connecting to this whirlpool of energy, he surpassed any of his best runs. And that day, Kunaq became the fastest creature in the One World.

He kept running, in the midst of a storm of images, emotions, voices, and thoughts. As these impressions organized themselves, he saw a silver energy image of his friend Atik running. Following his intuition, he used his purple source power to reach out to his friend. A glistening purple cord left from his source power, stretched out towards Atik, and touched his silver image. Immediately he felt what Atik was experiencing as he ran behind him.

"I will beat him this time!" In the whirlpool, Kunaq heard his friend's thoughts of trying to push through and catch up to him. He felt Atik's running style on his body. As he looked back, he saw his own puzzled face through Atik's eyes. He slowed down, and then noticed his own confused purple eyes shining brightly while Atik smiled and passed him. For a brief moment, Kunaq had received Atik's thoughts and running abilities.

He stopped. Breathing heavily, he closed his eyes and gathered his thoughts. He relived what had just happened, trying to make sense of what he had felt. Finally his breath slowed down. He was calm once more, for he had stopped thinking again and had remembered to just let go. With each deep breath, he engaged again the whirlpool within him. Then he opened his eyes. The purple in them flared. And he took off so fast a blurry essence of his body remained in place for a split second. He could still feel Atik's body in the whirlpool. As he let go, he gained Atik's abilities to run fast. Merging these abilities with his own, he increased his speed even more.

He catapulted past Atik, and looking back he saw the incomprehension in his friend's silver eyes: how could Kunaq be in front of him? This distracted Atik as he passed a mother phuru tending to her nest. His slight sound of surprise startled her. She let out a shriek that alerted all the nearby phurus. Then she thrust her beak towards Atik, who was focused once again —he needed to get out and get out fast.

Kunaq, now on the other side of the pond, realized what had just occurred. Still deeply connected to the whirlpool, he sent a mental message to his friend: *"Just let go, Atik. Let go completely. There is no body."*

He sent this message in the whirlpool via his purple cord, which was once again touching Atik's image. Atik's silver eyes flashed as he looked at his friend. Kunaq guided him to connect to his own source energy. As soon as Atik did, he and Kunaq ran as one. But Kunaq was standing still and Atik was evading frantic plunging beaks.

When Atik finally made it to the pond, he saw—through Kunaq's eyes— his own shimmering silver eyes. And at the same time he saw Kunaq's blazing purple eyes looking at him and smiling. It all made perfect sense. And it was because they had let go of tradition, of what they were taught to feel as normal. Letting go had elevated their powers. And now they would in turn teach all the Yachaq to truly let go of everything. To let go of their ways, their bodies, and their power. And to always welcome change.

For change would now be the Yachaq's new normal, the one thing that would remain forever so.

It was said—though debated by many—that this whirlpool of energy was similar to the tree roots that ran through the Magical Forest. They were all linked to one another beneath the One World's soil, connected to every- thing and everyone. Since the Yachaq were the first to learn how to tap into this internal energy fountain, the strongest and most direct route to the whirlpool lived within them.

The white elves could sense their enemy's weakness or their friend's strength. And the master elves could bond with someone else's energy line so profoundly they could mimic their power for a short period of time.

Because they were pure creatures with noble intentions, bonding to another being was done only if consent was granted or to save a life. Power was not at all important to the Yachaq; on the contrary, they thought it prevented change by anchoring them, weakening the purity and strength of their energy. So, they simply stayed away from mimicking the power of others.

What was clear was that all of the white elves were connected, sharing a vast depth of knowledge, fully aware of each other's energy and intentions. What was not clear, was how deeply they could connect to other beings.

Krons were not connected to each other the way the Yachaq were, but they wholeheartedly protected their kind. They were as big and as strong as a dragon and had humanoid features, long wavy hair, and slightly scaly but soft skin with golden undertones. They were divided into clans based on their skin color. There were eight colors: gold, blue, purple, red, orange, black, green, and silver. Their eyes were feline and the same color of their skin, which shone a lighter or darker tone based on their feelings. Their wavy hair was a different color than their skin—that of one of the other clans. It grew from their necks and backs as well as their heads.

Krons had small horns delineating their bodies—some even around their faces—which they could hide as they pleased and did so mostly during the day. A pure beast at night and almost human-like during the day. The tips of their chins and noses were very pointy, as if a horn had changed its mind and stopped growing. They had powerful tails and majestic wings. Eight massive claws grew on their strong leathery wings, starting near their shoulders and finishing about a foot from their torso, framing their entire wingspread.

Between each claw were razor-sharp scales. The Krons had full control of these scales, particularly during flight. They could turn their wings into powerful weapons in the air, capable of cutting through a mature tree just the way you and I would break a straw. When on land, they used their wings as capes by hooking them on the first claws. These capes made of wings then covered their muscular bodies, emanating a power that was as strong on land as it was on the air.

A golden Kron named Zarkon—the leader of all the clans—drove them to stand up for the innocent and to defend the One World. Zarkon organized the Krons within the clans based on their skills. By pure intuition, he taught them how to fight, to be strategic, and to focus. His heart was kind and his instincts to protect were strong, honest, and raw.

On a night when the three full moons were high, he saw a human child being tormented by a large warlock. He felt for the first time the urge to protect another life. Flying towards them, he picked the child up and while still in the air, he knocked the wicked warlock out far away with his tail. Then, he gently put the child down to let him go. The child's curly brown locks were all ruffled up from the flight and his eyes were wide open in excitement. He was ecstatic. He had actually flown! What a wonderful adventure!

Looking up at his rescuer, he signaled the golden giant to come closer. Zarkon, surprised, knelt down, curious to see what this little creature wanted. Then the child softly touched his blue hair and then the horns on his face, amazed by the softness of the scales on the Kron's skin. Finally, the child rested his eyes on Zarkon's green-gray cat-like eyes and smiled in gratitude. His smile was so broad and took up so much of his face, his rosy cheeks became as round as apples. After that, the child spun on his heels and took off, running and laughing and jumping in the air from sheer exuberance.

Still feeling the child's touch on his face, Zarkon's heart was so full of joy he felt the same rush he did when he flew. That was when he stumbled upon some yellow flowers. Without a thought, he fluttered his wings like a hummingbird and lifted off the ground, hovering in place. The power of his wings blew some pollen mixed with a few particles of the One World's magical powder into the air. The mixture whirled about while his body was suspended in the air. He was suspended right in the eye of the fair hurricane he had created, where the pollen and powder rapidly moved about. It became a yellow ribbon that dancing around him, getting closer and closer until he was covered by a golden blanket.

These particles pushed themselves into his skin almost intelligently, creating a golden undertone and immediately strengthening his muscles tenfold. He landed softly and felt the urge to eat some of the flowers. As he did so, his eyes shone golden for the first time. He became the only Kron whose eyes were not the same color as his skin. Now his body and his whole being became filled with the utmost strength, power, and love.

On the next night the three moons were full and high, all of the clans gathered in front of a field of gold. Zarkon taught the other Krons to eat nothing else but the flowers. Illuminated by the moonlight, they repeated what Zarkon taught them. They flew still, rapidly beating their wings, lifting particles in the air. As the golden pollen charged their muscles and their hearts, they sang in unison; they sang about protecting the innocent, about protecting the One World, and sang about love. It was a majestic sight!

From then on, with their new eyes, they were able to select the right flowers to eat and which ones to leave alone so more would grow. The flowers became extremely important for the Krons. Soon, if they stopped eating them their golden color would fade away and they would become too weak to fly. They would look more like giant lizards than the marvelous creatures they had become. For leading the Krons to their true nature, Zarkon became a Guardian.

This brings us to the sylphs. There were five sylph tribes, one from each of the five elements: air, water, fire, earth, and energy. These airy creatures had big eyes, bony sharp faces, and resembled humans but with three distinct differences. They had two translucent wings that sprang out from the middle of their backs. These wings looked delicate, glass-like. When they folded them against their backs, they would become invisible and disappear to the naked eye. Their hair revealed their element. And they were magical aerial creatures that could melt into their element.

Sylphs stood for nature, for justice, and for life—or rather living beings. The One World communicated with the sylphs through the five elements. As the One World's intent was to balance life, the sylphs were a means to carry this throughout its ecosystem. Though they were calm but playful, do not mistake them for fragile or weak creatures. Just as they were able to softly vanish in air, water, fire, earth, or energy, they were also able to manipulate their element and send strong gusts of wind, massive waves of water, fire bolts, giant boulders, and energy flares moving anything and anyone out of their way. They wielded their elements!

The air sylphs had fair skin, blue eyes, and fair hair that swirled like flowing locks of fog. Their wings looked like snow illuminated by sun rays. They were wind. They would vanish in a breeze, move fast without been seen, and reappear anywhere they wanted to go or the wind would carry them. That was something they particularly liked to do. To float with the wind, disappear, and travel through space, invisible to anyone. It was said that when you sigh, this meant that an air sylph had passed you by, without been noticed or felt, filling you with deep emotions of longing for love, a loved one, or home. They particularly protected and guided creatures that flew or lived in high altitudes.

Water sylphs preferred to live on, in, or near the water. Their skin glimmered with the different colors found inside a seashell, ranging from a pearly white to a deep purple. Their eyes changed colors, just as the seawater does, depending on how the sun hit them and on their internal mood. Their hair moved as if it were floating in the water, indifferent to the air, gravity, or wind—something the wind sylphs were not too happy with. When the water sylphs were not paying attention, they would send a quick gust of wind trying to move their hair one way or the other, but were never successful. If you ever feel a random gust of wind, it could be an air sylph trying to move the hair of a water sylph.

The water sylphs were able to disintegrate in any body of water and travel with the current to far, deep, and mysterious places. Interestingly, it was not important how much water there was or in which shape, they only needed one drop in order to disappear. If there were condensation droplets sliding on the wall, they could disintegrate into one of them, riding it to wherever they wanted to go. Some of the cold chills warning us of dangers can be attributed to the water sylphs, trying to guide us away from a scary situation. The water sylphs were tuned in with and ensured the safety and happiness of all water creatures.

Surprisingly, of all of the sylphs the fire sylphs were the calmest and the most in control. They were the tallest and strongest of the sylphs, almost Viking-like. They had powerful and defined muscles and sharp features, with reddish hair that ended up in small flames. Because mastering fire required full control of the mind and body, the fire sylphs had the best and most tolerant dispositions. Water and energy sylphs would run circles around them, playing tricks to try to get them to lose their temper, but to no avail.

All the sylphs of all the elements behaved almost like brothers and sisters, protecting each other, but driving each other crazy. The fire sylphs —fully aware when the mischievous water or energy sylphs were not paying attention—would send tiny fire spheres towards their behinds, making them jump up thinking an insect had bit them on the butt. Then they would look around to see who had done it, and would find the fire sylphs innocently meditating. They never suspected the fire sylphs were the culprits. As soon as they would turn back around, the corner of the fire sylphs' mouths would turn up slightly in a sly grin imperceptible by anyone who might be looking.

The fire sylphs guided and protected strong, big creatures whether they wielded fire or not, dragons being their particular favorite. Since the creatures they helped were big, most thought they did not need protection or guidance. But the fire sylphs knew that all living beings need help at some point in their lives, and were there for them.

With sharp, sometimes lumpy features, and eyes that resembled dry grass, the earth sylphs were the most balanced but the roughest looking of all the sylphs. Their long, occasionally spiky wild hair ended in what looked like hay, branches, vines, grass, or porcupines' quills. Their clothing was as wild as uncharted land, but helped them to camouflage in any environment, so well that they almost did not need to melt into dust, vines, trees, or rocks. On top of this, they were undetectable and left no footprints, so quiet and stealthy in their movements that it was impossible to hear them or spot them. If leaves were softly moved by a breeze, they would flawlessly resemble this while in hiding. This of course was an open invitation for the air sylphs to slow down the leaves' movements to a snail's pace, trying—to no avail—to see if they could knock the earth sylphs out of synch. The earth sylphs defended all earth creatures. As the One World was vast, there were more earth sylphs than any other kind.

The energy sylphs were good, had overall good intentions, but were the most mischievous of all of the sylphs. They loved playing tricks on... well just about everyone. When you touch someone and get shock, it is very likely that an energy sylph had something to do with it and may be giggling!

They were the least human looking, with gray almost translucent skin. Electricity flowed back and forth over the surface of their bodies, pulsing blue lines on their arms, neck, and faces. Their hair was an electric silvery white with sparks randomly exploding off the tips. If short, it would stick up in the air as static surged to its ends making it seemed they were standing up-side-down. Their eyes were a magnetic green, yellow, purple, or blue, softly flashing with every pulse, as if tiny flares of light reaching their eyes were feeding them power.

Never standing still, energy sylphs were constantly thinking about what to do next, always working on the next task. They guided and protected those with unique and strong powers. They understood energy. Energy in the One World was power...and power could lead some beings in the wrong direction. Sometimes the most powerful beings are the most confused and loneliest of creatures. The energy sylphs were there to help them when no help was asked, wanted, or given.

Sylph queens or kings ruled each of the elements, and guided their tribes to ensure balance and fairness was practiced across air, water, fire, earth, and energy. Each had a trusty right hand who led their strongest elemental sylphs to protect nature and all the living things within the One World's ecosystem.

Wayra was the queen of the air sylph and her second in command was Surux. He led the *air squadron* who patrolled the skies protecting its creatures.

Muyu was the king of the water sylphs, and his trusted leader was Mayu the strongest water sylph. He spearheaded the *wave squads* who were the protectors of all aquatic creatures.

The queen of the fire sylphs was Nina, and her right hand was Illapa; he was the head of the *five flames*, which rode on dragons and kept watch of all giant animals.

The earth sylph king was named Ut'u, and the head of the *seedling forces was* Tiksi. She ensured that all earthly creatures were safeguarded.

Micha was the queen of the energy sylphs, and Killa was her trusted confidant; he oversaw the *sparks crew* who looked after powerful creatures.

Surux, Mayu, Illapa, Tiksi, and Killa were the first sylphs to ever melt into their elements. This happened as they were all playing together when they were toddlers, before they could even speak. Their union was unequaled by most other sylphs, for they were selected by the One World and shared the same experiences. They were given the first right to pledge as Guardians of the One World.

Sylphs were purists. This meant that only sylphs from the same element could have a child. And they could have only one child. For centuries, this is how they strengthened their elemental powers. It was a rule that all sylphs happily followed. However, it came to pass that one pair of sylphs from different elements challenged those rules.

One day Qori, a member of the *air squadron*, closed her eyes as she decided to truly let the air guide her to where she was needed the most. While in mist form, she passed right through Ninan, one of the *five flames*, who was in the middle of a meditating session. Ninan breathed in Qori and opened his eyes for something inside of him had changed. Qori quickly realized what she had done. In shock, she softly moved apart from him, for she too was changed. Then Ninan whispered: "Do not go." And she found she did not want to move away from him either. In that moment, Ninan fell in love with Qori, and she loved him in return. They married in secret and had the first ever chimeras—mirror image twins from different sylphs tribes.

The chimeras looked exactly alike, but differed in their power. Ihxu was known as the nature sylph and had the combined powers of the water, earth and fire elements. Akiya was known as a sense sylph and had the combined powers of the air and energy elements. For breaking the only rule the sylphs imposed on themselves, the family was dishonored by the queens and kings. Still, they were included as part of the overall sylph family, because sylphs stood for all living beings and would never abandon one of their own.

But their love and union had repercussions for the leaders of their respective elements. Surux, the lead of the *air squadron*, and Illapa, the head of the *five flames*, each lost the privilege to pledge as part of the Guardians. It was decided that if they were not able to maintain tradition within their element, they could no longer be trusted to protect the One World. So in the end, only Mayu the lead of the *wave squads*, Tiksi the head of the *seedling forces*, and Killa, the leader of the *spark crew* became Guardians.

Unlike sylphs and the Yachaq, the tree nymphs were mostly seen alone. Known as dryads, they were majestic earthy creatures with hair made out of moss, a tree's crown, or leaves, deep heartfelt eyes, and elongated extremities. They moved slowly, with elegance and purpose, exuding an air of importance as they advanced steadily and with meditative movements. For all dryads took everything and anything around them into account. They were aware of activities and heard whispers that no others could, not even the Yachaq. And they would send whispers back to unexpected, yet eager ears.

Part of an inner circle that did not accept other magical members (at least, none that anyone had seen), dryads were very mysterious, but good and loving creatures. They were ancient, and possibly one of the first white magical creatures of the One World. Old songs tell the tale that, guided by the murmurs from the One World, they steered the creatures with white and black magic to find their powers.

The dryads had no concept of kings and queens. Four elder dryads oversaw the One World, as it was segmented into four regions.

Ruku the oldest oversaw the North. His chest looked like it was made of dark bark. His legs were covered with a cloak of grass, with tiny purple star-shaped flowers, and with shrubs. His yellow eyes were filled with age. From his head, the crown of a tree expanded outward as his hair. On it were there were leaves of vibrant yellow, brown, and green.

Paya oversaw the South. Like Ruku, her hair was also made from the crown of a tree, but its leaves were red, orange, and violet. Her long dress was made out of grey-blue and purple mossy lichens, her skin had a metallic green tone, and her eyes were icy blue and deep with emotion.

Uqi oversaw the West. His skin was of a dry ashen-white color. Smooth black bark covered his waist, elbows, and the top of his head. Dark, plain branches grew out of his head, fingers, and toes. The blackness of his eyes was as deep as his knowledge. However, do not let this or any color fool you, because he was a kind and gentle giant.

Mawk'a was the shortest of the four and oversaw the East. She was very lean and muscular and her hair was a huge, magnificent willow tree. Her eyes were a deep violet, full of joy and kindness. Small branches surrounded her neck. Curving downward, they grew thicker at her waist and twisted towards the floor like a flowing gown. This made it hard to distinguish between her legs and her garment of branches.

The elders would meet once every 33 years deep within the magical forest. They first connected their roots to share their experiences and what they had learned over the years. This meeting was a lengthy process that would take days and more, because after they shared with each other they connected with the roots of the Magical Forest's trees to pass along the information. It was at one of these gatherings that the elders decided that Mawk'a—the youngest of the four—would keep an eye on the efforts to ensure that the power of the One World would not be harvested by any of its creatures. She was to become a guardian.

Different from the raw and earthy beauty from the Dryads, the pegacorns were beautiful winged unicorns which used their horn to receive the magic from the One World. They provided beauty and merriment. Once you saw one, you were immediately filled with such a tremendous rush of happiness, you would cry out wildly or laugh out loud. After you regained control, you felt absolutely wonderful. And that was just from looking at them! If they allowed you to touch them... well, just imagine the most amazing feeling of pure joy and know that it would not compare to what that felt like. Pegacorns were incredibly strong. They would soar fast and nimbly through the sky at speeds far surpassing the dragons, the Krons, and the sylphs.

Even so, pegacorns were cautious creatures. Kawayu was the largest of the pegacorns and had the longest wingspan. For a long time, he led the pegacorns and taught them to stay hidden from all other creatures.

"The best way to survive is to trust no one," he would say.

Kawayu used his horn to camouflage himself, disappearing in plain sight. Or he would move any object to cover and conceal himself from the rest of the creatures. All other pegacorns followed his lead without questioning. And so they lived in hiding.

It came to pass that Unan, the smallest of the pegacorns, thought that they should not hide. But every time he tried to speak up, he was ignored or hushed. His small stature was like an invisible shield: others simply did not see him, and often spoke over him. But this did not discourage Unan, for it allowed him to keep to himself, and dare to show himself to the other creatures in the One World, without his fellow stopping him.

One day while he was out exploring, by accident, Unan ran into Urqu, the eldest dwarf clan leader.

The pegacorns had hidden for so long that at first Urqu did not recognize what he was seeing—a flying unicorn!

"I thought you were a myth," he half whispered once his memory recalled he had seen a pegacorn when he was but a youngster. Unan felt Urqu's stout heart, and realized that beyond the mountain of a wall that the dwarves put up as an invisible protective shield, deep inside, Urqu was a good creature. Indeed, he was not too different from the pegacorn's way of shielding themselves from the world.

For the first time, someone *saw* Unan. A small thread of happiness began to form within him and moved to his horn. His horn then shone a wonderful multicolored light, which in turn led to the first burst of laughter ever to come from a dwarf. It was a deep belly laugh and it was very contagious.

"What a wonderful thing it is to hear a dwarf laugh," thought Unan.

Urqu looked at the pegacorn, a smile still lingering on his lips, and he declared in amazement, "I heard you, my friend. I heard you in my mind."

Unan got close to the dwarf. And as a gift for hearing him, the little pegacorn touched a stone on one of his beard's braids with his horn. It turned instantly into a sparkling diamond. A new friendship was born and a new power discovered. The power to give joy.

When Unan returned to the pegacorns, he tried to tell them what had happened, but once again he was ignored—invisible. He looked at Kawayu and spoke to him with his mind. Immediately Kawayu hushed all other pegacorns and asked Unan to do this again. Filled with happiness, Unan's power grew, and this time all the pegacorns heard him at once. This automatically made him the new alpha of the herd. Kawayu willingly and with tremendous respect became second in command.

From that point on, two things happened. One, the pegacorns came out of hiding. Two, size and physical strength no longer ruled the pegacorns, but rather the ability to be heard and seen by other creatures. Unan taught the herd to speak inside other creatures' minds. They became so good at communicating telepathically, it felt as if they were speaking out loud. He also shared with the pegacorns his ability to create joy and happiness in others. This made Unan absolutely special.

Sometimes the small things are the ones that matter and can lead to big changes. The Apotequils were just that, the smallest of the white magical creatures. And they had power in numbers. Square heads framed their blue gem-like eyes. Their short square bodies had stocky limbs, with powerful arms that could carry potent spears. With unnatural speed, they could catapult their spears up into a cloud and instantaneously received the power of lightning. They could then guide it with their hands anywhere they aimed. In seconds, the Apotequils propelled rays that flashed as they blasted instantly whatever they touched.

Fast! The Apotequils were extremely fast and athletic as they ran up gigantic trees or boulders. Diving from the top, twisting and turning their bodies, they grabbed the spears descending from the clouds and ran again as if they had never stopped. Now, imagine hundreds upon hundreds of Apotequils coming towards you at once, shooting thousands of lightning rods. I would move away too! They were fierce lightning warriors, fighting for what was right, never giving up hope.

Khallma was the first Apotequil to command lightning. He was the youngest of 27 brothers and sisters (for the Apotequils this was a very small family) and always had to catch up to his older siblings. He was fast, but not the fastest; good, but not the best. One day, his oldest brother Q'axniy and his oldest sister Uskhay challenged all of their siblings to a fast-off. This year, Khallma had finally turned 15 years old and fast-offs could only occur when the youngest child came of age.

It was a two-day speed competition that took place in the Hulking Forest, which housed the largest and the fiercest of the non-magical creatures in the One World. In this competition, they had to pass through almost impenetrable and dangerous areas towards the center of the jungle where the giant trees lived, in order to capture their mother's first spear, known as the master spear. Master spears were only earned by winning a fast-off. The matriarchal master spear was one a mother had earned as a youngster; the patriarchal master spear was one earned by a father. It was almost impossible for one family to win a spear, and having two in one family was almost unheard of.

However, there were two spears in Khallma's family. This meant that two of the 27 children in his family could earn a master spear. All of the family members were excited about this event and the siblings teased each other about who was going to win the matriarchal spear. About who was the fastest, jumped the farthest, was the most agile, or the best gymnast. However, even though they loved Khallma, not one of them considered him as true competition, for he was the youngest, and it was very rare for the youngest sibling to win a master spear. They mostly disregarded him, always passing off errands from their parents to him, laughing.

He was sad, frustrated, and particularly mad at himself for not being faster. One of the biggest shames you could carry as an Apotequil was being the last in anything. His mother supported and encouraged him, though. She too was the youngest of 55 siblings, and yet had won the master spear.

While running the unwanted errands, Khallma would practice in private, away from his brothers and sisters. Leaping each time through higher obstacles. Running faster. Twisting and turning his body to get through impossible places. But still, he felt he was nowhere near Q'axniy's and Uskhay's abilities. The history told by the Apotequil's paintings on the Hulking Forest was that the majority of the time, it was the oldest siblings who won the spears. Knowing this pushed Khallma even further away from feeling he could win. Sometimes in the One World, a feeling is all you need to make things happen.

During one of these errands, while practicing twisting and turning his body to make it through an almost impossible space, he miscalculated. He fell hard on the ground, hurting himself. He lay on the grass, stunned, watching the clouds as they gathered above him, feeling small.

"Hmm! It is about to rain," he thought, imagining himself as the last one in the competition, the utmost feeling of sadness and failure filling him.

Raindrops touched his face, cooling his body and softly soothing the pain that had started to fill his heart. He remembered his mother's story of how she won the master spear and a small but hopeful smile formed on the corner of his mouth. A new feeling had emerged. But something made the experience of hope and encouragement feel extraordinary!

There was something different about these raindrops! Each one seemed filled with tiny electric bolts. When the raindrops hit his tough skin, the bolts seeped through and entered his body. Suddenly he knew he would *never* give up. In a flash, he jumped to his feet and forced the air out of his lungs, screaming "Noooo!!!!"

He refused to give up. When he breathed deep and filled his lungs with air again, his whole body was completely recharged, and so strong he took off, fast. As he ran, he noticed that the raindrops were slower than usual. That's when he realized he was running faster than he ever had before. Impulsively, filled with electric intent, happiness, and power, he grabbed a stick and threw it as hard as he could up into the clouds without missing one step or lowering his speed.

The stick pierced through a cloud, and as he felt a surge of excitement for what he had accomplished, a ray of lighting shot right back at him with tremendous force. His arms swung by reflect up to protect him, and instantaneously he felt a lighting pulse on his hands—lightening sparks were bouncing on his palms. This deflected it to the side, where it shocked the nearest giant tree while the stick bounced on the ground nearby.

Khallma was in awe! He lost his footing, which resulted in the craziest wipeout ever. He could not believe it! He had made and moved lightning! And he wanted to do it again! Which he did—many times. He returned home thrilled, exhausted, and bruised. And ready for the competition.

On the day of the competition, his siblings pushed him to the back of the line. They assumed that not only was he going to lose, he was going to place last. Once their mother uttered the fast-off tribal call, the oldest siblings dispersed and ran out towards the Hulking Forest without looking back, completely disappearing from sight. Out of habit, Khallma ran the old way, and was quickly left behind by his brothers and sisters.

For a moment, he thought that everything that happened was a dream. Shaking his head and exhaling, he stopped, closed his eyes and then took a deep breath. He remembered the exhilarating joy he felt before. A half smile filled with hope peeped on his lips. And then he saw his palms flash. He made a fist as he felt the energy of the clouds above him in his hands. And then he took off. He ran fast. Easily reaching and passing his siblings, who could not believe their eyes when they recognized that it was Khallma who passed them. Nor could they comprehend that it was he who threw spears that encircled and closed them in, preventing them from moving forward.

All the while, Q'axniy and Uskhay were having their own internal competition. They ran in parallel, and jumped at impressive heights when they realized that something was happening to their siblings behind. When they noticed that Khallma was near, they tag-teamed to ensure that he did not pass them. They threw large branches to block his path and let vines loose so he could get tangled. As if that were not enough, they sent big boulders down his way, or provoked colossals and sent these now furious creatures lumbering ferociously in his direction. These obstacles surprised Khallma, for he did not expect this from Q'axniy and Uskhay.

He didn't pause at all. Jumping an impressive height, he landed heavily on a tree, which broke off several sticks that he immediately picked up and shot into the clouds. Ten lightning rods shot back towards him at once. With majestic dance-like movements, he sent them into the path in front of his oldest sister and brother. Out of sheer shock, they stopped short. He glided past them, steadfast. He reached the center of the Hulking Forest in less than a day.

That day he changed the life of the Apotequils forever. He changed the fast-off to a lightning competition where age did not matter, and taught them how to wield a spear, transforming them into lightning warriors. Through all of this he was known as the last Apotequil to earn a master spear and the only one who could wield more than ten lightning rods at a time.

Wizards and witches also called the One World their home. They were very similar, but the few differences they did have were so pronounced that they considered themselves to be two separate species. You can understand this by thinking about the appearance of the stars. They seem the same from afar, but once you see them up close through a telescope, you realize that one is red and another is blue. And, if you had the power to see through the galaxies, you may observe that the red star was a cold planet and the blue star was a hot sun. Then and only then you can indeed confirm that these stars were nothing alike.

What the witches and wizards had in common was the look and flow of their magic. What was different was where this magic was summoned from.

With an out-in-out motion, the wizards would feel the magic in their environment, surrounding their skin. They would pull this bright white-blue thick gel inwards towards the center of their body and then redirect it out of their hands. When the wizards connected with their magic, their skin would glow as if touched by the moment.

On the other hand, the witches had an in-out motion. They would feel the magic in their core, and would push this wet white-blue light out from their hands. Their magic would illuminate their centers as if they were giving birth to it.

Once the magic reached the witches' or the wizard's hands, it would either dance from their palms creating fascinating and captivating spells or it would shoot out like darts of enchantments. Both had a unique connection with their magic and loved it as if it were family. In return the magic would sometimes caress their faces or their hair, or circle their bodies as they softly whispered a spell, breathing in its power, love, and intention. It was as if they spoke to it and it spoke back to them and what was said or shared was known only by them and maybe the One World.

Now, the funny story is that both the witches and the wizards found their magic at the same time; however, it happened under completely different circumstances.

All wizards appreciated their surroundings, but it was the wizard Benowit who first saw, really *saw* the beauty around him. His gentle brown eyes sensed more than the images that manifested in his brain. A glow flickered on the surface of everything and anything he laid his eyes on. Whispers emerged and engulfed his ears, silencing his thoughts. One day, attracted by what he saw, he walked impulsively towards a young leaf on the nearest tree. Softly, he reached his tawny index finger towards its glow. Immediately he felt it giggle. In reflex, he folded his finger away from the leaf. He smiled, ran his fingers through his curly brown hair, and when he reached again, he heard a soft hum.

The glowy substance changed shapes and hugged the tip of his finger, illuminating his whole hand. The light moved up his arm, along his neck, and then covered the rest of his long body. It felt much the way goosebumps do, running from one side of your forearm, down your back, to your whole body in less than a second. Closing his eyes, he lifted his head and let his whole body be filled with sensational magic. He then proceeded to gather it in and automatically let it flow out through his hands, and his spirit soared. The magic landed on a rock. He raised it up from the ground simply by looking at it, laughing because this was exactly what he had pictured in his mind.

At that same instant a few leagues away, a witch named K'antu was walking with her two daughters, Saywa and Urpi. They were having a wonderful loving time, when all of the sudden, Urpi accidentally tripped and fell in the funniest and most awkward way. The slow-motion way. And she made several crazy faces on the way down, while unsuccessfully preventing the fall. All of them started to laugh. Especially Urpi, who was laughing so hard that no sound was coming out of her mouth. Urpi then took a deep loud breath, her face a reddish-purple, and let out a loud crackle which made them all laugh even harder. At that instant, as K'antu watched her daughters rejoice in the moment, she felt such level of joy and love inside of her that her heart began to glow within her chest.

She felt and sensed the glow inside of her. Embracing her, connecting with her, and speaking to her without words. Her eyes were in a glaze and her mouth stayed frozen in a smile. Without knowledge or thought of what she was doing, she gathered even more of this blissful feeling inside of her, nurturing it with more love. As it grew, her core lit up more and more.

Once it reached a level where her daughters, now in awe, thought her mother was going to explode, K'antu raised her hands and in a tender way let this beautiful glowing gel flow out. As it did, it burst into a powder. Then it changed into hundreds of white butterflies and birds that swirled around the young witches, who were now smiling in amazement. This all happened while the echo of Urpi's crackle could still be heard.

The birds and butterflies flew towards the heart of the Magical Forest and all three witches followed them. This winged white magic found Benowit's floating rock and began to swirl around it. Both—the glow around the rock and the birds and butterflies—seemed to be made of the same material. Benowit noticed K'antu's hands were still glowing and real-ized that his own looked the same. He smiled at K'antu. While K'antu's daughters danced with the birds and butterflies, a new friendship was born between the wizards and witches. Both K'antu and Benowit taught the other wizards and witches how to connect with the powers that lived deep inside them or surrounded all living beings in the One World.

As time passed, the white magical creatures grew in their powers and learned to live with one another. One unexpected day, the One World sent out a message through the dryads that each white magical creature was to select a representative to join a secret summoning. Each species wisely selected the members who had discovered their primary powers. After all, these powers were in truth gifts from the One World. It was during this beckoning that the Guardians were formed.

It was a fellowship of ten. Kunaq represented the white elves, Zarkon the Krons, Mayu the water sylphs, Tiksi the earth sylph, Killa the energy sylph, Mawk'a the dryads, Unan the pegacorns, Khallma the Apotequils, K'antu the witches, and Benowit the wizards. Benowit became the strongest voice within the Guardians. In a sacred oath ceremony, the ten creatures pledged solemnly with their lives to protect their One World and its creatures. And to ensure that no creature would ever harvest its power.

For many, many years, the One World was at peace under the Guardians' watchful care. For a long time, the Guardians felt very content and happy that peace presided over this world. But then, as time passed and the peace continued, they began to become complacent. Too comfortable. Too trusting. They started patrolling the same places, the same creatures, and the same regions. The Guardians let their guard down.

And that was dangerous. Because there were many, many creatures who wanted what the guardians had. Who were not content with just the magic that came with their species. Who wanted to learn to steal extra magic from the One World. And as you may know, when creatures want something that another has but they do not, they are far more patient, more crafty, and more astute in their quest to obtain it than the other creatures might be to protect what they have. They never let their guards down, because they crave what they don't have. They watch and learn and experiment over and over and over until they perfect their abilities to steal or take by force that which they so desperately want.

Because of this danger, two more Guardians were called to pledge to protect their world—in secrecy so any creatures who might try to betray the One World would not know about them. They were not selected by their kin, did not participate in the oath ceremony with the ten, and were not formally part of the fellowship. For they would have to face many challenges in order to keep their oath a secret even from the ten Guardians. They would have to find out about the Guardians' plans, support them without been noticed, and follow their hearts. When tasks were hard, grasping tightly the rope of hope was the true connection that bound them to the One World.

The chimera twins, Ihxu and Akiya, were the two secret Guardians! And now I will tell you how it came to be.

The twins grew up fast, were kind, humble, and extremely powerful. They truly stood for all living beings and did nothing but protect those who needed them. The One World always kept a close eye on them. They were beautiful, but their beauty was not just internal. It could take your breath away just to see them. Nonetheless, few sylphs dared to speak to them because of what they represented, and what they carried—impure sylph blood and powers.

Pusaq, an energy sylph, liked to pull pranks on as many creatures as he possibly could in a single day; then, every day he tried to beat his record from the day before. He kept Ihxu quite busy for several years. As a nature sylph, she knew how this made other creatures feel, and desperately tried to help those poor creatures. Sometimes she would move the earth or a branch, shifting the position of the creatures so that Pusaq would miss. This only inspired him to pull more pranks. This went on for years. One day she decided enough was enough.

"I am going to stop this now," she said to Akiya, while Pusaq zigzagged his way around, shocking all on his path and leaving hairless scorched patches on many of the creature's butts. For the first time she sent large items to stop him on his tracks. Now Pusaq had to avoid boulders and earth mounds coming his way. He was loving it! It just made the game more fun for him!

Exasperated, Ihxu sent mini sandstorms, powerful gust of winds, and balls of fire. To no avail. He was fast.

"You need help?" Akiya asked a bit mockingly.

"No" she barked back. "I just … need … to figure out … where … he will be …next!" With every other word she heaved stones, tree stumps, water sprays, and fire spears towards Pusaq. Who was having a blast annoying Ihxu.

"Argh!" Akiya raised her eyebrows at Ihxu. "Sensing his next move here," she said a bit annoyed. "I can help," she sort of sang the last bit.

"I just need to relax," Ihxu said out loud to herself, ignoring her sister. She closed her eyes and took a deep breath. Pusaq saw this exquisite moment and took full advantage, realizing that he had never shocked Ihxu before. He sent an almost turquoise ray towards her derrière. She jumped so high, still with her eyes closed, and reached out with her left hand trying to grab onto anything to prevent the monumental fall that would happen next.

Pusaq just laughed and sped up his zigzag.

On her way down, Ihxu inadvertently touched Akiya's arm. In that instant, she linked with her sister's power and sensed Pusaq's next move. A branch from the colossal forest smacked Pusaq and he flew out of the way. Ihxu fell to the ground.

"Ahh!" All three said at the same time, but with different meanings.

Akiya was pleased, for she had also felt Ihux's power and connected with the branch that struck Pusaq. Like swapping an annoying fly, at first Ihxu was elated that she had finally taken Pusaq down. When that emotion subsided, she realized that she had actually connected with Pusaq and sensed what and how he felt. And Pusaq was pleasantly surprised that Ihxu had finally caught him.

"Good catch!" he said, smiling at her. She just looked at him, still processing what had happened.

"I am Pusaq." He extended his hand to help Ihxu up.

"I know," she said, looking at the blue nails on his hands. It was the same turquoise color that shadowed his zigzags. She took his hand.

"I am Ihxu."

"I know."

Smiling, he noticed green specs in her golden eyes and tiny freckles on her nose. From that point on they became inseparable friends. A friendship that over the years grew into a powerful and pure love for one another.

When Pusaq married Ihxu, his family were suddenly too busy to see him. And when they had their daughter Azel, his family stopped speaking to him. Azel was special. A beautiful, new kind of sylph, with larger wings and the ability to master all five elements.

For Akiya things were, well, different. Her powers allowed her to sense what her kin really thought of her, her sister, and her parents. She was confused, hurt, and sad. As a child, her kin disappointed her. This caused her to shut down all her sensing links to any sylphs outside of her family.

When she was not with Ihxu—which was rare—she was vanishing in the next breeze, floating and connecting with the One World, whose love she never had any cause to doubt. It was almost like turning on multiple channels, all on different frequencies, creating a pure and relaxing white noise. It was during one of these floats that she wandered off far into the Southern Seas.

Filled as she was with the power of the energy sylphs, water was not the best element for her to be surrounded by. Water makes the energy sylphs nervous. Some energy sylphs had electrocuted themselves when they had too much fun near water, leaving energy sparks on their hair as a reminder not to do it again. Akiya's strength was rooted more in her energy powers, and only recently had she learned to vanish with the air.

In her nervousness, Akiya started to sense around for some help. By mistake, she called on large water creatures, which translated her cry for help as the location signal of a potential meal. Luckily, she could catch the breeze these creatures made while jumping out of the water with their mouths open, and vanish just in time. But there were too many of them jumping too fast and too often for her to escape entirely.

Like swimming to shore and getting trapped in a set of waves so that as soon as you are able to come up for air, another wave is about to crash down on you. Akiya was caught between each creature's jumps. She had barely seconds to vanish before the next one would sense her and jump in her direction. This relentless rhythm did not allow enough time for her to focus on her sensing or on her vanishing skills in order to do more than momentarily avoid getting eaten.

In desperation, not knowing how many more cycles she could take, she sent her last cry for help to her sister. But it was not Ihxu who answered. Qucha, a water sylph who tended the large and more aggressive aquatic animals, rushed to her aid. With one wave of his hand, he created an enormous barrier around Akiya that the creatures could not swim. Next, he hummed strange tunes to them. Hearing his music, they immediately ceased their hunting.

Like Akiya, Qucha was a teenager. Fearless and fully attuned with these wild animals. He saw her— a chimera—and helped her because this is what sylphs were about. A purist, yes. But he stood for justice and life, and she was fighting for her life. She immediately understood his honest love for life, and in that instant, she loved him and what he represented. He recognized all that she was in her young life—her love, fear, vulnerability, and her wild power. He loved her instantly, and this love only grew as she became older and conquered her powers and most of her fears.

When they were older, he wanted to marry her and have a family. But that was the one fear she could not defeat.

Akiya's natural tendency to help, to enjoy life as it is forever evolving and unfolding, and to create balance in the One World was stronger than following silly rules set by creatures who were blinded by these same rules. The thought that any sylph could segregate and reject another sylph baffled her. It hurt her tender heart.

She knew that marrying Qucha would once again unleash these unpleasant feelings among the sylph tribes. She did not want to feel these emotions once more. She was already worried that her lovely niece Azel would find out and be deeply hurt the way she and Ihxu had been when they were young. So instead, she created an invisible energy field around Azel, to ensure that she would only feel the love and kindness coming towards her and their family, and never the judgement and hostility and fear of difference.

Then, she vowed to herself that she would never marry Qucha, but would always be by his side.

Both sisters continued to love and grow and expand their powers. They practiced in hiding, venturing sometimes far from their tribes to prevent any purist sylph from seeing them. In the One World, there was always one adventure happening after the other. So there was always an opportunity to put what they had practiced to the test.

One day, in the Hulking Forest, they came across a phuru that had wounded and was continuing to attack a dark elf who had been unkind to the giant bird. The dark elf was lying beneath the hysterical bird, unconscious as it kept savagely pecking at him. Ihxu calmed the bird down and guided it away from the dark elf while Akiya sealed the wounds with her energy. The dark elf woke up, and seeing the two sylphs next to him, he sent a pulsing sphere of dark earth to push them away.

He ran away from them but did not make it very far. His wounds were many and deep, and infected by the phuru's deadly saliva. After only a few feet he stumbled, and then fell to the ground. The chimeras ran to the elf and told him to stay still. Ihxu used her power to raise pure water from the depths of the One World's earth and Akiya used her energy to seal the wounds after she used air to cool down the pain and blow away the bacteria from the phurus' saliva. When the twins had finished their work, the wounds were gone.

The dark elf looked at them in silence as dust particles began to float in the air. He then jumped to his feet. Without a word nor looking back he ran fast as he could, away from the twins. Ihxu and Akiya looked at each other and smiled.

"Thank you, kind ladies for saving my precious and beautiful life," Akiya said to Ihxu mockingly.

"Well, you are most welcome affable dark elf," Ihxu answered, bowing. And they both laughed as they turned to walk back to their home.

Suddenly, a soft breeze caressed their hair. The chimera twins stopped walking and looked at each other. This was something that had happened to them since they were little kids. A breeze that made them feel great, loved, and connected to all creatures. They smiled and closed their eyes while the breeze softly blew on them, as if thanking them for their good deed. Then, they heard a quiet whisper. They both opened their eyes and looked at one another.

"That is new," said Akiya. Ihxu nodded.

The whispers grew louder, and soon they could feel the sound vibrating from the ground. They both kneeled, for now they knew it was the One World speaking to them.

"You must join the Guardians, and you must do this without them knowing," it said in its deep and airy whisper. "You must protect."

Ihxu and Akiya both nodded. Then and there, without question, they vowed to protect the One World and all its living creatures. They both knew that this request must be kept a secret and they also knew that this would be a challenge.

For now, there were twelve Guardians!

Creatures with Black Magic

As I told you earlier, dark magic also lived in this One World. And it was evil! The creatures with dark magic were as truly young and naïve as the ones with white magic. But the dark ones were impatient, and thirsted to expand their powers. They wandered the lands of the One World, scheming ways to reign, and particularly to control the Guardians. No matter how much these dark ones had stretched the boundaries of their freedom, the Guardians had managed to keep them under control. And this infuriated them.

These evil beings filled the spaces they called home with dark magic and cursed the land they lived on. They were always looking for an easy way to get more power, to rule, to command darkness, and to destroy the joy that filled all living creatures, especially the Guardians. They loathed the Guardians.

The most powerful of the dark creatures were the mist & water demons, the dark elves, the warlocks, the sorceress, and a vampire. These foul creatures personified the five elements of the One World: air, water, earth, fire, and energy.

Before I tell you more about them, I must warn you that darkness feeds on fear. So do not let any of these creatures scare you. For all creatures, good or evil, have a weakness.

Air was embodied by Phuyu, a mist demon that enjoyed controlling anything it was able to enter. A puppeteer. It would penetrate your mind by slithering its way through your nose, mouth, or ears. Not just to eat, but for fun, or to extract secrets or important information. While this illicit transaction took place, it would put you in a deep slumber, subjecting you to the most terrifying nightmares but still conscious of its commands. You had no choice but to lay still, very much like the effect a spider's venom has on its victims. Alive. Unable to move. Feeling everything that is happening to you.

Phuyu liked showing its prizes to its fellow dark creatures. Its airy tentacles would expand towards their heads. He displayed in their minds what it had just obtained, precious secrets, and the excruciating torment of his victim. The evil ones all seemed to enjoy this form of entertainment very much.

There was abundance in the One World and plenty of land to go around for all creatures. Yet Phuyu was born when two angry giants were fighting for land. They were greedy, and each sought to control and overpower the other. Their battle raged on for days, destroying the terrain around them because they both wanted something the other had. When they planted their feet on the ground, they left wells instead of footprints. Each flying fist that missed a face would leave holes on boulders. Throwing each other against the trees of the Hulking Forest, ripping the smaller ones from the earth and exposing their roots. These became weapons they swung with extreme force landing on white knuckles, jaws, or backs. The more they fought, the more blind and enraged they became.

In the midst of all the chaos and movement, they both saw a clearing, an opening for one final blow. With thunderous steps, these titans ran with all of their might towards each other. Sweat raining from their faces, arms, and backs as they drew back their arms, hands in a fist. Two synchronized hook punches parted the air in front of their faces and landed on their jaws. Massive powerful circular airwaves exploded outward, causing the hulking trees to bend backwards.

This was the last strike that ended the fight. And their lives. The force of it triggered an earthquake on the western Rocky Mountains. All of the dragons took flight as large rocks broke off, creating a massive avalanche of stone.

The giants used such strength in their last punch, that while their bodies lay still on the ground, their muscles continued to unleash waves of heat and energy. This rapidly evaporated the sweat on their skins, releasing a mist that hissed as it was born. Their death gave birth to Phuyu.

At first, Phuyu was small. A tiny thin cloud, no bigger than a human child. The first animal it saw was a colossal spider. He sped towards the eight-legged giant and entered it through its head, absorbing the spider's memories and fears. As Phuyu expanded into different parts of the animal, he realized that the more afraid the animal was the more control he had. First were the spider's eyes. Phuyu moved all of its eyes in one direction, to look at what he wanted to see. Next he experimented with the spider's fangs, using them to drip venom. And lastly, he bent one of the spider's legs backward until it broke in an awkward place.

When the mist demon had played enough with the hapless spider, he laughed and poured out of the spider's mouth like noxious fumes. He had doubled in size and thickness. With deep satisfaction, Phuyu lingered frozen into that shape, drifting on a breeze away from the terrified giant spider. He now realized he could take any shape or thickness it pleased, and he could control his victims as he fed on their fear and pain. And he realized one more thing: Phuyu was hungry!

In the same way that Phuyu lurked in the air, shapeshifting demons called Yaku lurked in the water. While the Yaku were in the ocean, river, or pond, they looked like a large snake. On land, they shapeshifted into different animals that could be mounted, so they could carry their victims to the water. Once these creatures were near the water—close enough to smell it or hear it—their skin would release a yellow sticky muck, gluing their victims to their bodies. Then they conjured an orb of water that would float in the air, and command it to cover the head of their prey and drown them. Once their prey was dead, then they would drag it into the depths of the water to devour them.

The Yaku preferred humans as a meal, particularly pretty young women. So they developed the ability to shapeshift into a handsome young man to attract and trap some of the most beautiful maidens. For this reason, peasants were always suspicious of strange men or animals near water, particularly if they had unusual amounts of sand or wet clay on their hair.

The Yaku were born out of pure disgust. Here is how it happened. One day, a beautiful young hunter was near the soft waves on the shores of the Southern Sea, cleaning the tip of a spear she had just carved by the edge of the Magical Forest. She was proud of her work and extremely happy that she had found a strong branch from the Magical Forest. Obtaining good hunting material from the Magical Forest guaranteed a meal, as it was told that this forest would always provide exactly what was necessary to those with urgent needs.

Unbeknownst to her, a deformed green snake was watching her closely. It looked like it had not eaten in a long time. It was extremely long with bumps and swellings that oozed a yellow, smelly liquid. Its deep purple tongue vibrated in the air as it hungered for the human. As it slithered closer to her, a leaf gently brushed one of the lumps on its body. The lump instantly released a foul odor as a yellow substance erupted from it. This killed all of the leaves nearby.

She smelled the snake before she saw it. Its smell and appearance repulsed her, causing cold goosebumps to rise on her skin. She covered her nose and mouth with her hand, but this did not prevent her from expelling the breakfast she had eaten a few hours earlier. As she was doubled over vomiting, the snake launched itself towards her, its smelly yellow goo spraying the surrounding area. Just in time, she looked up, saw the snake, and grabbed her spear. Out of pure disgust, she stabbed the snake in midair through its mouth before it could touch her. This kept the yellow spray away from her. But the smell of it all repulsed her even more. She ran into the waves and cast her spear with the beast impaled on it as far as she could.

At first its shiny blood tainted the shore like a green blanket. But soon after, the blood separated into long tiny droplets while the snake and the magical spear floated on the salty waters. Each droplet slowly morphed into what appeared to be smooth beautiful snakes. Eyes appeared on each of them. Then they awoke and moved about, admiring their own bodies and each other. Elegantly dancing by the large snake's body (their father) and the spear (their mother), they soon learned to change their appearance in order to catch a meal. The magical branch had transformed the hungry deformed snake into multiple beautiful hunters.

Tuj led the Yaku and was their best hunter. You can think of him as the head of the snake, since they were all pieces of the original deformed giant snake. They embodied the many that come from one. When one hunted and fed, they all experienced not only the hunting process but also the power that came from feeding. They learned quickly from each other, which made them masterful and powerful hunters. The more they fed, the stronger they all grew.

Tuj was sharp and had a cunning tongue. When shaped like a human he was a very attractive young man. He could convince the most headstrong maiden to elope with him, for he would promise love, a better life, protection, safety, and a family. He propelled emotions as deep as the Southern Seas towards his victim—almost palpable, projecting warmth and love. In truth, they were skin deep splinters that barely prickled his surface. He loved and care for nothing else but the Yaku.

Do you remember me telling you about the Yachaq? The white elves? They had a twin species. But these were as evil as the white elves were good. Laqha—the dark elves—roamed the dark earth of the One World. By nature, they were as beautiful as they were cruel and vicious. Stealthy loners, they preferred to drift on the shadows, ready to attack any living creature mercilessly. Shallow dark creatures with empty emotions, they ruled the dark forest and tarred its spirit with their very presence. The dark elves liked to talk about themselves, and they talked a lot. Their egos were so big they could almost be considered a separate being.

The Laqha were very well known for injecting fear into their prey while they expressed, in long monologues, how wonderfully terrifying they were. Their entire eye would turn dark when they were pulsating their power. It was gray shadowy dust. It disconnected their victims from their own life source energy, leaving them dry, lonely, and empty until it eventually killed them.

The Laqha looked just like the Yachaq, except they had light to deep ash-blue colored hair and hollow, opaque blue eyes. And now I will tell you the story of how the Yachaq and the Laqha came to be, and why they were so different from each other.

When the One World was very young, two creatures manifested in the middle of the Magical Forest. Male and female. Newborns. But already fully grown. They lay on the ground, with closed eyes, their feet barely touching, their faces only a breath apart.

A ray of light illuminated the female's body; the male's body was blanketed by a shadowy veil. They both opened their eyes at the same time. She saw a beautiful creature in front of her and immediately loved him. He saw a fair creature in front of him and immediately loved her.

Both knew at that moment that they belonged together, they were whole together, and must always be together. They raised their hands and touched each other's faces. He felt her soft skin. As she touched him, a spark of light from her hands started to lift the shadow on his face, filling his cheek and her hand with warmth. They both smiled. He saw how much more magnificent she looked when she smiled, and was amazed by her beauty.

Gazing into her light purple eyes he saw reflected his own face being freed. Her light released his shadow. His thoughts shifted from her beauty to his own. When that happened, the dark veil around him grew denser. It began to emit gray particles that looked like dust. Suddenly jealous of her fairness, he pushed her hand away. Her light on his face froze in place.

She saw more and more gray particles dance around him. She tried to touch him once again but his eyes became opaque. He turned his focus inward. As if by his sheer will, the dust particles gathered into a sheet that grew as it pulsated out from his body. Towards her.

Feeling the dust approach, her body expelled a sphere of light just as the last pulse was about to engulf her. Both powers crashed against one another. The explosive force of the collision propelled them away from each other. It dried up the forest where they were lying and created the great Aqu desert. This divided the Magical Forest in two. She was pushed deep into the southern portion and he was pushed far into the northern portion.

From that point onward, she was known as Achkyi. Even though her deep loneliness never fully left her, the Magical Forest comforted her. She felt loved and was accompanied by the life in the forest. Only one tear escaped her eyes. And this is how another white elf was born. Sut'u came to be Achkyi's companion and together they became the source of the Yachaq —the white elves—in the One World. Achkyi became the Queen of all the Yachaq.

His solitude and jealousy were so strong that rather than letting the Magical Forest heal him and return him to Achkyi, he continued expanding the dust flowing from his body. He dimmed the magic, engulfed the light, and left only dark magic in the northern forest. From that point, he was known as Uspha.

He turned into darkness the last remaining green leaf in the northern forest with such extreme satisfaction, it grew into another dark elf known as Yana. Yana had a darker essence than Uspha and every one of their offspring—the Laqha—had a darker and darker soul. This pleased Uspha, for it allowed him to control them and made him seem better, almost more beautiful. The darker they became, the more disconnected and evil they were, and the more power he had over them. With this power, the dark elf proclaimed himself the Dark Elven King, master of the Dark Forest, and ruler of the Laqha.

Just as the Laqha propelled magic from their bodies, the warlocks and sorceresses did too, but with minimal conscious effort or thought. Fire. This magic would seep mostly from their hands—a dark, thick, shapeless fiery liquid that they could send anywhere and touch anything with. Just as you might scratch an itch without even thinking twice about it—moving your hand and rubbing your skin immediately satisfying a voiceless request —they would lift their hands oozing black energy to satisfy a dark wish. As their wishes grew, so did their power.

One night as they all gathered around a fire pit, one warlock began gazing absent-mindedly at the flames. You see, fire has an unexplained attractive quality. The more you look at it, the more you are enchanted by it and the more you continue to stare. This was what happened to the warlock. And as he stared, without him even thinking about it, his dark shiny magic slithered towards the fire and touched it. Immediately, this fluid black snake acquired a golden shimmer. It grabbed part of the fire and raised it high against the dark night as if it were a mere bubble you could catch with your bare hands and blow away.

The warlock began to see what he could make the fire do. He changed it into different shapes. Each more complex than the last. First, the fire transformed into a simple sphere. Then a tree. Then a hammer that chopped the tree down and into planks. And then a boat made out of the fallen tree. Finally, he created the giant head of a ferocious lizard-like creature that swallowed the boat. He finished the spell with a dark blast of golden stardust.

All the other warlocks were in awe, including him. By accident, they had just discovered how to enhance their powers tenfold. In the beginning they used fire spells to guard their terrain by creating green, translucent fiery curtains. This prevented the Guardians from sensing what these dark creatures were doing and learning. Not too long after, they learned to suffocate and disintegrate life—even happiness.

The longer they used their magic, the stronger the warlocks and sorceresses became, and the more power they craved. They competed for absolute power, but the Guardians were always nearby to put a halt to their schemes. This infuriated the warlocks and the sorceresses.

Because he was the first to control his fiery magic, the originator of this fiery magic was superior to all others, and made himself their leader. Anyone who challenged him...well after a few tries that resulted in fewer warlocks and sorceresses, few dared to challenge him.

They called him Dashiok. And he was the first to sense the power within the One World.

The One World was the birthplace of the first vampire, which was also the first creature of the One World. He just existed. Alone at first. Not knowing what he was or how to live, roaming the One World in sadness and in anger. It was natural that he gravitated towards the other evil creatures once they appeared. Or maybe the other evil creatures gravitated towards him. But in truth, all creatures feared him.

He discovered and learned his true power by sheer instinct. He fed on the energy of others, absorbing or inhaling the magic from his victim's body, skin, pores, eyes...anything really. Then, he controlled this power for a short time. The more powerful the creature, the more he thirsted for and drank their energy.

He was also extremely fast. The Yachaq were the only other creatures faster. Which was good, since he craved the white elves the most, and hunted them for their power as much as for the thrill of the hunt. Consuming a large mass of energy and feelings from other beings was painful for him. He saw that it caused suffering, which was not his intention. He did it because he was hungry. But it was also addictive. The more he fed, the more he wanted to feed, and the more accustomed he became to the pain it caused him physically and for the suffering of others. For the most part, he was left to himself, since even the evil creatures were not sure if they were going to become his next meal.

They called him Yakar. Despite being the oldest creature in the One World, he had the looks of a young man—somewhere around eighteen years of age. But his eyes gave away the fact that he was not human at all, for they were feral. Fluorescent turquoise was the color of his eyes, and they would shimmer when he fed. His long, deep dark hair covered his moderately pointy ears, and he was incredibly tall. He feared and followed no one.

Creatures with No Magic

In this One World, there were creatures with absolutely no magic. This does not mean that they were helpless. On the contrary, they had to be more astute and innovative to keep up with the rest. For this world was harsh to the folks with no magic. To survive, they were forced to develop other abilities. Among them were humans, dwarfs, colossals, giants, and dragons.

The few humans that lived in the One World gathered in a small kingdom—one castle surrounded by humble villages. They were the last creatures created. It took many generations and almost extinction for them to learn how to remain alive. They lived at the base of the great Northern Mountains far away from the dangerous and the magical creatures.

This small kingdom was ruled by Elex and Alethea—descendants of the original families that had survived The Great Relocation. They ruled not just because they were the successors of the first human families, but because they were able to organize, influence, and survive.

Perhaps you are curious what I mean when I say "The Great Relocation." Listen, and I will tell you the story. You see, the great mountains of the north were not where the nine original families were first brought into existence. Initially, the humans were at the center of all of the One World's creatures. It was at the shores of the Southern Sea right at the rim of the Magical Forest.

There, the humans were not living. They were barely surviving, hiding in caves or holes. Only their bravest ventured out for food and supplies and each time fewer would return back. Fear, sadness, and despair fed their hungry bellies more than the mere scraps they were able to gather. Their hearts finally broke one evening when Elex, who was only four at the time, disappeared. They sent out scouting parties to look for him, risking their lives, trying to preserve their next generation. In this search, many many more were lost.

It was not until night, when the full moons were high, that the young child came back to them. His brown curly hair was ruffled up, and he was out of breath, but he had a huge smile on his face. When he saw his parents, he tried to explain what had happened.

"Big warlock...flying Kron," was all that the little one managed to say.

"No more!" said his mother. "We cannot survive much longer." Her words echoed on the elders' minds as she held her child tight, waiting for guidance. Only silence responded.

Finally one of the elders broke the silence, gazing at Dom's white peak in the distance.

"Yes," was all he said.

"But what can we do?" a tribe member asked.

"We need to leave," said a second elder.

"Leave?!" said another tribe member. "We can barely survive going out to gather fruits and nuts. How could we survive leaving? Where would we go?"

"There!" said a third elder, pointing at Dom's peak.

"No," another elder said. "We must stay here and learn how to survive. If the boy managed to return unharmed, there must be a way. Maybe it's a sign of good things to come."

"I agree," second another elder. "We know the dangers here. We do not know what other dangers lie in the mountains."

As they argued, Elex's grandmother was lost in thought. She suddenly realized it was the most dangerous creatures that thrived in the One World's warmer regions. There, the food was plentiful, the land was expansive and pleasant, and the magic was strong.

Finally she spoke. With authority.

"Here we are surrounded by creatures with powers that we do not have," she said. "We are insignificant to them. They stay here because it is warm and there is a lot for them to eat. We need to go where the magical creatures will not go."

"We will never survive crossing the dark forest," a fourth elder argued. "That is certain! We have survived here, but no one has survived in the Dark Forest. Remember. Years ago, some of us tried. And how did that end? All we did was to send our families to fail. The ones who waited near the forest's entrance heard their screams but never saw them again. And the return journey was just as treacherous. Only one made it back. And just long enough to tell us the story before perishing from illness and sorrow. So no! We are not doing this again."

"This is not surviving. This is dying in turns," said the first elder who had spoken.

"I will not allow it. My tribe will not go," said the elder who had first said no. Almost all of the other elders nodded in agreement.

"Yes," said the third elder. "I agree we must leave. I will allow it, and my family will go. Who will join me?"

The first and second elders to speak took a step towards him, and laid their hands on his shoulders. In unison, they said "We will."

Ultimately, only three of the original families—among them Elex's and Althea's grandparents—moved the few humans who followed them to the valley of the Northern Mountains. Together they convinced as many humans as they could to take this utmost dangerous journey. Their plan was to avoid as much of the Dark Forest as possible by going through the Aqu Desert. They knew nothing about this desert, but they decided to take their chances. The strategy was to travel from the warm Magical Forest, across the Aqu Desert, and finally through the Dark Forest towards Dom, the highest glacier of the Northern Mountains. If their calculations were correct, it would take them almost two months to get to Dom. If only they had magic.

Knowing that their journey would be arduous, they gathered as many supplies as they could carry, for they did not think that they would find human food in the Aqu Desert. And most definitely they would not eat anything that grew in the Dark Forest. These supplies would last them until they reach Aqu. There they would have to gather more for the rest of the journey.

They set off early one morning, just after dawn. They moved through the day and hid at night. They survived the creatures within the magical forest, always able to climb a tree to see the majestic Dom for guidance. That is how they knew they were traveling north. This part of the journey felt the shortest, but it was the same or maybe even longer than the distance from the Dark Forest to Dom. The farther away they moved from the warmth, the harder their path became. However, as you will soon learn, that was nothing compared to crossing the Dark Forest.

When they reached Aqu, the fine-sand desert, the first humans to touch its sands dropped and disappeared like a stone thrown on water. Desperate and frightened, the travelers turned back and made their way through the Magical Forest until they came to its last pond, not far from Aqu. There, they set up camp and began to look around for anything that could help them cross the liquid sands. To their growing dismay, they found nothing.

That evening as they sat around the campfires, they argued among themselves about whether to turn back. As they talked, they all came to agree on one thing. If by luck they survived the journey back, they still would not survive long if they continued to live the way that they had lived before embarking on the Great Relocation. It came down to impossibilities. They may not survive if they returned and they may not survive if they kept going. They all agreed that their only choice was to keep going and do their best to stay alive.

While the adults talked, four-year-old Elex wandered off, walking towards the largest tree he could find. In his young mind, he understood his family's need to cross Aqu. When he stood in front of the tree, he put his little arms around it and hugged it tight, all the while thinking of different ways to help. Growing sleepy, he found a big nook in the tree with a soft carpet of moss in it, just the right size. He curled up and fell asleep with a trace of dry tears on his dusty cheeks. And slept until his mother found him and brought him back to camp.

On the next morning, the travelers walked with heads bowed in thought and despair, back to the desert to try their luck once more. They passed many trees on their way. Remember, this was the Magical Forest and all the trees were magic. When they came to the border between the forest and Aqu, the very last tree there dropped one of its branches onto the fine sands. This tree had spoken to the tree that had sheltered Elex in its nook the night before, while he slept.

Elex saw the branch fall, cried out, and pointed at it, his eyes wide with excitement. When they heard him, all the travelers turned and looked, just in time to see the branch floating away on Aqu's fine sands! Then, the tree released large pieces of its bark to the humans. Piece after piece fell on the ground all around them.

Hope!

As the others began to gather all of the bark into a big pile, Elex walked over to the tree. He hugged it tight, tears of gratitude pouring down his cheeks, which looked like shiny red apples because of how his big smile covered his face. "Thank you," he whispered. "Thank you."

They set camped right there at the edge of the woods, and set about building small rafts and replenishing their supplies for the journey. After a few days, they set off across the desert. They soon discovered that the scorching heat that rose from Aqu's liquid sand was almost intolerable. Cherishing every drop of water from the Magical Forest's pond, they crossed the northwest corner of the desert in two weeks. Amazingly, they all made it to the Dark Forest. They had blisters and their skin was burnt and dry but they survived. All of them survived.

They had ventured across Aqu to reduce their time in the Dark Forest as much as possible. Now, there was no other choice but to travel north through it. They soon discovered that they had traded an eternal day for a never-ending night. And they almost didn't survive.

Not only was the forest damp and cold, but after only taking a few steps inside, they already felt lost. It was as if they were already deep within the woods. And they couldn't tell if it were day or night. Even after just a few days, it felt like weeks. They ran through their food quickly. The many creatures that roamed the forest were foul and devious. As the days passed, they would trick the humans. They would drive them deeper in, where they would try to separate them, and steal their food or other supplies. They toyed with them, taunted and tired them out, until some would finally run away from the group in desperation. Then the creatures would capture them. The rest of the travelers would not see them again.

One by one, their numbers were dwindling. The humans were disappearing fast. Even if they could find their way in this cruel forest, they had very little food and many days left before they could leave it. To some it felt like they had made a big mistake; these were easy prey for the dark creatures, who could sense they had given up and would easily cull them from the rest of the group. To others, the original determination to just make it through alive was beginning to fade.

Disheartened, some would look up into the tree canopy for a shred of light. This is when the forest itself would tease them. Within its darkness it would light up a sturdy branch high on a tree. They would think they could climb up and find the sky, see light. The forest would allow them to climb. But once they reached that one branch, the light would disappear. They would find themselves clinging to a slippery and impenetrable tree, and fall. While plunging towards the ground, they'd catch sight of a thick net of vines. In their last moments, they would understand that they would never be able to see the light, nor what they urgently needed to see in order to get out—Dom.

Even though the original humans did not wield magic, they did possess the power to make the greatest invention ever created by mankind. Fire. It kept them alive. When they entered the Dark Forest, Alethea's grandmother lit the bark from the Magical Forest. She maintained the flame alive during their time in these treacherous woods.

Soon, she was targeted by the forest. It tricked her and drove her mad so she moved fast and deeper into the forest. Three-year-old Alethea saw, and called out to her. At the sound of her little granddaughter's voice, she ran quickly back and handed her the torch.

"Keep it lit," she whispered. Then, she turned and ran deeper into the forest. She disappeared within the dark branches, which to Alethea looked like fingers closing over her. By instinct, Alethea walked the opposite direction, holding onto Elex's hand. Elex pulled on his mother's clothing, getting the remaining humans to follow him and Alethea.

Barely holding on, after a long time Alethea stumbled upon a weak little creek. She stopped short and her mouth flew open. Her blue eyes were shining bright against the torch and the red curls on her head were still bouncing when the other humans gathered around her and saw what she saw. The two children stood quietly holding hands, while they all looked at the running water. The adults knew this stream could only flow south. For all streams in the One World came from the great mountains of the north and fed the generous seas of the south.

They all knew in that moment that they were saved. They would find their way out of the forest by following the stream. And sure enough, this small stream of hope led the humans out of the Dark Forest and into the grand valley of Wallqa, the birthing place of the great Northern Mountains.

There, at the top of the valley, a crystal pond lay in the center of a semicircle. That is where they built a small castle. Gradually over time, a village grew and surrounded both pond and castle like a necklace. Humans became extremely sharp with innovation and negotiating. They learned to create and use impressive tools to help them get whatever it was they needed to survive.

The humans met the dwarfs in these Northern Mountains. The dwarfs had been in the mountains for thousands of years and understood these frozen rocky giants better than any other race.

Ruling within the guts of the mountains, Urqu was the eldest dwarf and ruled over all five dwarf clan leaders, Qhispi, Umi, Kachi, Kuti, and Thuru. He kept the dwarfs working and building inside the mountains. He made sure they maintained their tradition of finding treasures and precious strong metals, using them to create powerful tools, stunning gems, and fantastic buildings. Respect and tradition were established and handed down through each clan from elder to elder.

Over thousands of years, the dwarfs had grown unusually tough. They developed dense bodies capable of carrying boulders on their backs with surprising ease. They had sharp vision in total darkness. The deeper they dug within the entrails of a mountain, the stronger they became as a species. They even grew resistant to different types of poisons from the years of exposure to the toxic fumes they encountered while digging.

These subterranean beings created the most majestic cities. They embellished the caves' mouths with massive, glorious, ornate doors that reflected their master craftsmanship and wealth of knowledge about all earthly elements found within the mountains.

The dwarfs and humans did not necessarily like each other, but they learned to tolerate one another. For the dwarfs, the humans were an early warning if something terrible came out from the dark forest, reached Wallqa Valley, and headed towards the mountains. For the humans, the dwarfs had already done the heavy work—they had created the perfect hiding place in case something treacherous arrived in the valley.

Elex and Alethea were the first of their kind to engage with the dwarfs. Not necessarily a positive engagement, since dwarfs were known to be very difficult and stubborn, and displayed very little charm towards other species. But Elex and Alethea realized that having the dwarfs on their side was necessary for their survival.

So they sent spies to gather information that would help them to understand the dwarfs better. One thing the spies discovered is that the dwarfs liked to drink ale. It softened their hearts a bit, and brought partial smiles on their faces. (Something they would never admit if anyone dared to ask.) Elex and Alethea thought that just maybe sharing a good ale together might content their stout hearts and bring a sense of mutuality between them. It would not be the first time in history that a good ale had forged an alliance.

Urqu, too, sent spies to Wallqa Valley. From them he learned that the humans were creating new tools. Large contraptions that piqued his curiosity. Dwarfs were very interested in tools and engineering of all kinds. And since he indeed enjoyed a good ale, he thought meeting the humans over a nice pint might be a good way to learn more about these devices and how they could help the clans. So, because of the astute leadership of the three, the humans and the dwarfs made peace with each other and began to explore how they might be of mutual benefit.

The animals roaming the One World were giant beasts known as colossals. What they lacked in magic they more than made up for in courage, for they were immense and fearless. Most of them lived in or near the Hulking Forest, where the trees were wider than a house and taller than the towers on a castle. The colossals included many creatures, such as phurus, elks, reptiles, insects, amphibians, and felines.

Most of the massive reptiles, insects, and amphibians lived in the Dark Forest and fed off each other. Species eating species, where only the fastest and the smartest survived. A few lived in the Magical Forest, and these were beautiful, soft, and gracious. They still had to eat, of course. But in general, they were kind.

The felines were large and ferocious. A combination of lions, tigers, and cheetahs. These large cats would hunt together, eat anything that moved, and were extremely territorial. Of course, they considered their territory to be all of the One World. Even though the Hulking Forest was their main home, they were always moving from place to place, forcing the other creatures to learn quickly how not to get eaten. This kept most creatures moving from one area to the other. Thus, the One World was never still.

Magnificent elks would wander the edge of the Hulking Forest. These enchanting creatures were extremely fast, and had horns that looked like strong branches ending in razor-sharp points. They would use their horns to protect the forest from any newcomer who was not supposed to live there. Or any newcomer they simply did not want there.

The phurus were flightless birds two-and-a-half adult humans in height that liked to live and nest by the edge of the pond in the heart of the Hulking Forest. One of the first creatures of the One World, they primarily fed on large fish, with the occasional bit of algae to help their digestion. In general, these birds were docile, except when they sensed immediate danger. And they sensed immediate danger a lot. That is when they would blindly and repeatedly thrust their sharp beaks outward in all directions, to protect themselves. Making the probability of losing a limb while walking next to them pretty high.

The giants lived on the outskirts of the Hulking Forest, between the eastern floating stones and the coarse sand dunes east of the Aqu Desert. The huge rocks that floated closest to the forest had grass and elks living on them. The giants were able to move these rocks to create earthy ceilings, under which they made their homes. As they lived under these floating rocks, they turned them into dazzling works of architecture—constantly arranging stunning and delicate rooftops on them. These natural-looking rock formations concealed the giants from above. And you will learn why soon.

Giants were short-tempered. They could also be quite clumsy, especially when they were young. When they were building their houses, it often happened that a floating rock would slip out of a giant's hands, and bounce off the ceiling of another giant's house. Oh my, what an uproar this would cause! Immediate quarrels ending in fists, bruises, and more moving floating boulders crashing into other giants' houses. Soon the fight would invite all the giants to join in the neighborly event.

Overall, giants were loners within a community. As soon as they came of age, they would live alone in the houses they built. Even so, they always stayed very close to one another. They did not talk much to each other, or share their food, or their knowledge. But if there was any type of trouble from outsiders, they defended the whole community as one big fist.

The dragons were more sociable than the giants, and were organized into many clans. They lived in the Rocky Mountains of the west. These were the second highest mountains compared to the Northern Mountains and overlooked the multiple forests, the southern seas, the sand dunes, and the floating rocks. The dragons lived in the many caves that got created when massive boulders leaned against one another, or when one of the giant rocks fell, deeply denting or cracking the mountain's surface.

There were dragons always roaming the Western Rocky Mountains, and their many clans always worked together. The Superior Clan was the highest clan and commanded all of the dragons. This clan was led by Rrok, the largest and most fierce of the dragons. When the dragons were hatchlings, the Superior Clan decided which clan each belonged in, and placed them there.

They made sure that the strongest and the fastest hatchlings became members of the Warrior Clan—the highest honor for any dragon. To live and die defending the lives of other dragons was what all dragons dreamed of. There was one exception to this rule. The largest and fiercest dragon would always be the head of the Superior Clan. Only power can lead to power.

The Hunter Clan flew low looking for food, as they were responsible for sharing their catch and feeding all of the five clans. Giants were high on their menu, and this is the reason why the floating rocks were so important to the giants.

High in the sky you would find the Vigil Clan. Dragons needed a wide view from above of what could lurk nearby or in the Hulking and Magical Forests at the base of the Western Rocky Mountains. The Vigil Clan provided that, soaring over the landscape and peering down with their eagle eyes. They were the dragons' early warning system, and when they spotted danger they would alert all the clans.

The Healer Clan cared for all of the clans, and they were the smartest of the dragons. Their power was their ability to learn the weaknesses and strengths of a dragon's body. With this knowledge, they provided important information to the other clans. Ultimately, everything the dragons worked towards was to improve their strengths and remove their weaknesses. In the end, weaklings always become food.

THE WAR OF MAGIC

Magical Bindings

One thing that all creatures had in common, whether magical or not, is the need for power. And in the One World, magic was power.

Dashiok had just defeated another challenger. Satisfied with establishing once more his rank among the dark creatures, he wandered aimlessly into the core of the Dark Forest, where life itself was almost nonexistent.

His amber eyes were not focusing in any particular direction, as his broad body forged a pathway through the forest. His long reddish-brown fingers twitched with triumphant energy. His jaw-length blond hair was still messy and dirty from the duel. Thin lips stretched to form a sort of smile on his square coarse face. He looked average size for a warlock, but it was not his size or physical strength that caused fear in others. It was his eyes, which fired up when he was about to cast a terrifying spell. At this moment they were still burning with the joy of his last conquest.

After a time he came to a pit of darkness surrounded by dead trees and branches. There his feelings of adrenaline and rage peaked—he uttered a scream that triggered a dark liquid to ooze from his hands and slam into the dusky earth. These black streaks forked and dug into the dirt, and then ricocheted back, shooting fiery energy straight into his body. His scream of rage and victory became tinged with a hint of fear. His veins became inflamed as live embers coursed through them. They entered his hands, flowed into his neck, and then his face. There his fiery magic appeared as if a fiery Venus flytrap flower was closing from the inside of his face, the way it might close around an insect.

His scream subsided into silence. When his eyes filled with the powerful fire, he understood what had just happened. Before he could ponder it and practice with it, he heard a voice. It was a Guardian. The pegacorn Unan was flying nearby, trying to discover what had created such a magical disturbance.

Dashiok quickly ducked behind some of the black trees to hide. Dark leaves instantly closed around his body, further concealing him. He could hear and smell the flying unicorn, but he could not see him. The dense foliage—particularly in the core of the Dark Forest—was impenetrable. Even though he was invisible, he remained still, with half a smile on his face, for now he finally understood the reason why Guardians existed.

After Unan gave up the search and flew off, Dashiok tried again. This time he went about his magic in a more controlled way. He sent a small black thread, as thin as a needle, from his index finger to the black earth. When the magic ricocheted back to him, he felt the red embers running through his body. His face tightened with pleasure. An ashen circle formed on the ground around the black needle where he had just absorbed the One World's energy.

Flames covered his eyes and within these fires, he saw a strange symbol and then a war. He saw himself in front of thousands of creatures who followed him, ready to die for him, for he now was their new master.

Two things had to be done to manifest this vision and possess the power hidden within the One World's earth. He had to build an army. And he had to destroy the Guardians.

The fiery visions also clarified that if he did not lead the army, soon another would stumble onto this power just as he had. And that would mean he would have a true, equal adversary. Dashiok did not want this. He wanted the magic for himself. And now he knew that the only path to keep most—if not all—of it was to have patience. The desire to control how the energy was taken—and how much of it—was strong within Dashiok, for he and only he wanted to grant this power to the dark creatures of the One World. And the burning visions showed him exactly how to grant power and how to take the magic back.

Dashiok was particularly suited to this challenge. Because unlike all the other dark creatures, he understood others' need for power as well as their weaknesses. So when the time came to form an army, he would conjure attractive, binding negotiations. It was all done with black magic and a piece of the essence of each one who joined. An unbreakable connection that he, and only he, shared with all.

For a long time, Dashiok continued to return to the core of the Dark Forest to practice his new skill and gather more and more power. A lot of Guardians flew over the Dark Forest, which enabled him to figure out how much he could absorb without attracting them. The ground there was now filled with ashen circles. After many months, he went back one last time to finalized his plan and to obtain from the flaming visions the last steps of guidance. Also, he returned because he could not go long without absorbing more of the One World's energy.

On his way to the core of the dark forest, he was approached by Uspha. The dark elven king had sensed changes within the heart of his forest. The elf disliked anyone entering the Dark Forest without his permission. Almost floating towards Dashiok, his eyes became fully opaque as gusts of grey particles swirled around him. Instinctively, Dashiok adjusted his feet, ready to fight while the dark elf began to pulsate the grey particles towards him.

"Look," the dark magic within Dashiok whispered to him.

As he evaded one of the pulses, he looked at Uspha's grey veil and realized that the particles were made of the same magic he had discovered embedded within the Dark Forest. A black oozing ray shot out from Dashiok's hand towards Uspha's last and strongest pulse of dark magic. This pierced and transformed it to ashes, which now floated freely all around them.

Uspha tilted his head in disbelief, for Dashiok was able to control his magical pulse.

"How?!" demanded Uspha.

"I can be the provider," Dashiok's deep voice vibrated the floating grey particles.

"What do you want?" Uspha's opaque blue eyes narrowed.

"For the Laqha to fight alongside me and destroy the Guardians," Dashiok raised his hand, sending a smooth stream of black energy towards Uspha. "Let me show you."

Uspha took a step back but stayed still. He was curious, and the thought of becoming more powerful was enticing. The dark magical stream released itself from Dashiok and became as thin as the black bristles on the Dark Forest's pine trees. Uspha closed his fists as he looked at this stream spin in his direction. His veil was out once again. The stream touched both Uspha's neck and the dark earth, shooting amber coals of energy towards Uspha. His eyes turned completely black. Tilting his head backward, he took it all in. He opened his fists and a blast of energy shot out, pushing Dashiok backward.

Uspha turned to look at Dashiok and laughed deeply, still basking in the sensation that just a tiny piece of this new power had left in his body.

"You will provide to me first, and then to all of my children. Then when I decide we have enough, we will fight," he demanded.

"No," growled Dashiok. "I will decide how much you and your offspring can have. You will have more than them, of course."

"You cannot win without us," Uspha responded sharply.

"You cannot have this power without me. Still feel it in your body, don't you? You only have one choice. And to ensure you keep to this offer, I will bind our words."

In that instant, a stronger stream shot out of the palm of Dashiok's hands and swirled in the air to form a symbol. This was the fiery symbol that had been shown to him the first time he took the One World's energy deep in the Dark Forest.

As he moved his hands to finalize the symbol, Dashiok sternly looked at Uspha. The black magic twisted and turned until a crimson stream slowly circled in front of the dark elven king. It mesmerized him. He couldn't take his eyes off it. He almost forgot Dashiok was there, until the warlock spoke.

"I will grant you a power that you have never seen before. Will you and your offspring stand by me and fight the Guardians?"

At this question, Uspha's gaze shifted from the symbol to Dashiok. His body already thirsted for this power. He wanted more. Plus, he despised the Guardians. His lips curled at the thought of destroying them and ruling over the Yachaq.

"Yes."

"Very well." Dashiok moved his hands forward.

A faint shadow emerged from both of their bodies, like an echo. Dashiok incorporated it into the fiery symbol. Then, the symbol entered Uspha, who winced as it burned itself into the skin of his left collarbone. The symbol also burned itself into Dashiok's right palm. An alliance was born. And bound.

After his encounter with Uspha, Dashiok approached Ganrra, the strongest of the warlocks. It was quick for Ganrra to want more power and to become Dashiok's right hand. Together they lured all of the warlocks and quickly created binding allegiances as Dashiok transferred within them fragments of the One World's power. Each magical binding deepened the symbol on the palm of his hand. The earth's energy made them strong, but Dashiok controlled how much energy each creature received. Ganrra, of course, received a bit more, locking in his place in the power hierarchy.

The dark sorceresses soon followed, but this did not mean that it was easy for Dashiok to persuade them. Atiy, the commander of all sorceresses, was powerful, smart, and dark. She bargained for more than Dashiok could ever have expected. She negotiated to become his partner, his wicked queen, and the mother of all new warlock or sorceress born from this horrifying union. Once this binding was absolute, her coven swarmed the land, further eating up the One World's special powder.

Just as Dashiok foresaw, it was not long before the remaining dark creatures, the Yaku and Phuyu, wanted this power as well. Eventually, he repeated this ritual with all of the dark creatures. When the magic was transferred from the One World into these foul beings it would change its amber appearance for each creature. For Phuyu it would become an amber mist. For the Yaku, it would be amber waves. The Laqha received amber coals. The witches got amber electricity. And for the other warlocks it was amber flames.

Under Dashiok's command, the powers of these evil creatures evolved. When they first discovered their powers, they practiced and applied different types of spells. Fed by the One World's energy, these simple spells soon turned into curses. And they began to consume the earth's magic. Dashiok's army grew, while he aggressively fed them the magic within the earth.

As the magic was withdrawn, the once rich earth started to turn gray. As if death had been ground into a fine powder and scattered on the One World.

The One World cried, calling forth the Guardians.

The Duel

Dashiok soared as he built an army. This magical binding symbol was going to transform the One World forever. He had manipulated all of the dark creatures to fight for power, to fight for him. In the end, he controlled how much and how the energy was taken as all of the creatures were transformed into stronger and darker fighting beings. But Dashiok wanted them all. And he was still missing one.

With caution, he ventured to the Magical Forest to find Yakar—the only vampire in the One World—for the first time. The Yachaq roamed the Magical Forest, and the white elves were Yakar's favorite challenge and prey.

Dashiok was precise with his movements, for he knew that it was not the right moment for the Guardians to see him. Large amounts of the One World's energy coursing within him had transformed his body. A helmet of silver hair covered his head. His skin had a powder-blue hue, and he was bulky and muscular. The color of his eyes remained the same, but what changed was the darkness within them. Even when they lit up they were dark and raw.

Nature would move away from Dashiok while he walked through the forest with his hand extended out, feeling for Yakar's energy. He closed his eyes and deeply inhaled the smell of magic around him. Immediately he was filled with two fragrances. The pure magical essence of the forest, and Yakar's essence. Both tempted him. He thought how much more powerful he would become if he consumed either one or both. But he knew it was not time. He forced himself to become patient once again, and began moving towards Yakar.

Yakar was squatting high on a tree branch, looking into the woods at something only he could see. All of a sudden, his eyes shifted to see what was behind him. His mouth parted a bit when he felt the strong surge of power. He was ready to hunt. Quickly and quietly he leaped to a nearby tree, ready to face what was coming his way. He stood tall, trying to make sense of what his eyes had spotted.

"I see that you see me," Dashiok called to him. "I have come to make you an offer, so you can hunt and take all of the Yachaq roaming free in this pathetic forest."

Yakar continued to look at Dashiok, making no movement or sound.

"Let me show you, boy," Dashiok said as he raised his hand and let out a dark thin stream of magic.

Without hesitation, Yakar dove towards Dashiok. He absorbed this little stream, folded his body, spiraled, and landed several feet from the warlock. His turquoise eyes had a golden shimmer from the piece of new magic he just fed on. He dropped his head, bent his knees, and flew towards Dashiok. He wanted more.

Dashiok turned his magic into a whip that shoved Yakar out of the way. But the vampire landed on his feet and prepared to pounce once again.

"I can give you more and stronger energy," Dashiok told him. Yakar's eyes were focused intensely on the warlock.

"But to have more, you must join me and battle against the Guardians."

Again, Dashiok projected a stream of dark magic towards Yakar. In a split second, Yakar attacked again. This time all Dashiok could do was to change the small stream of magic into a shield. Yakar absorbed it instantly, landing right in front of Dashiok.

This was the first time anyone had ever gotten this close to Dashiok. Yakar was taller.

Yakar closed both hands into fists and inhaled deeply to feed once more. Dashiok's energy began to painfully rise to the surface of his skin. It hurt. He had been gentle with the vampire, hoping to win him over. But this time he did not hold back. He sent a powerful burst of energy that catapulted Yakar out of his presence.

"You have one last chance to join me or I will destroy you!" he roared.

Yakar's smile in response curled one side of his mouth, and his turquoise eyes were brighter and clearer than ever. He started to run at blasting speed towards Dashiok. He was hungry. He was ready to feed. And he wasn't play-ing. Dashiok created a black steel sword and thrust it towards Yakar. Yakar was fast and swerved around the sword without hesitation, moving closer to Dashiok. As he pivoted his body to face the warlock, he extended his hand and jerked it back, ripping out and absorbing a piece of energy deep within Dashiok.

Yakar slid to the ground, landing on all fours as he felt the rush from his recent feeding. When he stopped, he leaned back, with one arm straight up in the air behind him and the other dug deep in the ground. Thirsty for more, he looked at Dashiok. Ready to spring at his prey.

Surprise crept onto Dashiok's eyes. Yakar felt this little hesitation and dashed with immense speed towards him. As a knee jerk reaction, Dashiok extended his arms in defense and created a sphere of dark magic. It propelled him out of the Magical Forest and into the Aqu desert. When he landed, he realized two things. One, he had not known he could leap such enormous distances. This was a pleasant surprise. Two, he was absolutely displeased with this encounter.

"I will get you," he whispered with flaming eyes. His silver hair slithered around his head like his black magic, and all of the veins on his face pulsated with rage and power.

Alliances

The Guardians felt uneasy. The smell of dark energy had increased, for the air had thickened. This troubled their hearts. There were murmurs of an uprising. Dark thoughts were stirring within them and they decided to patrol the creatures with black magic more often. Their skin tingled as they hovered over the Dark Forest on these patrols. Something was very wrong. Different rumors reached their ears, but it was the dryad Mawk'a, who, after consulting with her brothers and sister, confirmed their fears.

The whispers told the dryads that the dark creatures were becoming more powerful and organized. Forces from different kinships had formed allegiances and had agreed to magical bonds in exchange for power—the One World's power.

Only one had learned what the Guardians thought no one could learn. There was only one head to this growing vermin, to this giant lice-like isopod. His name was Dashiok. A smooth operator who had managed to unite the divided. His overall intent was clear: he wanted to get rid of the Guardians, take all of the One World's power, and destroy anything good in this world. In secrecy, he had planned for this attack and now the one thing the Guardians swore to protect was in peril. Dashiok had formed an army one-hundred-thousand strong. Now the guardians were in the midst of a war.

Blood left the Guardians' faces once the last word slipped out of Mawk'a's lips.

War.

"How did we miss this?" asked the pegacorn Unan. The wings on the sylphs Mayu, Killa, and Tiksi stopped fluttering.

"It does not matter now," Benowit sighed, his brows furrowed in deep thought. "The real issue is what are we going to do?"

"We must unite," Kunaq the white elf answered. "We must fight! There is no other option. The Yachaq will fight."

"Agreed, but our numbers will be lower," said the witch K'antu.

"Even if we gather our best warriors...there are so many of them," Mawk'a said. "We need more."

"One of us is like ten of them!" claimed the Apotequil Khallma. They all looked down towards him and nodded.

"Aye!" Zarkon responded. "We need more claws!" He tightened his grip on his wings, which draped over his back like a cape.

"I can gather the giants to fight with us," Tiksi offered, suddenly inspired.

"Hmmmm," Unan mused. "I shall reach out to the humans."

"And I will gather the colossal!" said Kunaq.

"I will go to the mountains and speak with the eldest dwarf, Urqu," K'antu volunteered.

"I will join you," said Khallma. "I know stubborn. Only the dwarfs are more stubborn than the Apotequils. You will need all the help you can get if we are to convince them to fight with us."

"I can handle the dragons," Zarkon said.

"We must hurry!" Mawk'a said urgently. "For the whispers told us that Dashiok will attack when the three moons align in front of our sun, blocking its light. He seeks darkness to aid him during his attack. This alignment happens in four months!"

"Let us gather our armies in the Magical Forest and then travel together to the Four Edges," Killa the energy sylph suggested.

"Between all of us, we can influence the forest's magic to guard us. At least for a while," added Mayu the water sylph.

"So it shall be," Benowit said. "Be safe!"

"May the power of the One World guide us and speed our paths," K'antu said.

Each Guardian flew north, south, east, and west to their own kind, to round up as many troops as they could. They searched for the strong, the brave, and the willing. The willing can fight five times harder than most since they fight for something bigger than themselves. In this case it was the survival of their kind.

Quickly the Guardians reached the four corners of the One World and sent back troops fifty-five thousand strong to meet in the Magical Forest.

This was not enough! As the troops swiftly and quietly gathered, disguised by magic, the Guardians flew one last journey. They went to ask the non-magical folks to fight a magical war.

Tiksi went to the giants, for only an earth fairy could reach deep into the giants' hearts and help them understand that their whole community was at risk. This was a challenging task, since their first response was always with a fist. Camouflage was Tiksi's advantage, for the giants could not really tell where she was. So she avoided each massive blow. That was one of the reasons she thought she should be the one to speak with the giants. On the morning of the second week, after connecting with the strongest males and females of the community, Tiksi had managed to confirm the allegiance. She asked them to gather and lead their community to the Magical Forest.

Khallma and K'antu managed to obtain support from the dwarfs, though this took two months. Zarkon spoke with the head of the dragon's Superior Clan and within a few days was able to confirm their allegiance. Kunaq reached deep inside the colossals, obtaining support from the elks, phurus, felines, and reptiles. There was no support from insects and amphibians as they could not really understand what this was all about. Unan was the fastest to convince the humans, who to his surprise were ready to fight; but then again, once the humans moved to the north, they were always ready to defend their land.

All in all, they gathered an additional sixteen thousand warriors. This was done with the secret help of Ihxu and Akiya. It would have been impossible to convince the colossals without Ihxu's nature power, or to gather the dragons or dwarfs without Akiya's sense power. They also inspired the Guardians when they were thinking about who they should reach out to for help. All of the non-magical folks arrived in the Magical Forest on the night before the alignment.

In order to stay in contact during the war, the witch K'antu cast an incantation with help from Unan. This enhanced the telepathic powers from the pegacorn in order to connect the Guardians. They could clearly hear each other's thoughts regardless of the distance or the turmoil.

On the eve of battle, a total of seventy-one thousand creatures stood by the Guardians near the boundary of the Magical Forest. Just before the Hulking Forest, the Dark Forest, the Magical Forest, and the Aqu Desert met. This was known as the Four Edges.

They sat quietly by the fires in their camps or lay sleepless in their tents.

The only noises cloaked by the magic of the forest came from the humans and dwarfs sharpening their weapons. The dryads and nature sylphs climbed the trees to keep guard. They seemed like wild birds ready to sound an alert at the sight of danger.

It was a long, quiet, and restless night. The three moons were forming a line while the silence blanketed the evening hours. Surrounded by clouds of stars, the three moons were very close to becoming one large sphere. It was a majestic spectacle to see through the clearing between the magical branches. It was the last time the One World would look as it did the day before. It was the last night before the War of Magic.

War

Concealed by the three moons, daylight never reached the One World that morning. On the contrary, the day was darker than the night. Jingle-like noises fractured the silence. The nature sylphs were alerting them all by vibrating their wings. It was time. The dryads moved fast towards the Four Edges and the energy sylphs reached all creatures, alerting them to prepare for war.

The Apotequils climbed the trees while they moved closer to the edge where the Guardians were standing strong and powerful. The chimera twins stood unnoticed to the right of the Guardians. Behind the guardians were the Yachaq. No one heard the white elves. Throughout the night they had silently scattered through the whole group in order to protect them. Now they were a perfect white line of defense between their folks and whatever danger lay ahead. The Krons were next. A rainbow army barely hidden by the tallest trees in the Magical Forest. Their wings were tucked, and in unison they moved their sharp scales into ready position with a sound like swords unsheathing. The dryads, sylphs, wizards, and witches were standing in groups arranged from west to east right behind the Krons.

Of the non-magical folks, the first to be seen in full armory were the dwarfs. Their first line of defense had their shields and spears up and they were followed by stout warriors eager to fight, carrying an array of weapons—battle axes, longswords, and double blade picks. Behind them, making the dwarfs slightly nervous, were the colossals. Vapor escaped their nostrils as they shook their necks and kicked the earth in excitement. The giants were last and they tightened their knuckles preparing for a brawl.

Quiet. It felt that the Magical Forest took a deep breath, expanded and tightened as thousands of eyes looked forward in the darkness.

A quiet humming could be heard in a distance. Dashiok's army was close. As it grew nearer, the Guardians could hear the drumming of the dark army's feet stomping against the One World. It stopped once they reached the Four Edges.

"White army!" shouted Benowit as he turned to face them. Every single one of them heard his words clearly and knew that the dark army could not see or hear them under the protection of the Magical Forest.

"Today is not a dark day. Today will be filled with courage. Look around you. You are surrounded by your brothers and sisters. Release your fears for you are not alone. They are! Today is the day that we were united to fight. United to fight for the One World. United to fight for our kin. United to fight for our future. Today is a bright day, for today we will make a change. We will write the course of our history. Today is the day that we won!"

Seventy thousand voices roared "One World united! One World united! One World united! Ahhhhhhhh!" ending their chant in one heroic war cry.

Dashiok could smell them. He had changed even more. The tallest among the warlocks with long silver locks resting on his pale skin. His incandescent amber eyes looked as if yellow and red smoky substances were in constant battle.

He raised his hands and then thrust them downward, sending four powerful black rays to crash against each of the Four Edges. Enormous magical embers stolen from the One World reached him, and in a flash, he sent an astronomical amount of power to his army. Gray specs of dust exploded into the air as the One World shrilled in agony. The dark army grew and morphed right in front of their opponents.

Without hesitation, the white elves clapped their hands above their heads and bright rays shot out, creating light around them, blinding the dark army for a few minutes.

"Eliminate them!" roared Dashiok. Under his command, the dark army charged furiously. A mixture of dark elves, Yakus (some in human form and some in animal form), warlocks, and sorceresses ran towards the Magical Forest. Some of them were still undergoing the transformation from the rush of magic Dashiok had injected into them.

"One World united" screamed Benowit as all of the Guardians launched forward towards the Four Edges.

The war of magic had just begun.

Sand from the Aqu Desert flew in and buried the first line of dark attackers. The second, third, and fourth fell right onto the fine sands and were immediately engulfed in it. The fifth, sixth, and seventh lines stopped in their tracks to keep from falling into the sands. Then looked back in fear, ready to run.

The Guardians turned to look towards their right. Ihxu, with a wave of her arm, had asked the fine sands of the Aqu Desert to pour on top of the dark army. Akiya induced fear and confusion, with stretched arms and fingers pointing straight at the upcoming line of attackers. These attackers pushed back toward the dark army, some running in pure panic away from the Four Edges.

The Guardians and the sylphs were as surprised as Dashiok and his dark army. No one knew that the chimera twins were so powerful. The sylph queens and kings realized as much as the Guardians and Dashiok did, that the chimera twins not only were much more powerful than the purist sylphs, but that this type of power could win the war. It was in that instant that the sylph kings and queens understood their failure to fully accept the twins. The sylphs stood for nature, justice, and all living beings, but they forgot what they stood for when it came to the chimeras. They were not true to themselves, and they would need to win the War of Magic to rectify this wrong.

The guardians smiled as they charged forward energized by the power of the chimera twins. Spells from Benowit and K'antu flew towards the dark army, stunning several of them. Dashiok motioned Ganrra, his right-hand warlock, towards the twins.

The warlocks and sorceresses quickly released dark spells that harden the fine sands, creating solid bridges so they could pass. Dark elves floated towards the guardians led by Ushpa the dark earth elven king, who was looking for Achkyi, the white elf queen. Spears flew, at first unnoticed, towards the black sky. Then thousands of lightning rays catapulted down towards the Laqha, illuminating the Apotequils as they fearlessly stormed towards them. Dark spheres sent multiple Apotequils flying back towards the trees, while a hundred more stormed forward in their stead.

A ray of light shot straight towards Ushpa and he barely deflected it. Achkyi had found him first. He pulsed dark spheres towards her but she swiftly evaded them as she charged forward. The Yachaq, the white elves, had reached the Four Edges. White whips were slapping dark pulses out, while black spheres were darkening some of the light within the Yachaq.

Khallma led the Apotequils. He ran towards a massive troop of the Yaku crossing the bridge to prevent them from making it to the Four Edges. His oldest brother, Q'axniy, furiously threw sharp lightning rods, one right after the other, towards human-Yaku. The water demons were catapulting water with green sticky slime towards Ut'u, the sylph earth king. Ut'u created sand whips, snapping the Yaku one by one out of his way. Several Yaku, synchronized, sent multiple green spheres towards the king. Quickly he created a sand shield, but already it was weakening rapidly. A slime bubble was about to reach him when a large rock pushed the mucky water away just in time as he fell to the ground in surprise. Tiksi, the earth sylph, followed by the *seedling forces*, surrounded the king and fired back a massive sand storm filled with lightning, compliments of Q'axniy.

Several animal-Yaku were attacking the multiple elks, phurus, felines, and reptiles that had reached the Four Edges. They had managed to stick many colossals together in order to immobilize them. The phurus slashed with their beaks, while the elks used their massive horns to pick up and throw any of the Yaku who were getting close to the trapped group. Some of the felines and reptiles tried to rescue them by climbing on trees and jumping on top of the Yaku, but the Yaku pushed them away in mid-air with green slime.

Now Uskhay, Khallma's oldest sister, sent wide powerful lightning bolts towards a large group of animal-Yaku, melting away the slime that was suffocating some of the colossals. With the help of the remaining felines and reptiles, she was able to distract the animal-Yaku and free the trapped colossals.

Wizards and witches projected spell-like shots that tied, knocked out, or petrified anyone who crossed their path. The dryads used their mystical magic to put their enemies to sleep or give them hallucinations about happy feelings. This was something the dark creatures had never experienced. They looked even more fearsome when their smiles revealed sharp, dirty teeth.

Surux, the air sylph, led the *air squadron* as it vanished in and out, ambushing their opponents by trapping them in stationary tornadoes. Wayra, the air sylph queen, materialized and propelled many dark creatures away from the Four Edges at once. The *air squadron* moved fast, creating openings within the dark army. Suddenly, out of nowhere, a dense stream of water shot at Wayra and the squadron, trapping them in an endlessly swirling ball of turbulent waters. They tried desperately to stabilize themselves with their wings. They were drowning. It was Tuj and thousands of Yakus attacking them.

He smiled as he watched the air queen losing her breath. Qori, the mother of the twins, thrust out her arm and a strong gust of wind pushed Tuj and many Yaku several steps back. The ball of water fell to the ground hard and shattered, just as if it were made of glass. Gasps could be heard as air entered the lungs of the queen and the squadron. Wordless, the queen bowed her head to Qori in gratefulness.

Muyu, the water sylph king, and Mayu leading the *wave squads*, floated towards the Four Edges as they propelled water shots knocking down the dark creatures. Until they encountered Shuc, with a hundred dark elves by his side. Together they created one dark thick pulse, hitting the king and his warriors hard. Protecting his king, Mayu lost both wings and severely injured his leg from the impact. Not all of the *wave squads* made it—some used their bodies to shield both Muyu and Mayu from the pulse.

The fire sylphs shot fireballs and bolts towards the dark army. In a v-formation, Illapa headed the *five flames*, which included Ninan, the father of the twins, towards the Four Edges. Tactically, they launched fire bolts that blocked any dark magic from reaching members of the white army, particularly the non-magical folks. Nina, the fire queen, was shooting fire swords, as she flew and swerved between trees, dryads, Krons, and giants. They reached Shuc just in time as he and the dark elves gathered close to Muyu and Mayu to finish them off. Fire swords surrounded the dark elves as the water king, who had cuts and scratches on his thighs and face, helped move Mayu out of the way.

The *five flames* flew down fast, head first towards the dark elves. They inhaled deeply, raised their arms, and as they exhaled, pumped their fists above their heads, incessantly shooting multiple blue flame arrows towards the dark elves. In unison, and with sharp movements, the *five flames* flew up as dark rings blocked their path. They never stopped shooting blue flame arrows until they reached the first cloud. Half of the one hundred dark elves were on the ground. Shuc was still alive, screaming at the remaining elves, commanding them to send dark pulses towards the *five flames*. Nina's flaming hands were locked on Shuc.

Meanwhile, the dwarfs were using their axes to cut and their shields to block and stop the dark fiery streams the warlocks aimed towards them. Urqu and the five clan leaders, Qhispi, Umi, Kachi, Kuti, and Thuru thrashed with their longswords, double blade picks, and battle-axes. Striking each blow with purpose and intention, they were gaining on the warlocks. But the sorceresses joined forces with the warlocks and very quickly the dwarfs were split into smaller groups and losing their advantage. With a robust and powerful voice, Urqu commanded the dwarfs to regroup. But the blasts created from thousands of black fiery darts exploding on metal shields drowned his words, leaving the dwarfs disoriented and without a voice.

Umi was fighting furiously and taking down several warlocks when he saw Atiy, the sorceress queen, scouring the battlefield, looking for the dwarf clan leader. Her purple eyes immediately spotted Urqu. She raised her arms and thrust them forward, one hand in front of the other, shooting one massive black fiery lance towards him. Her black hair moving back in place revealed fuming eyes and a satisfied smile.

Umi took off his helmet as he ran towards Urqu, who was desperately trying to organize the dwarfs. With an agonized scream, he jumped up, his ax pointed at the sky, eyes focused on the black fire that was making its way towards Urqu. As he flew to save his clan leader, Atiy saw the redheaded dwarf about to defeat her lance. She shot several flaming darts towards Umi's exposed neck. Hearing his scream, Urqu pivoted just in time to see Umi's ax break the black lance that was going to pierce him, and the darts leaving Atiy's palms hitting Umi's neck and back.

"No, no, no, no, no," Urqu cried as he caught Umi, breaking his fall. He gently put the redheaded dwarf, his longtime friend, on the ground.

"My brother," he whispered. "My brother."

Umi smiled with contentment and closed his brown eyes. The war fell silent.

Micha, the queen of the energy sylphs, zig-zagged while Killa and the *spark squad* followed her towards the warlocks and sorceresses who were attacking the dwarfs. Urqu was holding Umi, while Thuru, Qhispi, Kachi, and Kuti were standing around him protecting their clan leader. For all had heard Umi's call and saw him die protecting Urqu. Thuru held a longsword with one hand as he fought back the black fiery weapons approaching Urqu. With the other hand, he shook Urqu's shoulder, telling him they needed to move, for Atiy's long body slid towards them. A cackle escaped her lips as she prepared for the final blow. She raised her arms again, but this time Micha send a powerful electric shock towards her and sent her flying out of the Four Edges.

There was no time to mourn. With the help of the energy sylphs, the dwarfs regrouped and together continued to fight the dark warlocks and sorceresses, who had lost their edge without Atiy's leadership.

The dragons announced their arrival by exhaling fire on Dashiok's army concealed within the Dark Forest. The warrior and hunter clans guided the dragons towards elevated altitudes. This was to their advantage, as they danced elegantly in the air, avoiding with ease any magic sent up to the sky while they marked their next target. Then, they descended fast, igniting their chests and shooting bursts of fire that burned broad, open paths through the trees and melting their branches.

The path they cleared revealed Zarkon and his army of Krons fighting the dark army. Zarkon's clan had crossed the sand bridges and were moving towards Dashiok. Unaffected by the dragon's fire, Zarkon was focusing on Dashiok. He used his wings to cut trees off, to smack Yakus out of the way, and to clear a path for the rest of the Krons. Rainbow warriors. The Krons moved forward spinning, opening and closing their heavy razor-sharp wings, flicking off members of the dark army as if they were mere twigs.

Fire and rainbows circled the enemy, expelling some of them and throwing others to the ground like brown leaves announcing the end of autumn. The enemy began to retreat.

Dashiok, still feeding on the One World, was enraged by the retreating members of his army and moved his pale index finger slightly. Vines rising up from the ashen ground and trees deep within the dark forest began to trap the deserters. Within these spider-like traps, Dashiok sucked their energy until all that remained were dry shapes of creatures who only moments ago had been fighting in his army.

"Fight!" he commanded. The surrounding creatures shrieked, snarled, and moved towards the Four Edges. He watches his army forming once again and smirked.

Zarkon ran with extreme force towards Dashiok and tackled him to the ground. Dashiok was shocked. This broke the warlock's black ties to the One World. Zarkon rolled and stood up, wings angled to the right, ready to strike once more. A deep, loud growl escaped his throat. It echoed and vibrated with the aid of his wings. This war cry was heard first by all Krons, next by the dragons, and then by all the white magical creatures. Dashiok slapped towards the ground and the force of his magic stood his body upright. The yellow in his eyes became more prominent, almost green, and his pupils narrowed. A sphere of dark magic manifested below his feet, raising him above Zarkon, who quickly adjusted his wings to pursue the warlock in flight.

Dashiok released a black thread that twirled below his feet as it fell gently towards the One World. Zarkon shifted to avoid the thread and focused on reaching and taking Dashiok down. The second he flew pass the thin thread, it slung itself towards him, tying his wings together. A free-falling golden rock.

He struggled to free his wings but the thread would move with intelligence, to avoid his claws and horns. A sudden, intense fire surrounded him, freeing him from this black spindle. He opened his wings just in time to slow his fall before landing hard on the One World. It was Rrok, the massive dragon and leader of the Superior Clan. He who had bathed Zarkon with incandescent red fire and was now in pursue of Dashiok.

Seeing that he was not going to win in the air, Dashiok started to descend. On the way down, he shot several black arrows to pierce Rrok's wings. Without losing his momentum, Rrok pivoted his massive body to avoid more of them. Rrok was hunting Dashiok. He flew higher than the warlock, gained the upper hand, and filled his lungs with air. His chest lit up in a reddish-golden color and he opened his jaws. A crimson flame projected out of the dragon as his beating wings held his body still.

All Dashiok could do was raise a shield. The impact shoved him downward forcefully. Still in the air, he barely managed to send a dark spear towards the massive dragon. Rrok simple shifted his body and sent multiple fire balls towards the dark warlock.

Zarkon pushed himself off the One World in pursue. His scales cut the air as he flew towards the dark lord. He was close. Zarkon could see that Dashiok was mostly defending himself, and he felt victory was near.

Dashiok hissed, sending a low and powerful growl that paused the dragon-Kron dance. Immediately the air became cooler and the light created by the white elves was dimmed by what appeared to be a massive moving cloud that scraped the ground. The dragons and the Krons felt this shapeless mass slide between them, and stopped. Cloaked by this thick mist, both Rrok and Zarkon could no longer see Dashiok. They were flying blind.

They felt this cold fog enter their noses. A cold iron rod that pierced and pushed its way through and into their brains. Pain. That is the last thing they felt to be their own.

Starting with Rrok and Zarkon, Phuyu, the mist demon, took over all dragons and Krons. Against their will, they began fighting for the dark lord, for Dashiok. Fighting their friends, the white army. The dragons and Krons attacked the sylphs and dryads. Many were lost, including Mawk'a who valiantly saved several earth sylphs, moving them out of the way of Rrok's red flames.

Floating a few feet in the air, Dashiok once more sent black shafts towards the One World, determined to take the last of its magic. He looked down and smiled, watching the white army become weaker.

Ganrra, Dashiok's right hand, was looking for the chimera twins. Before Dashiok provided him with the One World's magic, he had already been enormous. Now, a merciless giant, he was ready to destroy anything. For his master had filled him with rage. Inflicting pain in others caused him great pleasure. He was eager to explore his new body and powers. His stretched body still glistened from the One World's energy.

As he moved his hands, several black liquid rods branched out from his palms and slithered around his body. His eyes searched incessantly for Ihxu and Akiya. He sent his desire to find them into the rods. They gently entered the skin of his arms and legs, and then stabbed viciously into the One World's soil, lifted Ganrra from the ground, and walked him towards the mist, towards the chimeras.

The twins were fighting Phuyu. Ihxu created a thick shield of water that swirled around her and her sister but allowed them to see what was in front of and behind them. Phuyu attempted to break this shield, but it dissolved the mist before it even touched the water. Simultaneously, Ihxu manipulated the earth and fire to push away the dragons and Krons who were attacking them under Phuyu's dominion. While Ihxu protected their space, Akiya was in the center, eyes closed, using her powers to reach deep into Phuyu and end his control over the dragons and Krons. It was puppeteer versus sensing master. The chimera knew they would lose the war if Phuyu retained control of the dragons and the Krons.

Akiya had to figure out how to reach a creature that has no body, no brain, and no soul. She was struggling. But then she heard the One World reach her spirit and plant a memory. It was the moment when Ihxu sensed Pusaq for the first time because she touched Akiya's shoulder. The touch connected the twin's powers. She opened her eyes and saw her sister.

"Ihxu!" she yelled.

"Kind of busy here!"

"Grab my hand, hurry!"

"I can't! If I do, I may not be able to protect us!"

"Just *do* it!"

Ihxu grabbed her arm and at that moment the twins' eyes lit up, sending a clear veil which passed through all creatures in the One World and halted the war for a brief second. They were both moving their arms, controlling the water shield, deflecting the Krons and dragons, and sensing Phuyu. Together, they navigated through hollowness towards what could only be thought of as Phuyu's mind.

In this mind, they saw a machine made of rock with multiple wooden levers moving in different directions. The twins sensed that these levers were controlling the Krons and dragons. They pulled on them, but they were solid. Nothing budged. A buzzing sound surrounded them and forced them to focus on the war outside the water shield. Phuyu had sent more dragons and Krons to attack them. There was no time, they needed to free the levers from Phuyu's grip.

"Ihxu, the machine. It is rock holding the levers, right?" asked Akiya.

"It is rock…YES, you are right!"

Ihxu connected with the power from the earth, and a tiny pebble broke off the giant machine. The twins felt the shift within Phuyu and focused all of their powers on the machine. Turning the machine into thousands of marbles that spilled into emptiness, they released the levers. Each lever flew back towards its puppet, releasing the cloud rods that had entered the dragons and Krons. The mist demon became just mist mindlessly floating around the Four Edges.

The dragons and Krons had awoken. With fury they all faced Dashiok.

At that very moment, three thousand pegacorns flew in, carrying the humans on their backs, ready to fight the dark lord. The white army smiled in relief. Reinforcements were about to arrive!

Without breaking his connection to the One World, Dashiok roared for the black elves. Ushpa, the dark elven king, appeared next to Dashiok with his son Shuc and tens of thousands of Laqha. Together they sent dark pulses towards the pegacorns. The pulses did not reach the flying creatures, but they weren't meant to reach them. They were meant to alert the humans on their backs, and the warlocks and sorceresses behind them.

First, the sorceresses and warlocks brought forth large mechanical instruments. Some of these massive contractions would shoot enormous sharp iron spearheads on a wooden shaft with a bronze butt-spike at enormous speeds towards the white army. Others would launch spears, throwers, javelins, clubs, and maces with star-shaped heads made out of copper or bronze. As soon as Urqu, the dwarf clan leader, saw these weapons, his heart sank. Recognizing these machines, he looked up to the sky, for he knew what this meant. Betrayal!

In that instant, the humans flying on the pegacorns produced knives made of dark magic and began to cut the wings off these magnificent beasts. Unan, carrying the human king Elex, was the first to fall. Some of the pegacorns managed to throw off the humans, but most humans were able to take the flying unicorns down.

The humans had betrayed the white army.

Dashiok let out a loud laugh as the pegacorns fell from the sky and the white army recoiled. One thing that evil is really good at is finding weak creatures and infecting them with a thirst for power. The first ones to succumb were king Elex and queen Alethea. These were the same humans that had given their allegiance to the Guardians.

The twins felt the pegacorns' pain. They sent gusts of wind, electric rays, and fear into the human's minds, trying to throw them off the beautiful beasts. One by one, the humans fell except for Elex and Alethea. Then, synchronized, they turned to look at Dashiok. He was next! They raised their arms to attack. But Ganrra used one of his rods to strike them, breaking their shield and their bond.

Pusaq and Qucha, who were always near the twins, leaped and stood between them and the warlock, who was still sending dark liquid darts at them. Qucha used water to deflect the darts and sent water spears towards Ganrra, who broke them, causing splashing everywhere. Pusaq saw that Ganrra was wet and sent a powerful bolt of electricity at his feet. It electrocuted everything that was touched by water, including the large warlock.

In the middle of this, the vampire Yakar was feasting on the creatures from both the white and dark army alike. Though he favored the dark army, for Dashiok had plumped his creatures with the One World's magic. Drunk with energy and power, he was making a dent in the dark army. Dashiok saw him and remembered his unfinished duel. He raised his hand to strike. That's when he saw Ganrra get hit by Pusaq.

"Enough!" he screamed, as gray mist surrounded him and he released one of his holds on the One World. The dark nails on his free hand were almost touching his palm, creating an open fist where dark liquid swirled as it was filled with the One World's magic. The liquid fumed when he released it, boiled by the air surrounding his hand. These fumes intermingled with Phuyu, jolting the mist demon back to life. Phuyu hungered for revenge.

"Now!" snarled Dashiok.

Phuyu slithered fast, trapping the dragons and Krons again. Several giants fighting the dark army pivoted and swung a punch that hit some other giants. Almost half of the giants fell under Dashiok's spell. They became the second to betray the white army. Next the warlock pointed at Ganrra, releasing him from his electric prison.

Ganrra fell on his knees. One hand prevented him from completely falling to the ground. He raised his head, and through his dirty dark brown hair, he focused on Pusaq. Smoke exuded out of his body. He rose to his feet and walked calmly towards the energy sylph. As he got close, he broke into a run expelling from his hands a thick dark matter that targeted and engulfed Pusaq before he had a chance to react. It became a translucent black sheet that hardened the more he moved. He lay still.

Ihxu, who had once again joined powers with Akiya to fight Phuyu, felt Pusaq.

"No, no, no, no!" She repeated, guiding the water shield towards him. She sent sharp rocks and sticks at Ganrra while Qucha used a water capsule to lock him in place.

"Don't move, I will get you out," she urged Pusaq as she used sharp rocks to break the spell. Pusaq smiled. His mouth moved to create a wordless "I love you." That action completed the enchantment. The black sheet became solid gray rock, in which she could still see Pusaq frozen. He was still smiling.

"Nooooo!" Ihxu screamed.

Akiya tightened her grip on her sister. "No sister, we must stay together," she urged

Ganrra had used his black magic to break the water capsule and was now heading towards Qucha. Anticipating his move, Qucha sent a strong stream of water while Ganrra expelled his black magic towards him. Qucha froze it in midair. Surprised, Ganrra watched it fall to the ground.

"Hrmph!" he snorted, once again focused on Qucha. Again he shot his magic. Again the sylph sent the water. Again the mixture froze in midair and fell to the ground. This power interchange was repeated thrice more. Finally Ganrra passed by the first frozen magic on the ground and used his black liquid like a whip. With one hand he knocked Qucha down and with the other he expelled a thick dark matter. This time it swallowed Qucha.

"No!" whispered Akiya. She shot a powerful wave at the warlock, paralyzing him.

Then she ran towards Qucha, breaking the bond with her sister. He looked at her. All the love he had for her was in his eyes. The movement he made to look at her triggered the last enchantment. He was frozen in a gray tomb forever, in love with Akiya.

The chimera twins turned to fight Ganrra. They swept away many of Dashiok's warriors as they closed in on the giant warlock. Ihxu sent boulders and tree trunks at him, some reaching and injuring the black warrior. Akiya sent enormous gusts of fear and pain that bent the dark giant down.

But once again Dashiok intervened. He sent a powerful blow that propelled both twins back, breaking their hold on Ganrra. Ganrra was closer to Akiya and ran towards her.

She was just coming to when she felt the first blow from his whip hit her hard across her stomach. Sensing his next move, she raised her hands and created a power guard, blocking his next strike. It was her turn. Quickly she sent energy to his right leg, rendering it immobile, making him feel it was frozen, giving her the opportunity to roll away and evade another strike from his whip. Quickly, he manifested two dark pulses. One within his leg, freeing it from her magic, and the other towards Akiya, who evaded it fast.

She sent another powerful wave filled with fear energy but he blocked it. Then he sent black threads towards her, throwing her hard against a tree, tying her to it. He was creating a lance to finish her when he saw that the expression on her face changed. In her eyes, he noticed a shadow move. Instinctively he threw it behind, hitting Ihxu who was running toward Ganrra surrounded by several sharp stones and pointy branches.

"Gotcha!" Ihxu said, falling towards the ground. Several of her branches pierced Ganrra. Akiya sent energy towards her sister removing the lance, sealing, and starting to cure her wound from within.

"Argh!" Dashiok broke his connection to the One World and looked towards the chimera twins. He sent them a massive blast that knocked Akiya unconscious and mortally deepened Ihxu's wound. He was going to finish her when Benowit, the white wizard, blocked his magic. He was not far from the twins, fighting against Ushpa and the dark elves.

Shuc, the first son of Ushpa, moved near Akiya. He raised his hands creating a pulse towards her. She barely opened her eyes and realized there was a Laqha next to her.

"I will join you both my sister and my beloved Qucha," she thought. But Shuc removed Ganrra's magic that still held her tightly against the tree and gently took her away.

She was confused. Lifting her head she managed to look at the Laqha and realized that he was the same dark elf that they had saved many years ago in the Hulking Forest.

"I need to go back for my sister," she struggled.

"There is nothing you can do for her," he responded coldly.

"What? No!" Then it hit her. She was alone. She could no longer feel Ihxu. Her heart broke. She passed out once more while Shuc moved stealthily and carried her away from the Four Edges.

Benowit was now battling against Dashiok. He gathered white energy from the Magical Forest. A white ring enclosed Dashiok, which he blocked dexterously. Ushpa quickly moved towards Benowit, giving his master the time he needed. While Benowit fought against Ushpa, Dashiok now used both of his hands to finish absorbing the last of the One World's magic. Benowit was able to immobilize Ushpa quickly. Then he sent a powerful white energy ring towards Dashiok, breaking his hold on the One World. Dashiok was in disbelief.

"You dare challenge me, you white wizard?!" he asked insultingly.

"Yes!" Benowit stood tall.

Dark pulses and white rings began to clash against one another while Benowit and Dashiok faced each other. They fought furiously, both receiving blows from the other. This was a powerful match, and Dashiok knew it. But remember, Dashiok knew his enemies' weaknesses. And he knew Benowit's weakness all too well.

"You have lost, Benowit," he said. "Look around. See for yourself all of the suffering that has fallen upon your white army. Why would you let them suffer any longer?"

Benowit brushed his brow and looked around. He saw fallen pegacorns still fighting for survival on the ground. Krons and dragons controlled by Phuyu taking down his white army fast. Giants fighting giants. Humans fighting dwarves. He saw Ihxu on the ground lifeless next to many sylphs. His heart ached, as tears ran down his dusty cheeks, for floating all around him were the ashes of the One World.

Seeing Benowit's expression, Dashiok saw his opportunity and pressed on.

"You must stop this madness before more peril comes to your army... and to the One World."

At those words, Benowit shifted his gaze from his people to Dashiok. He knew they were losing. He knew they were all in peril, with little chance to regain any control now that the chimeras were gone. He also knew what would happen if they failed, what would happen if the One World was no more.

The white ring became stronger.

"If you will not stop, then you shall all die," Dashiok roared, sending the most powerful blast of black magic yet towards Benowit.

Remember, goodness was young, and youth is naïve. Dashiok was about to overpower Benowit and with him all good creatures, magical, and non-magical. While specs of gray dust were suspended in the air, the white wizard whispered the last hope for the One World.

"Indi ñami pacajurca,
lucerocuna inti shina ninanda punllayachin.
Kunan tutapi mana ñucanchigllachu canchig.
Ñucanchig cuyay sinchimari can,
shinami, cay sumag candotaca candajuni.
Ayllucuna magia shinami can.
Ama manchaychu,
cunan tutapi ninandami punllayachinga michagu shina."

It was a spell of pure love. A simple spell. The spell learned by all wizards from the time they were children. A night song, sung to younglings

before bed to keep their family together and safe. This simple song disinte-
grated Dashiok's blast effortlessly.

Enraged, Dashiok let out a scream of raw hate spoken in the language
taught to him by the flames, what we know today as the Ancient Language.
It was a magical curse, a spell to destroy the old wizard.

The powers of love and hate clashed, creating a mighty magical strike,
which reverberated into the One World's core, releasing the last piece of
magic deep within the earth. And breaking it apart into several pieces.

The One World was no more.

It was divided into eight worlds—seven magical worlds and one with
absolutely no magic at all.

See, love cannot be killed. Nor is it driven by power. Because love is self-
less, and the white wizard thought he had sacrificed himself, Benowit was
spared. The unicorns were sent to a new world to regain their wings and
create once more the magnificent pegacorns. The Krons and dragons were
sent to another, to strengthen their minds and hearts. Sylphs, Yachaq,
wizards, witches, and Yakar were sent to a yet another, in order to grow and
protect magic together. And the Apotequils, the giants, and the colossals
were placed in a world with enormous forests.

Now the dark creatures were also sent to different worlds, to repent.
Phuyu was sent to a world of watery fog and gray clouds. The Yaku were
placed in a world full of murky waters. And Laqha, warlocks, and sorceresses were placed in a dark world.

Elex and Alethea, the only surviving humans, were placed in the only
world with no magic, because they had committed treason in order to
obtain power. There they would be the first humans reborn and evolved
from the simplest of beings—from animals.

The worlds transformed over time. For instance, the sylphs understood
how they had lost their way even before the War of Magic. They had been
too focused on being purists and had ignored the only reason for their existence: to protect and love life. This meant *all* living beings. The chimera
twins were part of nature and when the sylphs shunned them, this weakened their true powers.

Some argue that it could have been possible to win the War of Magic if
they had chosen to accept and love the twins. Nevertheless, the sylphs
followed Akiya, the only surviving chimera twin. Who truly did not care
about being a purist. She cared for her niece Azel as if she were her own

daughter. And led her kind to create a new kind of sylph. More powerful and humble than their forebears.

Most forgot about Dashiok. Most magical folks tell tales that specks from his soul were imprisoned within the emptiness left by the spot where the One World once stood. Other stories say that his powers were beyond what anyone could ever guess or know. For now, what truly happened to him is one more secret that will be revealed at a later time.

Now that you know the tale of the One World, where you able to find more secrets?

CHARACTER TREE

One World

No Magic

Humans | Giants | Dwarfs

Colossals | Dragons

White Magic

Yachaq | Krons | Sylphs | Dryads
white elves | | air, water, fire, earth, energy |

Pegacorns | Apotequils

Wizards Witches

Black Magic

Phuyu | Yaku | Laqha

Warlocks | Sorceress

Vampire

WHITE MAGIC

Guardians

Kunaq	Zarkon	Mayu	Tiksi
yachaq	krons	water sylph	earth sylph

Killa	Mawk'a	Unan	Khallma	K'antu	Benowit
energy sylph	dryad	pegacorn	apotequils	witches	wizards

Ihxu	Akiya
nature sylph	sense sylph

Yachaq

Achkyi	Sut'u
queen	Achkyi's Tear & companion

Atik	Kunaq
	guardian

Kron

Zarkon
guardian

Gargon
Golden Clan leader

28 Sons	Sañi	Makaurrok
	daughter	dragon

Aline	Older **Brother**	Weak **Brother**

Pegacorn

Unan	Kawayu
guardian	2nd in command & fastest

👑 ~female   ♂ ~male

WHITE MAGIC

Sylphs

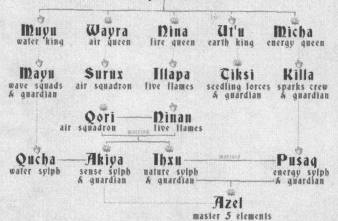

Muyu	Wayra	Nina	Ut'u	Micha
water king	air queen	fire queen	earth king	energy queen

Mayu	Surux	Illapa	Tiksi	Killa
wave squads & guardian	air squadron	five flames	seedling forces & guardian	sparks crew & guardian

Qori air squadron — **Ninan** five flames
married

Qucha	Akiya	Ihxu		Pusaq
water sylph	sense sylph & guardian	nature sylph & guardian	*married*	energy sylph & guardian

Azel
master 5 elements

Dryads

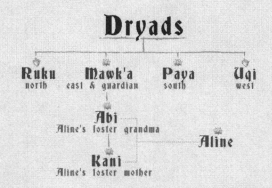

Ruku	Mawk'a	Paya	Uqi
north	east & guardian	south	west

Abi
Aline's foster grandma

Aline

Kani
Aline's foster mother

♀-female   ♂-male

WHITE MAGIC

Apotequils
Lightning Warriors

Khallma's mother
matriarchal Master Spear

Khallma's father
patriarchal Master Spear

Q'axniy
oldest son

Usqhay
oldest daughter

Khallma
guardian

12 sons & 12 daughters

Wizards

Benowit
guardian

Witches

K'antu
guardian

Saywa
oldest daughter

Urpi
youngest daughter

🌺 = female ⚘ = male

BLACK MAGIC

Phuyu
mist demon

Phuyu

Yaku
water demon

Tuj
head of snake

Laqha
dark elves

Uspha ——————— Yana
dark elven king   Dark Leaf & companion

Shuc

Warlock

Dashiok
Dark Ruler

magical binding

Ganrra
Dashiok's right hand

Sorceress

Atiy
Wicked Queen

Vampire

Yakar ———— Aline

♀-female ♂-male

NO MAGIC

Humans

3 Original Families

Elex ⚭ *married* Alethea

Mr. Grant   Mr. O'Moghrain   Amanda's Mother   Amanda's Followers

Amanda

Dwarfs

Urgu

Qhispi   Umi   Kachi   Kuti   Thuru

Colossals

Phurus Elks Reptiles Felines Insects/Amphibeans

Liyun

Dragons

Superior Clan

Warrior *Clan* Hunter *Clan* Vigil *Clan* Healer *Clan* Rrok

Kaurrok

Sani [Kron] ---- Makaurrok

Aline   *Older* Brother   *Middle* Brother

Giants

⚭ - female   ♦ - male

Made in the USA
Las Vegas, NV
25 November 2021

35269030R00159